NADINE DORRIES

Coming Home to the Four Streets

HEAD
of ZEUS

First published in the UK in 2021 by Head of Zeus Ltd

9 7 5 3 1 2 4 6 8

A catalogue record for this book is available from
the British Library.

ISBN (HB): 9781838939069
ISBN (XTPB): 9781800241961
ISBN (E): 9781838939052

Printed and bound in Great Britain by
CPI Group (UK) Ltd, Croydon CRO 4YY

Head of Zeus Ltd
First Floor East
5–8 Hardwick Street
London EC1R 4RG
WWW.HEADOFZEUS.COM

Coming Home to the Four Streets

Also by Nadine Dorries

The Tarabeg Series

Shadows in Heaven

Mary Kate

The Velvet Ribbon

The Lovely Lane Series

The Angels of Lovely Lane

The Children of Lovely Lane

The Mothers of Lovely Lane

Christmas Angels

Snow Angels

The Four Streets Series

The Four Streets

Hide Her Name

The Ballymara Road

Coming Home to the Four Streets

Standalone novels

Ruby Flynn

Short stories

Run to Him

A Girl Called Eilinora

An Angel Sings

Coming Home to the Four Streets

Chapter One

Liverpool

There was little need for Eric to guide his faithful cob, Daisy Bell, along his milk round. The early morning mist lay close to the cobbles of the Dock Road and the four streets but the mare knew each step of the route by heart and had never wrong-hoofed him as he dropped the reins to turn the pages of the *Daily Post* which, by arrangement, he removed from a bundle piled up on the pavement outside the tobacconist and replaced with two bottles of silver top.

'Morning, Eric. Red sky last night so that sun is going to get his hat on at last, eh,' called out a scurrying figure, bent forward towards the Mersey and wreathed in blue cigarette smoke. He gave Eric the thumbs up as he passed, on his way towards the dockers' steps. Eric lifted his white oilskin cap in greeting and, feeling the fresh air on his head despite his thatch of thick chestnut brown hair, replaced it quickly. He rubbed his chin and wondered should he give the float a coat of fresh paint when he returned to the dairy.

He's right, he thought. The weather must change soon. I can't leave the painting for much longer because the Dock Queen Carnival is only weeks away. Eric, Daisy Bell and the float played a central role on the day of the carnival. Cleared of wooden crates and bottles, bedecked in May flowers, garlands and with the large throne-shaped chair from Sister Evangelista's office draped in crimson velvet and secured by hidden ropes, they would transport the queen and her retinue along the Dock Road and around the four streets, beginning on the front yard of the Anchor public house where everyone was offered a free tot of rum by Bill and Babs.

This guaranteed attendance for some of the day by the men, reluctant fathers and work-worn dockers trying their hardest to elicit a second tot from Babs, no friend to the equally reluctant and work-worn mothers who resented the time she spent serving their husbands. The rum was freely dispensed but, unknown to either Father Anthony or Sister Evangelista, it was not provided out of generosity nor was it even the property of the Anchor. No, it had 'fallen off the back of a tramp ship', close to the dockers' steps and been stored in the Dohertys' outhouse, in waiting for the event of the summer.

The procession would be led by Father Anthony at the front, and brought up by the Union of Catholic Mothers at the rear, pushing prams. Children would be running and laughing alongside all the way to the finish in the large priory garden where, for one day only, the children were allowed to play and run free. Games were organised by Miss Devlin, the only teacher who was not a nun at the school, whilst the nuns and the women of the four streets served teas and home-made cakes in an old canvas army hospital tent which smelt of gunsmoke, mud and despair. The highlight of the afternoon was the blessing of the dock queen and the awarding of the prizes – threepenny bits – by Sister Evangelista. Goldfish were won, moles whacked and bells rang out as the first child crossed the finishing line at the end of each race. The carnival could be won or lost on the state of the weather, which became the focus of attention for weeks before.

Eric looked up to the sky. The rain had been relentless, but this morning there was definitely a lightness in the mist. He made the decision that he would begin painting as soon as he arrived back at the dairy and would take the week to paint a panel a day. He delivered every morning, even on Sunday, his wife, Gladys, having frightened away every young boy Eric had taken on as an apprentice. Even those from homes desperate for the money had never lasted longer than a week, terrified by her temper or frozen in her piercing glare.

Daisy Bell turned left and the Anchor loomed before them. 'Well done, girl,' Eric said, and her ears flicked forward as she recognised the affection in his voice. The public house was their next-to-last call on the Dock Road; the round ended at the top of the dockers' steps which led down to the Mersey and delivered to every house and business on the way. Eric enjoyed the meticulous order of the round which played well to his military training. Every day was the same. Same orders, same numbers of bottles out and empties back in and he was about to deliver a crate of six steri to the Anchor. There was no sign of the cellar man but Eric could tell by the bottles stacked outside the back door that the previous evening had been a lock-in.

As the float trundled across the cobbled yard, Babs threw open the door and greeted them with a wave. Her usual beehive hair style was tied up in a headscarf which resembled a turban, and the remnants of the previous night's eye make-up was smeared under her eyes.

'Busy night was it, Babs?' Eric asked as he inclined his head towards the bottles.

'The usual, Eric. You know what they're like around here. Complain they've got no money and just as soon as they have a quid in their pockets, they spend it in here and either throw it up down our jacksies or piss it up the wall on the way home. Don't ever ask me why I'm still married. If I had just spent a week in this place first, it would have been enough to put me off for life. Men!'

Eric shook his head; he often thought people must wonder why *he* was married, given that everyone knew and avoided his wife Gladys. 'It's a mystery to me, Babs. I don't know where they get the money from. Only half of the men in the pen were taken on every morning last week, so I've heard.'

She looked instantly guilty. 'Well, don't blame me, Eric, it's not our fault. I mean, we can't refuse to serve them, can we? I had to push Paddy Nolan out of the door meself last night. Cadged a bob off Ena, he did, because he said there was no money for the leccy at home and Peggy and the kids were in the pitch black, then moved into the back bar and spent it on Guinness as soon as Ena started singing "Danny Boy". It's Peggy and the kids I feel sorry for, but what are we supposed to do, close the bleeding place down?' Without waiting for an answer, she continued, 'And if we did, the buggers would only go and spend it down at the Sylvestrian and put their money over the bar there. At least in my pub it's not as far to stagger home and there's no prossies on the street to take whatever the soft buggers have left.' Babs took a long pull on her cigarette and flicked the ash out of the door.

Now it was Eric's turn to feel guilty. 'I'm sorry, Babs, I didn't mean to suggest...' he began.

'Oh Eric, no love, no, I know you didn't. It's just harder now that Tommy Doherty isn't around. If he thought anyone was drinking too much and the kids were going without, he'd march them back home. I've seen him many a time taking what was left of the pay packet from some soft sod and then their Maura would take it round to the wife the next morning. It's not the same since him and Maura left; the four streets are going to pot without them.'

Eric shook his head in dismay and changed the subject. 'I was thinking of painting the float for the Dock Queen Carnival. Is it starting off on your front yard as usual?'

Babs's face lit up. 'It is. I went to the first meeting with Sister at the convent – and honest to God, the whole time I was there I was waiting for lightning to strike, or the doors to slam shut and lock me in.' Babs, who lived in a warm public house with a large fire, had no need of a welcome dry hour in mass, three times a day for seven months of the year and was not a regular attender, laughed. 'Sister said, "So, ladies, who is organising the bunting?" Well, not one bugger answered. It was Maura did all that before she left, so I nudged Peggy who was sat next to me and said to her, "Peggy, can't you do that? Didn't you used to be the one helping Maura before she left?" and she just gawped at me.

'I tell you, no one was home that night and I don't know what's wrong with that woman, apart from the fact that she's married to Paddy and has seven kids with open mouths hanging around her ankles. Kathleen Deane was on the other side of me and she's the one half-raising those kids since Maura took off. So Kathleen can't do it, can she? She's making the cakes,

Maisie's sewing all the frocks with the little material they have, Shelagh is running around like a blue-arsed fly with half a dozen kids on her hips, trying her best, bless her, and Alice and Deirdre, they're running just about everything else trying to please Miss Devlin, who never stops with the orders, and Cindy, well, she's too busy running her salon. And there's another problem; there hasn't been a tramp ship in the dock for months. No one's got nothing.'

Eric felt breathless just listening to Babs. None of it was news to him. The widow, Maggie Trott on Nelson Street, had voiced her concerns to him about the carnival weeks ago. The dock board didn't pay enough of a weekly wage to feed a large Catholic family and everyone on the four streets enjoyed some luxuries in life courtesy of Captain Conor, whose mother, Ena, lived on Waterloo Street. On a regular basis, Conor's tramp ship haul was carried up the dockers' steps in the dead of night and it was his rum, from the Caribbean, which kicked off the carnival to a good start.

'I mean, where does Sister think the free tot of rum comes from when everyone's covering your milk float in May flowers? Or the fabric for the frocks, for that matter. They were made of shot silk last year, that Conor brought all the way from China. He sold it to a shop in town and kept a bolt for us, but he hasn't been home for months. His poor mam thinks he's drowned, but I said to her, Ena, stop being so dramatic; if he had, his body would have been washed up weeks ago, and we would have heard by now.'

Eric shook his head in disbelief. Ena was a soft and gentle soul when she was sober. As used as she was to Babs, he could only imagine her reaction.

'You can't help some people, Eric. Walked out of the pub, she did and hadn't even touched her drink – and that's a first, I'm telling you.'

Eric made the mistake of answering Babs, and could have bitten his tongue off before the words had left his mouth. 'Well, if there's no sign of Conor sailing in, could you ask the fellas in here to stop supping slightly earlier than they do and have a bit of a collection?'

'The only person around here, other than Tommy Doherty, who could empty this place out early, is your Gladys. I don't suppose you'd want to send her around at ten tonight, would you? I've already tried Father Anthony and that didn't work; I had to get Jerry Deane to half carry him back to the Priory.'

Eric shook his head. The truth was, he was so scared of Gladys himself, he dared not reply, so instead he said, 'Get yourself inside, Babs, before you catch your death, and I'll close the door behind you – go on, now.'

He handed her the crate of milk and pulled the door to, the smile disappearing from his face as quickly as it had appeared. To everyone on the four streets, Gladys and her reputation for ferocity was a source of amusement; to Eric, it was his cross to bear. He loaded the crate of empties Babs had given to him onto the wagon and, stepping back up felt the familiar dip as Daisy Bell readjusted her step to accommodate his weight.

'Walk on,' he said as he rested the reins on his knee and retrieved his tobacco tin from his pocket; he pulled out a pre-rolled ciggie and lit up before Daisy Bell pulled back out onto the Dock Road. He rolled five ciggies at the dairy every morning; four were for him and one was for Mrs Maggie Trott on Nelson Street, which was where he took himself for a cup of tea each day. He had known and admired Maggie since before the war and their morning cuppa was the highlight of his day.

He had one call-in before he turned and that was at the Seaman's Stop, a guest house for sailors. Here, Daisy Bell slowed to a halt without any instruction from Eric. He squinted to see who the woman was, standing outside the sailors' guest house and was surprised to see that it was Biddy, one of the housekeepers from St Angelus Hospital, fishing around in her holdall outside the door. Next to her, looking nervously around was Mary Malone, Deirdre and Eugene's eldest.

'Biddy, what are you doing here?' he asked. 'I could have given you a lift, for I delivered to your house half an hour ago.'

'I know you did, but I missed you. I came running out but you were already gone.' Eric turned his back to her to remove a crate from the float just as the door to the Seaman's Stop opened. 'Oh, Malcolm, there you are, I couldn't find my keys,' said Biddy.

Malcolm was wearing striped pyjamas and a dressing gown which had not fastened around his middle since before the war. 'Morning, Eric, Biddy – I wasn't expecting you,' said Malcolm. 'Oh, hello, Mary, what are you doing here?'

'She's coming to work for you,' said Biddy, in a no-nonsense-tolerated tone. 'She's seventeen now and Sister said if she had a job to go to, she could leave the convent.'

'I never said I wanted anyone working for me!' Malcolm protested. 'And besides, I thought Mary was taking the veil.'

Eric watched with some amusement as more words of objection formed in Malcolm's mind, but he was no match for Biddy.

'She went to work for Sister in the kitchens when she left school, but they've given up trying to make a nun out of her. Sister was hoping Mary would take a liking to the life of a postulant and you know Deirdre was always in competition with Maura and that's the only reason this poor girl was sent to work in the convent in the first place. Now that Maura's gone, Deirdre has no objection to Mary taking a job that brings in money, so the Lord's loss is our gain. The veil's not for everyone, is it, Mary?'

Mary shook her head, obediently, her expression solemn. As far as she was concerned, Biddy removing her from the convent to work at the Seaman's Stop had been her own salvation, a miracle indeed. Malcolm reached out to take the crate from Eric.

'You need to get this place shipshape and Bristol fashion and I can't keep helping the way I do. I've got my own job up at the hospital,' Biddy went on.

Malcolm looked offended. 'Biddy, I've managed this establishment on my own since 1945.'

Biddy was having none of it. 'Malcolm, when was the last time you mopped under the beds? And stop making fish faces at me – you can't answer me because you can't remember. Time for this place to have a good spring clean and Mary has been cleaning since she could walk.' Malcolm's mouth opened and closed, again. 'She has two freshly laundered pinnies with her and, if she's a good worker, on Friday night, you will need to put fifteen shillings in her hand.'

Mary blinked and smiled up at Malcolm, who was defeated. It wasn't Mary, Malcolm objected to. He had known her since she was born, the first to lie in the second-hand pram Eugene had bought down on Scottie Road. Eight more had followed Mary and Malcolm had watched her push the others up and down the street in the pram since she was old enough to reach the handlebars. She was wearing a coat at least three sizes too big for her and her chestnut hair, usually worn in a ponytail, had been tied in rags the previous evening in anticipation of her new job, long and thick, it now bobbed on her shoulders in tight ringlets. Her bright blue eyes were flecked with hazel streaks and appeared large in her thin face. She was not a pretty girl, but there was something about her that caught the eye. A calmness, a depth beyond her years. As she smiled up at him, Malcolm knew Biddy had won.

'There you are then, now move yourself.' Biddy squeezed past Malcolm into the hallway.

'It's a surprise to see both yourself and Babs out on the step this morning,' said Eric, who didn't often see Malcolm.

'I can't speak for Babs,' said Malcolm, 'but I'm here to stop whoever the bugger is keeps pinching my milk.' He glanced furtively from side to side, up and down the Dock Road. 'Three mornings this week I've been missing a pint of gold top. Doesn't take the steri, only the best for my little thief.'

Biddy's voice called down the hallway, 'Come on, Malcolm, the kettle is on. I have to be at work soon and we need to make a list for Mary.'

Malcolm rolled his eyes. 'I knew today was going to be a bad day,' he said.

'My advice is,' said Eric, 'just do as you're told. It's far easier in the long run.'

Malcolm turned to make his way down the hallway, saying, 'She means well.' And both men knew that if it wasn't for Biddy, lonely Malcolm would have disappeared inside himself long ago.

*

Eric felt a sense of anticipation as they headed towards the corner of Nelson Street and the mare increased her pace; she knew what was coming next. In Nelson Street lived a customer who always had a special treat waiting for Daisy Bell. He could still hear his Gladys's words ringing in his ears as he had left the yard: 'Don't you dare be giving anyone credit in the four streets, do you hear me? Especially not Peggy Nolan on Nelson Street. We sell the milk, we don't give it away.'

Gladys had no idea that he stopped and had a cuppa every morning of his life with the war widow, Mrs Trott. It was a mystery to him that no one had ever shopped him to Gladys, although he always made sure he left Maggie Trott's well-scrubbed front step just before the back gates began to click open and bang shut as women ran out of their homes, fastening coats and headscarves, checking pockets for change to light a penny candle to the dead and to answer the bells calling them to first mass. They left fires catching in grates and children sleeping whilst they prayed for ships to arrive, work to be had and money to be tipped into the bread bin.

Eric and Maggie had been taking a ritual cuppa together every morning since 1944, when she was already a young widow, her husband having fallen in battle. Eric, injured and invalided out, had wished every day it had been he who had taken the bullet, just to wipe the pain from Maggie Trott's eyes. Sometimes he glanced down the road, expecting to see Gladys running towards them, waving a rolling pin and screaming abuse, and he wondered what his reaction would be if she ever told him to stop taking his break with the widow Trott.

The dairy house Eric and Gladys lived in was situated halfway along the Dock Road and that morning, Gladys had sent him off with her usual kindly words. 'The last time that Peggy cadged a pint off you, she took four months to pay. You don't see her round here, offering to pay, do you? Oh no, if that woman had a shred of self-respect, she would be offering to muck out or sterilise the bottler, wouldn't she? To pay off her debts with a bit of graft. But not her, and she still owes us for eight pints. As lazy as her bloody husband, big Paddy. Thinks I'm here to pour our milk down the neck of her brats for the love of it. Well, we're not a bleedin' charity, Eric. Not that I'd want her round here mind, lazy 'aul bitch.'

There she was, complaining Peggy never came around to pay off her debts and then, in the next breath, saying she wouldn't be welcome. If Eric had a pound for every time someone had told him opposites attract, he wouldn't be on the cart today; he would pay Captain Conor to sail him away to somewhere exotic where he could sun himself and drink as much rum as he liked.

'Steady, girl,' he said as the excited mare almost broke into a trot. He pulled on his ciggie and turned his gaze left down towards the Mersey. The mist hugged the river like an unfurled bolt of dove-grey chiffon that was slowly sinking below the surface, but he could still make out the activity down below, though few were around. It would be another half an hour before the dockers' klaxon rang out. He watched as the tug captains made their way into the administration huts for tea and orders, the swooping seagulls waiting for the fish to come in from further north. Tug captains were the only men who rose at the same ungodly hour as Eric.

Eric looked right and saw Kathleen, mother to Jerry Deane, who had arrived in Liverpool from the west coast of Ireland, not long after her daughter-in-law, Bernadette, had lost her life in childbirth. A woman of wisdom, who had built a reputation for reading the tea leaves, she had become a pillar of the community and, along with Maura Doherty, had held the four streets together. But now Maura had gone and Kathleen, a woman in her sixties, struggled alone. She was leaving St Saviour's churchyard and walking with purpose towards the church itself. Funny, Eric thought, she's early today. He guessed she had been to lay flowers at the grave of Kitty Doherty and was reminded of Gladys's words the previous evening.

'They got very above themselves, the Dohertys, taking off to Ireland and opening up a business like that. I suppose Tommy Doherty thought if he drank in a pub every day, that gave him all the knowledge he would need to run one. A windfall my arse. Does anyone believe that story? Relatives in America turn up from nowhere with a baby in tow and give them enough money to keep them in clover? Not flaming likely! Well, you know what they say, don't you?' Eric didn't answer. He never did. 'A fool and his money are easy parted. My money, which no one will part me from, by the way, is on them both turning back up here with their brood of brats and tails between their legs before the year is out.'

'What makes you think they'll be back?' he had asked with a furrowed brow.

Gladys snorted as she placed a dish of bread-and-butter pudding next to his plate. To her credit, Gladys always served up a good evening meal, even though she did her best to ruin it with the venom that dripped from her thin pursed lips. Wiping a splash of hot custard from her hands onto her apron, she replied, 'Everyone knows, everyone thinks it, except you, soft lad. It was the talk of the butcher's when I called in this morning. Not one person around here thinks they'll last five minutes.'

'It's been a fair few months already, though,' said Eric. He shook his head in disbelief at having broken his own rule of silence at mealtimes, knowing it would certainly not end well.

'What would you know? All you do is collect milk, bottle it, deliver it and clean up horseshit. No one's interested in your opinion.'

It didn't matter what he did to prepare himself, Eric could never stop Gladys's words from stinging.

'And that story about their Kitty, going to look after

a relative in Ireland and just happening to drown by accident when she was there? What nonsense. What child around here can swim? Why would she even be near a river? One day, someone will get to the bottom of that story and when that day comes, we will all be the wiser for it.'

'God rest her soul,' said Eric and felt a genuine pain at Kitty's name being mentioned in such a way in his home. Kitty had been the sweetest child, her da's shadow, her mam's little helper and to have died at the age of sixteen, at the foothills of all there was to enjoy in this life, was nothing short of a tragedy.

'And then, to bring her body over here? Who paid for that, I ask you?' Eric didn't answer; Gladys wasn't asking him at all and had never, since the day they married, shown any interest in his opinion. 'In a carriage and a coffin and with all those flowers. None of that came cheap, I can tell you. Flown from Shannon into Speke airport like she was the queen. Well, Kitty Doherty is the only person from around here to have ever been on an aeroplane, I'll give her that. Kitty Doherty and the Beatles, who would have thought that, eh? Shame she had to die first and can't tell any of us about it.'

Eric had risen from the table feeling physically sick, the toxic atmosphere choking him. 'I'm just going to check on Daisy Bell,' he'd said as he made for the back door. 'I thought she looked a bit lame at the end of the round today.'

'What about your pudding?' she said to his back.

'I'll have it in a minute.' He'd closed the door behind him and gulped in the damp evening air, knowing he wouldn't be able to swallow another thing until he could erase the memory of her heartless words from his mind.

Now, on this fine morning, he raised his hand in greeting to Kathleen, who for a woman of her age walked with a youthful stride. Plump, with her white hair concealed in curlers beneath her hairnet, she looked over to Eric with a cheerful smile and, as she raised her hand in response, Eric felt washed over with shame at Gladys's words and disappointment that he had married a woman who could think such things about a hard-working, clean-living family like the Dohertys.

Mrs Trott was Eric's first stop on Nelson Street and she was at the door, waiting. He had no need to pull on the reins; Daisy Bell drew to a halt of her own accord.

'Morning, Eric. Not a moment too soon, I'm spitting feathers waiting for me tea – I used the last of what I had on yours.'

Eric slipped from the seat and, dropping the reins, walked over to collect his steaming hot cup. This had been their routine since he had returned from the war. Mrs Trott took the few steps from her doorway to Daisy Bell, holding the palm of her hand out flat with a sugar lump for the mare. She patted her on the neck and ran her fingers through the long, well-combed mane.

'There you go, good girl,' she said and moved back into the doorway, pulling her cardigan across her chest to protect her against the breeze lifting up from the Mersey. 'She'll have my hand one day,' she went on as she took a handkerchief from a pocket and wiped the sticky sugar residue from her palm. Her wire curlers protruded from the front of her headscarf and there was not a scrap of powder or paint on her face but it occurred to Eric that she was one of the few women he met on his round who, despite the early hour, still appeared glamorous at the start of the day. Her twinkling blue eyes and her full lips hinted at a generous and caring nature. 'I don't know why you gave that horse a cow's name,' she complained as Eric leant against the wall and sipped his tea.

He grinned over the rim of the cup. 'You're losing your marbles, you are. You said the same thing to me yesterday. Nice cuppa…' He held the cup up in a mock salute. 'Me losing my marbles, you say that every day, too.'

She chided him gently. 'One day, Eric, I'll sleep in and then maybe you might appreciate the sacrifice I make, getting up every morning to look after you two.'

Eric's heart swelled with pleasure; Maggie always included Daisy Bell whenever she referred to him and it gave him an inordinate amount of pleasure.

'Ah, well, that would be a sad day, I can't imagine how Daisy Bell would feel if we took this corner and her sugar treat wasn't waiting for her, it would break her heart, it would.' His words caught in his throat and he could say no more. They both knew he was referring to himself, not the mare. The air between them felt heavy and still, knowing as they did that it wouldn't be the lack of the tea that broke his heart. Maggie fractured the moment, distracted by something she sensed more than heard and he was grateful. They often did this, allowed their conversation to wander from matter of fact to flirtatious, but ending it as quickly as it began because neither had any notion where to go next.

'Don't look now, Eric,' she said, 'we're being watched.'

Eric made to turn and stopped himself just in time. 'Is it Peggy by any chance?'

'Aye, Peggy,' she said.

Eric dropped the last of his cigarette onto the pavement and stubbed it out with his toe, then took another swig of his tea. 'Here, hold this,' he said as he handed her the cup and then extracted a tobacco tin from his large pocket. He took out two cigarettes and passed one to Maggie. He glanced sideways up the street. 'Since Maura and Tommy left, my life has been much harder managing the likes of Peggy,' he said, shaking his head. 'Maura used to nip out and take an extra pint or two to give to Peggy if she thought the kids were going without. She would always say, "Put it on my bill, Eric." And then, she would get the money from Peggy in her own time, in her own way. I would get mine on a Friday night, as normal, and there would be no grief waiting for me back at home. She was a saint, Maura was. She knew Gladys made my life hell if I gave in to Peggy.'

'Isn't your life always hell?' asked Maggie, placing the cigarette between her lips. Their eyes met and held. As always, she looked away first. Despite the rumours that flew around the four streets, Eric never spoke about Gladys in a derogatory manner or confirmed what most knew of his life to be true. He flicked over her comment as if it were a page in a book he had no desire to read.

'Maura saved me from having to make excuses, aye. Step back into the hall, Maggie, it's too brisk for you to be stood on the step.'

Her comfort, her life, was always at the forefront of his thoughts. She did as she was told and took a step backwards as she took her petrol lighter from her pocket and, flicking the lid back, held it under the cigarette that dangled from Eric's lips. He inhaled the fumes from the petrol before he pulled up the flame and the stray ends of tobacco sizzled in the Rizla. Their eyes met and held again, despite the best intentions of both. They lived by the rules because Eric was a married man. This morning ritual was the closest they came to intimacy and, as she leant forwards, she inhaled the earthy smell of him, the morning air and Old Spice, cigarette smoke and horse. It felt to Eric as though the world stopped spinning on its axis, as if, for those captured seconds, he was someone else, sharing a harmonious life with someone who cared. This morning their eyes lingered on each other for longer

than usual before she drew on the flame herself, the lid of the lighter snapped shut and she slipped it back into her cardigan pocket. The moment was gone, over and done, until tomorrow.

'Yes, that was Maura all over for you,' she said. 'She kept this street in order, she did. Just look at the state of Peggy's nets. They were never like that when Maura was around. And I'll tell you what, Maura did get the money back off Peggy right enough; she made sure of it. She ran that house next door as well as her own. God love them, if there was a family that deserved good luck, it was theirs. Terrible thing that, losing their Kitty. I promised Maura before she left that I'd keep an eye out for little Paddy and the others. It's not the kids' fault they've got a mam and da like Peggy and big Paddy.'

Eric agreed. 'No, that's why I always feel bad when she asks me for the milk. Breaks my heart it does to see a kid go hungry.'

Maggie looked up at Eric. His shoulders were broad and he was a good eight inches taller than she was, his complexion lined and cragged from spending hours of his day outdoors, his eyes dark and deep and his hair, cut into a style only just longer than when he was in the army, poked out from under his waterproof white cap. If anyone saw them together, they would say 'there's a good-looking couple' and she knew it. A vainer woman than Maggie Trott would have relished such a compliment.

'You know what? You are a big softie, Eric,' she said, smiling up at him. 'Mind you, I'm not much better. Sometimes I think I only bake cakes every other day to make sure I can give some to little Paddy to hand them out to the kids. He loves my shortbreads, and God love him, they are so easy to make. No idea why his mother can't do it.

'I know Kathleen and Alice fed all the kids this Sunday; Kathleen said she had made too much and Alice had peeled too many spuds but they never did; they just knew those kids were on jam and bread all day because big Paddy, the lazy sod, barely worked last week.' She glanced up the road. 'Oh dear, Peggy will fall right out of that bedroom window if she leans any further forward to catch your eye, Eric! What are you going to do?'

Eric shook his head. If there was one thing he hated more in his life than anything else, it was having to say no to a woman asking him for milk he knew she couldn't pay for. 'What can I do? Our Gladys wants to get out on the round on Friday nights and do the collecting with me. She counts every pint out and every penny in since Peggy didn't pay up last time.'

Maggie pulled hard on her ciggie and then glanced up the road. 'If you do give her some, put it on my bill this week. It's her lazy git of a husband that's at fault, not her. If that man can get out of work, he will. Kathleen said yesterday, when she read my tea leaves, that Jerry was going to step in or those kids will be living on jam buttys forever more. Kathleen told me that one morning their Jerry and Tommy stormed up the stairs, dragged Paddy from his steaming pit and marched him down the steps. Now Jerry is going to try and do it on his own, before those kids get rickets – though God love them, the youngest looks like he has it already. Give her four steri, Eric, and I'll pay it; that way, your Gladys will never know.'

He fought the urge to reach out and fold her into his arms. Maggie Trott, kind, dependable, lonely. A bit like himself, even though he had Gladys at home. Maggie flicked her ash onto the pavement and under her breath whispered to Eric, 'Don't look now, we really are being watched and it's not just Peggy Nolan...'

Annie O'Prey never lifted the front room nets until Maggie Trott took out her cigarette lighter. That way, she and Eric never saw her as she watched their every exchange across the cobbled road. 'One day, his Gladys will catch him at that,' she said to her son, Callum, who had walked into the room behind her.

'I'm leaving for work now, Mam.'

She spun around to face him. 'What, now? The klaxon hasn't gone yet.' Her voice was laced with a hint of irritation at being caught spying on her neighbour but Callum couldn't have been less interested in what was happening across the road.

'I'm knocking on for Jerry,' he said. 'There's a full load of lumber in today and I want to make sure I'm taken on because I'm going to have to miss a day when Jimmy gets out.'

Her expression altered in a heartbeat, her eyes alight. Her firstborn, her Jimmy, her favourite had been mentioned. 'Oh, everyone will be up for a party that night!' Annie clasped her hands together and almost danced across the parlour.

Callum sighed inwardly. She had chosen to believe Jimmy's version of events, deliberately chose to ignore the pain of the poor man he had tied up, bruised and shaken, with a lump the size of an egg on the side of his head. He hadn't worked since and in a hard-working community, Jimmy's actions were a breach of common decency. Rob from the rich but do no harm to the poor was a well-established principle. The fact that Jimmy had crossed the line from scally to baddun was not a thought that had entered Annie's brain.

Callum shook his head; there would be no partying when Jimmy came home. Jimmy had broken the code of honour and for that the community would cast him out.

'Why can't I go with you to meet him when he comes out? Why won't you let me? Can't you get Jerry to take Jimmy on too?'

Since his own stint in prison, Callum, a good-looking boy, had managed to keep himself out of trouble and had been taken under the wing of their neighbour, Jerry Deane. Jerry had persuaded the gaffer down on the dock to take Callum on so long as Jerry guaranteed his good behaviour. Callum had sworn, to himself, Jerry and the priest, that he would work every day to repay this generosity and there was nothing and no one on this earth who could persuade him to do anything that would let Jerry down.

The O'Prey twins had earned a dockside-renowned reputation of stealing to order as soon as they realised they could run faster than anyone else, but in the past it had always been for a good cause – the back of a bread van emptied out so that a child on the four streets could have a birthday party; a delivery to the off-licence on the Dock Road, intercepted in time for Christmas. Their mother Annie, widowed young, had never been able to handle her boisterous twins and had long ago given up.

'You *are* going to meet Jimmy at the prison gates, aren't you? He can't walk out of that godforsaken place and travel all the way home, alone. It's three buses.' Annie's voice had taken on a note of pleading.

Callum thrust his hands into his pockets. 'Mam, if I don't meet him, he could be back inside before he got home! Of course I am. That's why I'm going to get as many hours in as I can between now and then – and that's the last day I'm giving to Jimmy.'

Annie frowned and pushed her glasses up her nose.

'Well, it's not his fault, is it?' she said. 'Ever since the priest was murdered, the police have not been away from these streets. They've put that horror of a bobby, Frank the Skank, on the docks since the sergeant married Miss Devlin and he's always walking up and down past our window.'

'Mam, if Jimmy stays clean he's nothing to fear from Frank the Skank. Jimmy was caught breaking into a betting shop in the Dingle. And don't forget poor Mary – he broke that girl's heart. Will he be doing the right thing there?'

Annie pushed Callum to one side as she walked past him into the kitchen. 'Not if I have anything to do with it. He was far too good for the likes of that girl. Our Jimmy deserves better than that.'

Now it was Callum's turn to feel angry. He carried a torch for Mary himself, but knowing she had fallen for his brother meant he couldn't do anything about it. To him, Mary was perfect. Annie could see she had upset her son, and whilst Jimmy was her favourite, Callum was the dependable son she needed to help pay the rent and the bills.

'Come on now, Callum, don't be like that. I'll fry a few rashers before you go, put something in your stomach; you can't do a day's work on an empty belly. You still have time to eat and be at the front of the pen.'

Callum followed his mammy into the kitchen. He had vowed that he would never again see the inside of a cell and resented having to take the day off work and three buses to meet Jimmy. His almost-impossible goal on the day he collected Jimmy would be to persuade his brother to become a reformed character and that a life of crime really didn't pay as well as the docks.

Eric walked to the cart and lifted Mrs Trott's milk from the crate. He noticed the net curtain across the road, which had been in place when he arrived, was now balanced on the top of an ornament. He placed his empty cup into one of Maggie's outstretched hands and the bottle of milk in the other.

'Seems as though someone was having a good look,' he said, flicking his head backwards.

Maggie sighed. 'Jimmy gets out of jail any day now. She won't get the chance to change his sheets before he's back in again.'

'Is that so? Can you get the news on those, then,' he asked, nodding and grinning at her wire curlers. 'Or, do they tingle if it's going to rain?'

Maggie grinned. 'Oh stop, will you! I'll be seeing you tomorrow then?' She always did, but she had to know.

He was reluctant to leave, to surrender to the remainder of the day. 'You will, as always. What would my morning be without you?' Two heartbeats skipped, the air held still, the seagulls silenced... Then, 'I'd be gasping for a cuppa,' and life returned to normal. He tore himself away and with his own heart heavy, walked briskly towards number 42.

Maggie watched him go. She patted the headscarf that was supposed to conceal her wire curlers. Maybe I should start taking my curlers out and putting on a bit of lippy in the mornings, she thought. She could count on one hand the times she had applied lipstick during the last two decades. Well, it was time for a perm so she would call in to Cindy the hairdresser on the parade and ask her for a lesson in the modern way of wearing make-up. It was all blue eyelids, sweeping eyeliner and shimmering pink lips these days and she had no idea where to start, but she could try. Unbidden, she imagined Eric in her bed – and the vision was so vivid, that, as she closed her eyes, she heard the mattress creak. Felt his hands, on which her eyes had lingered only seconds before, roaming along the length of her thighs, his lips, pressing down on hers, his breathing, deep and urgent, the smell of him, sweet and cold, the weight of his body, moving closer… His fingertips parted her willing knees – and just as that delicious thought grew in her mind, Sister Evangelista marched across the bottom of Nelson Street with Deirdre Malone following in her wake.

'Will I see you at mass, Mrs Trott?' Sister Evangelista called as she raised her hand. Maggie gave a guilty start and called back, 'You will indeed, Sister! I'll be on my way in just a minute.' She stepped back indoors and slammed the door, redemption from her wicked thoughts just around the corner, which meant that she was entirely free to indulge herself on another day soon.

Chapter Two

The west coast of Ireland

Maura deftly flicked her apron to the side as she moved swiftly between the bar and the Guinness barrel in order to retrieve a pewter mug, suspended from the wooden beam above her head. It belonged to her first customer of the afternoon, one of a small number of fishermen who frequented the inn on a daily basis and who always arrived with great ceremony. She was ready for him. He ignored the doormat she religiously beat each morning and stomped across the dark wooden floorboards she had polished on her hands and knees just an hour before, leaving puddles of muddy water behind him. He shuffled off his dripping oilskin and flung it onto the settle by the fire, never breaking his stride until he reached the bar.

Maura raised her eyes to the low ceiling, stained brown from peat smoke and clay pipes and bit her tongue. She had found the transition from docker's wife and queen of the four streets in Liverpool, to that of the landlady at the Talk of the Town Inn on the windy west coast of Ireland, a difficult one.

'Why would anyone call it the Talk of the Town?' she had demanded of her husband, on the wet, cold, wind-swept day they had arrived. She could barely hear his reply as the ocean roared behind them, only a moment's walk from where they stood. Their children, bedraggled, too miserable even to complain, huddled into their sides. 'There's almost nothing and no one here and we haven't passed a shop in miles. In the name of God, what flamin' town is it supposed to be the talk of? Where is the town, Tommy?'

She had stood with her hands on her hips and taken in the sparsity of stone cottages with weak spirals of grey smoke struggling to rise in the rain and blending without trace into the equally grey sky. The church, with its teetering gravestones facing the ocean, sloped down towards them and, huddling against the crumbling perimeter wall for protection, stood a sad and sorry-looking donkey that struggled to raise his head, or show any interest whatsoever in their arrival. Maura's dark eyes, offended by the sight of the dilapidated inn, locked onto Tommy's face and she realised, with a sickening dip of her heart, that her husband had been entirely duped.

'Tommy, speak to me, are we in the wrong place? Tell me we are, please,' she begged.

'I don't think so, queen,' he replied, his voice hesitant, a letter that they both knew he couldn't fully read, gripped in his hands. He was inches shorter than his wife and twice as wide and she fought the conflicting desires to knock his cap off his head, or comfort him.

Angela, their eldest since Kitty's death, sensing danger, inserted herself between them and slipped her hand into Tommy's. There were certain responsibilities Angela had assumed from Kitty, and one of those was to look out for Tommy, who could be far too trusting for his own good. A quiet man of simple needs, loving his family, football and friends, Tommy had bumbled through life until he had, late one evening, without any warning whatsoever, found himself standing at the doors of hell and nothing had been quite the same since.

'Da, where are we going now?' she'd asked, hoping the answer was not into the low, stone-built, partly-thatched building before them.

'I'm not sure, queen,' Tommy replied, his heart beating so fast it made him dizzy. Maura had ripped the letter from his fingers and scanned it with her flashing eyes.

'Oh, for the love of God, Tommy, tell me, is this it? Did you did ask the man how many people actually lived in this place before you signed the contract and handed over the money?' Her dark hair, free from the curlers she wore for most of the day in Liverpool, was pinned to the nape of her neck in a tight bun, her headscarf, tied into a knot under her chin, making her look much older than her forty years. 'Oh Tommy, by all the saints in heaven, what have you done now?'

For a brief moment, Maura thought she saw tears well in her husband's eyes, but with a blink, they were gone. Angela looked up into her da's face; she had seen the tears too and threw her mother a threatening glance. She squeezed Tommy's hand tighter, willing him to look down at her and say the only thing she wanted to hear, 'We've come to the wrong place, queen.'

Niamh slipped her thumb into her mouth and her free hand into her mother's, her eyes wide, while Harry rocked from side to side with the baby on his hip and the younger boys, tired from their long journey, flopped onto the suitcases that Tommy – carrying one under each arm and one in each hand – had dropped on the ground into puddles which splashed the shoes Maura had polished, ready to make a good impression on arrival at their new home. Each one of them was staring at Tommy, the man of the family who everyone looked up to. Tommy, who dragged men out of the Anchor and back into their own kitchens, tipping their money into the bread bin of a grateful wife and mother. Tommy, the man who organised the hauls from the tramp ship, got them up the dockers' steps and into his wash house, then distributed around the four streets before it was time to light the copper for the next week's washday.

Tommy was the close friend of Captain Conor who sailed the tramp ship *Morry* to the four corners of the world, and if it hadn't been for his meeting Maura on the day he arrived in Liverpool, Tommy might have been a merchant sailor himself. It was Tommy who studied the form of the horses and had the best tips in Liverpool, making him the man amongst men. Tommy, who lived with the darkest secret, shared with his best friend Jerry Deane. And if the residents of the four streets had an inkling what it was that Tommy had done, they would have chased him all the way to the gates of hell.

But Tommy was no longer in the four streets, this was a new world. He was out of his depth, in total despair and confusion, as he turned to face his family and replied, 'I don't know what I've done, Maura; all I know is, if we don't make a go of this, we've lost the bleeding lot.'

Maura remained as appalled today as she had been on that fateful morning and nothing and no one had managed to convince her that there were any more benefits for her children to living in a public house which faced out across the Atlantic, than there were perched in an equally damp two-up, two-down facing down across the Mersey in Liverpool.

'How are ye, Maura?' called the man who had soaked her floors, banging both of his palms flat on the bar. Maura's eyes fixed on the water that ran from the oil-skin coat onto her tapestry cushion. If one of the twins had done that, she would have flicked them around the back of the legs with the tea towel that hung from her waistband. She glared at her customer but he was impervious. His face broke into a grin and he removed his cap and shook it, sending water flying across the polished countertop and flopped it back on his head. Ignoring her lack of greeting, he continued unperturbed.

'God in heaven, it's mighty fierce out there,' he said as a chill damp breeze whistled through the bar when the door he had failed to close properly behind him blew open and banged against the wall. Maura flicked the brass tap on the barrel of Guinness and the black velvet liquid began to flow into his favourite pot. 'Where would Tommy be?' he asked. 'Don't be giving me half measures there now, will ye?'

Maura felt a familiar irritation wash over her. Tommy was over at the Deanes' farm, helping with the milking, and she had never given anyone half measures since the day they had taken over the inn. 'He's away milking,' she replied as she wiped the foam spilling down over the lip of the pot with the corner of her apron and laid it on the towelling bar mat. She had made a point of overfilling the pot, in order to avoid further criticism but he uttered not a word of thanks, just raised the pot to his lips and slurped away the foam, then took out his pipe and lit it.

Maura picked up the mop that stood permanently in the bucket in the passage behind the bar and wheeled it towards the wet puddles, pointedly slamming the door shut that he had left open. Flames from the peat fire in the huge open grate leapt up the chimney and then settled back down as the door closed.

'Born in a barn were you?' she hissed.

'Aye,' he replied between puffs on his pipe, 'as it happens, I was.'

Maura felt no inclination to laugh at his attempt at humour and besides, he was likely speaking the truth. Their only neighbours lived in a long stone barn, with a cow and a pen of pigs at one end, the family at the other.

'It's 1966,' Maura said to Tommy, after the first time they had been invited in, 'and it's the same as when we were kids, nothing has changed.'

Tommy had to agree with her. 'Aye, it's still a long way from Galway out here on the coast. Every one of their boys gone to America, too. Still, they have the money arriving every week, they aren't poor.'

Maura was not impressed. 'I'd rather have my kids by my side than the money,' she had answered, 'and you should know better, after losing our Kitty.'

She looked out now through the window next to the door, down over the road and towards the ocean. Raindrops the size of fat pebbles hurled against the thick, opaque glass, worn white with ingrained sea salt that had proved almost impossible to remove. She could count on one hand the number of days she had seen the sun shine since they had arrived and her heart felt so heavy it rooted her to the spot. This was it, the reality. The future she and Tommy had dreamt of and planned for.

They had willingly returned from Liverpool to Ireland, heading in the opposite direction to almost everyone else, to run their own business.

The tourists were supposed to be beating a path to their door and although the occasional American, in search of his or her heritage, had found their way here, they hadn't stopped for long, but returned to seek the hot fresh coffee, afternoon fancies and indoor lavatories in the Hardiman Hotel in Galway. Having sailed first class from America, the search for their heritage took ten minutes to complete. A visit to the church to light a penny candle, a blessing on a grave and a snap with a Canon camera to prove 'we were here', sufficed.

Maura very quickly discovered that they were wholly dependent on the small fishing community to keep things turning over. But as much as she hated it, they had no option but to go along with it. Tommy was running from his demons and she would run along with him, at her husband's side.

'We'll make it the best place for miles, Maura, you watch,' he had said as they opened the front door for the first time. 'They will be landing at Shannon and telling the taxi drivers to bring them straight to our door.'

But the bedrooms they had lovingly decorated and furnished stood empty and their dreams had turned to dust as their bank balance depleted, so Tommy had no choice but to help out on Liam Deane's farm to bring in some money. Liam was Jerry's brother and Kathleen's son, as good as their own family, and it was in the river that ran through their land where their beloved Kitty had drowned. They were bound together by an invisible bond and a knowledge of deeds that would never be spoken of but would hold fast for a lifetime. Liam and Maeve Deane were their only true friends in Ireland – all of Maura's own family were long since in America and lost to her and Tommy, an only child, had seen the passing of his parents. They had returned to the country of their childhoods to discover that, without those they had loved around them, it was a hard and miserable place.

The bar began to fill with the smell of pipe smoke, which suppressed that of stale ale and the smell from the jacks at the back of the inn – which Maura discovered was used by every inhabitant of the village as a sluice to empty their toilet buckets when the wind was too high to walk down to the shore. Nose held, she cleaned it daily with Dettol and a mop.

'Things can't be going as well as you hoped they would, if Tommy has to find work, helping with the milking.' Her customer blew the smoke from his pipe in her direction and Maura didn't dare look up, for her glance would surely kill him.

'Not at all,' she replied as she pushed down on the wooden mop handle with all her strength. 'How would that be?'

Her customer made her wait as he took a long sip on his drink and she pretended she wasn't waiting for his reply as she swung the mop back and forth, imagining his face on the end of it. He smacked his lips. 'Well, because Liam hasn't increased his herd and he was managing very well before. Maybe it is that your man was feeling a bit sorry for Tommy now; like, he wanted to help him out so, because sure, that would be the nature of Liam. He wouldn't hesitate to help out someone who was in need, so he wouldn't.'

'Unlike yourself then,' muttered Maura as she kicked the metal bucket back towards the bar. She guided it expertly through the hatch, behind the counter and into the back as she looked up at the clock. It was gone four. The children would soon be home from school. Having walked the two miles, they would be soaked through by the time they reached the Talk of the no flamin' Town, as Maura now called it. Very different from the ten-minute march from school gate to home in Liverpool with their lifelong friends. No longer did little Paddy, Peggy and Paddy's son, run into her kitchen with Scamp the dog at his heels and she missed him and his impish ways as much as she missed her friends. She'd fed him, looked out for him and guided his mother, simple Peggy. How she wished she could have banged that mop on the wall and called in Peggy from next door for gossip about the antics of the O'Prey boys.

Certainly, gone were the days of worrying about what she would make for tea on a Wednesday night if the money had run out before payday on Thursday, but with that had gone everything else too. Her friends, her life, her sparkle and, most importantly, her status. Here, Maura was an outsider. She heard the side door open and the rumble of feet up the half-stairs to their generous living quarters at the back, and she smiled, a rare occurrence these days: the children, safely home.

'Well, hello you lot. Yes, I'm fine thank you for asking.' She tutted and smiled again as she turned to walk into the bar – and almost jumped out of her skin as Harry, the eldest from both sets of twins, appeared before her. 'Jesus wept, Harry. You near frightened me to death! What are you doing stood there? Why are you not away up the stairs? I've left the Cidona on the table and the biscuits; did you think I'd forgotten? They will have eaten the flamin' lot if you don't hurry.'

She lifted up her son's cap and ruffled his hair, then stopped, as she saw a tear run down his cheek.

'Maura, I'm dying of thirst out here,' a voice called from in the bar as Maura dropped to her knees to face her son.

'Harry, what in God's name is wrong? Tell me?' Harry held out his hands and Maura's own hand flew to her mouth. 'God in heaven, who did that to you?'

Harry tried to speak, but his throat was tight and his tongue thick, no words came. Maura stared at the red weals across the palms of her son's hands and, as she turned him around, across the back of his legs too. Harry was Maura and Tommy's clever son. The sensitive,

41

helpful, caring boy who had assumed the role of junior parent since Kitty's death, whenever Angela let him. Maura threw her arms around him and pulled him into her.

'Maura!' a voice roared from the front. 'Have I to pour my own fecking drink? If I do so, I take it I won't be paying for it, will I?'

Maura pulled back and looked her son in the eyes. 'Harry, who did this to you?' she asked again.

The children attended the school of the Christian Brothers and Harry and the boys were in Mr Cleary's class, a civilian teacher who made Maura's flesh crawl. 'He's no Miss Devlin, either in looks or nature,' she had said to Tommy when they had signed the children up at the school.

Harry took in a deep breath and shuddered. 'Mr Cleary, with his stick.'

'Why? Why in God's name would he do that?'

Harry found his voice. 'I couldn't say the Hail Marys in the Irish, I got mixed up.'

Maura almost swore under her breath. 'Here, let me wash the blood away,' she said, turning on the tap. Harry flinched as she held his hands up under the running water and she heard the inn door open and close again, more voices, more demands for her attention, but she would not leave her son.

'Wait, can't you?' she shouted back. 'You won't die of thirst in five minutes!'

The response was a muted grumbling. She took a clean hand towel down from the shelf above the sink and ripped it down the middle. She pulled Harry's face into her apron and stroked his hair, muttering a prayer under her breath. 'You brave little soldier,' she whispered as she kissed the top of his head, inhaling the scent of him. Then, taking each hand, she wrapped it in the cotton, making a bandage. Her son looked up at her, his eyes brimming with a mixture of pain and love. Her breath caught in her throat. 'You go upstairs now. Have your Cidona and biscuits and when daddy is back from Liam's, we will talk about this.'

It was almost ten when Tommy riddled down the upstairs fire. ''Tis a small mercy, but one I'm grateful for that the boats are out in the morning,' said Maura.

The villagers lived by the tide and the light. As soon as it was fully dark, they made their way home, ready for an early catch on the boats or to lay the lobster pots, but it was not always so. If the fiddler or the storyteller called into the village, the wives and the children came too and not one of them left; at times it felt to Maura as though they had been taken over by squatters. The villagers drank until they could stand no more and slept where they fell, the wives and children too, with no catch the following day. Maura had resorted to dousing them with cold water, courtesy of her mop and bucket, to encourage them to move and her insistence that they left the inn and returned to their own homes had won her no friends amongst the locals, who knew no end to time, no urgency of need. Life was sun up, sun down, pots and boats out, pots and boats back in. Always, just enough to last until the next day. Life happened at a pace so slow Maura could barely comprehend how it was they existed at all.

As Tommy went to fetch peat sods to fill up the bucket, Maura washed up their cups in the small rear kitchen. She felt a sadness wash over her as she looked at her reflection in the mirror hanging next to the sink. She was ageing, she thought. Her face looked even thinner than usual. The sound of the wind and rain was so loud she almost couldn't hear the radio. She half smiled as she remembered how often the women on the four streets complained about the wind that blew up from the Mersey.

Tommy came and slipped his arms around her waist. 'Got you,' he whispered into her ear. She hugged her husband and for a long, still moment they breathed as one.

'I was just thinking to myself, how the women back at home—'

'*Here* is home,' Tommy corrected her.

'No, I mean back on the four streets.' She eased herself out of his embrace. 'They should try a day living in a house facing the Atlantic. To think how much we moaned about the river Mersey. You can hardly hear yourself think in here for the noise. Do you think the ocean has ever got as far as the front door?'

Tommy wasn't listening; his hands slipped down her back and cupped her buttocks as he began to kiss her neck.

'Tommy, stop, would you?' she protested as she pushed his hands away. On any other night she would have giggled and a play fight, which only ever ended in the bedroom, would have ensued. 'Tommy, we have to think. What are we to do about Harry and that brute, Cleary? Could you imagine him coming home with his hands bleeding like that if we were still living in the four streets? Sister Evangelista would never harm a hair on a child's head, even if Miss Devlin had sent him to her office.'

Harry had been so stoical when Tommy had returned home and applied the iodine to the bleeding, raw cuts on his hands. She'd had to fight back her own tears as well as wipe away Harry's. Her brave little soldier had turned a ghastly shade of white and she'd felt his legs buckle beneath him. Tommy had grabbed him and held him fast to his own chest. Maura saw the anger in his eyes as their son tried his best not to cry out again. Now Tommy released his hold and took his wife's hands.

'Maura, I got worse when I was a kid. The Brothers are brutal, all right, but they make a firm fist of turning us into good earners.'

Maura knew exactly what her husband was doing and

it was no use. He had done it every day since they had moved to the west coast. 'Save your breath, Tommy. You try to put a gloss on everything that happens here but you aren't going to make me feel any better. You can't put a shine on a turd and that man belongs in a midden. This is serious – and anyway, they teach you nothing. You can't flamin' read; if you could, we wouldn't be here. All you know, our Kitty taught you. Are you really such an arse feck?'

Tommy had the good grace to look embarrassed, if a little crestfallen, and Maura instantly felt guilty.

'Jesus, why did God make men such eejits?' she asked. 'They turn out good workers, I'll give you that, but Tommy, our kids spend more time in school on their catechisms and writing in the Gaelic than they do on their tables. This school is in the last century. I know for a fact it's not as backwards as this in Galway or Dublin. But here we are in the forgotten land, stuck behind the mountains where no bugger comes because the roads are too bad.'

Tommy bent to switch off the standard lamp by the plug. 'Aye, well, there's more to school than maths and reading and the Brothers, they run schools all over Ireland. They know what they are doing.'

'Tommy, are you mad? What more is there?'

Tommy sighed and gave in. He had been filled with his own rage when he had first seen Harry's hands and was consumed by an urge to put his coat back on and march down to the schoolhouse to give Mr Cleary a piece of his mind. But breathing deeply, he'd waited for the red mist to pass. The last time someone harmed one of his children, a murder had been committed... What was more, Tommy knew, as did Maura, it would only make things worse. 'Cleary comes in on a Friday night, I'll have a word with him then.'

Maura nodded. 'Aye, well make sure I'm stood next to you when you do.' They both knew which one of them the villagers feared the most and it wasn't Tommy.

In bed, Maura slipped into the crook of Tommy's arm and draped the other arm around his waist.

'It's better than me being on the docks, isn't it, Maura? Us being here? Better than always worrying when the next ship was coming in and if I'd be taken on. It's getting bad there, you know; the docks are only half as busy as they were.' Tommy always spoke more freely in the dark.

'Aye, but you always were taken on,' she said. 'You were one of the hardest workers. Like Jerry used to say, you're small and stocky, built like a brick shite house. You never went without a day's work.'

Maura, who set her alarm around the bells for morning mass and the Angelus, knew she should give thanks for what she had and be grateful and this she managed for most of the day, but, when the lights were out and she was lying in Tommy's arms, it was near impossible. 'I miss the four streets,' she whispered and the hot tears that prickled at the back of her eyes broke free and ran down her cheeks.

'Eh, come on, queen,' Tommy said. 'Don't be crying now. Isn't this what we wanted, to be back in Ireland, running our own business? Home is where the heart is, Maura.'

She buried her face into his chest to stifle her sobs. 'But our Kitty's grave, it's in Liverpool...'

And for that, Tommy had no reply. He had left his Kitty all alone in the churchyard, his precious eldest daughter and the best friend any daddy could have. How had he not thought of that on the day they left, when he had taken the flowers he had bought in the market to her grave? It would be her birthday soon and who would be there for her, to lay flowers on her grave now?

'I miss the four streets too,' he whispered. 'I miss the craic with the men, the games of footie, darts. And I miss work, I do; you don't get much conversation from a cow's udder. And the pub – I miss the Anchor. You are a grand barmaid, Maura, but it's a fact, Babs is better.'

Maura gave him a playful jab in the ribs. 'Oi, you, if that woman cried, there would be a landslide on her face, she wears that much make-up. Would you like me to start doing that, eh, chatting up the fellas in here?' She could sense rather than see his smile.

'Just think,' he said, 'it's the carnival soon. They'll all be revving up over there, getting ready. Remember how excited the kids all got with you organising everything and Angela helping Miss Devlin last year with the games and being so full of herself, she was unbearable to live with until the Tuesday after the Whitsun Holiday?'

Maura didn't speak; she was lost in her own memories of company and banter. She thought about the Friday nights when they all got together down at the pub, the friendships forged in adversity, the making of the bunting at her kitchen table, half of the women from the streets squeezing in and out of her kitchen, the steam from the kettle permanently boiling for more tea. Babies on breasts, women seeking tea and sympathy or simply a word of advice from Maura who was regarded with the same esteem and respect as Dr Cole or Mother Superior.

Tommy, wandering in his own thoughts, recalled the O'Prey boys, the fastest runners in the north-west, who helped him to run around the streets and houses with sacks of potatoes that had fallen off the back of a ship, tipping out an enamel washing-up bowl's worth to each house that was short of money, his heart pounding in case a bizzie walked up the road and caught them because he couldn't run as fast as Callum or Jimmy. But most of all, he missed visiting his Kitty.

Moving to Ireland had absorbed all their time and energy and it had occurred to him that, since they had got here, Kitty had faded. Even the sharpest of the pain in his heart, all that had remained from those dark days, had gone and he even missed it because it was this pain that kept his Kitty alive and, even though the priest was dead and gone, even though Kitty and all she had suffered at his hands had been avenged, he still didn't feel as though he had done enough.

As she so often did, Maura read his mind. 'I miss our Kitty so much,' she said.

Tommy placed his hand on top of Maura's shoulder and, feeling the coolness of her, pulled the blanket up and tucked it in around her. 'You're cold,' he whispered and rubbed her shoulder lightly over the top of the blanket. 'I miss her too, every single day,' he said as his hand casually slipped under the blanket to the familiar rise of her breast and rested there. 'There's no one here who really knew her other than Liam and Maeve and I hate to remind them of what happened. I know they feel responsible, even though they aren't. We will never know, Maura, how or what; we will only know that someone wanted Kitty dead. She knew, *we* knew, but they didn't dare come after us.'

There was a long silence, broken at last by Maura. 'Kitty isn't here…'

Tommy stroked his hand along her breast. 'Aye, because we don't talk to the same people Kitty did since she was a babby, the people who watched her grow. There's nothing here, no one, to bring her to us. Not one person who watched her play in the streets or knew her in school. She won't know this place, out here, won't be able to find us. One day I was visiting her grave and sat on the bench, the next I was gone. She won't know where I am.'

He felt a familiar pain rip through his heart and Maura felt it too and was instantly compelled to soothe it. Her husband, her lovely Tommy, was a man who had been through so much. He carried a guilt in his heart and she could only imagine how heavy it felt. There was no atonement to be found for the murder of a priest, no church in which to make confession. Redemption and the pathway to heaven was blocked for Tommy and they lived their life aware that there would no longer be a together forever. She shifted her weight and her lips found his. Her hand moved swiftly down to the inside of his thigh and slowly upwards as she gently caressed him. As was always the case, Tommy responded instantly, and their kisses held an urgent, life-affirming intensity. He would warm her shoulder when she was cold – and she would always be there, to take away his pain.

Chapter Three

On one day each week, Maura travelled all the way into Ballynevin to collect the post and to pick up butter, meat, sewing or mending. Other food was delivered to her from the shop in Ballynevin on the back of a van every other day. When they had moved to Ireland, she had never thought she would miss queuing outside the fish shop on a Wednesday morning, or the butcher's jokes and ribaldry as much as she did. Her weekly trip out now was reliant on one of the farm carts passing by, or the weekly delivery with the Guinness dray to hitch a lift back.

Her last stop of the afternoon had been to Mrs Barrett at the tailor's where Maura discussed the cuts Cleary had inflicted on Harry's hands in detail.

'Well, we can have that sorted in no time,' Mrs Barrett said. 'I have just the thing in my press for your Harry's hands. We are used to Cleary around here. He should be retiring soon, the age of the man.'

'Not soon enough for me,' said Maura as she placed

her overladen basket down on the floor and flopped onto the wooden chair on the customer side of the counter. No one just walked in, conducted their business and left. That would have been considered very rude.

'Shall I wet the tea?' Mrs Barrett asked. 'And while I'm at it, I'll find that medicament.'

While Maura waited, she gazed out of the window, past the wooden mannequin in the window wearing a man's suit that would only be bought for a wedding, followed by a lifetime of Sundays. She felt tears prick at her eyes and brushed them away with the back of her hand, irritated at her weakness. Pull yourself together, woman, she thought to herself. What the hell is wrong with you? Her thoughts returned to Harry and the cuts across his palms which were turning nasty. Every morning when she took the dressings off, she'd hoped to see an improvement, but this morning the hands had been hot, the wounds yellow and angry-looking.

Mrs Barrett returned, first with the tea and then with a dark green glass bottle with a handwritten label.

'Bridget made this and she's been the village seer at Tarabeg for as long as I can remember,' Mrs Barrett said. 'We don't need doctors here, not when we have Bridget.' She removed the cork stopper and smelt the liquid. Her head recoiled and her eyes watered. 'It has the kick of a mule, so it does,' she said as she passed the bottle to Maura who read the label. Apply with lint, and blow.

'What's in it?' asked Maura, squinting.

'I've no idea,' said Mrs Barrett, 'but Daedio Malone out at Tarabeg used it for years on his knees and he was dancing in the street at ceilidhs when he was well past a hundred. This will definitely do the job.'

Maura slipped the bottle into her basket. 'Well, I'm clean out of ideas myself and it can't make his hands any worse, that's for sure.'

On this particular outing, she had hitched a lift back with Liam Deane in his van. The light was fading as they turned onto the road that led out to the coast, the mountains slipping from green to grey as, laden down with provisions, she squeezed onto the front bench alongside Liam. She would only just make it back before opening time and, no doubt, her least favourite customer would be waiting at the door. But her heart was lighter now than when she'd left. There were letters in her coat pocket waiting to be opened and savoured at the end of the night when she and Tommy sat and enjoyed their nightly whiskey. She would open them, one by one, and read the contents out loud.

She could tell by the envelopes who they were from: Kathleen Deane, Liam's own mammy; Maggie Trott; one from Malcolm at the Seaman's Stop, which was somewhat of a surprise, but the thickest was from Sister Evangelista, who would be giving her all the news about the school, the mother's union and, even all the way across the sea, Maura would be told who was failing in their obligation to attend mass and be given chapter and verse about the carnival arrangements.

There was a letter from Peggy, too, and she had felt a sense of relief when she turned the envelope and read the name and address of the sender on the back. If Peggy was writing, all must be well, and last but not least, because it was bound to be trouble, a letter from the docks board.

'You have a wicked grin on your face,' said Liam.

'Have I? Well, I have letters from home, including one from your own mammy and that's always a treat. Nothing I can buy on any weekly shop would bring me as much pleasure as hearing all the news from back on the four streets.'

'We have one too,' he said. 'I'm not a man for the reading, though, I'll leave that to Maeve when I get back to the farm.'

Maura didn't question him further. She had no desire to embarrass him into owning up that he could read no better than Tommy. 'I'll wait until tonight to open ours. Tommy and I like to read them together,' she said. 'I'm so delighted there's one from Peggy next door – to think she was that organised to go to the post office and buy the airmail letter and then to even go back and post it. Peggy is obviously getting her act together now that I've gone and so, I suppose, every cloud does have a silver lining – because, God, she needed to.'

'Even we hear about Peggy in our letters from

Kathleen,' said Liam. 'Kathleen says she feels sorry for the kids.'

Maura sighed as the smile slipped from her face. 'I do miss those kids, especially little Paddy, and I do worry. I suppose the nuns or Kathleen will tell me if I've anything serious to be worrying about though, isn't that right?'

Liam nodded sagely. 'You haven't really settled here, have you, Maura?'

Liam dropped a gear and turned onto the narrow road which led to the coastal village. It was more of a statement than a question and it caught her off guard. The last of the daylight clung on stubbornly as the ocean roared to the left and the moon began to rise over the Nephin Beg and made ghosts of the mountains before them. The road ahead held another half hour of travel before they reached their destination.

'Why would you say that, Liam? Have people been talking? Have I not been putting on a good enough show? Jesus, why would I not settle? It's such a joy to wait on those miserable bastards all afternoon and evening.'

Liam roared with laughter. 'I've heard that you haven't exactly been making best friends with the locals. You'll have to forgive them, Maura, it's a man they are used to have running things, so you will have taken them by surprise, that's all.'

'Jesus, it's because I'm a woman, is it? It's their wives I would pity, if I didn't know they send their miserable bloody husbands down to me in the pub, to get them out of their way.'

'Maura, they are the men who keep handing you their money over the bar; you should be delighted their wives kick them out of the cottages. What would you be doing without them? You know, I wish your Tommy had spoken to me before you spent every flaming penny on that place. I'm not sure if you will ever get your money back – but you shouldn't bite the hands that are feeding you right now.'

Maura sniffed and pulled her handbag closer into her for comfort. 'I wish he had too. Get our money back, that would be a fine thing. Have you seen how many cottages are standing empty? Everyone is leaving. We're the only soft buggers that came back – and spent a fortune doing it. And it isn't just that place; I've gone backwards in so many other ways too. I miss the four streets, Liam. The people, the shops, the carrying on.'

Liam crunched the gears and the engine screamed out. Maura wondered would the old van make it. 'The carrying on?' Liam glanced at her with a puzzled expression.

'Yes, the carrying on. There's always something happening – and the bingo, God, I really miss the bingo. I was good at winning, often had the luck with me but I was never greedy, mind.' She sighed and, absent-minded, her hands patted the envelopes in her pocket, as if to reassure herself that she was closer to the four streets, just by touching them.

'The kids are happy though?' said Liam.

Maura snorted. 'I don't know, I daren't ask,' she said as her mind scrambled to remember the last time she saw her children laugh.

She was keen to change the subject. She knew she really should have said: no, the kids are as miserable as sin and when Liam probed her feelings, as he was doing now, the fact that Tommy had spent every penny on the rundown inn made her feel sick to the pit of her stomach.

'Maeve asked me to tell you she's expecting you and Tommy and the kids over on Sunday after mass and the kids always seem to have a grand time when they come to the farm.'

Maura smiled at the memory of their Sundays, their only day off. As soon as everyone was up, they headed over to Ballynevin for mass, avoiding the church next to the inn, and after, walked back to the farm with Liam and Maeve.

'That's it! That's when the kids laugh,' she said to Liam. 'When we come to the farm. It's the best bit of our week, Liam, and whatever the weather, the kids have a blast. Harry is beside himself that you are taking him out for the salmon again when the summer holidays come.'

Liam laughed. 'Angela insists she's coming too. I've told them, they can hold the landing net.'

'I don't think our Harry will be holding anything for a while; that Mr Cleary, he took the stick to our Harry the other day and you should see the state of his hands. He ripped the skin raw, he did.'

'Mr Cleary, you say? Aye, well, sure enough, I know what that feels like all right. He's been teaching the kids around here for as long as I can remember; the Christian Brothers brought him with them when they came from Dublin. They thought we were all peasants and they would need protecting.' Liam laughed at the memory. 'Anyways, it will only have been for Harry's own good. It did me no harm when he took the stick to me.'

Maura turned to look at Liam. She wanted to ask him, was he mad? Like Tommy, he couldn't even read but she said only, 'That's no way to teach a child, inflicting pain like that. I never saw the sisters so much as lay a finger on one of our boys ever, and the kids at the school in Liverpool? Well, they can't do enough for the nuns and every one of them is clever, especially Harry, and do you know, Liam, when our Harry told Mr Cleary where he was up to with his maths and English, Cleary didn't believe him and told him he would have to do it all again. No wonder he has no interest and is as miserable as sin.'

Maura chose not to mention the priest who was murdered, no one ever did, especially not Maura and Tommy. To mention his name was to give recognition to a man who had been an imposter in their faith.

'Aye, well, Harry will do fine. We all did.'

Maura swallowed down her exasperation. 'Liam,

your mammy told me you spent most of your time in the fields on the farm at home and you were out every night with your own daddy, poaching the salmon. Which is all well and good, but don't be giving out to me that you know what Cleary is like – you don't know what our Harry's hands look like.'

On the opposite side of the road an elderly man with white hair and beard, on a bike, raised his hand to wave and, as he did so, his bike wobbled precariously.

'In the name of God!' said Maura as her hand flew to her mouth and, just in time, the bike steadied as they passed.

'He's never fallen yet,' said Liam, who chose the diversion to end the conversation about Mr Cleary, aware he couldn't win.

Ten minutes later, Maura stood at the door to the bar, waving Liam on his way. As she watched the tail-lights of the van become consumed by the dark night, she felt deflated. 'You can't even read, Liam, what would you know,' she muttered.

Why couldn't Liam see that what Mr Cleary had done was very wrong? Only she and Tommy were indignant at the way Harry had been treated. She was Irish born and bred and she knew the ways well enough, but that didn't mean that those who had experienced better should tolerate less. Maura knew the difference between right and wrong and what Cleary had done to her boy was very wrong. A feeling of dread she had yet to acknowledge or identify, slipped into the pit of her stomach, made worse by the sight of her first customer walking towards her. There was still the fire to light, food to get ready for the children, and all the while the oaf lumbering up the path towards her would be barking out his demands: 'Get the fire, Maura. Fill my pot, Maura. Close the door, Maura.' She sighed. 'God in heaven, was it meant to be like this?' This wasn't the life she and Tommy had dreamt of.

'Get the door open, Maura,' her customer called out and she bit her tongue and fought back the urge to shout back, 'Open it your fecking self!'

Chapter Four

Paddy farted so loudly that it woke his wife from her deep and dreamy sleep. Her eyes opened wide and the vision of a twin-tub washing machine disappeared in a flash. Maggie Trott had taken delivery of one only the week before and Peggy, along with every other woman on the four streets, had formed an orderly queue in order to inspect it. Since then she had dreamt every night about owning one. Then the efficient rumble of a spin dryer vibrating on her kitchen floor was replaced by her husband's flatulent emissions. She turned her face towards Paddy.

'You dirty fecking bastard,' she snarled at him and, heaving her large frame up from the brass bedstead, threw back the old stained army blanket she had meant to wash in the copper boiler on the first sunny spring day. But that had been weeks ago and though there had been other sunny days since, somehow some inconsequential events got in the way and the blanket got dirtier and dirtier.

Peggy just didn't know how that had happened. Before the Dohertys had left for Mayo, she and Maura had washed their blankets on the same day every single year without fail. Peggy had no mangle, but she and Maura would carry the heavy wet blankets, one by one, out of her yard, down the entry and back into Maura's yard, feed them through the mangle and then carry them back in before throwing them over Peggy's line. There was never any knowing when a sunny day would appear, but when it did, Maura would bang her mop on Peggy's kitchen wall and Peggy would realise it was time to wash the blankets. She had meant to do it, the intention was there, as was the mangle, still standing in Maura and Tommy's yard, but as she often did with so many things in life, including in the man she had chosen to marry, Peggy had failed miserably and the bed bugs had breathed a sigh of relief.

She crossed the few steps to the sash window, her bare thighs slapping together because, although she was only forty, she tottered on arthritic feet. They were made worse by the excessive weight she carried, thanks to living on bags of broken biscuits while she fed what meat and vegetables they had to her husband and children. She flung the window upwards, allowing the sound of the church bells to fill the room.

'Jesus Christ, be quiet, will you?' Paddy muttered, almost under his breath.

'Stop your blaspheming, you fat slob.' Peggy folded

her arms across her winceyette nightdress to protect herself from the fresh breeze. Grey, almost threadbare and peppered with the occasional cigarette burn, it strained at the seams of Peggy's bulging frame. Dipping down, she stuck her neck out of the window and scanned the blackened chimney tops perched above the rows of two-up, two-down terraced streets to see who was awake and had coal to light a fire this Wednesday, the day before payday. Her eyes narrowed as Maggie Trott opened her front door to usher her large tabby cat indoors and stood as she always did in her doorway. Peggy watched as she pulled her long knitted cardigan to her body and scanned the street to see who was about. As the milk cart trundled around the corner, Maggie Trott quickly stepped inside.

'She's off to get the tea for him,' said Peggy.

'Who is?' said big Paddy from halfway into his pillow.

'Mrs Trott. I wonder if he knocks anything off her bill for that? I'm surprised his Gladys allows it.'

Paddy snorted with laughter. 'He's playing with fire, that one. If Gladys knew, she would chop his tackle off. Tell Maggie Trott to bring me one up next.'

'Tell her yerself,' said Peggy and, placing two fingers into her mouth, she sent out a piercing whistle to Eric. He didn't look her way and she knew it was deliberate. She waved her hands furiously to attract his attention.

'Wave your tits at him,' said Paddy. 'That'll make him look up.'

Peggy ignored him. 'I'll just have to wait until he finishes gassing and gets closer; Maggie definitely saw me.' Eric would take five minutes to drink the tea and he never dawdled for longer. 'Look at that, he's giving her a ciggie again. That must be their little arrangement, a ciggie for a cuppa,' Peggy tutted. 'I wonder who they are gassing about.' In Peggy's world, it was always who, not what.

Eric drank his tea and appeared to be in no hurry. 'Get a move on, will you,' she hissed. Peggy couldn't see the look of dismay that crossed Eric's face as he eventually took his leave of Mrs Trott and made his way along the street, depositing bottles of milk on each doorstep. He was getting closer and closer and, as he did so, his determination to keep his gaze fixed pointedly downwards, ignoring Peggy, became more obvious.

'Eric!' she hissed. 'Eric, up here,' as if he didn't know.

The brass bed frame creaked behind her. 'You're wasting your time. That tight bastard won't give you nowt,' said Paddy, heaving himself up the bed and reaching down to pick up his cigarettes and matches from the floorboards. He stuffed a ticking pillow, brown with old sweat and Brylcreem, down behind his back and slapped on the cap which had been hanging on the bedpost above his head.

'Me back's killing me. I've hardly slept a wink,' he said, doubting that there would be any sympathy from Peggy, but it was imperative he imparted the information.

He was laying out his stall for the day. 'Ouch, Jesus, I can hardly move.' He lit his Woodbine and, flicking the match, dropped it onto the floor to join the pile of dead ones already there.

Peggy tried to attract Eric's attention yet again; he was now only two doors away. 'Eric!' she hissed. 'Feck, Annie O'Prey will be off to mass if he doesn't hurry up and she'll see me. I swear to God he's walking slower than usual.' The sound of clinking bottles landing on steps marked Eric's progress until he was almost under the window. 'Eric,' Peggy hissed again, but he was stubbornly refusing to look up.

'Tell him you'll give him a quick leg-over in the wash house if he leaves us a couple,' said Paddy, and then he began to chuckle. 'No, don't do that, I'll have them all feeling sorry for me down the pub if you do for he's bound to refuse; the man is known for his good sense, even if he is married to Gladys.'

Eric couldn't have heard a word big Paddy was saying, and he knew it, which was just as well because Peggy's expression revealed that she might be about to lose her temper. But before he could say another word, Eric finally looked up. Peggy, spurred on by need, pushed her head well out of the window, holding onto her breasts with one hand and pushing up the sash window further with the other.

'Ah, you're a good man, Eric.' Her voice held an assumption that Eric noted in the tone of his response.

'What do you want, Peggy? You'll have the whole street out.'

Peggy tried a flirtatious giggle, but it had been a long time. 'God love you,' she said, 'what do you think I'd be wanting from a good-looking milkman like yourself? Would you just leave us a couple, for the kids' breakfast like, and I'll pay you on Friday.'

'Come on, Peggy,' Eric said, 'don't put me in this position. You know you owe me for eight as it and Gladys hasn't forgotten it.' He looked exasperated. 'Peggy, you're putting me in a spot here.' He was arguing with himself whilst Peggy, minus her teeth, grinned down at him. He knew if he gave her a pint of the steri, which had a flavour similar to evaporated milk, she would water it down and make it stretch to three pints and it would last her for two days. If she had any stale bread and a scraping of sugar, her kids would have pobs for breakfast. It was just the thought of the kids, hungry, that got to the man who was childless and felt the pain of it every day. Peggy's kids were half as wide as any others, with eyes that looked permanently haunted and hungry. They were fed by the street, by women like Maggie Trott and the nuns. Eric knew he had a moral obligation to play his part and he lifted four pints of steri out of his basket.

'You win,' he said, 'and don't worry about paying – you have an angel on the street who has covered it for you, because I can't just leave free milk, Peggy. Our Gladys, she doesn't trust me on Nelson Street now Maura has gone and isn't there to tip up the cash for others and she wants to come on the four streets collecting round on Fridays now.'

Eric saw the smile of relief slide from Peggy's face. She no more wanted to deal with Gladys than Eric did. 'You're a good man, Eric. God alone knows how a man like you ended up with a wife like that. Don't you be worrying, I'll find the money, somehow, no one has to pay for us.' She blessed herself; they both knew she had just lied and, as expected, the guilt kicked in. 'I'll call into mass, miracles do happen.'

Peggy ducked back under the window and, as it slammed down, the sound of the church bells faded.

Paddy laughed. 'Just think, if Maura and Tommy were still next door, you could knock on with the mop and get her to bring you round a quarter of tea from the chest they used to keep in the wash house and we could have a nice cuppa now.'

Peggy lifted down her dressing gown from a nail in the door and shuffled it over her shoulders. Paddy's words made her feel sad. She missed Maura every day. It wasn't just that she no longer had anyone to borrow the staples of life from, the tea, sugar, bread, or to provide her brood with a meal when it got really bad and they needed feeding, it was the company she missed and the routines. Maura had made Peggy attend mass on at least one day in the week and always on a Sunday. Maura made Peggy feel good about herself and so she had copied Maura. On the days Maura had washed her nets, Peggy did. When Maura lit the copper boiler, Peggy followed suit. But all too easily, without her guiding light, Peggy had become overwhelmed by the daily drudgery and battle and had very quickly become someone who forgot things and who couldn't quite manage.

Peggy had loved Maura for the true friend she was. And she was very sure she didn't love her husband, Paddy. On a day like today, when he was about to refuse to move from the bed and take himself down to the docks for an honest day's work, she imagined him impaled on the end of her bread knife. She'd had many such thoughts just lately, simmering below her veneer of incompetence, and they perturbed her. She was well aware that if she let the thought take hold, when the kids were crying and hungry, it could all too easily become a reality. She was brought to her senses as a tug passed out onto the river, blowing its horn, heading to the bar to bring down a ship to be unloaded.

'Come on you, get out of that bed,' she said and pulled the blanket away from Paddy, onto the floor. 'Hear the tugs? There must be a ship out on the bar waiting to come in.'

'You're joking, aren't you?' said Paddy. 'I can't go down those steps today with my back like this. It's killing me.'

'You might end up dead if you don't, for sure,' she said, 'and don't think I'm joking. As God is my judge, you will either walk down those steps to the pen, or if I have to, I'll bleedin' kick you down and you'll be rollin' down them and turning up for work on your fecking fat arse. How do you think I'm going to put food on the table? How am I going to pay Eric? How do I pay the rent and the coalman? We're weeks behind. Get out of that flamin' bed!'

Peggy slipped a foot into one of her frayed tartan slippers, which smelt almost as ripe as Paddy. The slippers, still damp from the night before, were the closest thing she owned to a pair of shoes, having pawned the ones Maura gave her before she left for Ireland. Picking up the remaining slipper, she bent over the bed and began to slap big Paddy on any part of his white, flabby flesh she could reach.

'You flamin' madwoman!' he shouted as, quicker than Peggy ever could be, he slipped his legs over the edge of the bed and grabbed his trousers from the bedpost. 'You're a feckin' mad witch, you are!'

'I might be mad and I may even be a witch, but I'd rather be both of those than a selfish, lazy fecking bastard who doesn't give a damn if his kids starve, because that's what you are, a fat, lazy, useless bastard!'

Her eyes were blazing and there was something in them Paddy didn't like the look of. He had seen it often of late. A fire, a thought, a fleeting glimpse of hatred, a hidden meaning that perturbed him. There had already been a murder on the four streets. The scandalous, shocking murder of a priest – and right at this moment his wife appeared more than capable of doubling that murder count. It crossed his mind, was it Peggy? But no, Peggy never lost her temper, that prerogative was his, often after a skinful he could ill afford down at the Anchor. He could never remember the night before; it was only the bruises on Peggy or the children which bore witness to his attacks or the upturned chamber pot, the broken chair in the kitchen. And his lapses had become more frequent since the Dohertys had left.

'All right, you crazy feckin' cow, keep your knickers on. I'm getting dressed, aren't I, eh?' He held up his trousers to her and, wincing, placed his other hand in the small of his back. 'Honest to God, queen, it's killing me.'

Peggy made a noise that resembled a deep growl more animal than human, but they both stopped dead as they heard a small voice behind them.

'I'll make yer tea, will I, Da? I'll wet the old tea leaves from yesterday if there's none, shall I, Ma?'

They turned, startled to see their son, little Paddy, in the doorway, his dog Scamp by his side, ears and tail down. There was no smile to match little Paddy's words, just a worried, furrowed brow. This morning the raised voices made his heart race with anxiety and his bladder weak. Before, whenever she heard raised voices, Auntie Maura would be straight in through the back door and either usher little Paddy and the others into her kitchen, or reprimand Peggy and Paddy until they stopped shouting; little Paddy no longer felt safe, now Maura wasn't there.

Peggy fixed a smile on her face. 'We've milk,' she said. 'Eric has left four steri on the step and isn't that just great? You fetch it in quick and I'll make everyone pobs, eh, how does that sound? We've got bread left over from yesterday to make it with, and a little bit of sugar.'

Little Paddy felt relief wash over him. He would do anything for his mother, but he hated it when she asked him to go out and steal milk from Malcolm at the Seaman's Stop on the Dock Road, while he still had his curtains closed. He felt physically sick lifting the gold top from the crate and would run as fast as his legs would carry him back to the house, with the milk precariously swinging in his hands.

'Go on, off with you,' she would say when she woke him early, extracting him from the tangled limbs of the brothers he shared his bed with. 'The greedy git gets eight pints and he only has six rooms, so he can't be using all of them. Hang around on the corner and when you see Eric cross over to the pub, you slip out, take one and leg it.'

On those days, little Paddy called into the chapel at the convent on his way into Sister Theresa's class. He felt weighed down with the guilt and compelled to confess.

He liked Mr Coffey, and the lady who was sometimes there, his friend, Biddy. Once he'd carried her bag from the bus to the Seaman's Stop and ever since then she would give him a barley twist, whenever she saw him. He really liked Biddy and it near killed him to steal the milk, in case she found out it was him. His mother, he knew, acted from a desire to feed them all, but he wondered, so many times, how it was his mother and big Paddy were so different from just about every other family on the streets whose kids managed to eat a breakfast every morning.

But now little Paddy finally grinned, for this was a good morning. Eric had delivered, little Paddy was spared and there would be breakfast before school.

'Go on, get your clothes on or some other little bugger will be stealing the milk from our step – it's like the wild west out there.' And Peggy roared with laughter as little Paddy went back into the second bedroom to retrieve the trousers Maura Doherty had bought him before she had left for Ireland. He folded them every night carefully and hung them over the brass bedstead. Maura had bought them two sizes too big and, initially, he'd had to thread string through the waistband because even the belt she bought with them was too big.

'Don't you be worrying, little Paddy,' Maura had said. 'They will fit you a dream by next year. Just don't go getting holes in the knees because I won't be here to sew them. Your mother's not the best with the needle.

If you're desperate, take them to Maisie Tanner's and say Maura said you were to go there, do you hear me?'

Little Paddy had nodded, his eyes wide. Maura had left him with so many instructions he was afraid that he was going to forget something. On the day he stood in Maura's kitchen, as she pinned up the hem of the trousers so that he would get more wear out of them, Tommy had sat in armchair by the fire, reading the *Echo*.

'Peggy will pawn those before the boat docks in Dublin,' Tommy said.

'Shush, you!' Maura had hissed at him. 'There, Tommy, doesn't he look just grand? Paddy, you'll have all the girls in the school after you, so you will.'

Little Paddy had blushed at the mere thought, but it didn't matter, nothing in the world could diminish the pride he felt at owning a pair of trousers with no holes and which had been bought from new, along with the shoes Maura had also bought for him.

Tommy had put the paper on his lap. 'You look proper grown-up, Paddy,' he had said. 'Best not to play footie in them, though, they won't last five minutes if you do.'

'I won't, never, I promise, Tommy,' he said and Maura had felt her heart swell for the little boy she had delivered herself in the front bedroom next door.

But it wasn't just little Paddy – she had bought clothes for the entire Nolan family.

'What's the use of us having money if we can't rig everyone out?' she had protested when Peggy made a half-hearted objection. As it happened, Tommy had been only half right. Peggy had indeed pawned the shoes and clothes Maura had bought for Peggy, but she hadn't touched anything of the children's, and when big Paddy suggested it, she had felt her blood boil.

'I'll pawn the blankets on the bed, the statue of the Holy Mother, even my mother's clock! I'd pawn you, you useless lump of shite, before I take the shoes off their feet. It's a shame I couldn't bear, Paddy, and I warn you: if I have to pawn the kids' shoes, don't you even bother coming back home.'

Now, before he put on his clothes, little Paddy flung himself flat on the bedroom floor, shimmied on his belly under the bed and opened the lid of the cardboard box he kept hidden there. Two small black eyes stared up at him. 'Max,' he whispered to the black rat, who obligingly pushed the rest of the lid off and, looked intently at little Paddy, as though waiting for his next words. Scamp shuffled flat on his belly and lay next to him. The dog and the rat were the axis of little Paddy's life now that his best friend in all the world, Harry Doherty, had gone.

'Stay here,' he said. 'I'll be back soon with some pobs and then you can come to school with me in me bag.'

Max, as if understanding every word, obediently hopped back down into his box and little Paddy replaced the lid. 'Back soon,' he whispered as he and Scamp wriggled back out from under the bed and headed down to bring in the milk.

Half an hour later the street came alive as the dockers' klaxon rang out, calling the men down to the docks and the calls went up from one back gate to the next. The marching men stopped at Peggy's. 'Oi, big man, are you coming out or what?' shouted Jerry who lived across the road in number 42.

Peggy grabbed the spoon from Paddy's hand as he was about to scrape the last of the milk-soaked, sugar-coated stale bread from the side of the dish and, opening the back door, threw his coat at him and pushed him out.

'He's coming now, Jer, just hang on there,' she shouted and then hissed under her breath, 'There's nothing for your break,' as she shoved an empty knapsack into his hands. 'Pretend there is and carry it anyway. You only worked three days last week and I'll have to go over the road to Kathleen and scrounge something to get these kids fed tonight. And understand this, you fat lazy slob, even if your back is breaking in two, you will be working every day from now on. There's no Tommy to carry you, no Maura to feed our kids when they are starving or invite us round for a roast. The rent hasn't been paid for weeks and it's time for you to pull your bleedin' weight.'

Paddy's reply was drowned out by the noise of the men at the back gate. 'Paddy, you got to dress yourself in time, what next, eh?' said Jerry, patting him on the back. 'Have you had breakfast?'

'He has,' shouted Peggy from the doorway. 'His belly is as full as a tinker's bra.'

The men roared with laughter.

'Don't worry, Peggy, I'll have him home before dark,' Jerry called back.

'Don't you dare, Jerry Deane. If there's an extra shift, you make sure he is taken on for it. He can work all night as well, for all I care, because he's a lot of catching up to do.'

She slammed the back door and felt the weight fall from her shoulders. A day's pay was in the bag, Jerry would make sure of that. Peggy placed her hand in the small of her back; the ache which had been there for so long was almost unbearable these last few days, but she never complained like Paddy did. She would ask Kathleen for some Anadin. It had been grumbling away for weeks and if Kathleen gave her more than two pills she would hide the rest in the bread bin. Her need was greater than Paddy's, for her pain was real.

Paddy grumbled all the way down the steps to the pen which was full, but there was no pushing or shoving. The gaffer would point to those who were known to be good workers, his own friends and the sons of his friends. Everyone else stood and waited, desperate to be taken on. The klaxon rang out, persistent and demanding, teasing the men with the promise of labour, larders to be filled, nights in the Anchor to be enjoyed. Those who weren't picked would make their way back up the dockers' steps and walk to the social, hearts heavy with worry.

'What's due in from out on the bar?' Stanley Tanner called out from the back to Jerry who, as usual, was first down, and always taken on.

'The mist on the water is so thick out from the basin, I can't make it out,' Jerry called back.

'We could do with the *Morry* – it's getting mighty close to the carnival and the fecking cupboards are bare,' Seamus grumbled.

'We may as well go back up – there's too many waiting down here to be taken on,' said Paddy hopefully. Jerry flicked the stump of his ciggie to the ground, ignoring him, and spoke to Stanley. 'Aye, Kathleen was complaining just the same. I thought Captain Conor would have been back before now, but Ena hasn't heard a thing.'

'What if he doesn't turn up between now and the carnival, Jer? What will happen?' asked Seamus who was always at the front with Jerry.

'I don't know, Seamus, but we've two weeks or so yet, so let's pray at mass on Sunday that Conor hasn't forgotten us and sails in next week.' He turned back to the men from the four streets, gathered behind him.

'Come on, fellas, let's get ahead before they move down to the Dock Road end. Looks like there will be work for all of us today.'

The men shuffled down to the front of the pen to be picked off, one by one by the gaffer, who winked at Jerry, acknowledging their conversations of the night before in the Anchor.

'I'm retiring, Jerry,' the gaffer had said, 'and I've told Mr Heartfelt it should be you who takes my place. That's the only way we'll keep the men of the four streets in work – because I'm telling you, the dock board has plans to knock the streets down and hand them over to Liverpool council for houses, like the ones they are throwing up in Speke. They're calling it slum clearance, the cheeky bastards.'

Jerry had almost spat out the Guinness he had been drinking. 'You're kidding me? Aren't you?'

The gaffer had shaken his head. 'The reason they've put Frank the Skank down here on our dock is because they're going to make life hard for us and we have to fight it. The docks are shedding jobs, not taking on.'

'Can he object to your choice?'

The gaffer, a man from County Mayo, shook his head. 'Heartfelt knows what's good for him. But he's up to something, so we need to keep an eye on him, just in case. You know the tradition is that every gaffer gets to name his own replacement, usually his son, but I only have girls and so I'm naming you.'

Now the gaffer pointed to Jerry, Seamus, Stanley, Callum and Paddy, as the pen gates slid open. 'Come on, lads,' said Jerry, 'we're on. The chicken is in the pot.'

The children were ready to leave the house for school and stood as a pack, dressed in the shoes and coats Maura had left as her parting gift. One huge upside of Maura's gifts had been the kids not having to share shoes and clothes, so they had all been able to attend school at the same time, much to Miss Devlin's delight and Peggy's, because it meant the house was empty and quiet each day.

Little Paddy chose not to walk to school with the others; he had to find an excuse to get back upstairs without his mother noticing. She had reluctantly learnt to accept Scamp but Max, found by Scamp soon after his best friend Harry Doherty left and seen by little Paddy as a partial replacement, would be a different matter entirely. He collected up the pobs bowls and was peering into the empty bread crock with a worried frown.

'Don't you be worrying now,' said Peggy. 'There's nothin' in there, but I'll go over the road to Nana Kathleen and see if she can lend us something. You won't go without your tea, I'll make sure of that.'

Peggy sounded more confident than she felt and little Paddy could hear the guilt in her voice. Maura had always helped her to manage her money, for money was a mystery to Peggy. It slipped through her fingers and, unable to add up very well, she had no idea how.

'Go on, lad, off to school, no dawdling. Why are you the last to leave?' asked Peggy as she slapped his cap onto his head and pushed him out of the door.

'Oh Mam, my bag!' he said, ducking under her arm and clattering up the wooden staircase. 'Max, Max, quick,' he hissed as he pulled out the box from under the bed. Max opened the lid himself and little Paddy dropped him into his knapsack. 'Here you go, pobs,' said little Paddy, opening his hand with the pobs he had kept from the bowls. He smiled as the rat made short work of his breakfast and slipped into the knapsack.

'For goodness' sake, Paddy,' said Peggy as he walked back into the kitchen. 'What's got into you?' And she thrust him out into the cobbled yard. She was in a hurry to finish the half-smoked Woodbine big Paddy had pinched off and left on the kitchen table, Peggy pushing him out of the door before he had time to slip it behind his ear. The effort of the morning, the sheer agony of getting big Paddy out and down the steps, the worry of making the bread stretch, the shame of begging milk from Eric... it was all almost too much. But at least Paddy was in work, all the kids were at school and she had half a Woodbine to look forward to with her broken biscuits.

'Ah, bliss,' she said as she bent over the flame in the range and lit the ciggie. She sank into the chair and inhaled deeply. All she had to do now was find her way through the day.

She kicked off her slippers and rubbed at her bunions as she thought through her options. She would ask Kathleen for help first. If that didn't work, she would have to go and see Sister Evangelista and hope to God she didn't send her to the priory. She could do without a lecture from the priest today, seeing as she hadn't been to mass for over two weeks. But she was the only woman in the street who had no footwear except slippers for the outdoors, a mark of shame that even Peggy felt as she knelt for communion. It was the lack of a proper pair of shoes that kept her from mass, but how could she tell either Sister or the priest that? She drew hard on the last shred of the Woodbine and savoured the hit of the tobacco entering her lungs. All she was missing was tea, her very best friend, food in the cupboard, fuel in the coal-hole, a means to pay the rent and the coalman, a pair of shoes, regular milk from Eric, sixpences for the leccy and the reassurance that big Paddy would be in work every day, for life to be a whole lot better than it was right now.

'Is that too bleedin' much to ask for, is it?' she asked the statue of the Virgin Mary, perched next to the clock and then, flooded with guilt, blessed herself and uttered a quick succession of Hail Marys. 'Ah, Maura, you were so much better with the words than me,' she said.

Maura would do the talking with Sister Evangelista

when Peggy was desperate for a winter jumper for one of the children, or a jumble sale coat. And then she had a thought which was so warming she rose and pushed the chair under the kitchen table. She would call into Kathleen's and ask her to help her write another letter to Maura though she hadn't answered her last one, yet. And maybe Maura might just send her a postal order in time for the carnival, because without the means to get her shoes back from the pawnshop, the shame would keep her from attending that too. The effort of standing had made her back twinge again and her eyes filled with tears.

'Don't cry,' she said to herself, 'you'll manage, don't cry.'

Chapter Five

All Malcolm Coffey wanted was to run his very lucrative little business, be a good host and to be left alone. His happiness in life was derived from the new television he had installed in his sitting room, the pools he filled out once a week, mass on Sunday, his morning tea with the *Daily Post* and his nightcap of the dark rum, courtesy of Captain Conor, which he kept in his Jacobean sideboard.

Malcolm had been amazed to see Biddy Kennedy so early and with her Mary Malone, whose cheeky brother, Malachi, was Malcolm's chief suspect as being his milk thief. He was as much a scallywag as Mary looked saint-like.

Now Biddy tapped the empty hook on the coat rack behind the kitchen door. 'Hang your coat here, Mary,' she said, 'then get the kettle on.' Mary, eager to please, obeyed instantly. 'Have you any word from Captain Conor?' Biddy asked Malcolm and a look of concern crossed his face.

'I haven't,' he said. 'The last I heard about the *Morry* was from a crew that was in here three months ago. They'd had word that Conor was sailing to the West Indies and they have pirates out there, they do. No one has had word since.'

Biddy pursed her lips, and tutted as she removed her cigarettes from her pocket. 'Everyone is in a right state. Maisie has been moaning that there's no material for the carnival frocks and Ena had to go to the doctor's to get tablets for her nerves, convinced the *Morry* has sunk – apparently she said that Babs had told her a body had been washed up on a shore somewhere in the world and it was probably Conor's.'

Malcolm gasped. 'No, surely not? Was that on the news?'

Biddy took out a box of matches and shook her head. 'Not very likely, is it? There's a lot of ocean and a lot of sailors! But it's been that long since she heard from him and Babs is in a flap in case her and Bill have to fund the rum for the carnival. Babs said she'll make it up to Ena and give her a free port or two to compensate.' Biddy sat herself at the kitchen table. 'Get your notepad and some paper, Malcolm, we need to make a list for Mary. She's here to clean your ornaments, not admire them.'

'Biddy, I don't need any help...' Biddy gave Malcolm one look and his protest faded away. He made his way to the tiny reception next to the front door and returned with the pad and pen and placed them in front of Biddy, at the same time as Mary laid two cups and saucers on the table.

'Would you like me to make you any breakfast, Mr Coffey?'

Malcolm was momentarily taken aback and attempted to stutter a reply.

Biddy sighed. 'Oh, close your mouth, Malcolm! Honestly, she asked did you want any breakfast, not a four-course meal, and given that this is a guest house it seems to me that maybe she should start learning now. Right, a bacon and egg sandwich for Mr Coffey, Mary, with lashings of HP sauce. Let's see if you can find your way around his kitchen. A bit of toast for me, queen.'

Mary made no reply but, glancing around the large kitchen, set to work while Biddy turned again to an impressed Malcolm. Maybe Biddy was right; maybe he could do with the help.

'Right, Malcolm, you are the only one who gets the telegrams when a crew is coming in, so can you send a telegram the other way like, to a ship? One that's still on the water.'

Malcolm shook his head. 'Tramp ships like the *Morry* don't have a schedule, so no one knows when they are going to turn up and they trade on the spot, but I do know the man in America who buys for Conor's ship. I can send a telegram to him if it helps?'

'That sounds like a good idea, though you'd have thought he would have got a message to Ena, wouldn't you? But anyway, let's go to the post office, Malcolm, and send a message to Captain Conor through this buyer fella. These streets need a haul, for no one has anything. The docks are only taking on half a pen every morning because there aren't many ships in and those that do come in have smelted iron and lumber and you can't toast a carnival or put a roastie in a child's belly with that, can you?'

Malcolm looked aghast. 'I'll be doing no such thing!' he spluttered. 'I won't be a part of anything crooked and underhand. I'll ask Captain Conor when his crew needs the rooms, but I won't be mentioning a haul.'

Biddy took a deep breath as Mary placed a teapot on the table. 'Kathleen Deane and her daughter-in-law, Alice, have been to see me. They're worried sick about the carnival so we must tell Conor what we need before he fills in the manifest.'

A haul was when an agreement was reached with a captain and enough cargo was slipped off the ship at night to sell on the black market, with some being kept for the dockers' families and widows. Biddy hadn't slept well the previous night. She'd thought the days of the hunger on the streets that she'd seen during the forties were over.

'I thought that with the end of the war and the busy traffic in the docks, we could rest easy, that there would be enough work for everyone forever,' she said now. 'But we can't, Malcolm.'

The smell of bacon filled the kitchen. Biddy had primed Mary on the way to Malcolm's. 'You'll cook Mr Coffey breakfast for him. I need to ask him to do something he won't want to do and, like with all men, it will be a lot easier if he is distracted by food to put in his belly.'

Mary now set a plate loaded with two slices of freshly sliced bread, dripping in butter melted by the hot bacon and fried egg with rivulets of HP sauce running down the sides, in front of Malcolm. Biddy winked at her; Mary had done better than she had expected. Now she would let his initial indignation melt away and compassion take over, while the smell of bacon wreaked havoc with his resolve and the warmth of it melted his heart.

Biddy felt the familiar pangs of pity wash over her as he took the first bite of his sandwich. His wife had been a fatality during the blitz, in the bomb that had dropped on Mill Road hospital, and their baby, not a day old, would very likely have been on her breast. They lay there still, buried beneath the concrete that covered those bodies unable to be retrieved. His parents, out shopping, had been killed in a direct hit two weeks later, so as Malcolm fought for king and country, he lost his entire family at home in Liverpool and returned to the dust-sheeted family home where the ghosts of everyone he had loved had waited in the shadows to greet him.

Biddy watched as he bit into the doorstep and a slow smile of appreciation appeared.

'Shall I pour the tea?' Mary asked.

Now it was Biddy's turn to be impressed. 'My, Sister has trained you well over at that convent,' she said as Mary poured the tea. 'Get a cup for yourself too. So, Malcolm, I want you to send that telegram and I want you to do it because your conscience will trouble you something wicked if you don't when you get to hear about all the kids who have gone hungry and how the carnival had to be cancelled. You don't want that, do you? We don't have long.'

'Biddy, you're putting me in a terrible position. I'm not a lawbreaker and I don't like trouble. I live my life a certain way, the proper way, with everything just so.'

'Tell you what, Malcolm, you send a telegram saying Jerry Deane is in need of a usual favour. That way, you aren't committing yourself to anything and Conor will know exactly what you're asking him?'

Biddy knew before the words had left her mouth that he would agree.

'All right,' he said reluctantly, 'I'll do it, Biddy, but on this condition: not one bit of whatever it is comes off that ship ends up in the Seaman's Stop, do you hear? I'll send your telegram today, for Mrs Deane is a good woman and if she has asked you, then it must be necessary.'

Biddy smiled. Her goal had been achieved. 'Of course I agree. And Maura and Tommy's house is empty, so we can store it all in their wash house out the back, just like we always have. Now get your coat, Malcolm, and

I'll come to the post office with you. Mary, here's your list. The rooms all have numbers on the door. Top and bottom each one out and then start on the dining room. You've done it with your mother enough times before.'

Mary gathered up Malcolm's empty plate and cup and obediently carried them to the sink,where she began to wash up.

'Did she take a vow of silence?' said Malcolm to Biddy.

'If she had, it would be a strange thing altogether, coming from a house with nine kids, isn't that right, Mary?'

Mary turned from the sink and smiled. 'I'll get cracking once I've cleaned up here,' she said.

Malcolm grinned. 'She may not be a nun, Biddy, but it seems you've brought me a saint.'

Chapter Six

O nce the door slammed shut, Mary leant against the range and gazed around the large kitchen where she would now be spending many hours. It was bigger than her mother's on Nelson Street and smaller than the convent kitchen at St Saviour's where she had worked for six mornings a week since she left school at the age of fifteen. Only those who were considering taking the veil and becoming postulants were allowed to work full-time and her mother, Deirdre, had made it very clear to her that this was her destiny. Mary had promptly burst into floods of tears.

'Send Malachi to be a priest, not me to be a nun!' she had howled.

'Don't be ridiculous, Malachi wants to be a docker like your da. What's up with you, Mary? Jesus and Lord above, you won't ever have a moment's worry in your life. Full board and everything paid for, no visits to the rent office for you. Why do you think the nuns are always smiling? Not a care in the world amongst them.'

Mary had stared at her mother, disbelieving, already knowing it was futile to object, already plotting an escape. As it was, Sister Evangelista had come to her rescue.

'Mary, I see no great calling in you, but work amongst us, spend time here observing our devotions and should you feel things change...'

Things did not change and Mary knew they never would. There was nothing special about Malcolm's kitchen, and she concluded resignedly that, whatever its size, a kitchen was a kitchen and the stage upon which her life's dramas were doomed to play out.

'There's no one else on these streets who has a son for a priest or a daughter for a nun,' her mother had begged. 'Try harder to see a way, Mary.'

Mary's taking the veil would bestow upon Deirdre a degree of respectability, an elevated position that she could achieve by no other means. Not by money or birth, or influence. Deirdre would become the mother of a nun and there was no greater status to be achieved on the four streets.

'I hope if our Mary does take the veil, someone writes to Ireland and tells Maura Doherty! That'll put *her* nose right out of joint,' she had said to Biddy, who kept a close eye on Mary. With no succour from Biddy, no endorsement of her plans, Deirdre played the same tune to her husband Eugene, who was equally ambivalent. Eugene was a beaten man, mild-mannered, afraid to express an opinion in his own house, so he simply said,

'She's a good girl, is our Mary; she will do what's right.'

On the rare occasion she was alone with her da, Mary would plead for his help. 'Da, tell Mam I don't want to take the veil – and if I did, the money Sister pays me would stop.' Mary was paid five shillings for her kitchen toils and she handed every penny over to Deirdre.

Eugene would fold his paper, lay it on his knee, rub his chin and reply, 'The thing is, queen, your mam sees a way here to get one over on Maura Doherty, who always lorded it over her when we got here, from back home. Queen of the four streets was Maura. You keep working in the kitchens and just say no, if Sister asks you about your devotion. Be polite, mind, and it will all pass, you'll see.'

In the end, it was Biddy who came to her rescue. When Biddy told Deirdre about Malcolm needing help and the extra money Mary would earn, Deirdre, with Sister Evangelista's blessing, reluctantly let her go. And now the Seaman's Stop was to be her salvation, not the veil as Deirdre had hoped. Mary and her red, chapped and work-worn hands had travelled from her mother's kitchen to the convent kitchen and now to Malcolm's kitchen – and she wasn't yet eighteen. She flopped down onto the still-warm chair vacated by Biddy. Leaning forward, she placed her head in her hands and rubbed her eyes.

'Oh Jimmy, where are you?' she said.

There were no tears; they had stopped falling long

ago. Sometimes it felt as though all that had happened to her in the past year was just a dream, but then at night, in the dark, she would remember, and it was as if she could hear his voice, feel his kiss, smell him. He was her first thought at the beginning of each day and her last as she closed her eyes at night.

It was all thanks to a tip-off from Malachi that Deirdre had caught Jimmy kissing Mary outside their back gate and she had let out a scream as she ran at the couple and prised them apart.

'Have you no shame?' she hissed as she dragged Mary through the gate into their own backyard and into the kitchen. 'What the hell are you doing? I cannot believe what I've just seen. Have you lost your mind, Mary? His reputation is notorious – if your father had caught you, he'd have had his guts for garters.'

They both knew this was patently not true, but Deirdre raged on. 'You know he's up before the magistrate every five minutes, don't you? And now he's tried to rob a betting shop, tied up a poor innocent man who was doing nothing but his job, almost killed him. He's turned an awful corner, that boy has. No one respectable speaks to his mother because of it.'

Mary's eyes had filled with tears as she stared down at her feet. She didn't care that Jimmy was regularly up before the magistrates, he had promised her he would change his ways after this last time in court.

'He said he won't do any more robbing, Mam, he's

promised me. He said he would go straight now.'

Deirdre looked incredulous. 'Promised you? *Promised* you? Did he say that to get you into his bed, did he?' Deirdre's expression had turned from one of anger to fear. 'Mary, a man will say anything, anything at all if it gets his hand down your knickers, do you hear me? Robbing is as natural as breathing to the O'Prey boys and they cannot change; all they can do is rob and lie.'

Mary had lifted her head. 'Callum has changed – Jimmy can too.'

Deirdre's eyes were wild at this point. 'Oh, ay, Callum's not as bad as Jimmy – at least he's down the docks, but I tell you, an old dog can't learn new tricks. It's in the O'Prey blood, for the father was as bad, not that Annie would ever admit it now.'

Mary had felt anger bubbling up inside her and blurted out, 'Mam, I'm almost sixteen. You and Da were married when you were sixteen. I'm old enough to make my own mind up. I love him, Mammy, and you chose Da.'

'Yes, yes, I did, but when I chose your father, I didn't choose a bloody villain, did I? I chose a docker who isn't afraid of honest hard work, now why can't you just do the same? I wanted better for you,' she wailed. 'I thought taking the veil would be good for you. Haven't you had enough of looking after kids? Aren't this lot enough for you? I thought I was saving you from this.'

Mary felt her anger slowly rise like bile in her gullet, but her response was calm and steady. 'No, Mam, that was you. Not me. No, not me.' She shook her head from side to side.

Mary could see that Deirdre was thinking, plotting, then her mother's eyes narrowed as a thought struck her. There was one question, one fear that had to be resolved there and then. 'How long has this been going on? Has he had his way with you? Has he? Tell me right now?'

Mary clenched her teeth together and looked down at her nails, bitten to the quick and cracked from hard work. Deirdre felt a panic rising. 'Oh, Holy Mother of God! Mary, I'm asking you, how many times has Jimmy O'Prey kissed you? How far have you gone? Jesus, tell me you aren't pregnant?' Deirdre was almost at screaming pitch.

Mary looked up at her mother, unable to stop the tears from flowing now. 'Mam, what do you mean, how far?'

Now it was Deirdre's turn to look embarrassed. 'Mary, you and me, we need to have a little talk about things for, honest to God, you don't understand. A few words followed by a few minutes with a scally like Jimmy O'Prey, they can ruin your life forever. You are never to be alone with him ever again, do you hear me? That's how accidents happen.'

Like most of the women on the four streets, Deirdre loved a drama and that day she had one all of her very own. 'God, my nerves are shot, I'll be down at Dr Cole's at this rate. Who would have thought it? You, kissing

Jimmy O'Prey and in broad daylight too! The shame of it if anyone had seen you. Mary, you promise me now that you will never see him again, because if you do I'll have to tell your da and he won't be happy, I can tell you. There will be trouble, Mary.'

Mary looked up and saw her brother outside the kitchen window, laughing openly at her discomfort, his hands and face pressed against the glass. He was too short to reach, which meant one of her other brothers was likely on all fours in the yard and Malachi was standing on his back. He had no shirt on and his vest was streaked with dirt, his face mucky and smeared. It would be her job at the end of the day to make sure each one of them was washed and scrubbed in the metal bath. She thought of her da and she knew he would indeed have been angry if he'd been the one to catch her with Jimmy. He was always giving out about Jimmy O'Prey, using his stints in prison as a warning and an example to his own sons.

Deirdre started putting lipstick on in the mirror over the fireplace. Her face was white, her hand shaking. She'd spoken to Mary through the mirror. 'You don't under-stand, Mary, your life can change for the worse with a lad like Jimmy O'Prey. Would you want to be knocked up, married to a jailbird not because you wanted to, because you had to? The shame of it, can you imagine? It would kill your father – and me, never mind him!'

Deirdre wasn't one for curlers during the day. She

was one of the most frequent visitors to Cindy's, the hairdresser on the parade, and was a disciple of the new order, sleeping in curlers at night and backcombing during the day. Her hair was short, bleached blonde with dark roots at least an inch long, and it seemed to Mary that no matter how many afternoons her mother spent in Cindy's chair, whilst Mary watched the children and prepared the tea, the roots were always there. Now Deirdre snapped the cap back on her lipstick, extracted her compact from her handbag and began to wipe the pad over her nose. She regarded her plain daughter.

'Never see him again, do you hear me, Mary? Never! If you only knew how miserable your life would become if you got yourself hitched to a boy like him.'

Mary felt lost, could her life be more miserable than it was already? How on earth could that be possible?

'Right, now get into the wash house where I know you will be safe from the likes of that scallywag and keep yourself busy. The washing is nearly done in the copper, so rinse and mangle it and get it on the line for me before the weather changes. I need to speak to Kathleen so I'm off to number 42.'

Mary had known that Deirdre couldn't wait to tell the women about what had just happened. It would have been a crime for them to witness it for themselves, but not to hear the embellished version from Deirdre. The fact that Deirdre had caught her and Jimmy kissing in the entry would spread across the four streets like a bush fire before teatime. Deirdre would be the centre of a drama, elicit the sympathy of the other woman for the cross she had to bear, the trauma of such a near miss and praise for the way in which she had averted a potential disaster.

Once the morning chores were over and the potatoes for tea peeled, the women of the four streets spent most of the day in and out of each other's homes, vacating one kitchen to reassemble in another, discussing something, anything – the murder of the priest, the price of fish, the state of Peggy's front step, the number of men taken on in the pen that morning – whatever it was that had occurred since the previous day. No one, though, ever gathered in Peggy's. Even women who had nothing were particular about which ashtrays they flicked their ash into, whose chipped cups they drank their tea from.

Mary hadn't waited for Deirdre to leave for Kathleen's; she'd dashed back down to the wash house, slamming the door behind her, wondering where Jimmy had gone. She could see no way out, no escape from the drudgery that was her life, which felt so much harder than it had even before Jimmy had first spoken to her. Jimmy had unexpectedly stepped into her life and from that moment on she had begun to dream and, for the first time, felt truly alive. She wondered, could she get the washing done before Deirdre returned and then head up to the bombed-out wasteland? That was where Jimmy would wait for her, she was sure.

It was where Jimmy, a handsome nineteen-year-old,

had first spoken to her, smiling down at her with an impish grin on his face and stealing her heart in an instant. His cap was low over his eyes, his smile full of mischief and promise. Jimmy did not lead the dull and boring life that Mary did and it showed. The air between them felt charged and so the clandestine meetings had begun at the back of the Anchor pub, behind the bins. They'd sit on the wall at the back of the bottle dump and Jimmy talked whilst Mary listened. He told her about all the bread vans he had robbed and the parties he had catered for in the four streets.

'No one would ever have had a party if me and Callum couldn't run so fast,' he'd said and told her of how they were behind all the shop deliveries which had gone missing, the minute the driver stepped into the shop and took a cup of tea. Jimmy wooed her, he impressed her, he stole her heart and, when he'd kissed her for the first time, she never wanted him to stop. In those six blissful weeks before Deirdre caught them kissing in the back-entry, Mary had fallen hopelessly in love with Jimmy O'Prey.

They managed one more meeting before Jimmy was sentenced. She had Malachi to thank for that too. 'He wants to meet you at the back of the Anchor right now, he has summat to tell you,' he'd whispered so no one could hear and then shouted, 'Chase me, Mary, bet you can't catch me!' and then run out of the back gate. After a startled moment, Mary had set off after him. She didn't care what happened next, or even if Deirdre came running after her – Jimmy had sent for her.

Callum had been standing with Jimmy, waiting for her, under Annie's instructions. 'I don't want Deirdre Malone in here again, giving me hell, so don't let him out of your sight,' she had ordered Callum. 'That woman makes me laugh, she does, never out of Cindy's, all high and mighty – she's Maura Doherty without the brains, that one, and her daughter is lucky that our Jimmy paid her a moment's attention. The cut of the girl! She isn't even pretty, a right plain Jane.'

Mary had been irritated that Callum remained with her and Jimmy and didn't move into the Anchor. As if he could read her thoughts, Jimmy had said, 'Would you look at him, he's me bodyguard. Taking me for my last pint, or so he thinks.'

Jimmy had laughed and Callum respectfully turned away, but not before he apologised, saying, 'Sorry, Mary. I'll be waiting by the back door, Jimmy.' True to his word he'd ambled across the backyard and stood in the doorway with his hands in his pockets, looking as though he would rather be anywhere else.

'Callum thinks I'm going down tomorrow,' Jimmy had told a stricken Mary, 'but I'm not. I always manage to wind the jury around my little finger.'

Jimmy hadn't kissed Mary within sight of his brother; instead, he'd turned to her and flicked her ponytail, saying, 'I'm sorry for all the trouble I've caused you, Mary. My mam gave out something wicked after your mam went to see her. And I mean, Jesus, it wasn't like we were official or anything, was it? I mean, we was both only having a bit of fun. It's the nineteen sixties – you'd think it was the dark ages the way your ma carried on.'

Mary had gasped, his words like an arrow that pierced her heart. Not official? But she thought that they had been. He had asked her to come to the house when Annie was out at the bingo, had kissed her a hundred times and she could remember every one. Not official?

'If – if they… How long will you be gone for…?' She'd had no idea what to say next, shocked by his disowning all that had passed between them as just a bit of fun.

'Oh, don't be worrying about me.' He'd been looking towards the door of the Anchor, obviously wanting to get away to the bar. 'If I do go down, it won't be for more than a year at the most.'

She'd tried to speak, but the rock that had lodged in her throat stopped her.

'Come on, Jimmy, let's go inside before you get Mary into any more trouble. Mary, your da, he'd be down here if he knew.' And Callum had walked over and taken his brother by the elbow to lead him away.

'Will I wait for you?' she'd asked, but she was speaking to Jimmy's back. He hadn't so much as touched her. The pub door opened and Jimmy had been swallowed by the noise and the smoke.

Callum had marched over to her. 'Mary, go home,' he'd said and she felt instantly ashamed of the tears that were rolling unchecked down her cheeks. 'He's my brother, but he's a baddun, he's half-mad and everyone knows it. There's no taming Jimmy. Go and find yourself a nice fella, one who deserves a lovely looking girl like you.'

And as Callum had walked away, her humiliation was complete when Malachi and some of his friends appeared above the wall and her brother had called out, 'Our Mary's been chucked, our Mary's been chucked,' and they all ran away, chanting. That had been over a year ago and still there was no sign of Jimmy's return, and every day she waited.

Malcolm walked out of the post office to find Biddy waiting outside. 'Did you send it?'

'I did and I have the receipt to prove it, here, look.'

Taking the sheet of paper from his hand she opened it out and read aloud, '*Awaiting your arrival. Please advise. Will inform Ena. Jerry Deane needs a favour.* Is that it?'

'It is and he will know exactly what it means. I don't mind doing this, Biddy, but I've told you, not a drop of it is coming anywhere near the Seaman's Stop.'

Biddy didn't answer. She would cross that bridge when they reached it.

'I think it might rain,' he said, looking up at the sky.

'I hope not,' said Biddy. 'I hate the rain, I do. It gets into my bones.'

Malcolm looked at her with concern; Biddy was the

closest he had to a mother and, if truth be known, he felt better for having sent the telegram to Captain Conor. His own mother would have told him to do the same. He could see with his own eyes that things were not as they had once been: Biddy was ageing and dockers with big families were getting poorer, as the dock board squeezed wages to make even bigger profits and fewer ships came into port.

'You know, Biddy, some of those women in homes where the men aren't being taken on must be out of their minds with worry, so concern yourself not, I was happy to send the telegram – if it helps out around here, it was the right thing to do. Now, shall we go to the café on the end of the parade for a cuppa.'

Biddy smiled. 'Good idea. And while we are there, I'll pop into Cindy's and get an appointment for Saturday. The best hairdresser in Liverpool, she is.'

Biddy linked her arm through Malcolm's as they walked down the Dock Road and Malcolm tucked her arm closer into his side. 'And you, Biddy, you're the best friend a man could have. I couldn't have asked for anyone better to have my back like you do. You remind me of Mam.'

'Oh, give over, you,' she said as she swung her handbag forwards and whacked him on his protruding belly. Malcolm gave one of his rare laughs.

'So you aren't cross with me about Mary, then?'

'No, I'm not at all. That was a perfect bacon butty.

You're right, Mary is going to make my life so much easier. I don't know why I'm so stubborn, sometimes.'

Biddy felt her heart fill with fondness. 'I never thought I'd hear you admit that. But you must understand Malcolm, I'm *always* right and if you doubt me, there's always Kathleen to read your tea leaves for confirmation. Oh look, there's Cindy waving through the window. Get me an Eccles cake to go with that tea and I'll be five minutes.'

Biddy could see that Ena was under the dryer and Deirdre Malone was sitting on the pink seat with a towel around her shoulders. When the bell jangled out over the shop door as Biddy opened it, the smell of perming solution and hair spray assailed her nostrils as she called out, 'How's our Mary doing?'

Cindy placed her fingers over her lips. 'Sshh,' and pointed to Ena, who was fast asleep under the dryer, head back, mouth open, top teeth hanging down.

'She will fit in just fine,' said Biddy, in a whisper, 'and I've no doubt she'll enjoy the extra money.'

'Do you want an appointment, Biddy?' asked Cindy, opening the book. And then, dropping her voice even further, 'I don't suppose Malcolm has heard anything from Captain Conor? Poor Ena is out of her mind.' Cindy nodded towards Ena. 'She hasn't heard from him for months.'

Biddy shook her head. 'Malcolm has just sent a tele-gram thingy. With a bit of luck we should hear something soon.'

Malcolm, heading towards the café, felt good. The clouds had dispersed, the threat of rain had gone, Mary had come to work for him, the sun might just be here to stay, Captain Conor would know he was needed and sail in – everything was going to be just fine.

Chapter Seven

Tommy poured the drinks whilst Maura slipped the paper knife into the top of the blue airmail letters and laid them flat on the top of the table, smoothing them out with the palms of her hands, wondering which one to read first.

'Let's be starting with Sister Evangelista, shall we?' she said. Tommy saw the look of pleasure and anticipation on Maura's face as she scanned the pale blue paper. It made him feel happy and it struck him that the letters from home gave them almost too much pleasure and highlighted how little of note happened in their daily lives.

'Well, imagine, Sister says they are choosing the Dock Queen attendants for the carnival this week, and she says that if Angela was at the school still, she would definitely have been chosen for the chief one, given how much effort she had put into controlling her temper of late. Well, I never, wouldn't Angela just have been delighted?' She couldn't help the disappointment creeping into her voice and looked towards Tommy.

'Don't,' said Tommy as he pulled the stopper from the top of the whiskey bottle and began to pour it into the glass. 'And don't be telling our Angela neither,' he said. 'She hates this bloody school she's in – and I swear to God, that effort to control her temper was short-lived. She's done nothing but complain since we moved here.'

He handed Maura her glass, half-filled with a generous helping of the warm amber liquid, to soften the sharp edge of his words. Maura took a sip and, placing Sister Evangelista's letter to the side with a heavy heart, picked up the next one. She would savour each letter as she went.

'This one is from Malcolm from the Seaman's Stop. God love him, he says that the streets aren't the same without us and he would throw a party if we would return home for the carnival.' Maura sat back and placed the letter on the table. 'Well, would you fancy that? Malcolm doesn't even go to the pub! He drives Biddy to distraction, for she loves a Guinness. She's been like a mammy to him since his own mammy died and poor Ena has ended up in his doorway more times than enough, three sheets to the wind. You'd think he would want to go and join them, wouldn't you.'

Tommy and Maura both blessed themselves with the sign of the cross and Tommy's eyebrows rose as his glass reached his lips. 'What else does he say? Does he write what kind of party would he throw, would the drink be free?'

'He says the work on the docks is drying up, that only half a pen is being taken on each day, there aren't as many sailors staying as there were.' Maura tutted as one hand flew to the crucifix around her neck. 'Tommy, it sounds bad, doesn't it?'

Tommy shook his head. 'It must be bad if Malcolm has written to you. He was always a quiet one and keeps himself to himself. His da worked for the dock board. That's how they got that big house over the road from the pub. Good money he earned. What does Kathleen say? Go on, read that one next; she might give us more of a clue what's going on. Is there news of Jerry? Any wins on the gee-gees? Has he been to the footie? Who's taken my place in the darts team? Does Jer still think Bill Shankly is the second coming?'

Jerry had been Tommy's closest friend, a friendship bound closer than brothers by the joint knowledge of a deadly deed. Neither man had ever spoken of the night the priest had been murdered and both were present, but it hadn't saved poor Kitty – and that was a sin they had to carry, the murderous end of the guilty priest.

Maura sliced open Kathleen's letter. As usual, she scanned the pages and read it herself before she began to read it out loud. This annoyed Tommy intensely.

'Go on, read it out, stop reading it to yourself,' he said.

'Well, sure this letter has dashed all my hopes that Peggy was doing all right without me. She's been to

Kathleen to borrow money for the kids' teas a few times and Kathleen and Maggie Trott are feeding them as much as they can. Shelagh has been saying she doesn't know how they are going to pay the rent because Paddy isn't getting out of bed half of the time and, Holy Mother of God, the carnival is on its knees. Kathleen says the only person doing anything is Eric; he's painted the float all nice, but there isn't a scrap of bunting made.'

Maura slapped the letter in the air. 'I don't believe it, it's all bad news.' She held it closer to her face. 'Kathleen has the kids over on a Sunday – she's doing two sittings, Jerry and Alice, Nellie and Joseph first and then she sends Nellie out to get the Nolans from the wasteland and take them back for a feed. She says they would go all day with nothing but bread and dripping if they didn't. Oh Tommy, God love them!' Maura looked upset. 'Kathleen says she's praying for the *Morry* to come in or it will be the worst carnival on the streets for many a year.'

Tommy let out a long whistle. 'As bad as that? Looks like we did the right thing, getting out when we did.'

Maura looked perturbed and sad as she opened the next letter. She had been looking forward to this hour all day and now she felt nothing but concern for families she knew as well as if they were her own. 'Let's hope there is happier news in this one,' she said as she opened out the sheet of paper. This time she read the contents out loud almost as quickly as she read them to herself.

'This is from the dock and harbour board asking us to sign the rent book back to them. They can't do that! The rent is paid in full.' They had continued to pay rent on the house, even keeping their furniture there. They had moved into the Talk of the Town with all they could carry, intending to send for the furniture, but never quite getting around to it. They were both aware, with the housing shortage in Liverpool, that once they signed over the rent book they would never get the house back and, even though the postal order Maura religiously sent to the dock and harbour board every Friday was money she could have well done with as she watched their windfall deplete, she had been compelled never to miss a week.

'And I'm not sure we should send the rent book back,' said Tommy.

'What, you mean not at all, never? We can't keep paying rent in a house we don't live in forever, Tommy. Do you know how much money we have left?'

Tommy shook his head; he never did. Money was a mystery to him. All their married life he had handed his pay packet over to Maura. She had given him his spending money back and they had always had a roof over their head, had never gone hungry as many did, thanks to Maura being an expert manager and lucky down at the bingo. It was a system that had worked well and Tommy hadn't had any intention of changing it until he took it upon himself to buy the Talk of the Town.

'We have just over one hundred pounds left from the money we got from America and we made one pound and six shilling's profit here last week,' Maura said now.

Tommy felt guilt wash over him and in need of another drink. 'I'm sorry, queen,' he said.

'Don't you be sorry,' said Maura. 'We will turn it all around, you watch. I'm not touching that money, though, Tommy. If we had to leave and go back, it's all we have. And we may have to make a decision soon, for you can't keep milking Liam's cows. That's not a living.'

They sipped their drinks, searching for a way to justify continuing to pay the rent out of the money they had left. They both knew they couldn't keep it up for much longer. Maura had never wanted her sons on the docks, but she was glad to keep the house for reasons unprobed and unidentified. Now, neither was willing to admit that they had made the biggest mistake of their lives.

'They must have got wind that we aren't living there, Tommy. It says here they prefer the house to be inhabited.' She folded the letter and placed it back in the envelope. 'They don't like to leave properties empty in case of burst pipes and irreparable and expensive damage.'

Maura shook her head. Her thoughts drifted to her house on the four streets. The carnival was coming. She remembered the excitement that surrounded the day, the games, the march and the knees-up in the Anchor pub when all the kids were in bed and being looked after by a variety of young girls who were allowed to stay up in order to babysit. It was always a highlight of the year. Maura organised the costumes, making a trip to the market for the fabric to supplement whatever fell off the back of the tramp ship.

'I miss the trips to the market. Do you remember the white silk dresses we had last year? And wasn't that just the thing, because the girls could use them for Holy Communion after,' she said aloud as she remembered she and Angela putting their best foot forward for a carnival without Kitty. 'Oh, Conor *must* be on his way back. It would be the first time he had let everyone down, so we have to keep paying the rent until then because, as God is my judge, they will need it to hide Conor's drink in the back and Kathleen will have to be the one to dish it out.'

Maura's voice had dropped an octave, even though there was no one to hear her. Without a doubt, the carnival would never be a day of fun and memories without an understanding between Captain Conor and the dockers. Just like at Christmas, the carnival fun arrived via wins on the bingo, Green Shield stamps, the butcher's and the biggest contribution of all, the goods that fell off the back of a ship. Maura had no chance to say any more because Angela appeared in the doorway.

'Mammy, it's Harry, he's really sick.'

Maura put down her glass and jumped to her feet.

'Is it his chest, queen? Is his breathing not right, is he wheezy?'

'No Mammy, it's his arm, it's hot all the way up and he's not making any sense.'

Maura fought to keep the panic from her voice as she laid Harry down on the settle, his body burning as his mind rambled.

'Get them off, Mam!' he cried, swatting at his arms as Maura removed his pyjamas.

'Tommy,' she said, 'go on, run. Get the bike out and get to the Deanes'. Ask Liam to take us to the hospital. Tommy, where *is* the nearest hospital?'

Tommy shook his head, feeling helpless and trapped. In Liverpool, he would have had Harry over his shoulders in a flash and marched down to St Angelus within fifteen minutes. 'I don't know, queen, but I'll go now.' And with one quick kiss on his son's head and the whispered words, 'Daddy will sort this out now, Harry. It's a doctor you need and we will have you better in no time,' he was out of the door and pedalling for his life, back to the Deanes' farm.

Maura had never seen one of her children look so ill and she had sat through many a long night and trips to St Angelus with asthma and bad chests, the curse of living so close to the river Mersey. Her heart raced fast as she filled up a bowl with tepid water and began to wash Harry's body down to reduce his temperature. Angela padded over to her mother's side.

'Angela, get me my rosary from the press,' Maura barked at her anxious-looking daughter. Angela didn't need to be asked twice; the sight of Harry's curls, plastered to his scalp with perspiration, along with his rambling and wailing, set her own emotions on edge.

'Here, Mammy,' said Angela as the rosary slipped from her hand to her mother's. Angela's dark hair fell long and unkempt down both sides of her face, her eyes were wide, her thumb in her mouth and her precious teddy under her arm. 'Here, Harry,' she whispered as she placed her teddy into the crook of Harry's arm.

'Good girl,' said Maura and smiled up at her. 'Now change this water, would you? Not hot, not cold, we don't want to shock him, just in the middle, for I have to keep washing him down to try and fight the temperature off.'

'Ma...' Harry opened his eyes. They were glazed and bright and for a moment they held Maura's.

'I'm here, Harry. Don't you be worrying now, just lie there nice and still.' Her son turned his head and looked about the room.

'Where's Da?' Harry croaked.

'Angela, get me some water for Harry to drink.' She knew they had to get fluids into him whilst he could hold it down. She placed her arm around her son's back and held the drink to his lips. Harry guzzled the water and Maura laid him back down. 'Da's gone for the doctor, Harry, he'll be back in a minute,' she said, but Harry wasn't listening. His temperature had rapidly risen again and he began to ramble incoherently once more.

'Mam, is Harry going to die?'

Angela had laid her hand on her mother's shoulder. She had never seen anyone that poorly before and Maura felt the question like a slap across the face. She stared at her daughter. 'No, Angela, he isn't. The good Lord has taken one from me, he won't be wanting another.' But the very thought that that would even be a possibility chilled Maura to the bone and she began to wash Harry down again. 'This water is hot already, Angela, bring me a jug of fresh.'

It felt to Maura as though the night would last forever as she waited for Tommy to return, raising her son's limbs one by one and running the cloth soaked in tepid water along each one, whispering comforting words as she did so, while Angela sat in the rocking chair and slowly rocked back and forth, her eyes never leaving her mother or Harry. Maura hardly realised it, but as she comforted her son in the dark and tense atmosphere, with nothing by way of light other than the peat blocks smouldering and a spluttering candle on the stone mantelpiece, her thoughts slipped from where they now lived to the place she thought of as home.

'Now, when you are better, you will be running straight up to the bombed-out site to play the footie, won't you? If I hear Jerry shout once more, "Harry takes a corner like Stanley Matthews", I'll be on the phone to Bill Shankly meself, do you hear me? I'll be saying to him, oi, Bill you don't even know it but your best player is here, knocking a ball about with the lads on the four streets and you haven't even noticed him yet.'

She stroked the wet hair back from Harry's forehead with the cloth as he burned up, muttering words that made little sense and she fought the fever bowl by bowl, cloth by cloth, as the clock ticked through the minutes and the fire fell into dust. Without being asked, Angela knew just when she was needed and helped her ma until they heard the sound of Liam's van pull up outside.

'Oh, thank you God!' Maura gasped, her voice catching in her throat and she blessed herself. Tommy took the stairs two at a time and ran into the room with Liam close behind and Maeve, Liam's wife, staggered breathlessly in after him.

'Come on,' said Liam who could see Harry was a very sick boy indeed, 'Tommy, you carry him down the stairs and we will lay him on the front bench of the van, across yours and Maura's laps. Maura, come on, down you go. Have you got everything you need? Maeve is going to stay here with Angela and look after the place. We knocked on to Pete Shevlin's and he's sent his cowman to do the milking for us. Angela, you go away back to bed and get some sleep before the others wake and you can have a day off school and help Maeve. Tommy, you lift Harry and take him down to the car. Do you need anything, Maura? Do you have your handbag?'

In the midst of the chaos, Maura almost smiled. 'You are Kathleen's son, all right, Liam,' she said, impressed, as she tied her headscarf under her chin.

Maeve helped Maura on with her coat and threw her arms around her as Tommy lifted Harry up and into his own arms. 'They will make him better at the hospital,' said Maeve. 'Sure they will that. I'd say send him down to Bridget on the farm, she has a potion for everything, but you'd never be able to get him there in the dark across the bog and up the bohreen until it's daylight. That's the worst of it, where Bridget lives in the sod house – even I can't find me way and there's so many goblins sleeping out there at night, one would surely grab at your ankles and trip ye up. Wicked, they are.'

Maura hugged Maeve back as Angela said, 'Can I come with you, Mammy?'

Maura bent down to her. 'No, Angela, I need you to be...' Her voice tailed away. She had nearly said, 'Be like our Kitty was', but she managed to stop herself. 'I need you to be a big girl and show Maeve how we do things and get the kids to school. Can you do that?'

Angela, nodded, knowing exactly what it was that Maura had been about to say.

Maeve took Angela's hand. 'Come on, there's a good girl. Will we make the tea?'

As Tommy walked past with Harry dangling from his arms, his head lolling on his shoulder, the teddy fell onto the floor.

'Take it,' said Angela as she bent and picked it up and thrust it into Maura's arms. 'He makes me better.'

'Go,' said Maeve. 'Off with you and God speed.'

Moments later, Maura and Tommy, feeling totally helpless, were sitting in the front of Liam's van as he drove it as fast as it would carry them on the road to Galway. As they passed through Ballynevin, they saw the lights on in the Post Office and Mrs Doyle, with her face up to the window, watching them as they passed.

'Why is Mrs Doyle up now at this godawful hour?' asked Tommy.

Maura's eyes never left her son's face, but she said, 'The cowman would have gone there to tell her what was happening and she would have telephoned the hospital to let them know we are on our way.'

Even though she couldn't see him, Tommy raised his cap to Mrs Doyle in grateful thanks. 'They *are* good people out here,' he said in almost a whisper as he placed his hand over Maura's and gave it a squeeze.

She looked up at her husband and their eyes met. She would not tell Tommy now, but if she had made a decision in the time it had taken him to get to Liam's and back – and, if their son survived this, nothing anyone said would change her mind.

She felt the tears prickle the back of her eyes as her son rambled and the van bumped and rattled along the road. She wasn't even sure if Harry would still be alive by the time they reached the hospital. In each village they passed through they were expected and someone was up and waiting in case they needed help. The jungle drums along the Atlantic coast road had heralded their coming. As they crept into one village, Liam slowed the van down, stopped at a gate, and just as he did, a door flew open and a couple Maura thought must have been at least eighty years old came running down the path. Liam wound down his window.

'A cool cloth for the boy and a tot for you,' the woman said, handing a damp cloth in through the window to Maura. Meanwhile, her husband unscrewed the van's petrol cap and, began to top up the tank from a large enamel jug. Maura was so grateful as she laid the cool cloth on Harry's brow, but she couldn't say so, words were beyond her.

'Here, knock this back, quick,' said Tommy and, taking the glass, she did just that.

The cloth helped to take the burning heat out of Harry's forehead and body and Maura wiped it around the back of his neck, down his chest and across the back of his neck again, then she dipped her head and looked out of the window at the old woman.

'God bless you,' she said. She wanted to ask how did they know they would be passing? There were no phone lines on this remote road. How did she know what they needed? The woman took one look at Harry and, reaching in, pressed something into Maura's hand. It was a whittled wooden cross.

'For the boy,' she said, watching as Maura put the cross in Harry's hand and wrapped his fingers around it.

'Thank you,' Maura said again.

'God speed,' said the woman, 'and don't be worrying any more; when this is over, you will be in the place where so many are needing your help right now. 'Tis an awful burden you have to carry.'

Maura's mouth dropped open and the only sounds in the van were those of Harry's laboured breathing and the petrol filling up the tank.

'I knew Kitty,' said the woman. 'I sent a potion for her when she was here. Sure, the midwife did her best for her, she was a good woman. No one could have done more.'

Maura grasped her fingers and squeezed them tightly. She had asked Maeve so often about what had happened with Kitty. She had delivered her baby in the convent laundry, hidden from view, and following the birth had been taken from there to Liam and Maeve, to give her time to recover and stop the police in Liverpool from making any connection between the murder of the priest and their unmarried, pregnant daughter.

'Kathleen is waiting for you back at home, 'twill all be over soon. Ye can't run forever, Kitty told me to tell ye, "Go back, he made a mistake, don't make him live with it until till the end of his days".' She inclined her head towards Tommy.

Maura felt her heart banging against her ribs; her mouth had dried, but there was no time to ask what the woman meant because now there was a bang on the bonnet to let Liam know the tank was full. Liam pulled out the choke, turned the key and within seconds, they were off again. Maura turned her head to look out of the back window of the van as they moved away and the woman raised her hand before she turned and Maura felt the breath she had been unaware she was holding leave her body.

'Was that the jungle drums as well, Liam?' she asked. 'Because they were very specific with the details.'

'Not really,' said Liam with a half-smile. 'That's Kathleen's eldest sister, my aunt. There's nothing about anyone she doesn't know. She taught Kathleen to read the tea leaves. Has the gift of the sight she does, she's the local seer. They have no phone – Jesus, they have no running water even. No one told them we were on our way through. She just knew we were coming and I knew I had to stop.'

Maura let out a big sigh and Tommy, never a man for public displays of affection, found his wife's free hand and, taking hold of it, squeezed it hard.

For the rest of the journey, Maura prayed over Harry; she had nothing else in her armoury. His temperature was the highest she had ever known in a child and his skin was wet and clammy. He had stopped rambling, was as limp as a rag, and no matter how often she whispered his name, there was no response. And, as she always did in times of need, she appealed to the Holy Mother for help. In the last miles of the journey, the only sound in the cab was that of Harry's laboured breathing and Maura's chanting.

'Hail Mary, full of Grace, the Lord is with thee; blessed art thou amongst women and blessed is the fruit of thy womb, Jesus. Holy Mary, Mother of God, pray for us sinners now and at the hour of our death and in the hour of our need. Please don't take my Harry,' she gasped and as she did so, Tommy once more slipped his hand into her own that grasped the rosary beads.

'We're nearly there, queen,' he whispered and she could just hear him over the noise of the rattling van.

'We had better be, Tommy.' She turned and looked into her husband's eyes and fear of gripped them both. It was unspeakable, beyond terrifying, and they were unequipped to take it. Having lost Kitty, there were no resources to call on: they knew that pain, that grief, and they could not face or survive it again.

Within a few minutes they were driving up to the door of the hospital. Liam pulled open the passenger door of the van and lifted Harry into his arms.

'He's worse,' Liam said to Tommy, as he half-ran, half-walked with him, protecting the precious bundle in his arms. In their haste, not one of them noticed the wooden cross as it slipped from Harry's fingers and bounced down the hospital steps.

Chapter Eight

The promise of sunshine held as May teased out the blossom on the trees in the churchyard and the priory garden. This particular Saturday morning, the sky had shone the clearest blue and the mildness of the air held the promise of a full day of play for every child who ran out of the house and headed up to the bombed-out wasteland. A football match, to end only when darkness fell, would begin as soon as every boy in the four streets, keen to be picked to play by Malachi Malone, the owner of the only ball, was up at the wasteland. Every boy except for little Paddy who had again made excuses to fall behind his siblings and almost had to leave Max under the bed in his box due to Peggy's watchful eye and the fact that his father was lying in his bed, refusing to rise.

Little Paddy had managed to take some crumbs from the bottom of the empty biscuit tin, a few sultanas, too precious to throw out and too few to serve any purpose, from the press and stole Max away with only seconds to spare before Peggy caught him. Peggy was at the kitchen table, the thick stub of a pencil in one hand. A scrap of paper lay on the table before her and a letter that she hurriedly shoved back into an official-looking brown envelope. She looked up as her son came into the room.

'Paddy, what the hell is wrong with you? Get yourself out of the door, right now. They've all gone out to play and you're supposed to be looking after them. Get up there before Malachi starts another fight with your brothers. Go on, get out.'

Little Paddy had slipped Max into his coat pocket and, as he wriggled in there, little Paddy, his heart beating wildly, placed his hands over the outside to conceal Max from Peggy's view. 'Mam, I'm only here because I want to help you. Da says he's not getting up today, that his back is bad. He said would you take him a cuppa tea up and I have to go and get him an ounce of Old Holborn from Simpsons in the parade.'

Peggy narrowed her eyes. 'Did he now? With what, may I ask? Does he think I have a magic pot in the out-house or a fecking tree in the yard that grows ten-shilling notes for leaves?' Peggy's voice was rising, but she lacked her usual energy and suddenly the heat left her face. She passed the back of her hand across her brow and said, 'Paddy, you need to get out. My nerves can't stand anyone around today. Go on, get out. Forget your da and the tobacco, unless I've not heard and Simpsons are giving it away for free now.'

Peggy pushed the chair back and stood up straight with her hand in the middle of her lower back. Little Paddy saw her wince with pain as he stepped closer to deliver the rest of the message from his father.

'Da also said to say his back is really bad, and he said the smokes help him, Ma...'

Peggy looked straight at her son and her eyes, for a brief moment, seemed far away.

'Is that what he said? Well, he should try having my back for a day. Funny how his only lasts until opening time at the Anchor, isn't it? Your father makes an amazing recovery then, every afternoon. Must be a miracle that. Don't you worry about your da, or his baccy, leave him to me, Paddy.'

Peggy's eyes softened as she looked down at her son. Not blessed with a daughter to help share the load, she often felt resentful towards those neighbours who did. The thought of Deirdre Malone, from Tipperary of all places, blessed with a firstborn like Mary, filled her with a burning sense of injustice. What was the Holy Mother thinking, leaving her like this, broke and with the worst case of fibroids the doctor at St Angelus had ever come across in a woman her age? With only boys she couldn't even get out to work because there would be no one to look after the little ones while she was gone.

'You gave Maura three daughters,' she often said to the statue of Mary in church and then moved swiftly into the confessional, having coveted what another woman had, a woman who acted like a saint towards her at that. And then Maura's Kitty died, breaking all of their hearts and Angela, the second born stepped into her place. It was as if God knew Maura would require a daughter in reserve and had then provided for the Dohertys a second time, with the hugest windfall they never knew was coming from their surprise relatives in America.

'If that isn't proof that wearing your shoe leather out running up in and out of St Cuthbert's in the name of religious observance delivers you the good life and a full purse, I don't know what is,' she had grumbled to big Paddy on more than one occasion before Kitty had died. But the Dohertys had paid a terrible price and now little Paddy stood before her with his pleading eyes, anxious expression and the winsome smile that made her heart melt and flip from despair to gratitude. She had her little Paddy and for that she was grateful, most of the time.

'Go on, Paddy, get out before one of your brothers walks in here screaming with a black eye. Haven't I enough on my plate to be dealing with, without another argument with Deirdre Malone to add to the list?' She picked up a decidedly dirty dishcloth and began wiping down the kitchen table, wincing with each outward stretch as little Paddy stood, frozen in a no man's land between his mother's despair and his father's ire. And he had more to say...

'Do we have enough money for the rent, Ma?'

Peggy, about to sit back down, stilled; his words hung in the air. He had been worrying about the rent for days. He knew exactly what she was doing when she sat at the table with the stubby pencil and he always checked on a Friday night when he arrived home from school. The rent book was kept in the press, in the little drawer under the bread crock, and little Paddy would slip it out, look for the ink tick in the box next to the date and if it was there, breathe a sigh of relief and slip it back into place again. But for three Fridays now there had been no tick. His ma usually left to pay the rent every Friday morning, straight after pay night on Thursday. She also took her curlers out to pay the rent, for Peggy, despite her ways, loved her hair. It had once been the feature that made her stand out amongst her peers. And although not as thick or as lustrous as it once was, it still made a statement when she removed her curlers. Peggy might stand in the rent queue in a coat with no buttons and her worn-out slippers, but her hair took on all comers from the dockside streets. However, little Paddy had noted that Peggy and her curlers had not been parted for the past three weeks and his heart had tightened in fear.

Peggy's eyes narrowed as she took in a deep and weary breath. She wanted to ask him why was he asking about the rent. What business was the rent of his anyway, being just a child, but she thought better of it. Her son was frequently bottom of the class at school, but at home there was very little that passed him by. Peggy's hand slipped over the pocket of her apron and felt the crackle of the envelope within. Little Paddy and Peggy, both hiding a secret deep in their pockets, held each other's gaze.

'Is Da going to go to work this next week, Mam? Will the rent be paid?'

Peggy shook her head, visibly irritated. 'Stop asking me questions, Paddy, I don't know, do I? It's not as if I have Tommy Doherty for a husband, is it? Your father was out at work every day because Tommy, who never missed a day's work, shamed him into it, and I can't keep going over the road to ask for Jerry's help. Jesus, I couldn't stand the shame.' Peggy's words stuck in her throat and Paddy could hear she was trying not to become agitated as he heard the rosary beads click in her apron pocket. 'Even Alice, a Protestant, doesn't have my life. Oh, there's something wrong there! She never sets foot in a church, not even her own. Full of sin she must be, and yet *she* has a husband like Jer and me – me, I have that fat lazy good for nothing upstairs!'

Peggy rolled her eyes up to the ceiling before she rubbed them with the back of her hands. Tommy Doherty had saved Peggy's life on a number of occasions and was the kindest man they knew. He had saved little Paddy and the kids more than once too, because the house walls were one layer of brick and noise travelled well. The moment Tommy had heard raised voices or the sound of a chair flying across the kitchen floor, he would storm up her back path, into her kitchen and heave big Paddy off whoever was on the receiving end of his fists. On more than one occasion, that had been Peggy herself, with the boys huddled in the corner, crying. Peggy felt lost without the Dohertys for many reasons. Peggy's eyes were red through lack of sleep and worry and her face was white, the only warmth in her cheeks a reflection from the red headscarf she wore tied around her curlers every day.

There was a time, in the days when Paddy did work regularly, when every now and then, on a week with good overtime, Peggy would call into Cindy's to have her hair done into a beehive and on those days little Paddy was so proud of his ma because she was almost like the other mothers. She would also go to the bingo with Maura, and nothing made little Paddy happier in the whole world than seeing his mother, smiling and excited, rushing down the yard to meet Maura and knock on for Shelagh or Deirdre. Oh, he loved her so much!

Peggy's shoulders drooped and the desolate sight of her, of the empty tin of Get Set hair spray on the mantelshelf standing next to the empty bottle of red nail varnish, a testament to better days, pained his heart, as did the worry etched on her brow and the sadness in her eyes. He knew something of how she felt, because he had lost his best friend too. He and Harry Doherty had been like brothers but he never said anything of this to Peggy; he knew she had enough on her plate. His head fell and he gazed down at the dirty, unwashed quarry tiled floor, covered in crumbs and half of the wasteland brought in on shoes. He was right, then. The rent hadn't been paid and that concerned him because he had seen Tommy Doherty storm up the stairs to his da's bedroom so often and heard him shout, 'Get out of that bed, you lazy bastard! Because if you don't, the rent won't be paid and the dock board will have the bailiffs round and all of you out on the street with every measly thing you own!'

Tommy would never have said that to his da if it weren't true and little Paddy had seen it happen, had walked past a family on the Dock Road, the ma crying, Eric the milkman coming to their rescue, loading their belongings onto the back of his milk float, Ena bringing the mam a glass of whiskey to steady her nerves. Maura had told him later that Sister Evangelista had sent them to a refuge on Upper Parliament Street to keep them dry until the Liverpool Corporation found them a house, but that the house would be miles away, out at Speke. Maura had bought them a bag of scones at Cousin's on the parade and asked Harry and little Paddy to drop them round to the ma.

'You take them, lads,' she had said, 'it will save her dignity that way. Better if I don't do it. God love them, they'll end up in Speke, now, miles from everywhere and everyone.'

Paddy had heard stories about Speke, the concrete new towns and the Giro cheques people lived on because they could no longer travel to work. He didn't want to go there, he wanted to stay on the four streets, next to the docks and the ships, forever. Max shifted to make himself more comfortable in his pocket and Paddy froze, sure Peggy would have noticed the wriggling.

Peggy put her hand on her son's head and ruffled his hair. 'Paddy, you'll be the death of me, honest to God. Don't you be worrying about the rent, I'll get it paid, I promise. Out you go, now, and don't be fretting about your da, I'll cadge him a fag from someone.'

Peggy closed the door behind him and took the letter from her apron pocket. She had worked out her sums on the back of the envelope and she first inspected her column of figures. This would be the fourth week with no rent paid and the letter made it quite clear what was about to happen to them if she didn't pay the arrears in full. The dock board were sending the bailiffs round and they would all be out on the street the following Friday and everyone would witness her humiliation and shame. Peggy's head felt as though it was filled with the candyfloss they ate at the carnival and she couldn't think straight. Her skin prickled with fear, as she pushed the envelope back down into her apron pocket. She opened the press door; it was empty. There was nothing in for anyone to eat, not even a broken biscuit. She blessed herself.

'Jesus wept, I'll have to go to Kathleen.' Kathleen would help her to feed the kids, she was sure, she would cross the road, swallow her pride and ask for help. As she closed the wooden doors, the ceiling thudded and plaster flakes fell around her.

'Is Paddy back with my baccy yet? And where's my tea?' Big Paddy's voice boomed down the stairs.

Peggy's eyes fell on the bread knife and rage threatened to consume her. The all-too-common vision of Paddy, impaled to the tip, his arms and legs flailing, a look of surprise on his face, filled her thoughts and she let them rest there for a few seconds before banishing them.

'There's no tea and no baccy because they cost money!' she shouted up the stairs.

'Oh, go on, queen, I know Shelagh brought you a cup full of tea leaves and sugar round last night; I heard her in the kitchen. I think it might help me back a bit if you have two Anadin to go with it.'

His voice, whining and pleading, fell into a void and the sun on the kitchen window caught the blade of the knife and winked at her. 'Go on,' it whispered to her, 'it'll be no trouble, I'll help.'

She had two Anadin left, but despite the pain in her back, she would give them to Paddy, just to stop him complaining. Her fibroids had been playing up since she had been on the change.

'We can have it all taken away,' Dr Cole had told her last year. 'Your uterus, it's just an empty sack now, Peggy, waiting to become diseased, so we may as well. Let me tell the consultant at St Angelus that you are ready.

He says in his letter he made you the offer last time he saw you.'

Peggy had shaken her head, made her excuses and left the surgery in haste. 'I'll have a think, but I'll be back soon and let you know,' she had said and had avoided both Dr Cole and the hospital since that day. Two weeks in hospital and four weeks in bed recuperating when she got back home to have it all taken away? How the hell could she do that? No, she would keep going for now.

Peggy sighed. 'All right then, I'll put the kettle on before the coal burns out.' The last of the Anadin was the least of her problems; the coal, now, that was a worry. On the way to the kettle, she began to remove her curlers. There was nothing for it; she would have to go to the rent office and throw herself onto the mercy of Mr Heartfelt. In the past, when a brown envelope arrived, Maura would come with her and Mr Heartfelt, who obviously had a soft spot for Maura, would have been amenable and open to discussion and a compromise. Today, Peggy would have to try to sweet talk Mr Heartfelt all on her own.

She threw the curlers into the enamel dish on the windowsill and ran her fingers over her scalp. A woman of no means and financially dependent on a man who refused to get out of his bed, all she had was her hair to help her. It was that or a pimp on the corner of Upper Parliament Street. Tears filled her eyes and she let them fall, one hand on the kettle, the other on the sink to steady her.

'Oh, Maura, what has become of me?' she sobbed, her predicament made worse by the fact that there was no one to hear her and no one to help.

Chapter Nine

Captain Conor was looking out to sea from the bridge of the *Morry* just as his first mate, whose nervous facial tic had earned him the name Blinks, arrived with his tray. The sea was calm and the port behind them rolled backwards into the distance.

'Ahoy, you had better drink this, now,' said Blinks, 'before we get out onto the ocean. There's a good splash of rum in it and it'll find your sea legs for you.'

'I hope there's not too much rum in here,' said Conor, raising one eyebrow and sniffing at the mug.

'If there is, you won't know anything about it when we sink. You've pulled a fecking fast one this time and we're all going to drown.'

Captain Conor put the mug to his lips and swigged back the contents. 'Have I ever let you down?' he demanded.

Blinks examined the map pinned on the wall. 'Have you set the course yet?'

Conor shook his head. 'Not yet, be my guest.'

The first mate screwed up his eyes as he examined the map. 'I've never in all my years sailed with a list like this on any ship – and to go all the way to Liverpool with one now, against all advice, is fecking reckless. We will have to set the course in a straight line, near as damn it. You were told to dump the cargo, not move it to port side – and it's made no fecking difference to the list that I can see. I can't bleedin' walk straight. No one can.'

Conor grinned at the sight of the horizon behind him. The ship was listing badly, but he had been sailing long enough to know that the skies looked good, the charts were promising and they should, on a wing and a prayer, make it to Liverpool full of a cargo the manifest said had been dumped overboard before they had reached Rotterdam.

'There's something in this for everyone,' Conor reminded his first mate. 'A hold full of rum, ciggies and a whole lot more which is no longer supposed to be there, it will mean a nice windfall for everyone. If any of them bellyache, send them to me. We're lucky that the ship's owner is insured and has taken the news in good heart. He's booked the dry dock in Liverpool and the accommodation for the crew. I told him we were taking on water and the load was uneven because he bought too much. He thinks half of it ended up at the bottom of the ocean in order to save his ship, which matters to him more than the rum.'

The first mate stepped out of the bridge and threw the dregs of his tea over the rails. 'Neither the money nor the time are much use to any of us if we are dead and lying in a watery grave on the bottom of the sea, Conor.'

Conor picked up his binoculars and looked ahead. 'I'll stay on the bridge until Liverpool, so stop your fretting. You'll all be buying me drinks in the Anchor soon. That telegram from Malcolm at the Seaman's Stop told us things are tough at home and we've a duty to get back and dry dock there, not in Rotterdam – and it's carnival time soon.' He smiled and Blinks smiled back.

'You have the luck of the Irish with you, Conor, but it's a good job it's May and not December. I have no doubt we will reach Liverpool safe and sound. We'll do four on and four off until we berth.'

Conor lowered the binoculars. 'Aye, well, I've cabled from Rotterdam and asked Malcolm to tell Mam I'll be back soon and told him to give a wink to Jerry Deane.'

Blinks asked Conor why it was he never sent the message straight to his mam. 'Surely she would welcome a telegram from every port? My missus would never forgive me if she didn't get the telegram.'

Conor shook his head. He had never sent his mam a telegram in all the years he had been at sea. 'Because it was the telegram boy who brought the news about my da, during the war. She would be a nervous wreck, just opening the door. And besides, my mam needs no excuse to be in the Anchor any more than she is. Set the course,

Blinks, let's head for home and, even with this list, keep those engines banked up and ramp up the knots.'

'Aye, aye, Captain. Liverpool, here we come, even if we limp in with the *Morry*'s fecking arse scraping along on the bottom of the Mersey.'

By the time little Paddy reached the entry, the kids were clear of Nelson Street. He could hear them starting a game of football without him up on the wasteland and the stragglers were way too far ahead for him to catch up. His heart sank. Little Paddy was lonely and had been since the day Harry and the Doherty kids had left to live in Ireland. It didn't seem to him as if anything was ever going to be the same again. As he watched the kids turn the corner, his steps were leaden and weighed down by his heavy heart. All of his life he had gone to the wasteland with Harry and the Doherty kids, always running and hiding from their grumpy sister, Angela.

Kitty used to mother them all and, being a mini Maura, guided them and made sure every game was played fairly and that they all got in through the school gates on time. Even Malachi had listened to Kitty, but then one day everything had altered. The priest got murdered, Kitty went away and then she died, and not long after that the Dohertys had left and nothing had been the same since. He was very sure that all of these things were connected, but no one ever spoke of it. On a morning such as this, he would have run into the Doherty kitchen and Maura would have quizzed him.

'Have you had your breakfast, Paddy?' He would lie, to save his mother from the shame, but Maura could always tell when Paddy was lying. 'Paddy, sit down at the table, now,' Maura would say and moments later a bowl of pobs would be set before him, or a slice of bread, soft and warm with beef dripping.

'Jeez, Harry, your mam has the sight all right!' he would say as soon as they left the house and slammed the backyard gate behind them. 'She could see that I was dying for the bread and dripping.'

This morning, with his belly empty, his eyes prickled as he thought about Kitty. Her funeral had had a profound effect on him. It was the first time he had ever peeped through the upstairs window to watch one. The children on the streets were usually confined to the back bedroom when a funeral was taking place, while the adults dragged their chairs out into the street as the cortege passed by. On the day of Kitty's funeral, the men had marched back up the dockers' steps and the klaxon had rung out in respect. The women had thrown buckets of water at the horses' hooves and the praying and chanting of the Hail Marys had risen up to the window where he knelt on floorboards, his face just above the sill. He was afraid, his mouth dry, and he wondered was that because he was the only person who saw what he had seen: Kitty, standing in the middle of the cobbles at the end of the street, looking down on her own funeral.

Did she see Maura, half-falling from her chair onto the ground? Did she hear her wailing and the gasp of everyone as Tommy collapsed and Jerry and Seamus and Eugene hauled him up onto his feet? Did she see the rain that fell from the skies and blessed the mourners? And when she smiled up at him, had she really seen him too?

He had spotted Kitty many times since, but he would never tell anyone in case they said he was mad and carted him off down to the priest, for it was well known that the priest had children taken away for being mad and they never came back. 'Gone over the water,' his mam had once told him when he asked about a young girl who had lived nearby. Everyone on the four streets knew she had been pregnant, but no one knew who by or what had happened to the baby.

'Moral indecency, that's what the priest at St Cuthbert's said. He arranged it. God love her, she will never get out of that place, so she won't,' were the words he had heard as the women gathered in groups in the street to smoke and chatter. And then, suddenly, no one mentioned her name any more, for she had had sex. She must have, despite her protestations and it must never be spoken about, for fear it would become contagious. It seemed to little Paddy that everyone, except himself, had forgotten her. He often thought of her because she had been so pretty and so studious, in and out of the presbytery every day with her books and her Bible.

'There are too many visitations of the Holy Spirit and immaculate conceptions around here for it to be true,' he had heard one of the women say.

'And to think, everyone thought she was going to take the veil,' he had heard his mam say to his da. 'She was never out of the priest's study.'

Paddy opened the green canvas army surplus bag that he had left in the outhouse and had collected on the way out of the back gate. When Max had finished his breakfast, he would transfer him into the bag whilst he kicked a ball around with the others, if Malachi would let him. It was Malachi Malone who decided whose feet could touch the ball and only the chosen few were allowed to play and the agreement was that Malachi was allowed to score the most goals of the day. Only yesterday, Malachi had become so bad-tempered with one of the boys who scored five goals in a row that Malachi picked up the ball and marched home with it under his arm, hurling abuse over his shoulder as he went. The disappointment of thirty boys on the bombed-out wasteland, especially those still waiting to play, was palpable.

'Aw, come on, Malachi, be a sport! If you want to go home for your tea, leave the ball and I'll bring it back later,' little Paddy had called as some of the younger boys began to cry and Paddy had felt for them. 'Come on, Malachi, don't be giving out like that now, be a good sport and let the little fellas play.'

But Malachi was crying hard, something boys over

ten years of age on the four streets never, ever did, not in front of other boys anyway. 'Feck off!' he shouted over his shoulder as thirty boys watched their elevation from boredom march away.

The canvas bag banged against Paddy's thigh as he walked, the buckle pricking the skin of his hand, thrust deep into his pockets to protect Max. He could tell that Max was sleeping soundly. He would leave his new best friend in his pocket until he got near to the wasteland before he transferred him to his bag. He trudged along, wondering would Malachi be in a good mood? Would a full day of play be on the cards before Malachi took his ball home? Would Malachi try to thump him or somebody else? As he turned across the top of the entry, he saw a woman shading her eyes with her hands, peering in through the window of Maura and Tommy's old house. Little Paddy thought for a moment and then, on a whim, he sauntered down the pavement and approached the woman.

'Hello,' he said, 'that's Tommy and Maura's house.'

The woman turned and looked down her nose at him. '*Was*,' she replied.

Paddy furrowed his brow. 'No, it's definitely theirs,' he replied and, without thinking, put his thumb in his mouth. Along with wetting the bed, it was the thing he was desperately trying to stop himself from doing. He had promised Maura he would before she left. It had been the last conversation she had with him.

'I won't be here, Paddy, to help your mam get the sheets dry. You know, she sometimes needs a bit of help, don't you? You promise me you will try, there's a good lad. Make sure you go every night, before you get into your bed, and keep the old brown ale pot next to you, in case you wake in the night.'

'I will, Auntie Maura, I promise,' he had said and he had managed to do just as she had asked. He never wanted to let her down especially after she said, 'You're such a good and special lad, little Paddy. The best in the four streets – along with our Harry, of course – you could be brothers, you two.' And he had felt so filled with pride to think Maura would rank him alongside his best friend and personal hero, Harry, that he hadn't wet the bed once since.

'Are you wanting Auntie Maura?' Paddy asked the woman now, feeling as though he was shrinking in size, caught as he was in the spotlight of the woman's un-friendly gaze. She peered down at him as though he was something that had crawled out of a half-eaten apple.

'Who are you?' she asked him.

Paddy grinned, this was a question he could answer easily. 'I'm little Paddy, I am. I live there.' He nodded towards the grimy front window of his house which hadn't seen a wash leather since the Dohertys had left and the front step was unscrubbed, didn't smell of Lysol and bleach like all the others. Paddy could see Mrs Trott on her hands and knees with a bucket scrubbing her step and willed her to look up and help him finish something he truly wished he had not begun.

The woman wrinkled her nose and, following his gaze, looked past Mrs Trott, down the street towards the docks. 'Well then,' she said, 'we are going to be neighbours. My husband and I are to live here, so your mother had better get her house in order before we arrive, I can tell you. Those nets are filthy and I'm not living next door to *that*.' She sniffed with distaste as she bent to look back into the window of Maura and Tommy's old house.

'What? How can you be doing that?' Little Paddy was about to say that his mother's nets weren't filthy, but he knew better than to start an argument he couldn't win. He looked down the road and saw Annie O'Prey, her gleaming white nets twitching at him from the side of the window. He felt in need of protection and for once was reassured to be under the gaze of the four streets' nosiest neighbour. The woman peered down at little Paddy again, her face a picture of distaste.

'I think the women of these streets need to know that Margaret Wright is moving in.' Paddy sucked harder on his thumb. The woman had decided he would be as good a way as any at getting the message across, but his silence made her wonder. She felt a need to fill the silence his lack of response had created. 'My husband is the new police sergeant, been promoted he has. He's going to be in charge of what goes on at the docks and I can assure you, bringing order around here will be his first challenge, especially with the O'Prey boys living here. We will be your next-door neighbours, young man, and I'll tell you this for nothing: my husband is a man who enforces law and order and we aren't stupid. Nothing anyone says or does gets past my Frank. Do you understand that?'

She bent down until her face was on a level with his own. Her red lipstick had bled into the cracks in her skin that ran away from her top lip and Paddy was transfixed by the faint orange line on her neck where her foundation ended and the white skin on her neck began, for it resembled a noose. She was also now obviously struggling to maintain her composure.

'What is up with you, boy?'

Paddy swallowed hard, now beyond speech. She turned her head towards Annie O'Prey, still peering around the nets in her window, and refocused her gaze. One of Annie's boys, Jimmy, was due out of Walton Jail any day now and Paddy guessed she might know that because she smiled a cold and meaningful smile in Annie's direction. The net curtain fell abruptly and Margaret Wright turned back to little Paddy, who was deeply regretting his decision to talk to her.

For a brief moment, Paddy lost his focus and suddenly he could see Kitty; she was standing at the end of the street, watching him. He froze and stared until his eyes stung and blurred and then, despite not wanting to, he blinked and she was gone.

'Have you got my meaning, boy?'

Seeing Kitty's ghost was far preferable to this encounter any day. His instinct was to run, but his feet felt as heavy as lead and refused to move.

'They didn't make my Frank a sergeant for nothing, you know. You had better let your mam know that.' She leant in closer towards him, narrowing her eyes, and he felt a strong desire to clutch hold of his langer before he wet himself. He had been doing so well, but this woman, she had the power to undo all Maura's good work. He could see the curls of dark hair escaping from under the rim of her bottle-green felt hat. The women on the four streets didn't wear hats, they wore wire curlers held in place all day long with a headscarf and they only ever came out for the bingo, mass, or a bit of a do down at the Anchor or, in his mam's case, on rent day. His eyes narrowed back at her – it was the best he could do.

'You tell your mam that we are moving in next door in the next few days if Mr Heartfelt gets his act together. We are just waiting for the rent book to be handed over.' She pulled herself upright. 'Do you know why they are still paying the rent? It's very odd. I know they had a windfall, but if they aren't coming back, why would they be doing that? Is there someone else living in there who shouldn't be?'

Paddy blinked. He was truly confused and had no idea what the woman was talking about.

'Lost your tongue, have you? Well, here's something else to pass onto your mam: if there's anything knock-off arriving in this house on a regular basis, it had better stop right now. Do you understand? Makes sense to me that an empty house must be getting used for something, so fencing, I reckon. That's why the nets are still up. Well, you make sure your mam knows I'm onto them. The robbing can stop, because Frank Wright is moving in, those nets can be washed, that step scrubbed and the playing on the bomb site, that can stop too. Have you got that? Make sure your mam knows that we will be in before the carnival. I think we can improve the standards around here no end and it will make it a better community for all to live in.'

Paddy nodded, his thumb was now thrust so deep in his mouth it protruded out of the side of his cheek. There was nothing knock-off in their house – no one trusted his mam and da to keep anything safe – but Tommy and Maura's wash house and scullery had indeed been the trading post if there had been a haul and he knew the woman was bang on. The house was empty now, but as soon as the *Morry* came into dock, that would change. He knew that there were empty wooden tea chests, still in Maura and Tommy's outhouse. Not a scrap of tea in them, though, or his mother would surely have had it.

He had slipped in himself once and tried to scrape some out for her, when he had found her sitting at the kitchen table, crying. He had tipped up a case and, pulling away the thin paper lining of the chest, to his joy extracted enough to make his mam a pot of weak tea every day for a week. She had been so grateful she even stopped crying and hugged him. That had been the week after Maura had left.

The woman folded her arms, peered down at him and sniffed. It had occurred to her that either little Paddy wasn't about to cough up, or he was so stupid he was of no use to her. She had no ill feeling towards the boy, but Margaret was disappointed that the best the dock board could do for her Frank, following his promotion, was a house on Nelson Street. Margaret hated rats and therefore hadn't wanted to live so close to the river.

'I can tell you,' she said, 'if housing wasn't still so short, we wouldn't be moving here, but needs must.' She wasn't really talking to him as she looked up and down the street. 'They will be building the new houses soon and then we'll be off. All this lot, they will be razed to the ground and the rats along with them.'

Paddy instinctively clasped his hand over his pocket – and felt a shock run though him. Max was gone! The woman took one long look at little Paddy, who wasn't quite sure if, by rats, she had meant the large river rats that ran along the bins and the top of the yard walls, where he had found Max, or the residents of the four streets. He stood frozen to the spot. Max, where are you? he thought, as he crossed his legs.

The woman sighed. 'These streets have a dreadful reputation.' She slipped her handbag into the crook of her arm and clasped her leather-clad hands together.

'Goodbye, young man,' she said. 'Remember what I said and make sure your mother knows. My husband won't be tolerating litter like that in the gutters, either.'

Paddy took a deep breath as Kitty appeared from nowhere, behind the woman's back. He thought Kitty had come to save him and Max, but it was too late, he could tell where Max was by the warmth on his shoulder and by the look on the woman's face that she had seen him.

'Oh my giddy aunt!' she screamed, lashing out with her handbag and thumping little Paddy on the chest. 'Get that disgusting thing away! Look, look, you've got a rat on your shoulder!'

She raised her arm to hit him with her handbag again and this time she was aiming straight at his head. Worried that Max might be hurt, little Paddy staggered backwards. The woman was now puce in the face and her voice had risen to a shriek, the veins on her neck bulging as she stepped towards him, her handbag flailing in the air.

'Frank!' she screamed at the top of her voice. 'Oh, Lord, I had no idea it was this bad, they're everywhere, overrun this street is. I have to tell Frank, you disgusting beast!' And without another word the woman turned and ran down the road, apparently unaware that Kitty was right behind her.

He wondered if Kitty, like him, wanted to laugh at the sight of the woman retreating, but Kitty had disappeared as quickly as she had arrived. The nets on Annie O'Prey's window quivered as little Paddy opened his knapsack and, without the need for instruction, Max hopped straight in. Annie's nets dropped again and, with a quick glance, Paddy checked that there was no one else in the street before turning to face the wall, unbuttoning his short trousers and relieving himself against Maura and Tommy's house.

Little Paddy placed one hand on the wall as he leant in and felt the cool brickwork against his forehead. He had just seen the ghost of Kitty, for far longer than was usual, had been thumped with a handbag by a strange woman, Max had almost been killed with a swing from the same bag – and he hadn't even got down his own street to the bombed-out wasteland yet. Something about it all made him feel just so sad and he knew it was Kitty. She had appeared because she'd sensed he was frightened, and he had instinctively known that. Why did everything have to change, he thought, as he buttoned his trousers back up, ready to run around the entry to the back gate and tell his mam everything. None of it would be news his mother wanted to hear.

Then he heard a voice and, looking up the street, saw Auntie Kathleen seeing Nellie off from number 42. Her granddaughter would be off out with the girls. They would gather together and divide into groups, each taking a street, where they would knock on doors and ask, 'Can I push your baby up and down the street, missus?'

They would reassemble at the wasteland, comparing knitted bonnets and judging the prettiest babies whilst their mothers rinsed out enamel buckets that lived under the kitchen sink, changed the dirty Napisan water and filled washing lines full of fluffy white terry towelling squares before they peered over the walls to check whose were the whitest.

Kathleen saw little Paddy and made Nellie wait. She called out to the boy, 'Hang on there, little Paddy, love,' and disappeared back inside. Seconds later she was back and thrust something into Nellie's hand. The girl waved to Paddy who ran down the street to meet her, his bag firmly held so as not to jolt Max about.

Nellie grinned as he approached and Nana Kathleen exclaimed, 'Thank God we caught you, Paddy! I was keeping something for you. I was only thinking at mass this morning how I haven't seen you all week. Is your mam well? Maggie Trott was asking, only we haven't seen her since she came to the meeting about the carnival. She's not been out for a natter or to have her leaves read.' Before he could blink, she continued, 'Jerry left without the time to eat his toast so will you have it?' And without waiting for an answer, she thrust a slice of bread the size of a house brick into his hand.

'Go on, Paddy,' she said, 'you'll be doing me a favour. I hate throwing good food in the bin.' And Paddy immediately forgot about his encounter with Margaret Wright. The melting butter and jam were calling out to him and, within seconds, butter was dribbling down his chin.

'Ah, God, that's lovely that,' he said as he licked his lips and grinned up at Kathleen.

The sound of Nellie's laughter wiped from his mind the harsh and deeply worrying words the woman had spoken and the message he was meant to deliver to his mother. For a brief moment the sheer sweetness of last summer's strawberries erased his worries about the unpaid rent, but the sight of Peggy running across the road in her slippers, calling Kathleen, soon reminded him. Scamp was hot on her heels and she didn't appear to notice little Paddy at all.

'Kathleen, can you do me a favour and lend me two and six? Big Paddy's been that sick, we've had short weeks and, honest to God, I haven't a potato for the kids' tea or a drop of tea in the house.'

Kathleen sighed inside, but smiled outwardly. 'Of course I have, Peggy. Now, do you want to come into ours for a cuppa? I'm just giving your little Paddy some bread I was about to throw out because our Jerry didn't eat his breakfast.'

Paddy grinned up at his mam, his face smeared with jam and butter, his eyes alight. Peggy's stomach grumbled so loudly they all heard it and Nellie looked at her gran, with pleading eyes.

'I've more where that came from if you've room for a slice of toast with the tea too.' Kathleen, large and round, eyes twinkling through her glasses, betrayed not a hint of irritation.

Peggy had known kindness like this from Maura every day of her married life and had sorely missed it, but now she felt self-conscious. 'Well, if you have the time, Kathleen...'

'I do that, so come on away in. Alice,' she shouted over her shoulder to her daughter-in-law, 'put that kettle back on before you go to Cindy's.' And then she remembered what she had seen as she had stood at the door with Nellie. 'It's Alice's hair day,' she said by way of an explanation, as though they didn't know who Cindy was. 'Now little Paddy, who was that woman you were talking to?'

'What woman?' asked Peggy.

'She said she's the police and she's moving into Maura and Tommy's house.'

The two women looked at each other, their faces the picture of shock. 'Are you sure she said that?' asked Kathleen.

'Aye, I am,' said Paddy. 'Mam, she said you had to wash the nets and clean the step and there was something else too...' Paddy frowned and thought hard. 'Oh yeah, he said, no more playing on the wasteland, no more thieving – and something about a fence.'

'Paddy!' Nellie, waiting for him to cross the road to the side of the wasteland, called his name from the kerb as Kathleen and Peggy looked at each other, horrified.

'Well, the cheek of her! Was she calling us thieves,

then?' Peggy looked wounded. 'That woman needs to wash her mouth out. Who the hell did she think she was talking about?'

'Little Paddy, did you get a name, love?' Kathleen's voice was urgent, pleading and coaxing all at the same time. 'Did the woman say who she was at all?'

Little Paddy took a deep breath. 'She did.' There was silence. Kathleen dared not speak again and she placed her hand on Peggy's arm to silence her. The event had occurred not five minutes since and if they gave little Paddy enough time it would come to him, eventually. So they stood, they waited and little Paddy blinked and frowned; he looked back across the road, he pursed his lips and then, as if a light bulb had been switched on inside his head, he blurted out, 'She told me her name is Mrs Wright and her husband's name is Frank.'

Paddy also wanted to say that he had seen Kitty and Kitty had been trying to tell him something, but the look of complete horror that now crossed his mother's face and the tears that sprang to her eyes made him think twice.

'Dear God, can my life get any worse?' Peggy blurted out. 'Kathleen, it's Frank the Skank who's moving next door to me! Jesus, I think I'm going to faint.'

'No, no you're not, you just need a bit of breakfast. Get inside,' Kathleen ordered Peggy, and then she called down the hallway, 'Alice, knock on to Shelagh with the mop and you need to run to Cindy and tell her you have to cancel your hairdo. This is an emergency. We need the women round for a powwow; I may even have to read the leaves for we've got a big problem to sort out. Off you go, kids, and thank you, Paddy, you're a very clever boy.'

Paddy grinned with pleasure. Nana Kathleen had said that in front of Nellie and everyone knew how clever Nellie was.

Peggy turned to face Kathleen. 'You know who it is, don't you?'

Kathleen pushed Peggy along towards the kitchen. 'I do, he shopped the bizzies who were in on helping us on our docks and got them sacked – and not only that, not one of them can get a job because the minute Frank hears about it he has a word with whoever is taking them on. Some of them have left the police and are trying to get work elsewhere, but he has eyes in the back of his head and he finds out somehow. He's a bad, bad egg that man. Jerry has told me that the men who work with him are the only people who dislike him more than we do.'

Peggy wasn't listening; she had sunk deep into the well of her own despair. 'I'm doomed,' she wailed. 'I'd rather throw myself in the Mersey than live next door to him; 'tis the only thing left to me, Kathleen.'

Alice came to the kitchen door, her face still and calm, hiding her resentment at being told to cancel her hair appointment. The waters ran deep with Alice and no one ever knew what she was thinking. 'I've knocked on. Is it true?' she asked.

Kathleen nodded her head as she herded a crying Peggy past her.

'Frank the Skank?' Alice asked. 'Didn't he get promoted to sergeant because he grassed on the dock police?'

Peggy turned to her, stricken. 'Yes, yes, he did and they are moving in next door to me, into Maura and Tommy's house!' Peggy almost shrieked the last words as tears sprang to her eyes.

Kathleen rolled her own eyes and shook her head. 'Alice, is there a drop of brandy in the press? Peggy needs it in her tea. Jesus, if it's true, we all need it, for there'll be no more hauls from the *Morry*. I mean, that's not robbing – Conor gives it to us and it's up to him what he does with his cargo. Isn't it?'

Alice smiled. 'Not quite, Kathleen, he lists it on the manifest when it's being unloaded and the dockers count it off short.'

Kathleen waved her hand at Alice. 'Oh, I know that, I know, but it's not as if it's anyone's livelihood or the crown jewels, is it? I mean, he buys it cheap and sells the leftovers and no one gets hurt, Alice. Not so with the likes of Jimmy O'Prey. Now, when he gets home – which is any day soon, so Annie tells me – that's who Frank the Skank should be worried about. He's turned into a real bad lad, he has.'

Kathleen shook her head. Every family depended on the hauls that came up the dockers' steps. Every wedding, christening, party, birthday and bit of a do was, in some part, courtesy of Captain Conor and the odd crate that fell of the back of any of the other ships. It was the means to dignity, to happiness and survival for the large Catholic families who depended on the docks and the measly wages of the dock board to earn a living.

'Frank the Skank moving into the four streets is very bad news, Alice,' Kathleen said, 'so we have to stop this happening, somehow. We need to get our heads together and this will be down to the women to sort.'

The back gate clicked and Shelagh's footsteps and those of the other women close behind her sounded on the cobbles in the yard. Shelagh would have knocked on to Deirdre, Deirdre to her neighbour and so on down the line it went. Even those who didn't or couldn't answer the call would knock onto the next kitchen to let them know the white smoke was rising, so everyone to Kathleen's house.

'Line up the cups, Alice,' said Kathleen. 'Brandy in first.' She took a large gulp herself, straight from the bottle, just as the back door opened.

'By God, it must be bad news,' said Shelagh, her eyes opening wide, 'the cut of you. You have the brandy out already?'

'You've no idea how bad it is,' said Kathleen. 'Frank the Skank and his wife are moving into Maura and Tommy's house!' And as she began to measure the brandy into the cups, Maggie Trott came into the kitchen.

'Oh, that is bad news for all of us,' exclaimed Maggie and they all turned to look at her.

'Do you know them?' asked Alice.

'Oh, I do,' said Maggie, 'and Frank the Skank is a nasty piece of work.'

Peggy staggered and Alice caught her before she fell, then Maggie eased her into a kitchen chair.

'That's it for me,' wailed Peggy. 'My life is over and done, it can't get any worse than this.'

Kathleen placed a cup in her hand. 'Here, drink this, queen, get it down you.' Peggy knocked back the brandy in one and pushed herself up from the chair.

'Peggy, where are you going?' asked Maggie Trott as she walked towards the door. Peggy turned around and looked at the women now assembled in the kitchen, some with babies in arms, some carrying a plate with biscuits they had made that morning. Peggy looked at their faces, their hands, work-worn, like her own. But each one of them had a husband in work and their rent was paid – *they* were safe. No one missed the rent, for the street would provide food if a family ran out. On cold nights, shovels of coal would be donated to a family that had none, but the rent, that was a different matter altogether, everyone paid the rent.

'Peggy, are you all right, love?' asked Maggie Trott. 'You've taken your curlers out.'

Peggy couldn't reply; she could not share her secret or her shame. She looked at their faces, their worried frowns; she couldn't tell them about the letter. It was the final humiliation. No one had ever been evicted on Nelson Street, but then, no one else had dirty nets or a fat lazy oaf for a husband who lay in his bed all day long, inventing any excuse not to work. The faces of the women she had known almost all of her life appeared distant to Peggy. She could have told Maura – she could tell Maura anything – but not Kathleen who would be disappointed with her. Not Deirdre – she would be straight down to Cindy's and have it all over the street – and not Maggie, she would expect it.

'Is Biddy coming?' she asked and her voice sounded light, strange, even to her. She could tell Biddy who was kind and wise as Kathleen.

Maggie Trott was the first to answer her. 'I doubt it. I saw her nipping into the betting shop on the parade with Ena not ten minutes since. Come on, Peggy, it's not that bad. We will put that one in her place as soon as she arrives, won't we, Kathleen? And anyway, how can she be moving into Maura's? Maura has the rent book and she said she would keep it going for a year in case Tommy has made a mistake.'

Deirdre sniffed as she picked up her teacup. 'All right for some, isn't it? I'm surprised Maura doesn't keep a set of rooms in the Grand Hotel and let a family who needs that house have it. I mean, she's that la di da now since they came into money.'

Kathleen pulled out a kitchen chair and sat herself

down. 'Hush your mouth, Deirdre, you have no idea how much money Maura and Tommy have or what their plans are. Peggy, sit down again; eat your toast and stop your worrying, we will sort this.'

'Is there no toast in your own house?' asked Deirdre, who was silenced by an icy glare from Kathleen.

'Come on Peggy, we'll have a gas,' said Maggie, but Peggy shook her head. 'I'm all right now, and I have the copper on,' she said and walked out of the back door, leaving them all open-mouthed. They all knew that was a lie, because Peggy had her washing line full on Monday, along with the rest of them, and Peggy just about remembered to do the wash then. She would never do one twice in a week.

Peggy wiped her dripping nose with the back of her hand. Her tears had made her feel hot and flu-like and the pain in her back was sweeping around her abdomen to the front. She steadied herself with her hand on the yard wall and then, when the pain subsided, made her way out of the gate, feeling as though the sky had fallen onto her shoulders as she realised that, in all the commotion, Kathleen hadn't given her the half a crown for the children's tea and big Paddy's fags. She had forgotten in all the fluster of the news and the arrivals into her always busy kitchen. Peggy had written to Maura with Kathleen's help but had received no reply and that almost broke her heart. It must be that Maura was settled in her new life and no longer had any interest in Peggy or her troubles. The rent office was open until twelve, that was the reason she'd had to leave; she would need to get down there without Maura to help her and beg to keep the roof over their heads – and she had to succeed. The alternative was not worth thinking about.

Mary had returned home only to find the house empty and the dishes piled up in the sink. Malcolm asked her to return at four, to help him make the evening meal for the guests he was expecting. She had slowed her pace as she walked past Annie O'Prey's back gate but all she could hear was the tinny sound of the radio on the kitchen windowsill. No sign of Jimmy being back home, or Callum, for that matter. She knew Callum had been taken on down at the docks and was under the wing of Jerry Deane.

'Jerry is going to be the gaffer down there any day now,' she had heard Eugene say to Deirdre the previous evening. 'When that happens, there will be more work around here on the four streets for the likes of us. He's got Callum O'Prey taken on every day already. The gaffer has as good as handed over.'

Deirdre had been wrapping up potato peelings in newspaper to burn on the fire and glanced from the corner of her eye at Mary, who was darning one of the boys' jumpers. 'He's not a total waste of time like his thieving git of a brother, then?' she'd said.

'Callum? Not at all, a grand worker he is. Whatever Jerry says, goes with him. There you are, Mary, now there's a good husband for you. Try flashing your eyelashes at Callum. He earns a full week's wage every week.'

Now, as Mary removed her coat, she glanced up at the clock. She had been at Malcolm's since six for early breakfast for the crew who were leaving on the morning bore at ten past eight so she had been up since half past five and felt tired and in need of her bed. But looking around the mess in the kitchen she knew it could not be left, so she rolled up her sleeves and, turning on the tap, filled the kettle ready to wash yet another bowl of greasy dishes.

Chapter Ten

Peggy had been given short shrift at the rent office as she handed over her rent book to Mr Keeble there. It had been given back to her just as quickly, a gesture which came as something of a surprise to her.

'Mrs Nolan, you have given me the book, but there is no money in it,' said Mr Keeble.

'Yes, I know,' said Peggy, looking behind her to see if anyone had followed her in. 'I wondered if we could have a bit of time, like. You see, it's just that my husband, he has a bad back and he's under Dr Cole at the minute.'

The rent man raised his eyebrows. 'Really? Knowing the size of your husband, that must be very uncomfortable for Dr Cole. Now Mrs Nolan, you know as well as I do, all arrears have to be dealt with by Mr Heartfelt. I have no authority in this area, I'm here to take the money, record and bank it, that's all.'

'Yes, I know,' Peggy had stammered; she would try anything to avoid a meeting with Mr Heartfelt, who might be so in name, but was certainly nothing like it by nature. Peggy's voice dropped. 'Mr Keeble, is there a way it would be possible just to wait for that for just a week? You see, I've sent a letter to a friend for help and I know she will reply just as soon as she can. My husband, he's waiting for an appointment at the hospital to come through, but you know what the post is like, it's shocking, and he can't go back to work until he's been seen by a specialist. Dr Cole said it's the worst case of a bad back he's ever seen in all his years as a doctor and if he did go down to the docks, it would kill him stone dead…'

Her words trailed away as Mr Keeble, who appeared to be a man for whom no excuse would hold the remotest element of surprise, gave her the courtesy of his ear, but not his attention as he opened a letter and began to read it. Peggy sensed she was not being listened to and rambled on to an uncomfortable stop. Mr Keeble peered at her over the top of the letter.

'Finished?' he asked. Peggy nodded, she was speech-less, a rare event in itself. 'Good, well, I am afraid I have to inform you, yet again, that I cannot deal with this here. You are into your fourth week of arrears and, as you know, Mrs Nolan, from our encounters in the past, that is not good news. I can accept payment, but not excuses. You must see Mr Heartfelt yourself. You won't be needing directions, will you, as you've been there plenty of times before. I'm surprised you aren't on his Christmas card list, you must be that well acquainted.

He is there this morning and I will telephone him and tell him you are on your way.'

He glanced back down at the letter in his hand and then, looking back up at her under his cap and over the top of his glasses, asked, 'I don't suppose you know why it is Mrs Doherty keeps paying the rent on the house next door to you, do you?'

Peggy's mouth opened and closed. She shook her head. She had no idea. She was desperately confused. 'The policeman, he's moving in, his wife said so.'

'Yes, that's right, and we need the rent book back from the Dohertys, so if you hear anything from them, tell her to get a move on, would you?'

Peggy shook her head; he was confusing her further and she didn't want to see Mr Heartfelt. She was searching for something to say, words that would stop the clocks, allow her to think, to find a way out of the mess they were in. Everyone avoided a visit to Mr Heartfelt. His nature was in itself a deterrent to arrears and his own brother-in-law was the bailiff and known for his unpleasant ways. Maybe she should swallow her pride and throw herself on Jerry's mercy.

'I have to go right now, do I?' she said.

'You do indeed, Mrs Nolan. You will have received the letter, I'm sure. Mr Heartfelt is meticulous about such things; we often comment on how strange it is that all the medical mysteries of the world appear to have colonised around the Liverpool dockside streets.

And we have the worst of everything any doctor has ever seen, did you know that? It's a wonder the streets aren't like a ghost town and that anyone can get out of bed.' He began to laugh at his own joke, but the sight of Peggy, her forlorn expression, the tears he saw spring to her eyes, her obvious innocence and her lack of gumption lay on his heart like a hand on a fresh bruise. He leant across the counter and, taking out his cigarette packet, shuffled out two cigarettes and passed one to Peggy.

'Look, Mrs Nolan, at least with Mr Heartfelt you have the chance to put your case. This is the first time you've been to see him without Mrs Doherty, isn't it?'

Peggy took the cigarette and, leaning over the counter, accepted the light from the match he struck. She drew on it hard before she blew the smoke out to the side. 'She did; she was better than me at explaining.'

Mr Keeble nodded understandingly. 'Oh, I know that, you weren't the only one. You see, she had a way, did Mrs Doherty, and whatever she promised Mr Heartfelt, people delivered, so he trusted her. Is there anyone else you can take with you? I'm not allowed, or I would offer...'

Peggy shook her head. He understood; no one liked others to know they were behind with the rent, it was an excruciating shame.

'Look, you go down there with a plan, tell him how you can manage it, but do yourself a favour, don't go telling him your husband has a bad back, he's heard that one plenty of times.'

Peggy smiled gratefully. 'I'll try,' she said. 'Thanks for the cigarette, Mr Keeble.'

Peggy felt strangely dizzy, she still hadn't eaten.

'I'll phone him now, Mrs Nolan,' he said as turned to leave the office.

A trainee cashier, who had overheard the conversation, said loud enough for Peggy to hear, 'I'm sure he'll put the kettle on and plate up a fancy for her!' He laughed loudly at his own joke.

'Now, now,' said Mr Keeble sharply, 'I can tell you that the last thing Mrs Nolan wants to be doing right now is heading off to see Mr Heartfelt.'

Peggy had heard them and her face flushed. Mr Keeble looked apologetic and she heard him whisper something sharp in tone to the apprentice who wrinkled his nose. That made it obvious to Peggy what he thought of her. He was all of fifteen and yet, because he was well fed, in a job and wearing clean, ironed clothes, he thought he could speak to Peggy as he would to a dog. She walked out of the rent office to make her way down the dockers' steps to the administration building, dumb, deflated and debased.

Callum had never wanted to see the tall wooden gates of Walton Jail ever again, or hear the jangle of the keys,

the turning of the four locks followed by the sliding of the
four bolts. He'd felt sick to the pit of his stomach as the
small door opened and Jimmy stepped out into the bright
sunlight. Callum was filled with shame at the memories
of the time he had spent there. Since he'd got out, Jerry
Deane had been like a father to him, had showed him that
hard work paid and it was his fervent wish to ensure
that Jimmy turned over a new leaf, that he had walked
out of those same doors for the very last time too.

Seeing his brother, Jimmy's face lit up and he ran
across the road to greet him.

'Hey, did Mam send a butty? I haven't had any breakfast yet.' He slapped his brother across the back of his
shoulders and sides and Callum couldn't help himself;
he grinned as he thumped his brother back.

'She did, but you've just flattened it.'

Both boys laughed out loud as Callum removed the
bacon sandwich from his jacket pocket. Jimmy ripped
off the paper and bit deep into his breakfast. 'Oh that's
good, I've missed Mam's cooking.' The squeak of the
bus brakes could be heard in the distance. 'Where have
you been, Callum? I was in there a whole year and you
never got brought in once. I told the guards, when our
Callum gets here, you can put us in the same cell.'

Callum pushed his hands deep into his pockets. 'I've
kept out and that's the way it's staying. I'm never going
back in that place again.'

Jimmy stopped chewing and gave his brother a

quizzical look. 'You must have been practising the running, or you've got smarter at not getting caught!'

Callum looked at his brother with interest, his identical twin, his complete other half, his mirror image. Inseparable, they'd been; five minutes had divided them at birth and yet it felt to Callum as though a million miles separated them at that moment.

'I've been too busy to be caught at anything, Jimmy. I'm earning an honest living down on the docks. Jerry Deane took me on, and if you talk to him, tell him you want to go straight, he'll give you a chance like he did me. You don't want to be back inside that hellhole again, you said so yourself.'

Jimmy looked at his brother as though he were speaking a foreign language. 'I don't,' said Jimmy. 'You've only been on the docks, that's all you've been doing? You've gone straight? I thought Mam was just holding out on me, keeping secrets.'

Annie had never missed a prison visit to see her son, but Callum had refused every invitation, though she pressed him.

'Callum, do you not want to be seeing your brother, just for five minutes?' she would say. ''Tis shocking and shameful if you don't, and I'd gladly give up one of my visits so that he could see his brother for a change. There's no news I have that he is interested in, but you, you have it all.'

Callum was resolute. 'I'll see him when he's out, Mam,

and not before. I will never walk through those doors again.'

Annie knew better than to push Callum, and besides, she really did not want to relinquish even one visit to her son. 'I suppose it's just as well; no one can tell you two apart and they might keep you in, thinking you're our Jimmy.' At this point, Annie would chuckle to herself, but there were no smiles from Callum, just a shiver that ran down his spine.

'You want me to work down on the docks? Where Da died?' Jimmy said now. 'You think I'm going down there to wait for a crane hook to knock *me* on the head? Are you mad? I'm not working down the bleeding docks, now or ever. It's a death sentence.'

The sound of the bus pulling into the bus stop turned their heads.

'The bus, quick,' said Callum.

'I'll race you,' said Jimmy, grinning.

Callum let him win and they leapt onto the platform and swung around the pole, just as they always had as boys. They gripped the chrome bar and watched as the tall and forbidding wall of the prison receded into the distance. Jimmy grabbed the pole with both hands and leant backwards out into the fresh air as Callum grabbed his cap and saved it before it fell into the road.

'Feck, it's bloody fantastic to be free and out of that shithole of a place,' Jimmy shouted up to the sky.

The conductor approached them with his ticket

machine banging on one thigh, the saddlebag for collecting the money on the other. 'Language, please. We have ladies travelling on the lower deck.'

'Dock Road, please,' said Callum, taking a ten-shilling note out of his pocket. The conductor took it and, lifting his money bag up from the bottom, shook the change until the coins he wanted shuffled up to the top. 'Ah, there you are, the half-crowns always slip to the bottom. You're the big fella today, then,' said the conductor, 'flashing the brown one.' He smiled and handed Callum the change, as Callum slipped the tickets into his pocket. 'Don't lose those,' the conductor said. 'The inspector gets on in two stops, and you,' he pointed towards Jimmy, 'swear on my bus again and you're off.'

As the conductor walked away, Jimmy scowled and whispered under his breath, 'Cheeky fecking bastard.'

Callum glared at him. 'Jimmy, stop, he means it. You'll have to walk the rest of the way home if he throws you off.'

Jimmy grinned. 'No I won't,' he said and, opening his hand, flicked out a one-pound note.

Callum's eyes opened wide. 'Where did you get that?' he asked.

Jimmy laughed. 'It was sticking out of your man's pocket and I lifted it.'

Callum was speechless, his heart pounding as he looked down the bus to see if had anyone noticed Jimmy holding the note. Jimmy grinned from ear to ear.

'You're home,' Callum said as he stared out at the shops and warehouses they passed until they came towards the houses. He just wanted to alight from the bus as fast as was possible. He willed every inch of the journey to go faster so that he could dismount in one long stride. He held his hand up to Eric who was travelling in the opposite direction on his round and waved at him as he passed. He saw Ena walking out of the butcher's and making her way towards Cindy's, where she called in most days for a natter, and then he saw Mary, cleaning the windows in the Seaman's Stop. She stopped and stood still, staring at them. Callum gave her a half-smile, half-raised his hand, but she didn't acknowledge him because it wasn't Callum she was looking at. The bell rang out.

'The four streets,' shouted the conductor and Callum was off the platform, long before the bus had stopped. As he strode out ahead, hands in pockets, leaning forwards, Jimmy caught up with him.

'Callum, what's up with you? I'll spend the pound on fish and chips for all of us tonight. Straighten your face, will you, or Mam will want to know what's up wit' you; I don't want to tell her I robbed a quid before I got home, do I?'

Callum didn't answer; he wanted to say that he would choke on fish and chips paid for with money that would get the conductor into trouble when he returned to the depot. His anger simmered as he walked and he felt the need to run as far away from Jimmy as possible. The sight of Mary, her crestfallen expression, her lack of a wave back added insult to injury. He spat out the question he had to ask his brother. The question that had leapt to the front of his mind the moment Jimmy walked out of the prison gates.

'Have you written to Mary while you've been inside? Are you going to be seeing her, let her know you're out and home?'

Jimmy had had to run to keep up with Callum. He was slightly breathless as he answered his brother. 'Mary? Mary who?'

Chapter Eleven

'Er, hello, I'm Mrs Nolan, Mr Keeble was calling down for me,' Peggy said with a tremor in her voice to the rather prim-looking lady seated behind the tall oak counter, with a typewriter in front of her and a pile of brown envelopes on one side. Peggy recognised the envelopes; one was nesting comfortably in her cardigan pocket. 'I'm looking for Mr Heartfelt, please.' She had been through this process, met this woman before, but always with Maura doing the talking. Then, Peggy had felt no fear. Today was very different. She swallowed down the acid that was burning the back of her throat, thanks to adrenaline and a lack of food. She felt a shiver run through her aching bones and placed a hand on her belly, used its heat to still the now-persistent ache in her abdomen, which seemed to travel all the way around from her back in a belt of dull pain.

The lady behind the desk appeared not to have heard her the first time, so Peggy tried again. 'Hello,' she said, a little louder this time, 'I'm looking for Mr Heartfelt.'

The woman ceased typing and peered at Peggy over her spectacles. 'Are you now? I'd never have guessed.'

The sarcasm was lost on Peggy, but she realised that the woman knew very well why she was there. The rent man, Mr Keeble, must have kept his word and telephoned ahead and so at least she was expected, that was something, she thought. It took every ounce of strength to stop herself from visibly shaking, her tears from falling, weak with gratitude for a kind gesture from someone who was almost a stranger and didn't even live on the four streets.

The woman pushed her wooden swivel chair back, stood, and then opened a large black ledger on the desk. 'What is your name please and the purpose of your visit?'

Peggy knew the woman knew why she was there, so why was she asking, unless it was to shame her? She dropped her voice to a whisper. 'Mr Keeble sent me, I've to see Mr Heartfelt, didn't he tell you? About the arrears.' She almost whispered the last three words but when the door behind her opened and in walked Frank the Skank, it was clear he had heard her.

Peggy's heart stopped, the jugular vein in her neck throbbed. Two young women walked in behind him, so smartly dressed they must have come down from the shipping offices. They were very definitely not from the Dock Road. Peggy moved closer to the dark oak counter, her fingers clutching the edge for balance, and lowered her voice even further.

'He wrote to me, I have the letter, here.' She retrieved the envelope from her pocket and pushed it across the counter. 'I've come to see him about the rent.'

The woman didn't lift her eyes from the ledger. 'Name?' she asked, her fingers poised over the columns in front of her, ignoring the letter Peggy held out.

'Peggy Nolan,' said Peggy. She wasn't used to such hostility and was very sure Mr Keeble would have mentioned her by name. All the women in Peggy's life were friendly, Kathleen, the friendliest of all now that Maura had left. Maybe she should have confided in Kathleen, asked her to come with her. She would have done a better job of explaining things. The women on the four streets supported each other, they had their moments but they were used to a crisis, knew that each day work was provided, each week a pay packet arrived, did so by the grace of God. That, at any time, illness or accident could wipe away their security in a heartbeat, and when this happened, everyone gathered round.

They had all done it so often for Peggy but she had never had the means to give help in return. No one knocked on Peggy's door to borrow a scrape of dripping or a cup of sugar, they knew there was no point. The street would feed her children tonight if she asked for help, she never worried about that, but she would cling to her last shred of dignity, she would not tell anyone how far in arrears she was with the rent.

The woman, obviously irritated at having been

interrupted in the middle of her work, said, 'What is the reference number on your letter?'

Peggy looked confused. 'Sorry? I don't know what you mean.' She glanced sideways. Frank the Skank was now openly watching her and his amusement was ill disguised.

The woman peered at Peggy for a very long second over the top of her winged spectacles. 'Give the letter to me,' she said and held out her hand. She picked up her handkerchief before she took it and wrapped it around her fingers. Peggy's own hand shook as she passed the envelope across the counter and slipped it between the folds of white cotton. The woman flicked it open, gave the letter a cursory glance, then ran her finger down a column of numbers in the book. And to Peggy's utter embarrassment and horror, announced at the top of her voice, 'Ah yes, quite significant rent arrears, it would appear. Wait there, please, and I'll call Mr Heartfelt down to see you.'

She let the letter flutter to the desk and then, peering distastefully at her handkerchief, dropped it to one side of her typewriter. Peggy blushed from her toes to her scalp and willed the floor to open up and swallow her.

Frank grinned viciously and, holding Peggy in his glare said, 'I thought so.'

To their credit, the two young ladies appeared to be totally occupied with their own shoe leather, but Peggy was in no doubt that they had heard every word. Meanwhile the receptionist's eyes never left Peggy, not even for a moment, as if she expected Peggy to lean over the counter and steal the discarded handkerchief. She picked up a large black telephone receiver and dialled a number. 'A Mrs Nolan to see you in reception, Mr Heartfelt,' she said. 'It's about her rent arrears.'

Peggy felt as though she was standing on a precipice and she knew she had to move away from the edge, because one breath away was darkness and a fear that made her heart race. The thoughts, you are alone, there is only you, ran through her mind and, taking a deep breath and holding onto the oak counter by her fingertips to steady herself, she managed to look upwards and fix her gaze on the large wall clock, and holding on, the ache in her belly throbbed.

Mr Heartfelt took twenty minutes to arrive and although there were two chairs in the reception area, Peggy was not invited to sit. Frank the Skank, though, was offered not only a chair but also a cup of tea. Once Frank had settled himself down, the only sound in the office was the clatter of his cup on the saucer, the angry clashing of the typewriter keys and the ting of the bell when the carriage reached the end before it was returned to the beginning again.

Mr Heartfelt arrived and looked around the reception area; his eyes alighted on Frank the Skank. 'I'll be half an hour, don't go,' he said to him.

Frank removed his helmet and said, 'That's fine by me. I'm being well looked after here.'

It occurred to Peggy, even in the midst of her panic, that there was something unusual about the familiarity between Mr Heartfelt and the police sergeant, who was acting as though he owned the reception area, and winking at the two young ladies who had discreetly shuffled as far into the corner as they could.

'Are you ladies for the secretary's job?' asked Mr Heartfelt and both women nodded. 'Good, I won't be long with this.'

Peggy looked down at her slippers; water had soaked into the toes and the fronts were now a different colour to the backs. She remembered Maura's parting words to her, 'Peggy, I won't be here, but you have to act as though I am. If you get into a difficult situation, you have to ask yourself, "What would Maura say?" and if that doesn't work, promise me you will go to the convent and speak to Sister, or the priest.'

With Maura's words in her ears, Peggy took a deep breath and, looking up, presented her bravest face. Mr Heartfelt avoided looking directly at her, pushing back wayward and unusually long strands of hair over the top of his bald head, flattening them into place with the palm of his hand. Peggy's heart sank. Mr Heartfelt, unlike his name, was not kindly. It was a cruel trick. His face was extraordinarily long and thin. He wore a knitted Fair Isle sleeveless jumper over a crisp white shirt with a maroon tie fastened so tight his Adam's apple protruded over the top. He carried a buff-coloured folder in the hand that was not concerned with his balding pate.

Peggy's eyes rested on the folder, knowing that her life and that of her parents and grandparents and those who had arrived through the gates of the Clarence Dock in 1848, during the time of the Irish famine, lay in that folder. They had come straight to the docks and every one of them had been employed by the dock board ever since. The house they lived in had belonged to her mam and da and to theirs before them. For over one hundred years, since Nelson Street was built, Peggy's ancestors, all hard-working dockers, had lived there and the rent book was passed down from the eldest of one generation to the next. She was about to alter the course of her family history and all because she had married a man her father had begged her not to.

Her heart sank at the expression on Mr Heartfelt's thin face. She thought of the last time she and Maura had been here together; they had laughed on the way home, Maura making fun of Mr Heartfelt all the way. 'Why the long face, Mr Heartfelt, it's only the rent?' Maura had joked, mimicking the way he looked and spoke and the laughter had been such a tonic that Peggy had felt much better. Today, however, he did not greet her with the smile he always had for Maura and went straight to the point.

Peggy tried desperately to speak, for something about the look in his eyes had rung an alarm bell and she instinctively knew she had to ward off his words with some of her own and her mouth began to engage before her brain had time to think.

'H-hello, Mr Heartfelt, you wrote me a letter—' There was a loud crash and the ping of a bell from the direction of the counter. Peggy almost jumped out of her skin and stopped mid-sentence. She looked back at the receptionist, whose smile was openly mocking. The noise had been made by the typewriter carriage as she'd slid it forcefully along to the end.

Peggy turned back to Mr Heartfelt. What had she been saying? She had forgotten. Her mouth was dry, her head was spinning, black spots were swarming before her eyes. She had been out of the house for hours, had stood for so long, waiting, and she desperately needed to use the bathroom. Frank the Skank was shaking his head at her disapprovingly.

'Mr – Mr Heartfelt, I would just like to explain...'

But he held up his hand and stopped her. 'Mrs Nolan, I wrote to you asking you to call in to see me and I'm very sorry to be the bearer of bad news—'

Peggy's panic reached her mouth as the words spewed out. 'Oh, please, don't you be worrying, I can pay the arrears off, I'll have no trouble doing that. No, we just need the appointment at the hospital to come through so that someone can look at Paddy's back and then it will all be back to normal. He's sick, you see.' Peggy's head swam and she put her hand out to steady her against the wall; it landed on a drawing pin. She flinched and, pulling her hand back, rubbed it hard. A spot of blood appeared in the middle of her palm and she smeared it away.

Heartfelt paid not the slightest attention, simply thinking to himself, if I don't get the rent book back from the Dohertys this one will do. In fact he hated this part of his job. It was a massive inconvenience – those who had inherited rent books were the worst. He looked over to Frank who nodded in his direction with a knowing half-smile and he recalled their last conversation.

'We will get you the Dohertys' house. The trouble with these people is that they feel a sense of entitlement, as though the house is their own,' he had said to Frank. 'Think it's their right to keep it, even when they can no longer pay, because the rent book gets passed down the line. It's a bloody nuisance.'

'Is that why the Dohertys are still paying?' Frank had asked.

Mr Heartfelt had shaken his head. 'I've no idea what's going on there. I know they came into money, but they bought a pub in Ireland and, by all accounts, it's not doing too well. Maybe they are coming back?'

Frank had scowled. 'That's not part of our agreement; you owe me.'

Mr Heartfelt had looked nervous. 'Frank, we can't draw attention to ourselves, can we? I've written and asked for the rent book from the Dohertys and I've sent a bailiff's notice to the house next door. You will get your house, two weeks, tops. You wait and see, it will all be done, Frank. You just get on with your end of the bargain.'

Mr Heartfelt could see Frank's unwavering gaze, his disconcerting eyes, watching every gesture. Yes, this was definitely the part he hated; he much preferred to use letters and his brother-in-law the bailiff but he had to press on.

'Mrs Nolan, you are now into your fourth week of arrears and I have noted from the clocking-in sheets that your husband has not worked a full week for six months. This concerns me. Under normal circumstances, Mrs Doherty would be with you and I would be very willing to accept a payment plan, as I have in the past.'

Peggy looked so drained of colour he realised that she had moved beyond taking in anything he was saying. He pulled a sheet of paper out of his folder. 'It does clearly state on the back of the rent book that, if you are more than two weeks in arrears, you have to present yourself at the administration building for an appointment to discuss matters. You haven't been anywhere near.'

Peggy felt as though the world were spinning. She looked at Mr Heartfelt; she could make out the movement of his lips, but could no longer hear the words he was saying. She couldn't breathe and the pounding in her ears moved into her head and beat against the sides of her brain while the pain around her lower back and across her abdomen was sickening in its increasing intensity. She needed two Anadin, she had forgotten to ask Kathleen. He held out another brown envelope towards her.

'Mrs Nolan, please accept this letter as your notification of eviction. It is the dock board policy to give you a further seven days' notice. If the rent isn't paid within that time, the property must be emptied within forty-eight hours. If not, the bailiffs will be on your doorstep at 10 a.m. on Friday the twentieth of May. They will board the house and seize whatever is left inside. I suggest you go straight from here and visit the Liverpool Corporation offices in search of help. They will contact the Salvation Army to ask for temporary accommodation for you and your family; please note, it may be that you are not accommodated together.' He was reading from the letter he would have sent, but he might as well have been talking to himself.

'You then need to make your way to the Giro office in Bootle and tell them you have no access to money or accommodation and, finally, I will telephone children's welfare this morning. I have already made enquiries and am aware you have young children who may have to be taken into care.'

Peggy felt as though she had been punched in the face a hundred times. Surely this could not be happening? 'My husband – my husband – if we aren't in the house, he can't get down to the docks to work... he can't do anything else.'

Mr Heartfelt sighed and shook his head. 'Mrs Nolan, if he worked, you wouldn't be in this position. These are dockers' houses, owned by the board, and a condition of service is that the dockers actually work, and you make regular payment. My advice to you is to prepare your children before the children's welfare department arrive at your door.'

Peggy's world crashed and shattered at her feet as she heard the sound of a woman's voice, a shout. Her head turned. The woman who'd shouted was one of the two who had been waiting for an interview. A frown crossed Peggy's face; the young woman was running to her, Peggy, to catch her. But why? Just before she hit the dusty wooden floor, the last thing she saw before darkness blessedly claimed her, was the grin that passed between Frank the Skank and Mr Heartfelt.

Chapter Twelve

Alice was on her way to Cindy's when a car, an unusual sight in itself, made its way slowly up Nelson Street, lurching from side to side over the cobbles. Alice recognised Mr Keeble as the driver almost instantly, but her jaw dropped when she saw that it was a rather pale-looking Peggy in the passenger seat. She waved him down and he drew to a halt and wound down the window.

'She fainted in the administration hut and I was bringing her back up home.'

'Are you all right?' Alice asked Peggy, who didn't answer her.

'I think she could do with seeing the doctor,' said Mr Keeble and Alice boldly said, 'Would you mind taking us? I'll just collect Kathleen.'

And before Mr Keeble could answer, Alice had run back into number 42 and shouted, 'Kathleen, it's Peggy! Get your handbag and your coat on, we're going to the doctor's in a car.'

*

Kathleen had never got used to calling Brendan Cole, *Dr* Cole. She had known him since the day he was born back home in Ireland and now he greeted her warmly when she arrived in his surgery, but not as warmly as he would have done if she had been passing him on his way into mass on a Sunday morning, back in Ballynevin. Like many before him, Brendan Cole had arrived in Liverpool as a houseman at St Angelus and never returned home to Ireland. Here in Liverpool, he had never lost his keenness to impress and remain professional at all times.

Brendan Cole listened to Peggy's complaints about her shortage of breath and her aching veins with the patience of Saint Patrick himself, before he gave her a thorough examination behind the screen while Kathleen sat and waited on the other hard-backed chair beside his desk. Peggy had told Kathleen and Dr Cole about everything, but not about the bailiffs.

'Your heart sounds fine, but it is a bit fast and your blood pressure is too high. Your nerves are in a bad way, Peggy,' he said, as Peggy fastened her blouse. 'Are you feeling OK back on your feet? Maybe I should just give you an internal and check those fibroids. Did you go back to the clinic? Are you bleeding heavily at your time of the month?' he asked, wondering if bleeding from the fibroids had caused an anaemia that had brought on the faint.

'I'm going to have them out, when I've got time,' she

said, trying to remember when exactly it was she had had her last period. 'But I've no bleeding to speak of; the tablets they gave me worked a treat so there's no need for an internal.'

Reassured, Dr Cole smiled. 'Sit yourself down next to Kathleen,' he said in a voice that was loaded with the sympathy he felt for all the women who lived around the docks and were married to underpaid stevedores.

'I have a lot on my plate, doctor,' said Peggy, as she flopped onto the chair, which creaked loudly in protest, 'haven't I, Kathleen?'

'She has, you've no idea, Brendan – sorry, doctor,' said Kathleen taking hold of Peggy's trembling hand, and holding it tight.

Kathleen had been rolling pastry when Alice ran into the kitchen. 'Oh, Holy Mother of God, what is it?' Kathleen had asked as she flaked the pastry from her fingers and rubbed her hands on her apron.

'Peggy must have been paying the rent and fainted in the dock administration offices. She's outside in Mr Keeble's car and he'll take us to the doctor's.'

Katheen slipped her arms into the coat Alice held out for her. 'Paying her rent, today? She must have missed Mr Keeble when he called on Friday night. I've never said a word to anyone about the number of times we feed those kids, Alice, and Maggie Trott hasn't either, because we know that if we're feeding the kids, then Peggy is paying the rent to keep a roof over their heads which is what matters. Even Peggy isn't stupid enough not to pay the rent. Right, I'll go with her and you go and check on the kids. They'll be up on the wasteland, so make sure Malachi isn't beating the living daylights out of any of them.'

'Kathleen, I'm supposed to be having my hair done…'

But Kathleen wasn't listening. 'I've kept all the fatty bits from the meat and the rind from the rashers for Scamp.' They were already alongside the car. 'Hello, Mr Keeble, thank you so much for this and for waiting, it's very kind of you.'

Kathleen let herself into the car, slamming the back door. Alice saw Mr Keeble wince as she did so and sighed. She would miss her appointment with Cindy. 'And my hair's a mess,' she wailed, but no one was listening as she made her way to rescue Peggy's kids.

Alice had almost reached the wasteland when she bumped into Mary, who was hurrying down the entry and Alice could see she'd been crying. 'Mary, are you all right? What's up, love? Is it Malcolm, I know he's a stickler for the rules.'

Alice's voice tailed off as Mary shook her head. 'Malcolm is a dote,' she said, fishing in her pocket for a handkerchief. 'It's not Malcolm.'

Alice linked her arm through Mary's. 'I've got to check on Peggy's kids and I was supposed to be having my hair done, so honest to God, I really do have something to cry about, look at the state of me?'

Mary looked up at Alice's hair and smiled. 'You look lovely,' she said.

Alice smiled back at the young waif next to her. She had watched Mary grow up and had always felt as though they had something in common; and if Alice had been raised in a house and a community where people cared, she often wondered, who would she be? In recent months it had occurred to her that she would have been like the diligent, deep and thoughtful Mary. She had travelled a very hard road to get to where she was and never a day went by when she wasn't grateful to be accepted by everyone around her.

'Come on,' she said, 'you walk with me and if our Nellie is watching the kids, let's go to the café and have us a cup of tea and a custard slice; do you fancy that?'

Mary couldn't speak; she was so touched by Alice's kindness, she was sure she would erupt into a fresh bout of tears if she tried to. Alice squeezed her arm. 'Come on, over that cake you can tell me all your troubles. I'm sure you know I've had enough of my own over the years – and one thing I've learned is that nothing is ever as bad as it seems, especially when you've talked it out over a custard slice.'

Peggy shuffled forward on the chair and a wooden leg beneath her groaned. 'Doctor, the Wrights are moving in next door to us – you know, Frank the Skank, the policeman even the other policemen don't like – can you imagine?' She almost shrieked the words. As she said it out loud, she could barely believe the nightmare she was living. She had told no one she couldn't pay the rent and had no idea how she had got into this mess, had gone weak with relief when Kathleen had said to her, 'Fancy missing the rent man last night, Peggy. If you had paid it then, you wouldn't have had to go down those steps.'

Peggy could not have been more grateful for Kathleen's mistake; all she had left was her dignity and to that she would cling like a drowning woman.

Now she said, 'I was wondering, doctor, if you could write a letter to the dock board and get it stopped, them moving in, on account of my nerves? They might listen to you. You could write that them moving in will make me very sick, that I might die, or something.'

She knew she should tell him they were being evicted in a week's time and if that happened, nothing mattered anyway. But if she said it out loud, it would make it real and it would definitely happen; if she just kept it quiet, maybe she could sort something out in the time remaining. Maybe Maura would send her a postal order. Maybe she could pawn enough to hold them off... Her voice had trailed off and she knew the answer before Dr Cole spoke, so she lunged straight into the remainder of her woes in an attempt to persuade and deflect him.

'And if all that wasn't enough going on, it's my

husband, Paddy. He's a lazy git; he won't go to work and so he hasn't had a full week in six months and we've got no money. He won't get out of bed, we've got no food in and I can't go to the priest again. You must know about Paddy; he says he's coming down here every week and you are waiting for him to be under a doctor at the hospital, a specialist, and it's all taking so long...'

Peggy reached a tearful crescendo and Kathleen pushed a handkerchief between her fingers.

'How are you keeping up with the rent, Peggy?' she asked.

'I'm managing,' said Peggy as she dabbed at her eyes.

As Kathleen watched Dr Cole writing down everything Peggy had told him, she thought how like his father he had become. Every day of the week, Brendan Cole had half a dozen Peggys in his surgery, women who came to see him about problems which had little to do with their health and more to do with the circumstances they lived in, so the sight before him today was a familiar one. Peggy blew her nose noisily into the handkerchief, dabbed at her eyes.

'I'm sorry, Mrs Nolan,' he said. 'I can't write a letter to the dock board instructing them what to do with their own property, I just can't. I can have a word with your Paddy, though, if you think it will help? Because I *have* seen your husband and I think there must be some mistake. I can find nothing wrong with his back and I certainly haven't referred him to the hospital.'

Peggy gasped and looked as though she were about to faint again.

'Look, there are two solutions to this problem. The first is for me to have a word with Paddy. I'll check him out again, but I'm afraid that isn't going to have any impact on how often he goes down the steps, or on who your new neighbours are, so you will have to think of something else to deal with that one. Have you spoken to the dock board, to Mr Heartfelt?'

Peggy looked horrified. 'No, no, I'm not going there, I'm not, ever again.'

'That's where she was, Brendan – I mean, Dr Cole – she must have been asking them herself, were you, Peggy? Is that why you paid your rent down there?'

Peggy lied to her friend for the second time and nodded.

'And what did they say?' asked Dr Cole.

Peggy looked up. 'They didn't get a chance, I fainted,' she said.

'Well then, you may simply have to consider keeping yourself to yourself when they move in; don't give Sergeant and Mrs Wright any cause to address you.'

Peggy repeated his advice disbelievingly, 'Keep yourself to yourself...' while she screwed up her face in a look of amazement. No one, absolutely no one on the four streets, kept themselves to themselves. Even the children joked that sometimes they forgot where they lived or who their actual mother was, they spent so much time in and out of each other's houses. Mothers likewise joked that they forgot which kids were their own. Kathleen could see this was all going nowhere.

'Are there no tablets, doctor?' she asked.

'For bad neighbours?' Dr Cole almost smiled at his mother's old friend. He remembered the Deane farm where they got their eggs and milk, he could almost smell it if he closed his eyes. He and Liam had attended the village school together but while he had studied and studied, Liam had been just the opposite, had hated school with a passion, preferring milking and hay making to composition. 'Well, Peggy, I can give you tablets for your nerves, but I would rather you tried to sort the problem out for yourself first.'

'What would you give me?' Peggy looked interested.

'He means the Valium,' Kathleen said to Peggy in a half-whisper. 'You don't want to be taking those, they made Alice sleep all day, when she was bad, you know, before...'

Dr Cole shot Kathleen a look which was clear in its meaning; she was to stop talking. Dr Cole knew all about Paddy and his bad back, his gastric stomach, his gout, his lungs, his terrible headaches. He was in the surgery almost every other week, looking for an excuse not to report for work. He decided that if Paddy's behaviour was having such an impact on Peggy, it was time to be a bit firmer. He would threaten to really send him to the hospital.

Peggy's lip began to tremble again at the thought of

the state they were in. She had never felt so alone in her entire life. The fear of the mess she was in, the challenge ahead, made her feel as though she were detached, floating through each scene of her everyday life. Surely, this was a bad dream and soon, she would wake? A picture of herself and the kids out on the street, with their furniture piled around them, came into her mind…

'Look, Peggy,' Dr Cole said, 'when you feel yourself losing control, try and take some deep breaths and put into perspective what is happening around you instead of panicking; you will feel much better for it. Tell your Paddy to come and see me.'

Peggy looked deflated. 'I would be a lot better, doctor, if Maura were still here. I do miss her and it's as if everything just keeps going wrong all the time.'

'Ah, Mrs Doherty… A lovely woman. She's moved back home, hasn't she?' he said to Kathleen. Dr Cole felt deeply sorry for Peggys in his surgery, women who came to see him about problems which had little to do with their health and more to do with the circumstances they lived in, so the sight before him today was a familiar one. When help was needed he had women he could call in on, and Maura Doherty had been at the top of his list. Peggy wasn't the only one who missed her. 'Tell your Paddy to come and see me, Peggy, and maybe you should drop Maura a line, a nice letter back would be something to look forward to; she's always full of good advice and wouldn't that just make you feel better now?'

'Oh, I did, Dr Cole. Kathleen helped me to write a letter, didn't you, Kathleen? I just haven't had a reply. I think Maura is busy getting on with her new life now.' To Dr Cole, she sounded deflated. Only Peggy knew it was despair.

Dr Cole gave her an encouraging smile. 'Listen, if you stop sleeping, or find your nerves are getting worse, come back and see me, because we can't have you fainting again.'

'Thank you, Brendan – I mean Dr Cole,' said Kathleen. 'And when you are writing to your mammy, send her my best; a kinder woman never walked this earth, Peggy, 'tis no wonder he became a doctor himself.'

Brendan Cole allowed himself a smile as the door closed and then picked up the phone to his receptionist. 'Can you get me an outside line, Cynthia? It's an international call. Give me ten minutes, please, and if you could just pop to the post office for me, with today's hospital referrals, that would be grand.' He waited for Cynthia to make contact with the exchange and then to buzz him, once the operator was on the line. He knew that the Dohertys had bought the Talk of the Town – Maura had told him on her last visit to have Harry's chest checked and he had thought it the most ridiculous idea, but had kept his opinion to himself. He would ask his mammy to see that Maura dropped Peggy a line. She lived in Galway with his sister for half of the year and she had a telephone. He had an idea that Peggy needed a ray of sunshine in her life, something which, in his experience, could deliver better results than the little yellow tablets they might have to resort to if Peggy didn't improve.

Chapter Thirteen

Eric began his milk money collection at six o'clock every Friday evening, but when it came to the local shops and businesses, he called on a Wednesday, straight after he had finished his morning round on his way back to the dairy. His last stop was always at Cindy's, the hairdresser. There was no fancy name painted on the hoarding above her window, it was simply *Cindy's* and if it hadn't been for the sink with the rubber spray hose attached to the taps, two pink overhead dryers, the swivel chair perched in front of the large mirror and the spider plants along the windowsill next to a display of light-faded *Woman's Own* and *Woman's Weekly* magazines, no one would have known what service Cindy offered inside her shop which was on the end of a row of pre-fabricated units, hurriedly erected after the war.

Nelson's parade boasted greengrocer's, butcher's, fish-monger's, a hardware store, Simpson's the tobacconist and paper shop, the chippy, Cousin's the baker, the betting shop and, finally, the hairdresser. Cindy was the only woman who worked on the parade to wear make-up and sheer stockings every day, had a hemline which appeared to be creeping upwards at an alarming rate, and she never went to church. Cindy wasn't married, by choice and there wasn't a woman on the four streets who didn't know that Cindy was taking contraception. Yet, despite the fact that she was often whispered about over kitchen-table gatherings, not one of them had withdrawn their custom as a result. This was due, in large part, to the fact that Cindy had covered herself in a veneer of respectability and credibility, provided by good-looking Reg, her long-suffering boyfriend, the well-respected local garage owner and mechanic who, it was said, popped the question every Saturday night, half an hour after the official Anchor closing time and five minutes before he hopped into her bed.

Reg was the closest the community had to a success-ful self-made man, evidenced by the fact that he was never slow to put his hand into his pocket in the pub. People were in awe of the hours he worked, the cash he flashed, and the number of young men he employed who called him 'the big boss man,' and, despite all his obvious attributes, his absolute failure to persuade Cindy to walk up the aisle astounded everyone.

'She's strong-willed, that one, but surely not strong enough to resist the likes of Reg? Who could do that? Tell you what, he can slip between my sheets any day,' Peggy would say in the presence of Maura and, for all her holiness and jangling of rosary beads, Maura laughed as loud as all the others.

'Peggy, stop, would you!' Maura would exclaim in mock condemnation, and in order to outrage Maura even more, a sport in itself, Shelagh would chip in, 'She got that wrong there, didn't you, Peggy? She means between her legs, Maura, not her sheets.'

And that would make the tea spray from Maura's mouth and the laughter would be so loud the children would run in from the backyard to see what all the noise was about, then someone would shoo them back out with a broken biscuit in hand and put the kettle back on. When the women ran out of others to gossip about, or times were hard and problems tough, as they often were, they always had the tales of Cindy to cheer them up. There was only one woman on the Dock Road who didn't experience a tinge of jealousy in the company of Cindy, or spend hours discussing her audacity, and that was Eric's wife, Gladys.

'She's not normal,' Gladys, with her sallow skin and curled thin lips, would often say to Eric. 'With all that muck on her face. If it wasn't for the fact that Reginald is a well-respected businessman and desperate to make an honest woman out of her, she would have a name for herself, that one would. That man saves her with his intentions alone. She's very lucky indeed that she has him – half the girls around here would love to be in her shoes. He could have anyone he wants, so God alone knows why he bothers with her. Brazen as you like she is, her skirt near up to her knickers. It's a disgrace. Brazen.'

Eric fought not to frown. He had often thought that Cindy was a delight to look at, a feast for the eyes and a free and independent spirit, someone to be admired because, as Maggie Trott had often said, 'No one leaves Cindy's company without feeling all the better for having been in it – and it's not just the hairdo that does it.'

As Gladys agitated, Eric had often thought how much more civil life would be if every man were lucky enough to be married to women like Maggie Trott or Cindy.

'How do you collect that one's money?' Gladys had barked at him during her last rant about Cindy, squinting and looking sideways at him. Until recently, that look would have made Eric feel quite unwell. His mouth would dry, his bowels turn to water and his heart would race, but no more. Her bite had lost its sting of late and Eric had no idea how or why. It was as if her words now ran over him, rather than piercing him with their malice as they once had.

'She leaves it in a used envelope underneath the empties,' he'd lied. If he had said, 'I call in and we have a good old natter and a laugh,' he wasn't quite sure what Gladys would have done next.

★

Cindy tapped her cigarette ash into the sink with her polished nail and, with expert precision, turned the tap on to extinguish the butt before she flicked it into the bin behind the sink. Then, turning the tap off, she shook in a liberal grey cloud of Vim and began to rub to remove the smell of the ash and perming solution from the sink before the next customer came in. She had over an hour until Maggie Trott arrived for a perm and set. The entire process would take three and a half hours and Cindy often commented that she spent more time with some of her customers than she did with members of her own family.

Glancing in the mirror, she frowned at her reflection. She wore her strawberry blonde hair backcombed into a cloud that tucked in just behind her ears. Reg often complained about the amount of time Cindy spent on her own hair.

'Reg, if my hair doesn't look marvellous, why would anyone want to come to my hairdresser's, for goodness' sake? I'm a walking advertisement,' she would retort.

Turning off the hose, she rubbed her hands down the front of her coverall to dry them and patted an errant lock of hair back into place. Her make-up looked dewy from a morning spent with an overhead dryer blasting out into the small space, so she took out her handkerchief and dabbed her nose. The colour of her skin complemented her hair, and powder-blue eyeshadow enhanced the bright blue of her eyes. She was pretty and she knew it and was proud of the fact that she had passed twenty-one and was still single, a rare bird indeed on the Dock Road.

'By the time we get married, I'll be collecting my pension,' Reg joked, every time she rejected him.

'Reg, I keep telling you, stop asking me,' she would reply, as though Reg bored her. But he would do it again, with a bouquet of flowers in his hand or as he had last week, with a new Ingersoll watch in a padded box. He had bought the ring two years ago and she had told him to keep it safe somewhere, but that he was never to ask her again with a ring unless she gave him permission. The women of the four streets often begged her to regale them with this story.

'Well, you're playing a very dangerous game, my girl,' Kathleen Deane said to her, more than once. 'He'll be getting down on one knee to someone else one day soon. You're playing with fire, you are, Cindy.'

Alice, her daughter-in-law, had taken a different approach when she had been Cindy's age and, a woman of few words, she would smile at Cindy, approvingly.

'If I had my time again, I wish I'd told our Paddy to stick his ring up his arse too,' Peggy had once said.

'Really?' Deirdre had replied. 'And where is that ring Paddy hooked you with, then, Peggy?'

Once again Peggy had found herself on the wrong end of the laughter, until Maura had patted her hand and chipped in, 'Who needs a ring when you have a heart as big as and better than any diamond, like our Peggy has, eh?' And the laughter had stopped dead.

Cindy matched her disdain for marriage with an equal degree of kindness towards others and there were plenty who were in need of it. She was admired by the women who would sometimes call into the shop, not to have their hair done, but to while away the time and natter, because a natter with Cindy made them feel better – and whether Cindy had a customer in the chair or not made no difference. On the rare occasion when Maura had had her hair cut, Cindy would tell her, 'Come in on Wednesday morning when I'm quiet and I'll do Peggy for free – just check her hair for nits the night before for me with your toothcomb,' and no more needed to be said.

Cindy was a phenomenon. She was on birth control, had faced down the priest and come to no harm. She still lived and breathed, had not been struck down by lightning, and the priest, despite frequent references from the pulpit to the evils of vanity, fumed in vain. Cindy was a walking miracle and, what was more, she and Reg went out at night together – he never went to the pub alone. He bought her presents, obviously adored her – and not one woman could quite work out how it was she did it.

Now she popped the Vim tin on the shelf at the back of the shop, as the spin dryer came to the end of its cycle and she began to remove the washed and bleach-stained towels from the day before, just as the shop bell rang.

'Eric, love,' Cindy exclaimed as he walked in, the coins in his leather bag clinking, the collection book in his hand with the pencil wedged in a thick brown rubber band to keep the page open. 'I thought you were a customer and I was thinking, please God, no, I can't be doing with anyone arriving early today – it's me washing and cleaning day and if I don't get these hung up now, they won't be dry for the morning. How are you?'

Eric opened his mouth to speak, but no words came out. He frowned, his head tilted slightly to one side. He was about to say, 'I'm just fine, Cindy, how are you?' as he always did, but the words had stuck in his throat.

'Eric, are you all right, love? The cat got your tongue?' Stepping forward, she placed her hand on Eric's arm and gently caressed his shoulder. 'Eric, love, what's wrong?'

Eric looked into Cindy's kind and welcoming eyes and his guard slipped somewhere deep down inside him. A tear silently trickled out and rolled down his cheek. Cindy took him by the elbow and, pushing one of the overhead dryers to the side, sat him down on the chair. She didn't ask any further questions, she didn't need to. Enough tears had been shed in Cindy's salon for her to know what to do next.

'Right, you sit there; I'll go in the back and make us both a cuppa. I've got a nice bottle of the Irish for times like this and I'll put us both a good splash in.' She gently ran her hand up and down his forearm, gave it a gentle squeeze. 'You just sit there and catch your breath,' she said and left him for the few minutes she instinctively knew he needed alone.

Five minutes later, when she returned, there were no tears to be seen, just a thoughtful Eric, gazing out of the window, watching women bustling past, heads bent low against the Mersey breeze that whipped through the parade like a wind tunnel.

'Isn't the morning awful? It's going to pour down soon,' said Cindy, placing the cup and saucer in his hand. 'Mind you, best we have it all now, out of the way before the carnival. And no point in anyone getting their hair done today, it's wrecked by the time they've walked home.' She sat down next to him, balancing her own cup and saucer on her knee and watched as he took the first sip of his tea. 'Don't be signing any important papers after drinking that,' she said, 'I've put a double in yours.'

Eric managed half a smile and allowed the burning liquid to run down his throat and settle into the pit of his stomach. The combination of tea, whiskey and sugar restored his equilibrium. Cindy didn't ask him what was wrong: she knew, if he needed and wanted to tell her, he would do so, in his own time. They drank the tea together and, as he had run out of his five cigarettes, he accepted the offer of one of her Embassy filters. He settled back in the chair and looking at Cindy, raised a smile.

'You feeling better now?' she asked.

'I am,' he said, 'I'm like a new man, whiskey in the tea and an Embassy filter instead of a roll-up, don't be...'

He stopped. He was about to say, 'Don't be telling our Gladys,' when he realised that he couldn't care less if Cindy did. 'Are you going anywhere nice tonight?' he asked, keen to keep the focus away from himself. Cindy placed a pink lustre, cut-glass ashtray on the arm of the two chairs between them and laughed as she blew smoke into the air. 'Eh, you, that's my line, not yours.' She nudged his arm and the tea slopped over his cup into the saucer.

'You can drink that out of the saucer,' she said.

Lifting it to his lips with one hand, he said, 'Waste not want not,' and slurped the overspill.

Cindy sat back in her chair. 'I say that to every customer, you know, to get the conversation going, as if that was ever a problem around here. I reckon I know everyone's life story.' Eric raised his eyebrows over the rim of his cup. 'Oh yes, I do. All the ins and outs, the trials and tribulations. The women who get the backhanders, the black eyes and the backstreet abortions. They sit in that chair there and tell me. I brush away as many tears as I do clumps of hair from the floor.' She nodded towards the chair in front of the mirror and then, turning to Eric, said, 'And do you know what? I will take every word of it to my grave.'

It was Eric's turn to smile. 'Thanks for the tea, Cindy, but I'm all right. I think I'm just tired.'

'Or you just need a laugh. As it happens, me and our Reg, we always go to the Anchor on a Wednesday night and many other nights; never see you in there though, Eric. Why don't you come and join us tonight? I promise you'll have a laugh.' She deliberately didn't mention Gladys. 'Go on, why don't you come down? We'd love to see you, so come and have a drink with me and Reg.' She pushed the point because she could see, instead of Eric waving it away, the thought had landed on a perch in his mind.

Cindy was an expert in communicating and said no more. She slipped her cigarettes into her front pocket as the bell jangled and the door opened.

'Biddy, love, I haven't seen you for ages, I thought you must have deserted me.'

'I'm in need of a perm, Cindy, but I haven't time for that right now so can you fit me in for a cut and can I book in a perm before the carnival? Oh, hello, Eric, do you come here to get your hair cut then?'

Eric stood and laughed. 'No, I do not. I'd come out smelling like a French tart's boudoir, thank you very much. It's the barber for me.'

'Oi, cheeky bugger,' said Cindy, laughing. 'Come on, Biddy, sit down. I've got time.' As she took the cup and saucer from Eric she said, 'Don't you be forgetting what I said, will you, now?'

She gave Eric a knowing look and Eric replied quietly, 'No, I'll bear that in mind, Cindy, I will. I might just take you up on it,' knowing that he would never in a million years have the nerve to tell Gladys he was off to the pub. The consequences would be too great. Gladys would purse her grey lips and her serpent tongue would do its worst.

Cindy smiled and held his gaze for a moment. 'You do that. Even if you just pop in for a quick pint with us, it would be lovely to see you, Eric.' She turned to Biddy and said, 'Come on then, give us your coat, Biddy. And shall we give it a quick set? I can blast the dryers on full? Don't mind me if I faint from the heat, I always come back round.'

Biddy began to giggle. 'She's a case, that one is, Eric. Get away with you Cindy. Only if you have time, and it's no trouble.'

'See you then, Eric,' Cindy called out and he was back on his cart and halfway to the dairy before he realised that Cindy hadn't paid and Gladys would want to know why he was short when she cashed up the takings.

Chapter Fourteen

It had taken seven long days for Harry to land back on safe shores, during which time Maura had been warned a number of times by the doctors at the hospital that he could lose one of his arms or even his life.

'The poison has travelled high and fast, I'm sorry to say; he has septicaemia and he's a very sick little boy,' the doctor had said and the expression on his face held no sign of hope.

Maura hardly slept but sat by her son's bed for all the hours the hospital would allow her and fretted and wept for the hours they would not, her rosary beads never leaving her hand. On the eighth day, after twenty-four hours with no temperature, Harry ate food for the first time. Now he was almost ready to be released.

'He was asking for you and little Paddy as soon as I came on duty today,' Maura's favourite young nurse said as Maura sat down beside her son's bed. 'I gather he was awake long before dawn which is why he's sleeping now! I'll fetch you a cuppa from the kitchen. Did you get a lift here?

'I did,' said Maura, her eyes never leaving her son as she gently pushed his fringe back from his face. 'Liam brought me. Sister said I can stay until twelve today. Liam has gone to the market and he'll take me back.'

'Hello, who is this then?' said the nurse as she flicked the brake on the linen trolley off and pushed it away from the bed. Her eyes were fixed on the sister's table in the middle of the ward and the woman who had walked in through the ward doors. Visitors were forbidden during the morning, without express permission from sister and the woman appeared to be in deep conversation with the staff nurse on duty. 'Ah, looks like they know each other,' said the nurse and turned back to Maura. 'Would you like a bit of toast? Did ye have time for a bite before you left home?'

Maura's stomach rumbled at the mere mention of food. 'I did not. I was so busy making sure everything was set up for when the kids got up, I forgot about myself.'

The nurse smiled. 'I thought as much. I've seen more meat on a butcher's pencil than there is on your bones. I'll be back in a jiffy with a bit of tea and toast for yourself.'

As the nurse walked down the ward, Maura watched her go. She felt her heart fill with gratitude for the young woman who had cared for Harry with as much attentiveness and affection as she would have one of her own. The staff nurse called her over and Maura noticed that the visitor asked her a question before she walked down the ward towards Harry's bed. As the woman came closer, Maura recognised her as someone she had occasionally seen at the Sacred Heart church on Sunday mornings when they went to mass with Liam and Maeve.

'Hello, Maura,' she said. 'You don't know me, but you know my son well enough back in Liverpool – he's Dr Cole and I'm a good friend of Kathleen's.'

Maura's face lit up just at the mention of home. Dr Cole had brought Harry safely through most of his late-night asthma attacks. His mammy was smartly dressed and carried a handbag looped over her arm. Her brown felt hat was held in place with a pearl-topped hatpin and her face resembled Kathleen's with cheeks as soft and as puffy as fresh pats of dough and eyes as twinkly blue as only Irish eyes can be.

'Does Dr Cole know Harry is here?' asked Maura, confused but at the same time, delighted.

'No, he doesn't, but he did telephone me earlier and asked me to see how you are, so when Liam told me the news, I wondered should I pop by and see how you were for myself? I live in Galway now for half of the time, with the wayward younger daughter. She's not married, you know, lives a shocking existence, goes out to pubs and dancing and all the rest of it and doesn't care who knows it. The rest of the year I live in Ballynevin with the sensible daughter, the older one. The wayward one tells me that everyone who lives in Galway is wayward and I'm thinking, from what I've seen so far, she's right.' She smiled at Maura. 'She does it to tease me. She's a nurse here in the hospital.'

Maura laughed, but felt anxious; she didn't want sister to think she had invited someone and get herself into trouble, or have her visits curtailed. 'Did the staff nurse—'

Mrs Cole interrupted her. 'Did she say I was allowed? Oh, aye, she did. Brendan did some of his training here and my daughter is one of the staff nurse's friends so they all know the Coles here. Your lovely young nurse, now, I don't know her, but she said she's fetching us both a nice cuppa.'

There was a second chair by the side of Maura. 'Sit down, would you?' Maura said, with as much breath as she had left. Her mind was working overtime. Dr Cole had phoned his mammy to ask how she was? It didn't make any sense to her at all.

'Have they told you when he will be home?' Mrs Cole asked as she studied Harry's face.

'Aye, if his temperature stays down, today we can go back home soon.'

Mrs Cole studied Maura whilst she spoke. 'And where would that be then, home?'

Maura made to answer, 'The Talk of the Town,' but the words stuck in her throat and she swallowed hard. Her son had been at death's door and God had given him back to her. She would not thank him with a lie from her son's sick bed. Mrs Cole appeared not to notice.

'Isn't that just the thing? Brendan is always trying to get me to move to Liverpool – and God knows, I would like to, it has that many shops I'd never be out of them, for I love the shops, so I do. It's the reason why I love to spend half of my time here in Galway, but our Brendan, he's there, in Liverpool, and well… It would be an obvious choice, wouldn't it? So many things there to make me happy. Have you ever been in Blacklers?'

Maura smiled. 'I have, many a time. I couldn't afford anything like, but I love to look.'

Mrs Cole looked impressed and laughed out loud. 'Nor would I afford anything after a week, I can tell you. Every time I go to visit Brendan, which isn't very often like, because he just loves to come home for his holidays, I'm spent up within days – all on the kids, mind, and he gives me such a telling-off, so he does.'

'They would all make you very welcome,' said Maura, fully realising that Mrs Cole would hardly be likely to become a resident of the four streets, even if she did live in Liverpool.

Mrs Cole patted Maura on the arm. 'Well, isn't that just a lovely thing to say? But, you see, the thing is I've spent the greater part of my life in Ballynevin. I know it, I have my daughter and my grandchildren there and so I could never leave, now could I? But, it's not just that, not just the family; I know every single person I pass on the road every day, every building. And the seasons, well, nothing they bring holds any surprise for me and I like that. I know it's how it's meant to be and, you know, if people need me, if they need a bit of help, they know where to find me.'

Maura knew that feeling too; it had been her life on the four streets...

'And, my husband,' Mrs Cole went on, 'he's buried in the Sacred Heart churchyard and so that's that, isn't it? The thought of leaving him there, well, it's impossible. I never could go away and leave him, could I? It would be like deserting him. No, I'm tied to the place, so I am. Leaving him in death would be like leaving him in life, could you imagine? No, I would never be happy living anywhere else; I would fret and life, well, it's too short to live somewhere you're not happy, isn't it?' Maura thought of Kitty, and her heart folded in guilt as she realised how long it had been since she had taken flowers to the grave of her firstborn.

'Oh, and see what's my memory like! Brendan says would you drop a line to your old neighbour, Peggy; he thinks she could do with a word from yourself, to cheer her up like.'

Maura was speechless, remembering her decision on the way to the hospital that dreadful night. Harry opened his eyes. 'Mammy, can I have a drink of water?' he asked.

'Mammy, is Paddy coming?'

Maura smiled and shook her head. 'Have you been dreaming, little man? Paddy is back in Liverpool, with Auntie Peggy.' Harry looked disappointed and Maura turned back to Mrs Cole.

'Will you thank Dr Cole for asking about me?' she asked.

'Oh, I get the impression you will be doing that yourself before too long,' said Mrs Cole and Maura knew she was right.

The children ran out of the school and down the cinder path to the sound of a brass bell being rung between the boys' and the girls' entrances. Angela was surprised to see Tommy standing by the gate.

'Da, what are you doing here?' She clutched her composition book in one hand and her hat in the other. Her long pigtails hung down her back and the pink ribbons, which had been neatly tied into perfect bows that morning, trailed limp and straight down over her shoulders. It struck Tommy in that instant that she had Kitty's eyes. Kitty, his Kitty, harmed by a priest, at the hands of another man in authority. A frisson of anger ran down his spine.

'Where is Mr Cleary, queen?'

'He's there, Da, ringing the bell.'

Tommy looked up and saw a small, stocky, red-faced man, holding a brass bell by a wooden handle and ringing it for all it was worth. Tommy frowned, pulled his cap down tight onto his scalp and in a tone harsher and gruffer than was normal, said, 'Get the kids, Angela. Don't be asking me any questions and take them up to Liam's van, he's waiting. Get out of here.'

Mr Cleary had spotted Tommy and the ringing of the bell lost its pace and ferocity. The news of Harry and how desperately ill he had been had soon reached the ears of everyone around. Tommy walked slowly and purposefully towards his target as his eyes met that of yet another man in a position of trust who had harmed one of his children and his gaze never left the defiant face of his son's abuser.

'Da...' Angela's voice trembled; she sensed danger and didn't like it one bit. She was aware that, one by one, the children had stopped screaming and shouting and the cinder yard fell silent.

'Who is that?' a voice called out.

'It's Harry's da,' came the reply.

'What are you wanting?' Mr Cleary shouted.

Tommy didn't reply as a sea of children parted to let him through. His fingers closed over the large penknife in his pocket. He had taken a knife to a man before. A priest. A man who had defiled his daughter, and he had taken his life. And every day since he had repented in his own private prayer. He had never been really sorry. The community of the four streets had gathered around and protected him and his family. They had paid the worst price imaginable. The dark days. The worst days, the days they had run away from to a place where another man had harmed one of his children.

The curiously intent children before him stumbled backwards, faces fearful as a murmur rippled through the yard. He extracted the knife from his pocket and, with one gesture, flicked it fully open and the blade glinted in the sunlight.

'Da!' Angela screamed as he drew level with Cleary.

'What are you wanting?' Cleary demanded, but Tommy could see he was trembling.

'You hit my lad. You ripped the skin off his hands with a stick.' Tommy's voice was cold, his words, very matter of fact, betrayed none of the emotions coursing through his veins.

Sweat was breaking out on Cleary's forehead. His hand visibly shook and the bell rattled, but despite his fear he attempted to hold his ground. 'Aye, and what of it? That's what we do here. Spare the rod, spoil the child. Do you not read your Bible, man?'

Tommy felt strangely calm. 'Aye, we take it very seriously over in Liverpool, it's an eye for an eye – and my lad, he nearly lost his life. Here's how we take our revenge in Liverpool,' he said as he pressed the knife against Cleary's throat.

The white stubbled flesh depressed as the Adam's apple bobbed furiously up and down. Cleary backed away, almost stumbling until he hit the wall, but there was no escape. Tommy walked faster and pinned him against the wall and with his right foot, bore down hard on Cleary's own. Cleary was no match for Tommy, a docker all of his life. His face was close to Cleary's as he hissed, 'Say your prayers, you evil little man.'

Cleary began to cry and the bell left his hand, clanged on the ground and rolled to the side. Tommy had lost his senses; his breathing became laboured and his nostrils flared. One press, that was all it would take. He would avenge Harry – and Kitty, their Kitty, he would feel the belated joy of revenge for her too.

'Da, come back!' It was Angela and her voice cut through his rage. 'Don't, Da, please, please don't.'

She was crying now, but was it Angela, or was it Kitty? He was momentarily confused and in being so, the red mist parted. He heard the sound of running water which jolted him to his senses and he was aware as it splashed onto his boot that it came from Cleary.

'Go on, piss yourself, you pathetic bully,' he hissed as he flicked the knife shut and put it in his pocket. No, he would not spend time in jail for the likes of Cleary. Removing his hand from his trouser pocket, he raised his fists and, just as a look of total shock crossed Cleary's face, he hit him straight between the eyes. The only sound after the impact of knuckles on skin was that of Cleary hitting the ground and lying in his own puddle, followed by the sound of children whooping and cheering.

Angela reached her father's side and took his hand. 'Da,' she said, 'what have you done? Mam will kill you, so she will.'

Tommy turned and walked away from the sight of Cleary, groaning and crying like a baby on the floor. 'Oh no she won't, queen,' he said to Angela. 'Your mam will be delighted.'

'She won't, Da, she'll definitely kill you, she will.'

Tommy let out a laugh; for once, his Angela was very wrong.

'I've news, Angela; you are never going back to that school again. Tonight, Liam is taking us to Galway and we will get the train to Dublin and the ferry to Liverpool. We are going home, kids, so go on, get into the back of Liam's van.'

At that very moment he felt an overwhelming urge to get to his Maura, to take her there and then; he longed for the night to fall when Maura would know just how much of a man he had been and she could show him how grateful she was for protecting their family. There would be no refusals, no excuses, and besides, wasn't it time for another child anyway? He felt life surge through his veins. They could never replace Kitty, they could never try, but it was time for new life, that was what mattered. They were going home to Liverpool and Tommy would make sure that there would be a new Doherty arriving not long after.

Chapter Fifteen

Malcolm was waiting at the door for Biddy to arrive, holding a telegram in his hand. Mary had left and, in celebration of the news, Malcolm had opened the bottle of rum he took a tipple from last thing at night and had it on the table with two glasses waiting.

'What the hell is up with you?' asked Biddy as soon as she saw him standing there. 'Where's Mary?'

Malcolm took her coat and handed her the telegram. 'Here, read this.'

Biddy took the sepia-coloured envelope which, of course, Malcolm had opened without a single tear with his silver knife and she walked towards the kitchen as she read. '*The* Morry *has list. Needed repairs. Wink. Home soon. Jerry be Ready. Tell Mam.* What in the name of God does any of that mean?' she asked Malcolm as she looked up.

He began to pour the rum. 'In truth, Biddy, I have no idea, but I sense it is good news for the four streets, the store cupboards and pantries of the houses and, if I'm not mistaken, there will be rum, knowing Conor. The *Morry* is sailing in!' He raised his glass.

'What is a list?' asked Biddy as she reached out to take her glass.

'It's when a ship has taken on water, or has a badly stored hold, or it has taken on too much cargo.' Malcolm winked.

'What's up with you, winking at me like that?' asked Biddy. 'Have you something in your eye?'

Malcolm looked exasperated. 'No, Biddy, that's what Captain Conor says in his telegram – he's sending Jerry a wink. My bet is that this is going to be a good haul and just in time for the carnival too.'

Biddy smiled as she took a sip of her rum. 'Right, well, I'll drink this and then I'll go and find Ena and tell her, put her out of her misery – and you never know, she might walk home sober tonight.'

'Oh, I doubt it,' said Malcolm, 'but at least she'll be happy.'

Cindy cursed at the hot water that hit the back of her hand just as she tipped the Aunt Sally cleaning fluid into the bucket of steaming water. 'Damnation,' she said as she rubbed at the skin and before she continued, fanned out her long and elegant fingers and checked her nails for chips. It was the end of the day and she was ready for an evening spent sitting in front of the fire in the Anchor with Reg.

She thought about Reg now. Maybe she should say yes the next time he asked her to marry him. She looked around her. But who would take over the salon? She doubted if anyone would: there just wasn't enough money in it. She heaved the metal bucket out of the sink, ready to wheel it into the front and mop the floor, when she heard the bell above the door ring. Cindy took a deep breath; the salon was closed and she was in no mood for a delay right now. She wanted to spend some time on her own hair before she and Reg went to the Anchor. The bell rang again.

'Hang on, I'm coming, keep your knickers on!' she called out and screwed the top back on the bottle of Aunt Sally then walked out into the shop.

The men down on the docks had knocked off over an hour since, but Jerry had been tipped off by the gaffer and he and a few of the men hung about on the steps.

'A ship is out on the bar, waiting on the bore; due in over a week ago, they said. It has a bad list, been struggling, and needs to come in as soon as possible. The harbour master wants it to go straight into the dry dock, but the captain is said to be insisting on docking here to unload first. He's asked for it to be brought down to berth for two weeks, emptied, checked, and then go up into dry dock for repairs. And the gaffer said it would be of interest to all of us.'

Seamus had punched the air. 'Yes! It has to be Conor, doesn't it? Who else would it be insisting on docking here.'

Jerry was squinting under his cap, peering down the river. 'I hope it is Conor, but the gaffer didn't know the name of the ship or the captain because that miserable bastard, Heartfelt, wouldn't tell him which ship it was and said he would give him a copy of the manifest only once it had left the bar and was on its way down.'

Big Paddy spat his tobacco to the ground. 'Heartfelt's a slimy git.'

'I'm surprised you remember his name, Paddy,' said Seamus. 'I'm sure to God he's forgotten yours, we see that little of you down here these days.'

Paddy looked wounded, an expression he had perfected over a number of years. 'Honest to God, Seamus, if you had my back, you'd know about it.'

A couple of the men at the rear guffawed at Paddy's response and he had the good grace to blush.

'Is it worse in the mornings then, Paddy?' asked Jerry.

'Oh, aye, terrible in the mornings, gets better as the day goes on. I'm a martyr to my bad back, Jer. There are some days I just can't get out of my bed. Dr Cole says if I don't take it easy, I'll be an invalid before my pension is due.'

Jerry resisted the urge to laugh. Kathleen had told

him what Dr Cole had said to Peggy when she was in the surgery with her. 'That's a God-given illness you've been handed out there, then, one that improves by night-time so you can still get down to the pub. Holy Lord, if I am to be afflicted with anything, please make it Paddy's back!' Jerry clasped his hands together and made a mock praying gesture to the sky and laughed out loud.

'How's your Peggy managing for the money?' asked Callum, his voice full of concern.

This was a conversation Paddy didn't want to have. He knew that the dripping Peggy had put on his bread that morning came from meat Jerry had paid for and the enamel bowl Peggy had scraped it out of was from Kathleen's own kitchen. He did a good job of persuading dockers who had supped deep into their cups to buy him a drink of an evening; indeed, he could walk into the Anchor with empty pockets and then struggle to find his way home after a night of ale on the back of other men's generosity and he never went hungry. As was the tradition of the streets, the men, the workers, were fed first and best. There was no response from Paddy to the question every man had been asked by their own wives, 'How is Peggy paying the rent if Paddy isn't working? We can't ask her, so did Maura give them money, or what? She must have something to be managing on if he's not going down the steps and clocking on.'

On days when he did work, Paddy had left early on

a number of days, having cadged a sixpenny bit off someone under the pretence that the kids needed food and took it straight to the betting shop. The luck had been with him one afternoon and he had won ten pounds. He kept the money hidden deep in his pockets and had kept himself fed on pies and paid for his own pints from the winnings. He hadn't thought about the rent, but Peggy must have been paying it somehow, otherwise they would have been out on their ear. Paddy suspected that Maura and Tommy had sent Peggy money and she had kept it hidden from him. Well, two could play at that game.

The men, aware of Paddy's discomfort, fell silent, bored with waiting, not wanting to take out their tobacco tins and roll up a damp cigarette as the evening mist rolled up the steps from the Mersey or remove the half-smoked stubs from behind waxy ears in case they should be seen lighting up from down below.

Eugene was the first to see it and punched Jerry on the arm.

'Would you fecking look at that! Isn't that Conor's ship?' he whispered as the funnel of a steamship loomed and listed, creaked and groaned, chains clanking and ropes banging on the deck as, like an old and weary ghost, it emerged from a dense patch of mist. Captain Conor's ship looked every day of its age.

Jerry grinned. 'It is, Seamus, one blue funnel, three stripes, two masts and the answer to our prayers has arrived. The next thing I have to do is meet up with Captain Conor or his first mate, Blinks, and find out what they have on board. If he's been out to the Caribbean, it'll be full of rum and, knowing Conor, he will have brought plenty back to make the ladies happy.'

Callum placed his hand to his brow and watched as the tugs expertly guided the ship in. 'Will he have to pay tax on the booze, Jerry?'

'Oh, the owner of the load will be paying it, not Conor. Our job will be to get our share up the steps smartly and stored along with whatever else he has for us and then doled out without Frank the Skank or anyone else noticing. Then we have to take the rest to sell at the market and via other means,' Jerry tapped the side of his nose, 'to make Conor his cut.'

Big Paddy looked panicked. 'We'll definitely get our rum off, won't we?'

Jerry slapped his hand down on Paddy's shoulder. 'We have plenty of time to get organised, Paddy, but the only way you will see any of it is if you pull your weight. If there's a haul coming up the steps, I won't be taking any prisoners. Seamus, who can we get?'

Seamus looked up towards the streets. 'There won't be a man not wanting to help when Babs and Bill find out Conor's down there. I mean, he does know the carnival is next week and I bet he's got everything the women need to get the float ready.'

Jerry dipped his head and watched as the tug captain

on the bridge called down to the crew on his own boat and they eased the *Morry* into berth. There was a ship already in the second dock further up, waiting to be unloaded, which looked more promising than the lumber ships of late. It had been there for four days and yet not a single stevedore had been allowed anywhere near and the bottom of the gangway was guarded by two dockside policemen. Jerry scanned the dockside and Seamus could almost see the cogs in his mind turning.

'Look,' said Jerry, 'the police aren't interested in Conor; yet normally they would be all over the dock like a rash when the *Morry* sails in.'

'Yeah, whatever is on that other ship, someone is waiting for their own cut and it isn't us,' said Eugene.

Jerry was deep in thought. 'Aye, well, we need to get those policemen to take a stroll down to the Clarence Dock while Tommy and I organise getting the load up the steps and into Tommy's outhouse.'

Callum took a ciggie stump out from behind his ear and pushed himself back into a cut-out in the wall. 'We don't have those look-the-other-way bizzies any more, do we, Jerry?'

Jerry shook his head. 'We don't. Frank the Skank grassed on them, and what intrigues me is why the Skank is now stood, guarding the gangway, whilst the *Morry* sails in and no one is batting an eyelid. Something is going on down there and I have no idea what it is. But I intend to find out.'

★

Cindy pushed back the long tails of the brightly coloured fly curtain.

'Who's there? I'm closed,' she said as she flicked the light switch back on. 'Oh, Mary. Heavens above, I didn't expect to see you here.' Cindy smiled at the girl. 'What can I do for you, Mary? I'm closed.'

Mary wanted to run out of the shop, but the money in her pocket burnt into her hand. 'I'm sorry, Cindy,' she said and her voice was so low Cindy could hardly hear her. 'I've been saving up and I was going to come in on Saturday, but Malcolm is busy and I can't and, well, I just wanted to look nice.'

Cindy smiled. Alice had warned Cindy to expect Mary when she'd finally made it to have her own hair done.

'Mary has a special fella in mind, Cindy,' she'd said. 'She's only young and she needs a bit of a confidence booster. I've told her to start here with you; I said there was much she could learn from you and that she needs to be more like you and less like me.'

Cindy had seated Alice under the dryer and had fetched them both a cup of tea. 'I'm up for that, Alice. I think we should try and help her or that poor girl is going to be washing dishes and peeling spuds for the rest of her life – and, of course, there's Deirdre to deal with. She's always seen Mary more as free help than a daughter – and that dreadful brother of hers, Malachi, is treated like God in that house, can do no wrong. Leave Mary to me, this sounds like a bit of a project that's just up my street. Who's the fella?'

Alice raised her eyebrow and through a sardonic smile said, 'Jimmy O'Prey' and no sooner had the words left her mouth, than the tea left Cindy's.

Peggy had made her way down the Dock Road, pushing the old pram, and went as far as her legs would carry her. She knew there was a pawnshop where she would be unlikely to be seen. No one on the four streets ventured that far down. It was also known as the part of the road where prostitutes plied their trade but what Peggy hadn't been prepared for was how blatant they were.

She had taken the blankets from the beds, thanking God it was May, and the coats Maura had bought for the children. Hopefully she could buy them back before winter... The blankets were piled up high on the pram, disguising her shame, because it was acceptable on the four streets to pawn blankets in the summer, or ornaments; some even pawned Sunday-best suits and frocks, if they had them, but children's shoes were deemed to be beyond the pale – only the lowest of the low did that and it was the level to which she had descended. She had taken the shoes from the children's feet and left her boys at home, crying, desperate to play on the wasteland. Out there, they could forget about groaning bellies; sitting at home with no light and no money for a television, it was all they could think of.

'It won't be for long,' she had said to little Paddy. 'You need to keep yours, though, because I need you to run messages and help out.'

Little Paddy was relieved but still pleaded on behalf of his brothers. 'Mam, is there no other way? They can't go out and play with no shoes on.'

Peggy, her desperation growing, her patience waning, had snapped, 'Paddy, stop it, would you! I need you to help, not hinder. What choice do I have? Your father didn't work one full day last week. We'll get three days' pay on Friday but I need that for the rent and whatever I can get for the shoes to put with it.'

'Mam, you said we'd paid the rent!'

Peggy shouted, 'Shut up, shut up, would you? Just shut up!' And she'd begun to cry, loud sobs racking her body. Little Paddy was terrified; he had never seen his mother so near despair and he was scared stiff. He'd thought that as his da was out of the house and down on the docks today that she would be happy.

'Mam? Mam, shall I go and borrow some tea from Shelagh?' He was desperate to help.

'No, Paddy,' she'd said, 'just do as I ask, that's all I need for you to do to help me. I know what I'm doing. I'll find a way to pay the interest and get the shoes back, honest to God, just please, please don't give me grief.'

Little Paddy didn't believe her and she could see it in

his eyes. She didn't believe herself, but this was the only thing she could do and say right now. All that was left to her was this, or to sit on the chair and wait for the bailiffs to arrive.

A string bag, suspended from the handle of the pram, banged against her thigh as she walked along the road. In it was the only cutlery they had in the house and in her hand another knitted string bag contained her mother's clock, wrapped up in an old copy of the *Echo*. She had picked the statue of the Virgin Mary up off the mantelpiece, intending to take it too and then put it back down again. The Holy Mother had looked Peggy straight in the eye and when Peggy thought she saw her frown, the guilt that shot through her sent her mind into a frenzy; her breathing had become rapid and her face hot as she blessed herself.

'What in the name of God has become of us?' she had whispered. She put it back and, delving into her apron pocket, clasped the comforting rosary beads as they clicked through her fingers.

The children had been sitting on the stairs when she'd opened the kitchen door to leave and she had avoided their desperate expressions, but she could not unhear their miserable sobs. Still, Peggy wouldn't allow them to play out, barefoot. Never in a million years would her children be the only barefooted children out on the street.

'I'll get you some plastic sandals as soon as I can, I promise now,' she'd said. 'It's nearly summer and with some of the money I get for this lot, I'll buy you chips. So come on, cheer up.' She was attempting to cheer herself up as much as the children.

Paddy had held her gaze, his face full of concern. 'Ma, can I do something? Do you need help? Can I help, Ma?'

'Paddy, you can help me with the chips when I get back and I'll make sure I get enough for everyone to have a saveloy each too.'

Her children had looked up at her, their eyes filled with the kind of adoration reserved by the masses for the pope. Oh, she would not let them down. Knowing the women would be in their houses, preparing the tea for their own families and away from the street, she'd opened the front door and, pushing the pram before her, slipped out. She had taken the one and sixpence she had left to her name, money Kathleen had given her to help with food for the tea, knowing that unless she could find more, they would be turned out of their house on Friday. To keep a roof over their head and food on the table she would sell herself down on the docks. Everyone knew, when Annie O'Prey had fallen on hard times, it wasn't a cup of tea and a slice of Annie's famed Victoria sandwich that the coalman had stepped inside for. She would never admit it now, but the black handprints on Annie's backside half an hour later had been a dead giveaway. Annie had paid for a hundredweight in kind and Peggy knew of others who had done the same in desperate times.

Now, if she couldn't get what she needed from the pawnbroker, there was nowhere else for her to turn. She was days away from losing her home and the children's welfare would take her children into care when that happened. All she would be left with was big Paddy – and what a thought that was. Her children were hungry. She would sell the clothes off their backs, the shoes off their feet – and if she had to, Peggy would sell herself.

Now she wandered down the Dock Road, looking around her, watching carefully, and then she saw it happen before her very eyes. A woman stepped out from a closed shop doorway and a man approached her. They spoke and then she opened a door in the wall and they disappeared inside. Peggy sighed; this woman was not wearing slippers. She wore heels, a fancy coat and her hair was done.

The visit to the pawnshop almost robbed her of the last of her dignity, or so she thought.

The pawnbroker picked up each shoe and checked the soles. He put the blankets on one side. 'I don't suppose they've had a wash?'

Peggy looked down at her hands.

'Well, in that case, I can't give you much because if

you don't come back, I'll have to get them to the wash house before I can sell them. Three shillings for the blankets and ten and six for the shoes.'

Peggy gasped. 'Is that all?' It had hardly been worth the long and exhausting walk.

'I'll have to get this lot resoled. It's a business I run, not a charity.'

Peggy felt as though she had been winded. 'But why? They're made of good leather?' She was in shock; she had guessed at three pounds at the very least. She was depending upon that amount to call off the dogs. To persuade Mr Heartfelt that she could return with more and to let them stay in their home because they had nowhere else to go.

'Leather is leather,' the pawnbroker said. 'No one from around here has ever brought me good leather. They don't even know what it looks like.' He laughed out loud and then, with little compassion for the bereft woman standing before him, asked, 'Am I taking them, or not?'

Peggy looked over her shoulder and out of the window. Normal people living normal lives were bustling past. Workmen on their way home to a tea on the table. Old, invisible women, returning from mass, children answering the call to return home for tea; and she thought of her own children, huddled on the stairs and hungry. And very soon there wouldn't even be the stairs to sit on.

'Take them,' she said as she placed her mother's clock

on the counter and the man peeled away the layers of newsprint.

'Ah, now you're talking,' he said. 'I'll give you a fiver for that – it's an original.'

A thrill ran through her. She could deliver chips to the kids after all, and saveloys too – and surely this would be enough for Mr Heartfelt. Frank the Skank and the threat he and his wife posed had faded. She would rather keep her home with them as neighbours than have no home at all. It had come to that.

'I'll take it,' she said, and as she pushed the clock across the glass-topped counter, she heard her mother's voice, 'That clock's been my pride and joy; it was your grandmother's, so don't you ever let it go, do you hear me?'

Peggy's breath caught in the back of her throat. If she died before she got the clock back, and if she had the last rites and went to heaven and her mam was there, what would she say? Was her shame on earth not enough? Must she take it with her? The pawnbroker placed the money in a brown envelope with the items listed on the front and ripped a corresponding page out of his book. Peggy took it and slipped it into her coat pocket.

'Aren't you going to check how much is in there, that I haven't short-changed you?' he asked but Peggy didn't answer him; she could do no more. Turning, she headed for the door and, lifting the brake on the pram, set off towards the four streets and the chip shop.

★

Mary sat in the chair, with the cape around her shoulders and Cindy undid the ribbons on the bottom of her pigtails and let her hair fall onto her shoulders.

'You've got lovely hair, Mary,' Cindy said, looking at the girl in the mirror. Mary had never been into Cindy's, or any hairdresser's, in her life. Deirdre had always cut her hair in the kitchen, along with the boys'. 'Does your mam know you're here?' Mary shook her head. 'I thought as much. Was it all Alice's idea?'

Mary managed a half smile. 'It was. She said I had to be more like you and the best way for that to happen was for you to give me a modern haircut.'

Cindy grinned. 'Well, she's not wrong there, I know all about haircuts. Have you seen this one?' Cindy picked up a magazine and began to rifle through until she came to the page she was looking for. Mary gasped and her hand flew to her mouth. 'I know,' said Cindy, looking proud of herself. 'It takes someone bold to have that cut, but look at her cheekbones – they're the same as yours. You're a chrysalis, Mary, and with the right haircut, a butterfly will appear.'

Mary's eyes were wide. It wasn't just the things Cindy said, it was the way she said them. Cindy was totally confident in her own skin and Mary realised that Alice was right: Mary *did* want to be like Cindy.

'Don't you dare go and knock on his mam's door,'

Alice had told her when she'd unburdened all her woes, that Jimmy was out of prison and had made no attempt to see her. 'I did exactly that; I knocked on Jerry's door and it's the wrong thing to do. Oh, I know I'm happy now and you are too young to know or remember, but we've been to hell and back along the way and I took people with me. Do not be me, Mary. Be more like Cindy. You go to Cindy and get her to make you look so fantastic that when you walk down the street with your head high, everyone looks at *you*. And if you do see Jimmy O'Prey, you look the other way and ignore him, do you hear me?'

Mary had looked as though she was about to burst into tears. Her mouth was full of custard slice and her eyes were huge. 'I can't,' she'd said, through flakes of puff pastry, 'I love him.'

Alice had instantly felt guilty. 'Mary, I know you won't believe a word I say, but believe me, love has to work both ways; if it doesn't, it will only bring you years of heartache. Look, if you really want him to notice you, let's make you unmissable. I suggest you start with a visit to Cindy and then we'll get to your wardrobe. I was your size once and, honestly, I have some lovely clothes I brought back from America which just don't fit me any more and never will again. We'll see if there's anything there, shall we? It's good stuff too and will fit you a treat, but first, the hair! Let the transformation of Mary begin. Jimmy O'Prey, eat your heart out.'

Alice had held her cup in a mock toast and, despite her tear-stained cheeks, Mary had laughed as she picked up her cup and toasted Alice back. For the first time in her life she'd felt as though someone had not only noticed who she was, but could see her dreams and knew who it was Mary really wanted to be.

As she made her way back home, with the pawnbroker's money safely in her purse, Peggy stopped and watched at the dock wall until the woman and the man she'd seen earlier emerged from the doorway, the deed obviously done. The man, who was well dressed and wearing a gaberdine mac, went away down the street while the woman walked over to another man who was leaning against a lamppost on the opposite side. She handed him what looked like money. He counted it and gave her some back and the woman walked away to the next lamppost swinging her handbag back and forth provocatively.

Peggy watched, mesmerised, then a voice behind her asked, 'Fancy a go? Short of a few bob? I saw you coming out of the pawnbroker's. That pram looks lighter than when you went in.'

Peggy almost jumped out of her skin. It was the pimp; he'd crossed the road while she stared at the woman. 'What? No! I mean...'

He looked her up and down. He had customers who liked their ladies on the larger side and while she was bedraggled-looking, he would bet she scrubbed up decent. She was what? Maybe forty? 'Look, my name's Fred – you don't need a second name. That there is Stella and she'll show you what to do. You go home, love, have a wash and do something with your hair, then get yourself back here and it'll be five quid in your pocket for each punter. It's busy and I've got a couple of girls off so I could use you.'

Five pounds, Peggy thought, maybe she would get enough to pay the rent arrears off in one night. But the children were hungry, they needed chips, so she would see to them first.

'Oh, and put a pair of heels on, no slippers on my patch.'

Peggy's heart sank. She walked away and didn't turn around, pushing the pram with her head held high and her slippers flapping on the pavement, her humiliation complete. She couldn't even sell herself, wasn't good enough for that, because she didn't own a pair of shoes to her name.

There was a queue in the chip shop and it was almost an hour before she arrived home to be greeted by a cacophony of noise. The pain in her abdomen had increased with a vengeance as she'd stood in the queue. She decided that it was worse when she stood and when all this was over, when she had saved her family and they were out of the woods, she would return to the doctor and let them take it all away. What a relief that would be, the rent up to date and a life without pain.

Little Paddy had done all that he could to stop the boys from crying and complaining, he'd even resorted to using Max, letting his brothers hold him one by one, but after half an hour little Paddy's last resort had lost its appeal. He went out to the entry and dark thoughts ran through his mind. His mother wasn't coping and he didn't know what he could do to help. He'd thrust his hands into his pockets and, as he did so, looked up to the Dohertys' bedroom window. She was there and he'd whispered her name.

'Kitty? It's all going bad, Kitty.'

Tears had filled his eyes as the street lamp flicked on overhead and the day relinquished its hold...

'Little Paddy?'

It was Peggy in the entry, pushing a pram. He could smell the vinegar-soaked newspaper and he laughed with relief. 'Mam, I thought you weren't coming back!' he said.

'Where's your da?' she asked, turning the pram in through the gate.

'He's not home yet,' his voice falling again, along with his hopes, for his mother looked dreadful. As Peggy walked into the house, the complaints the children had stored ready for her return were all silenced by the smell of the hot chips. Even Scamp flew out from under the table.

'I put Max away,' whispered the second-youngest to his brother.

'Sit still, everyone,' Peggy said as she and little Paddy handed the newspaper parcels to the boys, all sitting in a row of wriggling excitement. The youngest licked the fat off the paper and smeared newsprint all over his face. The others began to giggle at the sight, their mouths stuffed full of chips and the room was filled with laughter.

Then suddenly Peggy felt water run down her legs. 'Oh, Jesus God in heaven!' she exclaimed, her eyes stretched wide, both hands on her back in an attempt to suppress the huge ache that had suddenly seized her.

'What, Mam?' asked little Paddy.

'Nothing, Paddy,' said Peggy, 'I'm caught short, that's all, and I need the outhouse.'

The children were so eagerly stuffing chips and saveloy into their mouths that not one had noticed the puddle of water on the floor. The deep ache came again, sharper and longer. Peggy, in a state of confusion, walked towards the back door, her slippers soaked and squelching. She had to get to the outhouse as quickly as she could, biting down an all-consuming urge to scream.

And with it, Peggy was thinking: no, no, no, please God, no, this isn't happening, it can't be! But she also knew that no amount of denial would alter a thing; she was about to deliver a baby! She had done it many times before and the pressing urge, deep in her abdomen, was unmistakeable. She shivered, feeling as though ice was running through her veins, and nausea consumed her as she lunged towards the back door. Her sons, high on the excitement of hot food, had not noticed her dilemma, not even little Paddy.

Peggy reached the outhouse door and looked over the wall at Maura's empty house, feeling a powerful need for her friend. She blinked when she saw Kitty at the upstairs window. She often did, but had never told Kathleen or anyone else, in case they thought she was going mad, but she had no time to think about that now; she was panting furiously, out of breath, a baby was coming and it was coming fast.

Chapter Sixteen

Eric had hoped he could slip out of the dairy and in through the doors of the Anchor before Gladys arrived back from her sister's over in the Wirral. Cindy's words had barely left his mind since he had been in her shop. 'Don't forget, you know where me and Reg are if you fancy a drink and a natter, we've only got one life, Eric.'

One life... those words... His breath caught in his throat as he placed a kiss on the warmth of Daisy's neck. Was this it for him, this one life, lived in dread and fear of stepping back indoors? Spending more time in the stable with his horse than any man should? Counting the minutes until he could make an excuse to head to his cold and lonely bed in the back of the house? As though sensing his thoughts, the mare bent her head and pushed her nose against his shoulder.

'Oh, Daisy,' he said, 'thank goodness I've got you. There's nothing I wouldn't do for the very best girl in my life.'

He almost leapt out of his boots as Gladys's stinging voice sliced through the air. 'Charming, I'm sure.' Her tone was unmistakeably acerbic and accusing. 'I fall in behind the horse now, do I? Well, I have to say, I'm not surprised. Her intelligence is about at your level, so I suppose you've something in common.'

Without knowing where they came from, alien words now fell from Eric's mouth. 'That's as may be, but *you've* a face like a horse's behind,' he muttered and then, instantly regretting it, finished his words with an exaggerated cough.

'What's that?' said Gladys.

He took a long deep breath and turned to face his wife's puckered grey lips and fake orange cheeks. Her dyed black hair with its tight curls lay almost flat against her scalp.

'Is it true, you gave that Peggy Nolan on Nelson Street milk? I know it is, so don't try denying it. I've done the accounts today and there's two pints missing and two ticks in Nelson Street not crossed and accounted for from last week.'

Eric sighed. He'd given Peggy the milk a few days ago and, of course, she hadn't paid as she had promised and he'd done it in secret, without telling Maggie.

'I thought you were off to your sister who lives on the Wirral?' he said, attempting to change the subject.

'Eric, we have been married for twenty-five years. Her name is Pauline. Why do you insist on calling her "your sister who lives on the Wirral"? Is it because it bothers you that she married a man who can keep her in a lifestyle I can only dream of?'

Gladys knew how to deliver maximum hurt in the fewest words possible to cut him down to size and leave him speechless. Pauline, the younger sister, had married Dennis, a bank clerk from Hoylake who, following the war when there was a general shortage of men, rose quickly through the ranks despite his mediocrity, to become manager at the Hoylake branch he had worked in before he was called up. Milkman, bank manager; Daisy, Austin Seven; detached house, end-terrace dairy. Pauline and Dennis lived on a tree-lined street that ran down to the shore while Eric and Gladys lived a stone's throw from the docks and no matter how hard he tried, he couldn't match the lifestyle of the bank manager.

With a glance at his wife, Eric lifted Daisy Bell's water bucket, slipped back the bolt on the stable door and pushed it open, forcing Gladys to step backwards as he carried the bucket to the outside tap. He had intended to say, 'Sorry, Gladys,' as she stepped back, but instead he kept his mouth closed.

'You stupid idiot, you almost knocked me over there. Close the stable door behind you,' barked Gladys and banged the door shut, spooking Daisy Bell.

'She's not going anywhere while she's eating her mash,' said Eric, turning the tap full on to drown out her voice.

But Gladys wasn't going to let the subject of Peggy and the milk drop.

'Well, did you? Did you give our hard-earned money away? She still owes us for eight pints and you know that.'

Eric took a deep breath; there was no point in his denying it. 'Yes, I did, but she promised me I would be paid on the collection round and I just haven't been able to catch her since.'

'What a surprise. Well, on Friday, it won't be you going, it will be me.' She glared at her husband and Eric could see the thoughts running through her mind as clearly as if she had spoken them. Gladys would take huge delight in knocking on Peggy's door and that delight would only be increased if Peggy couldn't pay and had to ask for extra time.

'Gladys, they don't have a lot in that house. Don't you be going and making a show of her, that won't get you anywhere.'

Gladys was impervious to his pleas, as he knew she would be. 'I didn't come down with the last shower like you, Eric, so I'll be doing the Nelson Street round this Friday.'

Eric's heart sank. He felt on the edge of despair. 'Gladys, you can't get blood out of a stone. If she doesn't have it, she doesn't have it. Please leave it to me, Gladys. I'll get it. Everyone always does with Peggy, eventually. She's never had the bailiffs round, so she has that much to her credit.'

Gladys snorted in derision. 'That was only thanks to Maura Doherty. Now she's left, and mind, who could blame her – living next to that lot, it was only a matter of time. The Nolans probably drove the Dohertys away. They are the most notorious family around here, apart from Annie O'Prey and her thieves for sons, and you, soft lad, give out the free milk like it's a charity we run here.'

'The Dohertys left because they had a windfall, as you often observe, 'twas nothing to do with the Nolans,' he said and, under his breath, '*I'd be off meself if we had one. I would and that's a fact.*' An image of himself and Daisy Bell, walking along a shore, leapt into his mind; the sun was shining and there was someone walking along beside him, he just couldn't tell who.

'Leave it to you to collect it? What will *you* do? Take a crate with you and give her another half a dozen for free? "Here you go, Peggy, take the bleedin' lot, why don't you, Peggy. Have it all, go on, take the horse too, Peggy, because I'm a flamin' big eejit I am".'

As Gladys mimicked his voice, Eric glanced away. Suddenly the familiar barbs from Gladys didn't hurt or embarrass and that surprised him, because they had been doing just that for the past twenty-five years.

'Well, not bloody likely! I'll be dealing with that Peggy – and if she doesn't pay, I'll be getting the bailiffs onto her myself. No one takes *me* for a mug!' She turned on her heel and marched back towards the house.

Eric sighed. Oh, no, no one ever does that, Gladys, he thought. They take you for many things, but never a mug. He tried one last time. 'Please, please, leave Peggy to me. If she doesn't pay, I'll speak to Kathleen Deane; she keeps an eye out for Peggy since Maura left.'

Gladys loved the conversations when Eric pleaded with her best of all. It made him look weak and pathetic and wasn't her life bad enough, having to live on the Dock Road? Could the straw she drew have been any shorter? Could her sister have done any better if she had tried? The moments when Eric begged were one of the few pleasures she had in life. She stopped and looked back over her shoulder.

'You are a waste of good air, do you know that? You are the most pathetic specimen of a man I have ever known in my life, and that's saying something because the streets around here are full of them.' She stared at him, waiting for a response, but there was none. Disappointed, she turned away.

'Your trotters and mash are on the table,' she called back as Eric carried the water into the stable, asking himself the usual question: was it normal to have been married for as long as they had and, for the last twenty of them, to have been spent loveless and in separate rooms? He had no idea.

Eric was a shy man, he never spoke of such things as sex, but he knew other men had it and he didn't, which had come as a surprise, given that Gladys had been so very keen to lure him up the aisle with promises of a wild and reckless love life once he had been allowed to do battle with the tops of her suspenders. It was Gladys who had unbuttoned her blouse and encouraged him to explore, not him, and the night of his downfall had been filled with such passion, too. They had been dating for only three months when he had been called up and when he had walked her home after telling her his news, they had stepped into the pool of darkness alongside the bins.

The news of his imminent departure had turned Gladys into a much more accommodating girlfriend. She had always been very insistent on setting boundaries before the day his call-up papers had arrived. 'Not until we are married, Eric,' she would whisper into his ear as his hands cupped her buttocks and Eric, always a gentleman, had obeyed her every command. This night, however, Gladys was on fire as she pressed herself into him and things advanced too quickly for Eric to ask himself the question, *what is going on?*

She startled him as she placed his hand firmly on the most private part of her body, a place he had never thought he would ever be allowed to roam free. He froze in astonishment, the act robbing him of his breath, and her next words were, to Eric's total amazement, 'Marry me, Eric, if you want to go any further.'

Eric was stunned and recoiled, but she grabbed his arms and pulled him back into her, lifting her woollen skirt which had slipped back down to her knees, and replaced his hand. 'Marry me,' she'd said, pressing his hand harder into her, his fingers as frozen in movement as a dead man's.

'When I come back, Gladys,' he had said, his voice sounding thick, not at all like his own, his senses dulling, then all he was aware of was the warm mound beneath his hand. It was as if nothing else in the world existed right at that moment.

She grabbed his free hand and pressed it to her thin breast. 'Go on, Eric...'

Suddenly Eric was alarmed; the speed and direction at which events were moving were faster than his reasoning could keep up. 'No, Gladys, we can't, it isn't right.'

What he meant was that Gladys wasn't right. Eric was young, he was about to do his duty to fight for king and country. The fog in his mind became thicker as he tried to work out how and why he was here. The truth was that Gladys had singled him out, not the other way round. She was the only girl he had been brave enough to approach at the dance and that was because every time he looked over to the chair she was sitting on, she was already looking his way, and smiling. He'd thought that, as she was alone, she would be grateful for the offer of a dance, but that was all. He was a nervous kid and he looked it. If he survived the war and came back alive, he was determined that he would set his sights on Maggie, the popular girl who worked in the grocer's on the Dock Road and lived on Nelson Street. She wouldn't look twice at him now, but maybe if he returned a hero, he might stand a chance.

Gladys could sense his resistance, had known it was there for the past three months. Their evenings had followed an established pattern. They attended the weekly dance in the church hall, then he walked Gladys home and pecked her on the cheek and said thank you. Her behaviour on that fateful evening was a wild deviation away from the norm. Unbeknown to him, she had received strict advice from her mother.

'Get him to marry you,' her mam had said. 'That way, if he doesn't come back, you will at least get a payout and maybe a pension until someone else takes you, but it will be a struggle, Gladys. You don't have our Pauline's looks.'

Her mam's words were ringing in her ears as she felt Eric resisting. Without another word, she raised her thigh, pressed her heel into the wall, placed her hand over his own and pushed hard against him. He gulped hard.

'Marry me, Eric, before you leave and then I'll be waiting when you come home on leave. I can make you the happiest man on earth before you go and then you know there will be something to return for.'

She'd kissed his lips, hard, pushed her tongue into his mouth and pressed it against his own and Eric, confused, felt the picture of Maggie slip from his mind, to be replaced by a pounding, relentless urgency in his loins. The inside of her thigh was warm and soft, surprisingly so in comparison to the rough, calloused skin on her hands. He didn't answer her question, he just said her name, 'Gladys', with a hint of reproach, as she placed his hands within easy reach of the unknown. He could feel the heat of her, scorching his fingertips, coaxing them into life.

'Marry me,' she'd whispered in his ear, 'marry me,' and, as she pushed herself harder against him, as his fingers slipped inside her, he knew he was beaten. He was seventeen, had never even fully kissed a girl. She had hurled him rather than pushed him over the edge. He plummeted down into a world beyond reason and he suddenly wanted more. It was too late for Eric whose passions had got the better of him. It was time for Gladys to be the startled one as he had grasped her hand and pressed it into him. He moved up and down against her, pushing his own hand deeper and deeper with the same rhythm as his loins against her hand, and now he was the one who didn't want to stop and, as the blissful relief came, he shouted out, far louder than he had meant to, 'Marry me, Gladys!' Aware only of the blood pounding in his ears and his shortness of breath, he said again, 'Marry me,' only slightly quieter this time.

'I'll have to, Eric,' she had replied, with no hint of emotion, 'I've got no choice. I'm not a virgin now, you've ruined me for anyone else, you have...' She'd removed his hand with rather less grace than she had placed it there and, with the briskness he was more used to, brushed her skirt down and back into place. 'Meet me at the town hall tomorrow at half past twelve and bring your call-up papers with you. We'll both go in our breaks and then we can be married on special licence.' And just before she turned in through the gate she said, 'We'll move into the dairy with your da after; I'll pack tonight.' In a flash she was gone and Eric stood scratching his head and wondering what on earth had just happened.

When Eric finally returned from the front, Maggie was a widow and even more beautiful than she had been all those years ago. Gladys, never a good-looking woman, had travelled in an entirely opposite direction. Her lips had become as thin and as mean as her nature. Objecting to sex was something she became accomplished at once the first few years were over and no baby arrived. The message was given loud and clear: 'Get your hands off, enough of that messing about,' and he had long since given up trying.

Nothing he ever did made Gladys happy. Some men managed it with their wives, but not he. If only that night in the entry long ago had never happened. He would have returned home a single man, the Widow Trott would have been available and, who knows, he might have stood a chance of happiness.

'She landed on her feet that one,' Gladys had once said to him referring to Maggie. 'Married, widowed and she only goes and inherits from his mam and dad and she got the widow's pension. Won't ever have to work, can afford her rent without lifting a finger. No wonder she hasn't remarried. She doesn't need to. Didn't get herself lumped for life like I did.'

Those words rang in Eric's ears day and night. Gladys would rather he had not returned from the war, would have preferred a widow's pension. And when he and Daisy Bell were making their way home to the dairy along the Dock Road one mid-morning, he suddenly heard those words as clear as the mare's shoes beating out her rhythm on the cobbled road, she wanted you dead, she wanted you dead, she wanted you dead.

It was that day, those words, that made him realise for the very first time there was nothing worth fighting for...

Chapter Seventeen

Mary was lost for words as she stared in the mirror; she had chosen the boldest cut and an urchin stared back at her. Her eyes were wide, her cheekbones high and she was all but unrecognisable.

'I love that!' Mary finally said as she touched her hair. 'My da will too. I'm not sure what Ma is going to say – but it doesn't really matter as long as Jimmy notices me, that's all I want.'

Cindy grinned. She was more than happy with her work and it had transformed Mary. 'Leave your mam to me, Mary. Jimmy… now that's a bit more difficult. You do look irresistible. But Alice is right – don't you go chasing him, don't ever do that. And she is right on the other thing, Mary; this time next year when you're sat in this chair having a trim and I say to you, "Remember that crush you had on Jimmy O'Prey?" Do you know what you will say to me?' Mary shook her head, her newly revealed eyes open wide. 'You'll say to me, "That soft lad? I don't think so!"'

Mary shook her head, but she couldn't resist laughing, not something she often did. Alice and Cindy were wrong and she would show them; she loved Jimmy O'Prey and she knew, once he saw her again, it would be just as it had been before he went down.

Cindy was brushing up and Mary said, 'Here's my money.' She held out the note and a few coins. Cindy waved her hand away.

'No, I'm not going to take it, Mary. You go and spend it on some make-up in town. If Alice is going to give you some nice clothes, well, it goes to say, doesn't it, you need a bit of tutty, too.'

Mary stepped forward and took the brush from Cindy's hand. 'Then let me,' she said. 'Honestly, I'm used to clearing up.'

Cindy allowed her to take the brush. 'Go on, then, I won't refuse a bit of help, and I'll finish the sinks.' As she was doing so, she looked at Mary – and an idea lit a light bulb above her head.

As Mary made her way out of the parade, she stared into every shop window she passed to admire her hair. It wasn't just a haircut – it had made her feel six feet tall, beautiful, grown-up and it had put wings on her heels. She would knock on at the Deanes' and thank Alice and maybe Alice would have time to show her the clothes. Her heart felt light; she had not only enjoyed the haircut, but Cindy had also spoken to her as though she were her equal – and no one spoke to Mary like that. She was always there to do something for someone else. And she had loved Cindy's shop, a microcosm of pink and whiteness, of scents and potions, a little world all of its own in the middle of the bleakness that was the docks and rows of terrace houses.

She heard voices ahead of her outside the betting shop, among them one she recognised. She looked, and her heart beat as fast as a train because Jimmy was standing with a group of young men and two girls in the doorway.

'Come on, lads, I'm closing now; you've got your winnings so have a good night,' said the man who ran the shop as he locked the door. The group began to walk towards her with Jimmy in front. This was her moment! Now he would see her… He was talking to the man next to him but, as he came alongside and looked straight at her, his name stuck in her throat. Jimmy's brow furrowed; he thought for a second and then recognised her just as one of the girls ran alongside him and linked her arm through his.

'Are you going to spend your winnings on me now, Jimmy?' she asked.

With a sheepish grimace towards Mary, Jimmy raised the peak of his cap before turning to the girl on his arm and kissing her full on the lips then saying loudly, so that Mary heard every word, 'You're my girl, aren't you? Of course I am.'

Chapter Eighteen

Peggy delivered her baby in seven minutes and, throughout the process, she called for the only women in her life who had ever cared for her or shown her any love: her mother first, her grandmother who had raised her in her early years in Ireland, then Maura and finally, in a cry of desperation, her husband.

'Paddy, Paddy, come home!' she gasped as the rising moonlight lit the dark cobbled yard. The stale air of the outhouse, disturbed and shaken by her panting and anguished gasps, felt cold on her hot skin, as violent tremors racked her body, but she felt no pain, just a burning urgency to be somewhere safe.

'Mam, Mam, Nan,' she gasped but there was no response from her long-dead relatives. No matter how much they had loved her in life, they were of no use in death. Peggy felt their presence in her heart, thought she saw Kitty as a cool hand passed across her burning brow, but there was no one there, no hand to grasp onto, no one to hold her upright, no Maura whispering, 'Hang on, Peggy, we're almost there.'

Putting her hands out to support herself on the cold brick walls which were damp, even in summer, she looked upwards and saw the stars through the missing tile on the roof. As a contraction subsided, an icy coldness ran like a glaze from her head downwards and needles of pain began to penetrate the palms of her hands as she pushed harder against the wall to keep herself from sliding down onto the sodden, earthy floor. Outside, cats howled and fought for scraps in the entry as bin lids lifted and crashed down again. It was that time of the evening in stable homes where routine begat comfort and order.

A dog barked in a yard in one of the houses further down Nelson Street and Peggy held her breath as footsteps scuttled down the entry towards the house.

'Paddy,' she gasped. 'Paddy, is that you?'

The footsteps slowed and then stopped. 'Peggy?' a voice called out. 'It's Mary, are you all right?'

Oh, thank God, help was here! For the briefest moment Peggy's heart soared with relief then she recognised the voice and her hopes were dashed as fast as they had risen. It was Deirdre's daughter, Mary. Deirdre, the last person Peggy would want to see the dilemma she was in – her children without shoes, the disorganised mess in the kitchen and the mantelshelf bare, her pride and joy, her mother's clock, gone. She would judge the lack of food on the press, the missing blankets and cutlery. And when this baby came there was no coal to heat water, no clean towels to wrap it in. Help was on the other side of the gate, but it was help neither her pride nor self-respect would allow her to take.

With every ounce of strength and willpower she had, Peggy held her breath, resisted the urge to pant. She stood stock-still until the footsteps continued on their journey and the silence surged softly back. Peggy was trapped in a nightmare and her mind began to wander and dart about.

'No, no, no! Please no,' she sobbed as tears ran down her face – and suddenly she was no longer in the out-house. She was up in her bedroom, with the fire lit and Maura sitting on the end of her bed with little Paddy in her arms.

'Your firstborn a boy, isn't that marvellous?' said Maura. 'And would you look at that head of hair! Sure, he's nothing like his father.'

And they had both laughed as the midwife went about her business, making Peggy comfortable. A candle burnt on the windowsill, to let the street know little Paddy had arrived, one for a boy, two for a girl.

'Maura,' Peggy gasped, 'Maura!'

Maura had sent for the midwife with every one of Peggy's deliveries and Peggy had run to fetch the midwife for Maura. On occasion, the midwife busy elsewhere, they were the only two there, in that special hour when the smell of a newborn and new love filled the room, often in the early hours when all the cleaning up was done, the baby on the breast or lying in a blanket-lined drawer. Then, the fire lit and tea in hand, they talked of their hopes and dreams for the new life they had brought into the world...

Scamp scraped his paw at the outhouse door and whined and Peggy, dragged back into the moment, just at the point that her body could hold on no longer, reached down, and caught her baby in her hands and then fell backwards onto the wooden plank seat, wondering and amazed that her child was the longed-for daughter at last. She knew to wait; she had birthed seven children. The great contraction was to come when she would deliver the placenta and she knew it would come in its own time, just as her daughter had. She reached up for the grubby ribbon tied around the neck of her blouse, yanked it out and, using her teeth, ripped it in half to tie the umbilical cord. Then she took a wire curler out of her apron pocket and using that and her teeth, separated her daughter from the placenta.

Sighing loudly and spitting, Peggy pulled her uncomplaining bundle up onto her chest and wrapped her cardigan around her, holding her against her as she rocked. Her eyes were wild, her face flushed and she felt a huge sense of relief and panic, all at the same time.

'The bailiffs are coming,' she whispered into the side of her daughter's face. 'I prayed for you, I wanted you,

I've asked and asked the Holy Mother to send you, but you've come too late; they will take you off me now, they won't let me keep you. I can't let that happen, I can't.'

Her baby snuffled and Peggy, holding her away from her, looked down into her face She was struggling to breathe and so Peggy sucked the mucous from her nose and her airways and spat it onto the floor. Her daughter gasped, her first full breath, opened her eyes, and looked straight into Peggy's own, which were bright with tears.

'I'm sorry,' she said. 'I can't keep you, you can't stay here for there won't be a here; we will be out on the street.'

Mary had almost reached her back gate. Her thoughts, initially troubled by the sight of Jimmy with another girl on his arm, had turned to relief in the blink of an eye. She had expected to feel devastated, but between Cindy's proposition as they left the salon together and her own transformation, she felt as though she were standing at the crossroads of her life and for once the choice was hers to make.

Cindy had said, 'You know, Mary, I often wonder what will happen to the salon if I get married and have a baby. Reg isn't going to wait much longer for me because I'm a stroppy mare and he puts up with a lot!' She'd grinned down at Mary. 'Look, what I'm saying is, I could do with training up someone to take over from me and I like you, Mary; I think I could trust you, so, if you fancied a change from scrubbing floors and washing dishes…? I liked the way you chose your style; you have a boldness and you remind me of myself when I was younger. Alice was right, Mary, choose your own destiny. And honestly, it doesn't have to be one of misery and nappy buckets, not until you are really ready for it, anyway.'

Mary's mouth had opened and closed. Cindy had laughed. 'You don't have to answer me now. Off you go before I have your mam down here wanting to know where you are. I know you help a lot at home, everyone knows that, and I'll tell you what: whoever does run this place for me, will get the flat upstairs because I'll be moving into Reg's house.' Cindy grinned. 'Oh Mary, if you could only see your face. Go home, think about it and come and see me when you're ready, but honestly, I think me and you would make a great team. And remember, the only way to shape your own destiny is to control it. It's your life, no one else's.'

With a smile on her face and her eyes lit with excitement, Mary had left Cindy, full of anticipation for all that could lie before her. And then she'd passed Jimmy outside the betting shop. Seeing him kiss the girl full on the lips, in the same way he'd kissed her, had pierced her feelings like a pin in a bubble and she'd gasped; she had just told Cindy she loved him with all her heart, said she knew he was just scared of her mam and da, that was why he hadn't come to see her. But that was no longer true. She'd turned and watched the group as they walked away, Jimmy with his arm around the girl, and at that moment it dawned on her that she'd been set free. She'd lived a year in madness, waiting and hoping and dreaming of Jimmy and yet, here he was, and she couldn't believe that she had been so stupid, so willing to hitch herself to a cartload of strife. To think of walking in her mother's footsteps and hope and pray that her firstborn would be a girl in order to lighten the load as the years progressed. Why would she wish her misery on another?

As she made her way back to Nelson Street, Mary had felt the thrill of a different life opening before her. Cindy's salon. Cindy's salon. She would be exchanging one bleach for another, boredom for company, and soap-suds for sophistication – but, most of all, chores for creativity. She saw Eric the milkman running across the road towards the Anchor and he did a double take and then raised his hand towards her in greeting.

'Lovely hair, Mary! Did Cindy do that?'

'She did, Eric,' she shouted back and then she amazed even herself as she called out to him, 'Do you like it?'

'I do indeed. You look thoroughly modern, Mary, absolutely gorgeous,' he called as he passed her.

'Thank you, Eric,' she responded as her heart swelled. Never in her entire life had anyone before called her gorgeous. 'You have a good evening, Eric,' she called and almost laughed out loud as she thought: who has

Cindy turned you into? She almost floated home, until she reached the back gate of the Nolans' and thought she heard someone call out. She stood and listened, called, 'Peggy? It's Mary, are you all right?' but there was no reply and, deciding it must have been a cat, she walked on.

As she approached her own gate, her footsteps slowed as she recognised a figure waiting in the shadows; Jimmy. She frowned. It couldn't be Jimmy – she had just seen him heading off towards the Anchor. As she drew closer she realised it was his twin, Callum. The way he carried himself, the manner in which he hung his head, was one of shyness and reticence, totally different to his brother who walked like he owned the four streets. She stood still, afraid to approach, knowing it was herself that Callum was waiting to see but she had no idea why. Callum sensed her hesitation and moving away from the wall, walked towards her.

'Mary, I thought it wasn't you for a moment; I thought the light was playing tricks, but it *is* you.' He looked sheepish, glancing down at his boots.

'Was it me you were wanting?' she asked, her heart racing. 'I've seen Jimmy; I mean, I just saw him down on the parade, with a girl.'

Callum grimaced. 'Ah, I wanted to see you first, to warn you. That was Franny; she lives down the Dock Road. I didn't want you to see for yourself and as soon as I knew they were going to the Anchor...' His voice trailed away, and then he looked up at her. 'I think he treated you badly and I wanted to warn you, that's all.'

'Oh, I don't want to see Jimmy at all.'

Callum was taken aback by Mary's answer. He had not been able to get the look on her face when she had seen them on the bus platform out of his mind. It had not been him she was looking at, it had definitely been Jimmy.

'I don't want to see Jimmy.' She said it again, just so that he was sure.

Callum looked up and straight into her eyes; her words had lit a flame in his heart.

'Mary, your hair looks lovely.'

Mary blinked and smiled. Cindy had said that and Eric and now Callum, the third person to see her, had said it too.

'It's so modern.'

She felt dizzy. It was as though, when her hair was swept away from the salon floor, so was the old Mary too. She made to speak but was stuck for words. No one ever told Mary that she looked lovely and it was all becoming too much too fast. She had been shown a new life, fallen out of love and told she looked lovely for the first time ever and all in the space of half an hour.

Callum could see she was confused and knowing it was now or never, he tried again. 'Mary, would you give me a chance? I am not my brother... Would you let me take you to the picture house in town?'

Mary clasped her hands together. 'The picture house? I-I'd love to,' she said.

'Saturday night?' Callum asked. Mary nodded her head and it felt very much lighter and a bit odd to her. 'Shall I ask Eugene if I can take you?'

Mary thought about that for longer than she would have done only hours previously. What would Eugene say? Well, there was a great deal she would have to tell Eugene herself over the coming weeks, she was sure of that. Jutting her chin and straightening her back she said, 'No, *I* will do that.'

Callum raised his eyebrows; he wanted to do things properly. 'Are you sure?'

She wasted no time in replying. 'I am, I'll speak to him first, before Mam.'

In that moment Mary made a decision: she wouldn't ask Deirdre, she would *tell* her she was going to the picture house with Callum and that he was calling for her – and why not, hadn't she said herself that at least he worked down on the docks? She would also tell her that she was going to work for Cindy. She wouldn't mention the flat, or that Cindy was thinking of marrying and having a baby of her own, and she wouldn't let Malcolm down, she would give him good notice. Cindy's words came into her mind, '… *the only way to shape your own destiny is to control it.*'

Mary smiled at Callum; there was something about his self-effacing manner that appealed to her.

'I'll knock on for you then?'

Jimmy had never taken her anywhere. Had never knocked on for her or spoken to her with thoughtful care and consideration in the way Callum was now.

'I'd like that, Callum, thank you.'

Not knowing what to say next, they stood and smiled at each other and Callum felt his heart race. He wanted to talk more, ask her more, but he hesitated. *Steady does it*, was the thought that entered his mind and he knew, instinctively, it was the right thing to do. Mary was not like the other girls on the four streets, she wasn't cheeky and confident. He remembered her playing in the street, always the one looking after her younger brothers, not running off with the other girls to the wasteland. He had felt sorry for her then, had hated Jimmy for the way he treated her, but not now. Admiration, respect for her dignity and something he was still unsure of, was what he felt now.

'Saturday, then.'

Mary nodded her head, not trusting herself to speak because she felt as though if she and Callum began a conversation, it would not end, but go on forever, and she knew that this was the beginning, that it would be Callum for always and, not having the words, she hoped that her smile, the pleasure in her face, told him all he needed to know.

★

Peggy had managed to get upstairs with the baby unremarked, and now she sat on the edge of the bed and wailed in despair; she had no idea what to do. She looked into the face of the daughter she had prayed for with every pregnancy, had hoped and longed for over the years, and the baby's perfect little face looked back up at her.

'Look at you, I've nothing for you but the street, for they'll take you off me when we get turned out.'

The tears poured down her face as she held the baby to her cheek and drew in the smell of her. How could life change so fast? This time last year the arrival of this baby would have made her the centre of attention in the street, the first girl after seven boys. Presents would have arrived through the door, home-made matinee coats, a plate of biscuits, a cake, a trail of women with their own babies would have walked in and out of the kitchen, to talk to her as she lay on the settle that would have been dragged in from Maura's. They would have brought shovels of coal to tip in the bucket, a posy of flowers from the greengrocer's to put in a jam jar on the windowsill; the boys would have gone to Kathleen's and Maura's to be fed and washed and return home to sleep.

The house would have been scrubbed from top to bottom by an army of women and Mrs Keating would have brought her a delicious lunch in every day. Twice a day, someone would have called in for her nappy bucket, replacing it with a clean one, and whoever was washing would have collected Peggy's too. In the afternoons, she would have lain there, her precious daughter on her chest, wallowing in the bliss, the peace, the cleanliness, the daily grind and responsibility of a family assumed by others, because on the four streets the arrival of a new baby was an occasion, a celebration.

She would have rejoiced in the silence, the lack of pressure to get up and carry out one of a never-ending list of chores. She would have listened to her mother's ticking clock, inhaled the delicious stew someone would have put on the range. Because that was what having a baby in the four streets was like. The women had nothing, but together they could create their own luxury. Her daughter would have been passed from mother to mother to be admired, or nappy changed and their own babes would have been laid on the bed with Peggy whilst they too met the new arrival.

Oh, it was not supposed to be like this! No child on the four streets ever came into the world like this, into this hopelessness, alone in the outhouse, not into this despair.

'I can't do this to you, I can't face it,' Peggy sobbed, knowing there was only one way out from this, only one escape. She felt the edges of her mind blur and, laying the naked baby on the bed, rose and walked over to the press and removed a small drawer from the top. It contained very little: the boys' christening gown and the odd undergarment that she owned. She took out the only fresh clothes she had for herself and changed and then wondered what was the point. She took an old nappy from the drawer and ripped it apart. Bending down, she placed it into the clean knickers between her legs, sobbing for the past and the future she could no longer have. She wrapped the other half around the baby and took out a grey and rough towel and wrapped it around her.

She picked up her baby, who lay uncomplaining, eyes wide, and smiled through her tears at the small folds of fat on her knees.

'I should call you biscuit,' she said. 'It's what you've been fed on, but someone else can do that now.'

Laying her daughter in the drawer she moved with extreme difficulty into the boys' room and pushed the drawer under the bed next to the cardboard box that little Paddy kept there. The boys were beginning to get restless downstairs, moving about. They would hear her, they could find her, and by the time that happened she would be gone. It hurt to walk and she felt light-headed, but with absolute clarity she knew what she had to do. They would all be better off without her. She was not good enough to be their mother, could not face the shame of the bailiffs and everyone knowing what an awful failure of a woman she was in the four streets full of perfect, uncomplaining women, whose children never went without a meal. Women who, even in hard times and short work, did not have to pawn their children's shoes and their mother's clock.

At first, the boys didn't notice her walk into the kitchen. She put her arms in her coat and, removing the money that was left from what the pawnbroker had given her, laid it down on the press. And then little Paddy saw her.

'Mam? Where are you going now? You haven't had your chips, I kept them there.' He pointed to the draining board. Peggy drew on every ounce of reserve she had to carry her through the next sixty seconds. She had no idea what to answer and then it came to her.

'I'm off to Shelagh's to take the pram I borrowed back,' she said. 'Look after your brothers for me, Paddy, be a good boy, they need you.' She stood and stared at her children and a frown crossed little Paddy's face; there was something about her tone, her manner, that sent a frisson of fear running across his scalp.

'Mam?' he said, but she turned her back on him, opened the back door and walked out of the house.

Chapter Nineteen

Shelagh was in the middle of the same end-of-day chores as every other woman in every kitchen on the street. The large enamel bowl in her sink was filled with hot soapy water as the scouse pan soaked on the wooden draining board next to it, ready for a scouring with wire wool and soap. In the scullery, one by one her children had washed their knees, hands and faces and now sat on the floor in front of the fire, listening to the radio. The kettle had been refilled for the third time in a row and was coming back up to the boil as the day's washing, draped across a wooden clothes horse, stood open before the fire, absorbing the heat and drying the washing which had been brought in from the line; above her head the pulley was filled with lines of steaming terry towelling nappies.

Shelagh leant her back against the draining board and, slipping her hands into her front apron pocket, sighed, wondering would Seamus be back in time to help her with the big pan. She hated the wire wool she used to clean it, which dug into her red and cracked hands like shards of glass and made her cry out in pain. The only two comfortable chairs they owned were filled with children and even though the veins in her legs pulsated and throbbed she knew that there was no point in shooing them off and sitting down herself, because within seconds she would need to be back up again for one thing or another. A woman's work was never done.

Little Paddy didn't knock before he entered Shelagh's kitchen; knocking was unheard of in the four streets. Earlier that morning, she had baked biscuits and there had been over thirty children in her backyard with hands open and little Paddy and Nellie had helped Shelagh to dish them out.

'Can I have two please, Shelagh?' Malachi had shouted out across the assembled heads. 'If I can, I'll let your Anthony be in charge of the ball all day.'

Shelagh had shaken her head. 'If I tell your mam what you've just said, Malachi, she wouldn't believe me. That's called blackmail and you'll end up like Jimmy O'Prey, you will, in and out of the nick.'

Malachi had scowled. 'And she won't believe *you*, Shelagh, that's why I said it,' he said, the smile on his face not quite reaching his eyes.

Little Paddy and Nellie had overheard him and Nellie looked so upset at his cheekiness that little Paddy had felt the need to intervene.

'You don't deserve any at all, Malachi,' little Paddy

had said, but the other boy had scowled and then delivered a quick kick to little Paddy's shin.

'You're barred from the game,' Malachi had snarled at little Paddy, who then knew there was no point in him heading back to the bombed-out wasteland that day.

'Paddy, what are you doing here at this time?' said Shelagh as little Paddy closed the door behind him. 'Has your mam sent you to scrub my big pan for me?' Shelagh smiled down at him, but the smile quickly left her face when she saw the worry etched across his, the tightness of the pale skin across his cheekbones, his eyes wide and concerned.

'Shelagh, have you seen me mam? She went out ages ago; she said she was going to yours to bring the pram back and she hasn't come home.'

Shelagh took the cigarettes out of her apron pocket and lit one. 'Paddy, I haven't.' She blew her smoke high into the air. 'But surely you must have misheard her? There's a bingo on down at St Cuthbert's tonight. I bet she's gone there, eh? Was her hair done, love?'

Little Paddy shook his head; he felt very confused and very scared.

'When your mam borrowed my pram earlier, she didn't say what she wanted it for and I didn't ask; I just said, as long as it's not for coal, Peg, because our baby's got to sleep in that pram tonight, and I could do with it back soon. Do you know what she wanted it for?'

Little Paddy didn't want to betray his mother or lie to Shelagh and so he shook his head again.

'Tell you what, let's see if your mam's put the pram back.' Shelagh opened the back door, little Paddy following her, and they went into the wash house. Blocking the path to the copper boiler, as it usually was, was Shelagh's pram. 'There you go, she's brought it back and taken off to the bingo, so stop your worrying, Paddy. Honest to God, sometimes you look as though you're carrying the weight of the world around on your shoulders. Go back home, go on; she'll be running back up your path with her winnings soon, you mark my words.'

Little Paddy felt relieved; his mam hadn't lied – the pram was returned.

'Don't suppose you want to scrub my pan for me, do you? I can't with these hands, they'll be bleeding all night if I do.'

He looked towards the gate and thought of his brothers. 'You look after your brothers, Paddy,' his mam had said. But the pan would take him just five minutes. He pulled up his sleeves. 'Come on then, Shelagh, I'm as strong as Popeye, I am,' and they both laughed, his worries gone, as they walked back into Shelagh's kitchen.

Alice tiptoed into the kitchen, having settled Joseph for the night and picked up the tea towel to dry the big scouse pan Kathleen had just scrubbed. Kathleen was cleaning down the range, Jerry was at the table, about to finish his supper and head over to the Anchor and Nellie was reading in the armchair next to the fire. Kathleen couldn't have been happier to hear the news from Jerry that the *Morry* had berthed.

'When will you know what she's carrying?' Kathleen had asked her son.

'I'll find out tonight, Mam. My guess is that Captain Conor will do what he always does, put his crew in the Seaman's Stop with Malcolm, pop in to see his mam, Ena, throw his kitbag in her hallway and head down to the Anchor looking for Tommy and me to give us the news. So I'm away to see a man about a dog as soon as I've finished this, and give him the news that Tommy has gone and 'tis me and Seamus now,' said Jerry as he blew on a steaming hot spoonful of food. 'Seamus is already in the Anchor, and big Paddy and Eugene. High on the news, they were, and desperate for a pint of the Guinness to celebrate.'

Kathleen tutted. 'How does Paddy afford the Guinness? He barely works. I don't know how Peggy is managing. It would be better if he didn't work at all, at least then she would get some help from the welfare. As it is, they exist on starvation money, neither one thing nor the other.'

Jerry lifted the spoon filled with potatoes and scrag-end of lamb to his mouth. 'I've had him in three days this week, Mam. I've told him, if there's a haul from the *Morry*, there's nothing for him if he doesn't pull his weight and work a full week. I'm not having part timers if I take over as gaffer.'

Kathleen was not impressed. 'Three days this week, Jerry, one day last week – a family can't survive on that. You keep on at him. Poor Peggy, she has one heavy cross to bear.'

Jerry's spoon scraped against the plate as he made short work of his supper, eager to leave and get down to the Anchor. 'Paddy loves his rum, and he knows the *Morry* is always good for it. Alice, don't wait up for me.'

Alice looked none too pleased at this announcement and Jerry knew it as he skipped round the table and hugged his wife, who was not a fan of outward displays of affection.

'Get off,' she said as she shrugged his arm away.

'No, I won't,' said Jerry, hugging her tighter against his chest, making Nellie giggle. Jerry knew just how to wrap Alice around his little finger. 'Oh, Alice, go on, it's not drinking I'm doing, it's work. You are the best wife in the whole world and if it was anyone but you, I wouldn't bother. And besides, if I don't go, who else is going to make sure we get the haul up the steps, eh?'

'Oh, go on, Jerry, get out of here and out of our way; we know what you're like! Just don't come back without good news about the *Morry* and the carnival,' said Alice as she pushed him away. 'Your mam and I have only gone and got ourselves landed with the bunting, as well as decorating the float and the cake stall, so your mam's reading the riot act in this kitchen tomorrow and getting everyone moving.'

Kathleen wiped her brow with the tea towel. 'Honestly, I've such a funny feeling today, like something is out of sorts. I've felt it in my waters since mass and I saw it in Shelagh's tea leaves when I read them earlier. I didn't say anything to Shelagh, mind, only that she would be pushing another baby around soon, her and Seamus. God, they have enough already, will they just stop the shenanigans? I said to her, just cross your legs and tell him to sort himself out. Peggy did the same, mind; it didn't bring her much luck, God love her, but at least it stopped her having another baby.'

'Mam, you never did!' The anguished cry of her daughter-in-law filled the room. 'I never heard you say that.'

Alice, the product of a brutally strict upbringing would never discuss anything remotely private, with anyone. The only Protestant to live on the four streets, she was grateful not to be a Catholic, for confession would have presented Alice with a difficult challenge. Her first response to any priest asking her if she had sinned would have been to ask him what business was it of his?

Kathleen, with her back to Alice, raised her eyebrows, pursed her lips and pointedly rolled her eyes to Jerry, nodding her head in the direction of Alice, a gesture Jerry chose to ignore as he glanced over to the fireside chair to see if Nellie had heard. As always, Nellie was sitting forward in the chair, elbows resting on the wooden arms, her fingers in her ears, absorbed in her book. An only child for a long while before Joseph arrived, with a lively imagination, Nellie lived her life vicariously through the characters in her books.

Jerry sat back down as Kathleen placed a bowl of bread-and-butter pudding covered in hot, thick, yellow custard down on the table and Kathleen bent her head into his line of vision, silently mouthing something at him in an exaggerated manner, her lips pursing and stretching. He looked down at his plate. These conversations always went the same way: Jerry told Kathleen he couldn't hear what she was saying and to speak up, quickly followed by Alice chirping in with, 'She can't, Jerry, she's talking about me. If she speaks up, I'll know what it is she's saying, won't I, Jerry? And I'm not supposed to, am I, Kathleen?'

And that would be it – by trying to avoid the very situation he did not want to be involved in, he'd find himself slap bang in the middle of an almighty row between the two women of the house.

Kathleen gave up trying to get Jerry on side and answered Alice instead.

'What in God's name is wrong with you? Do you think the stork has a particular fancy for the four streets, given how many babies are dropped here? Do you think it favours Shelagh and Seamus because it gets a cup of tea and a couple of lemon puffs for its trouble? There's no shame in what I said. Seamus and Shelagh make their babies the same way as everyone else and she's getting too old to be carrying on so they need to cut it out. It's only for Shelagh's own good. I don't care what they get up to, but they have more than enough mouths to feed. Jerry, you agree with me, don't you?'

Jerry played it safe. 'Mam, don't involve me. What do I know?'

Kathleen huffed and gave her son a look that had turned his blood cold when he was just a boy. She continued, unperturbed, 'Anyway, before I was so rudely interrupted, Alice...'

Now it was Alice's turn to roll her eyes towards Jerry, who, sensing an escalation in the banter between the two women, glanced at the clock to see how long it was until he would be able to escape. There was a slap of card on paper as Nellie slammed her book shut and, looking up, grinned at her da. They were very much on each other's side, himself and the child he shared with his first wife, Bernadette, who had died shortly after giving birth to Nellie.

Kathleen carried on undeterred, 'I definitely saw it in there, in Shelagh's leaves, a very dark cloud, right in the middle of the bottom of the teacup. And if I see it, I say it. That's why the women from around here come to me and not Mrs King on Upper Parliament Street. I give them the facts, facts that are true,' she finished with a flourish as she removed her handkerchief from her apron pocket and began to wipe furiously at her steamed-up glasses.

'Isn't that the whole point of a fact, that it's true?' said Alice with more than a hint of sarcasm.

But Kathleen was on one of her rants and no longer in the mood for interruptions. 'Be quiet, Alice. I don't see that cloud very often, so I don't.' She pushed her spectacles back up her nose and peered down at Jerry as she walked closer to him, her brow furrowed. Round and matronly, Irish eyes often twinkling, tonight, Kathleen looked concerned.

'Oh, Mam, don't be doing that to me,' said Jerry, digging into his pudding. 'Could you take a look into the leaves and tell me about the ship that's berthed down on the docks that everyone seems to be so secretive about? No one batted an eyelid tonight at Captain Conor's ship docking – the police were marking the one already in but it hasn't yet unloaded and nor do we know when it will be. It's very odd.'

Kathleen leant towards her son. 'I saw that ship and the police at the bottom. I said to you, didn't I, Alice, we've not seen that one here before.'

They all stopped as they heard the click of the back-yard gate. Seconds later little Paddy stood framed in the doorway.

'Paddy, what are you doing here?' asked Jerry. 'Your da is in the pub with Seamus and Eugene.' His immediate thought was that big Paddy had failed to tell Peggy where he was going and little Paddy was looking for him.

'Kathleen, have you seen our mam?' Little Paddy asked Kathleen. 'Only she went out ages ago to take Shelagh's pram back and she hasn't come home yet. Shelagh says she will have gone to the bingo, but I don't think she has.'

Kathleen looked at little Paddy as though he had grown two heads. 'What are you talking about, gone to the bingo on her own? Never. I would have known about it if she had. Had she done her hair?'

Little Paddy shook his head.

'Where are the kids?' asked Kathleen. 'Are they at home?'

Little Paddy lowered his head. 'They are, but they have no shoes so they can't go anywhere.'

Kathleen thought little Paddy looked extraordinarily pale, and in a kind voice asked him, 'Paddy, have you had your tea? Have you had anything today?'

His voice perked up. 'We had a biscuit from Shelagh and Mam brought us chips and saveloys before she went out.'

'What, for all of you?' Then to Jerry Kathleen said, 'She borrowed one and six from me to buy in for the kids' tea and that lot would have cost at least five shillings for all of them. Paddy, why have the kids got no shoes? Sure, they are running around in the finest shoes they ever owned that Maura bought for you all?'

The boy said nothing. He could not say the words,

'She took them to the pawnshop.' He was old enough to know the meaning, to feel the shame his mother felt and hated himself for feeling relieved that he was still wearing his.

'Where's Scamp?' asked Peggy. 'Is he with her? Sometimes he follows her when she goes out.'

He shook his head. Scamp had been lying by the side of his bed when he left, refusing to move, and little Paddy knew why. He and Max had become great friends and Scamp was probably impatient for Paddy to get him out of his box.

Jerry said to his mother, 'Try the bingo, Mam.' The tone of his voice was enough. Jerry didn't want any more to be said in front of little Paddy or Nellie, and the look he gave Alice said as much. 'Tell the kids Nana Kathleen is on her way, little Paddy.'

The boy retreated from the kitchen but as he reached the door, he turned and ran back in. 'Kathleen, can I have those carrot tops and the cabbage scraps please?' He pointed to the vegetable scrapings on the newspaper.

Kathleen gave him a half-smile. 'Have you still got that pet rat in your pocket no one knows about?' Little Paddy's eyes widened in alarm. 'Don't worry, lad, I won't tell anyone.'

'How did you know?'

'It was the way he nibbled your ear and looked very comfortable indeed on your shoulder the other day – it was almost as if he lived there. Go on, away, take these with you.' Kathleen rolled the paper up and gave little Paddy the parcel. 'I'll be twenty minutes because I'll call into St Cuthbert's on my way. Tell the kids Nana Kathleen is bringing them some sweets from Simpson's and I want washed knees, hands and faces and everyone clean and ready for bed by the time I get there. If any one of them plays up, I'll give their sweets to whoever was the best-behaved – and tell them I mean that.'

The back door slammed shut and Kathleen watched little Paddy run down the path. Peggy must have pawned the shoes – and there was not a woman she knew who wouldn't sell herself before she would be forced to do that. Things were far worse than she'd thought.

Jerry ran his hand through his hair. 'Those poor kids. Where do you think Peggy is, Mam? And the kids' shoes...? Holy smoke!'

Kathleen had taken a jar down off the press and was counting money out of it onto the kitchen table. It was the jar full of sixpences, the price she charged for reading people's tea leaves, and she made almost as much as Jerry did from it. Added to that, she received regular money from Liam and Maeve and the farm in Ireland, which was still Kathleen's in name. With only Nellie and Joseph to feed, the Deanes were one of the better-off families on the four streets.

'I'm guessing Peggy *has* gone down to the bingo. And something is seriously wrong – where the hell did she get the money from for chips and saveloys? I told you, didn't I, that something wasn't right because I saw it in the leaves.'

Jerry was back at the door. 'Mammy, go and see Sister Evangelista – she will know what to do about Peggy, don't you take it all on your shoulders.'

Kathleen shook her head. 'I daren't do that, Jerry. For all Peggy's failings, she loves her kids and she's terrified the welfare will take them off her. I can't be the one responsible for that happening. If the nuns are involved, it has to be Peggy's doing, not mine.' She took her coat down from the back of the door and slipped the coins into her pocket. 'You go to the Anchor and see if you can get that haul up the steps – we need something to put everyone in the mood for the carnival. Alice, can Nellie come with me?'

Nellie was instantly on her feet and at her grand-mother's side.

'Of course she can; I'll be here with Joseph. But Kathleen, as soon as you know where she is, let me know. I think you're rubbing off on me – I have a funny feeling too. I'll see you back here later. Go on, go.'

Jerry smiled at his mam and, as he did almost every day, he thought how lucky he was to have a mam like Kathleen. His household was as solid as a rock, built on his mother's common sense and good management. There was a time in his life, with his new baby in his arms and his wife dead, that he had wanted to die himself. And then, Kathleen arrived and there was no doubt she saved him. Jerry was well aware how easily life's events could drag you down and almost drown you. Things had even worked out with Alice, after the rockiest of starts.

'Everyone should have a mam like you,' he said to his mother, 'I don't know where Nellie and I would be if you hadn't come to live with us.'

Kathleen fastened her headscarf under her chin. 'One thing I have learnt in this life, Jerry, is that more often than not, when you reach rock bottom, even if no one knows you are there, someone steps out to give you a hand back up. I don't know how or why, some say it's the angels at work and I'm inclined to believe them myself, for I have no idea what it was that made me get on the boat and come to Liverpool, but I had a feeling, so I did, and I have that feeling again right now, only I can't fathom what it is or what I'm supposed to be doing at all.'

Jerry hugged his mam and kissed the top of her head. 'Mam, whatever it is, you will be wherever you are supposed to be – you always are.'

Kathleen pushed her son off. 'Go you, and come back here and tell me good news about Captain Conor. Alice, we'll be back in half an hour.'

Kathleen could move fast for a woman of her age and with her eyes to the floor, her arm linked through Nellie's, they left Nelson Street and headed towards St Cuthbert's Hall on the Dock Road where the bingo was held.

'Nana, look!' Nellie pulled on Kathleen's arm. 'Isn't that Peggy down there?'

Kathleen looked over the wall to where Nellie was pointing. Her eyesight wasn't good and she squinted to see where Nellie was pointing. 'That's the dock down there, Nellie, don't be ridiculous. Peggy will be at the bingo hoping to turn one and six into a quid.'

Nellie shook her head; she was sure it was Peggy. The woman's hair was not in curlers and she was talking to another woman, a woman Nellie had seen down there before. When she'd asked Jerry who she was, he had replied, 'A woman of the night, Nellie, and not someone you should ever speak to.'

Peggy and the woman were huddled together, talking at the back of the administration building, and Nellie kept looking backwards as she was swept along by Nana Kathleen. She had a funny feeling something was wrong and that woman down on the dockside – she was sure it was definitely Auntie Peggy.

Chapter Twenty

Maura and Tommy had never before made love in a bed that wasn't their own and she had found the experience both frightening and exciting all at the same time.

'I'm not sure if we can,' she had whispered, terrified of making a noise and trying to work her dates back in her mind. 'When am I due?'

Tommy, a man who always depended on his wife to ensure they did not make love on the days she was likely to be caught, for fear of another pregnancy, had thrown caution to the wind. 'I don't know and I don't care,' he had said as he pulled her towards him.

'Tommy, have you lost your senses? And you've left the light on; what are you thinking of?'

Maura had also only ever made love to her husband in the dark and the urgency of his need was confusing her. It felt as though she was in bed with another man.

'Maura, how did you feel when we were leaving Liverpool to move back to Ireland and start our great big adventure? When I made the biggest mistake of my life and bought us the Talk of the no feckin' Town? Were you happy? Was I happy?'

'I don't know, I'm not sure, there was so much to do, with the kids and everything...'

'Maura, if we had been doing the right thing, nothing would have mattered, so how did you feel? Think, remember!'

Maura had no idea what had just possessed her husband, a man of few words, to own up to a mistake. Usually he had to be worn down into submission first.

'Scared, I suppose,' she blurted out.

'Aye, me too. What do you feel like now? Tonight, here in this bed and breakfast?'

Maura's face broke into a tentative smile. 'Excited.'

Tommy threw his head back and laughed out loud. 'Yes, so do I. That's because we are going home. We should never have left. It was the money, it went to our heads.'

Maura pulled a face. 'Well, it won't now because there's hardly any left.'

And Tommy had almost told her his secret, the news it had half killed him to keep from her for days.

'Tell her now,' Liam had said to him as they shook hands.

'No,' Tommy was defiant, 'I'll tell her on the deck, as soon as I can see Liverpool,' and since that conversation, the secret had burnt in his mouth desperate to escape and each time he almost told her and didn't, he felt a sense of atonement for his mistakes of the past.

The only time Kitty was ever spoken of was late at night, in the dark, in bed but not tonight.

'Maura,' Tommy said, 'it's time to look to the future, for all of us – and I can't think of a better way to do that than with a new babby, can you?' He had pushed Maura's dark hair away from her face. 'Don't you be looking like that,' he said, noting the sadness that crossed her eyes. 'No one can ever replace our Kitty, but a new birth, that would be exciting for the others and especially for Angela. It might make her smile and you, you're not too old yet, missus.'

Maura had grinned. 'You have a nerve, you. If we weren't sleeping under someone else's roof, you wouldn't get away with that.'

Tommy had silenced her as his lips found hers and, as it had been throughout their married life, Maura was lost. Despite the fact that they had been together for all of the years they had, he could still make her insides flip over at his gentlest touch and that night, he was like a man possessed. Maura knew, as the first watery light of morning had slipped in though unfamiliar curtains, that she was with child...

'Mammy, are we nearly there?' asked Angela as she lifted her head from her father's chest and rubbed her sleepy eyes. They were in a taxi which Tommy had hailed at the Pier Head to transport them on the last leg of the journey home. The cobbles of the Dock Road rumbled beneath the tyres as the taxi jolted along past the tall red-brick warehouse buildings that towered above them.

'We are, Angela, can you smell the Mersey?' said Tommy. They had been on the road since before first light and they were all exhausted, but as the ferry had drawn closer to the shore and the lights of Liverpool sparkled before them, Maura had perked up.

'Would you look at that,' Maura had said to Tommy. 'The Liver Birds. Tommy, we're home!'

Her eyes had filled with tears at the sight of the three graces and the skyline of Liverpool that lay before them. Tommy had slipped his arm around her shoulder. 'We are, queen, and I never thought I'd say it, for I will always be an Irishman through and through, but Liverpool is where my kids belong and that is where my heart is. Fancy that! I call a country that produces wet potatoes, home.'

Maura felt the familiar grip of guilt tighten around her heart. 'What about the money, the inn, is it gone forever, do you think?'

Tommy had fixed his eyes on the shore. 'Maura, I have something to tell you. Liam bought it, not what we paid for it, but enough to make a difference to our fortunes and I ask you, what more do we need?'

Maura had pulled away from him. 'What? You sold it to Liam? For how much?'

Tommy couldn't help himself, a grin passed across his face and he picked up one of her hands and slipped it under his arm. 'Maura, we have almost five hundred pounds! I have a hundred in my pocket and four in the bank so we are going to be just fine.' Maura was speechless. 'I have just one condition, mind; I have eight of it for the season ticket for the football for the lads and myself – our Harry, he deserves that.'

'Five hundred pounds…' She let the words roll around her mouth. 'Five hundred pounds, Tommy, that's such a relief! Why didn't you tell me? I've been worried sick about whether or not you'd be taken on down at the docks or if we would have enough to manage until you got work.'

'Because I wanted to show you that I'm not the useless eejit you think I am, that's all.'

Maura squeezed her husband's hand. As the realisation sank in that all was not lost, Maura had felt a thrill of excitement run through her while the ship blew its horn to let Liverpool know they were approaching as the jetty came into sight.

'It's a good thing, Tommy, to know where we belong. It's good for the kids too. They know everyone on the four streets and everyone knows them; there's no one to judge them, everyone has the same. We all know what it's like to go without and kindness comes from that. It may have cost us to find it out, but at least now we know where we belong and isn't that a richness in itself? And to think, we have the five hundred pounds to add to it! I feel like the luckiest woman in the world.'

Tommy felt a lump in his throat. Any other woman would have made his life a misery for spending all they had on the Talk of the Town and only getting half of it back, but not his Maura, who always looked for the good in every situation.

Now, as the taxi passed by the shops on one side and the warehouses on the other, Maura's thoughts turned to more immediate problems.

'Tommy, I hope to God Kathleen is still up to get a drink for the kids. I'm gasping meself.'

Tommy nuzzled her neck. 'Mind if I nip down to the Anchor, queen? Let them all know I'm back like. Just for the one.'

Maura knew she could trust Tommy and that he would keep to his word, that it would be just for the one; nonetheless, her answer was unequivocal. She looked straight into his eyes and said, 'No, you flamin' can't. You can get this lot unloaded into the house and get the fire lit – we left coal in the hole, if it's still there – while I take the kids to Kathleen's.'

Tommy leant over and whispered, 'I'm not done with you yet, Mrs Doherty. Don't think you are off the hook tonight.'

Maura elbowed him in the ribs. 'Tommy, stop! Do you think I'm as big an eejit as you are?'

'Ah, go on, Maura, will you? Let me have one jar, for

I'm desperate to see Jer and it's darts night, so they will all be in there. Can't have the lads thinking I've snuck back like a thief in the night, can I? They'll think I have something to hide. Let me be the big man for just one night, buy everyone a pint. Besides, I need to know what ships are coming in, what work is on. No time to waste.'

Maura was losing patience with him. 'Something to hide? You have,' she said, and there was no mercy in her tone. 'Tell them about the monster, Cleary, how our Harry nearly died, and then there'll be no question why we've come back home. Or, if you like, tell them that it rained for six months and we've all grown a set of gills.' Her voice caught and she turned and looked out of the window, not wanting Angela to see the tears that had sprung into her eyes.

Tommy slipped his hand across her back and kissed her on the cheek. 'You're tired,' he said. 'Go on, Maura, just one pint and I'll give you a treat when I get back home.'

Maura squirmed away from him. 'Tommy, the kids! Do you have no shame? And have you not heard, big-man-buying-everyone-a-drink, a fool and his money are easily parted?' Tommy grinned and kissed her on the neck again. This time she elbowed him sharply in the ribs.

'Don't you dare try and get your own way! No, Tommy, you are not going to the pub. You've lived in one for the past six months, it won't hurt you to have a night off. Help me drop the kids at Kathleen's and Angela and Niamh can sleep in the bed with Nellie, the boys on the floor.'

They were both steeled for the fact that there would be no beds aired in their own house and that they would struggle to get warm for a couple of nights until the bricks of the house had warmed. It was months since the fire was lit and the house would be damp through.

Harry was the next to wake up and in an instant had his mother's attention. 'How are you feeling, little fella?' she asked him.

'Are we here?' He asked the same question they had all asked repeatedly since they had left the Talk of the Town.

Tommy ruffled his hair. 'We are, lad, look out of the window.'

Harry leant forward and rubbed the window with his jacket for a clearer view. 'Da! There's the docks and there's two ships in. Oh, I've never seen that one before, it has two funnels. I'm going to be a sailor, Mam, when I grow up,' he said to Maura.

'Oh no you are not, Harry, you are never going to be out of your mam's sight for that long, I can tell you.'

Tommy gently nudged Harry away from the window. 'I've no idea what that ship is,' he said, 'but Maura, Captain Conor's is next to it and you know what that means?'

'There's the Anchor, Da,' said Angela, and as they

coasted alongside the pub, someone walked out of the door, throwing a light out onto the yard in front.

Tommy rubbed his hands together; he hadn't felt happier since before Kitty had died. 'Aye, aye!' He leant closer to the window. 'Maggie Trott's walking into the Anchor with Cindy and Reg – things have changed around here, Maura, since we left.'

Maura sat bolt upright and pushed Angela out of the way. 'Mind, let me see,' she said as she peered through the window. 'It is, and she's wearing heels and where did she get that coat from? I have never seen Maggie in the pub ever!'

'Well, maybe she was just waiting for us to leave before she let her hair down. Turn right here, pal,' Tommy called to the taxi driver.

Maura's eyes never left Maggie Trott. 'She's been mourning her husband that long. I never thought I'd see her in the pub in a month of Sundays, maybe she has a new fella?'

'I've no idea, Maura, but I'd find out and come back and let you know if you let me go for a pint...' The taxi driver caught Maura's eye in the rear-view mirror; they all knew Maura would not be able to resist that line. 'I'll catch up on with what's what, all the gossip like, and I'll be back in no time to tell you it all. Go on, Maura, you know you'd be in there yourself to find out if it wasn't for the kids.'

Maura rolled her eyes. 'Oh, go on, you! Just get the

cases in, drop me and the kids at Kathleen's, and off you go.'

'I'll drop you back on my way down, pal,' the taxi driver said.

Tommy exclaimed, 'Would you mind? That would be just grand and save me the walk.'

And at that moment, Maura knew. 'Hang on a minute! The pair of you planned this, didn't you? Did he ask you to do that when he called you over at the Pier Head? Tommy Doherty, you think I came down with the last shower, don't you?'

She leant forward with her hand on the driver's seat as they pulled up outside 42 Nelson Street and he protested, none-too-convincingly, 'What, me? No, I know nothing! But welcome back home to Liverpool, everyone!'

Kathleen felt moved to tears and covered in shame when she walked into Peggy's house, carrying seven paper bags of Simpson's mixed sweets in her hand. Three of the children were sobbing and little Paddy was trying to placate them. The fire was out, the range was dead, it was dark and the house smelt of hopelessness and despair.

'Have you not switched the lights on, Paddy?' said Kathleen as she took in what was before her and sprang into action. 'Nellie, take the coal bucket and go down to the coal hole and see what you can find. If there's none, go to Shelagh and tell her I'll send little Paddy round with a bucketful from ours to replace it tomorrow.' Kathleen flicked the toggle on the switch, but there was no light.

'The meter ran out,' said little Paddy.

Kathleen opened her purse and gave him four six-pences. 'Top the meter up, Paddy,' she said and shouted after her granddaughter, 'Nellie, bring me some milk and tea and sugar from our house.' Then, as she placed the sweets on the table, she turned to the Nolan boys. 'Has everyone washed their hands like I asked?' The row of little boys nodded their heads, barely able to believe their eyes. 'Right then, here's your sweets.' The boys stopped their crying and, wide-eyed and excited, began to take their sweets from the table.

'Did you find Mam at St Cuthbert's?' asked little Paddy. 'Is she coming?'

'I did,' Kathleen lied. 'She just had a few more games to go and then she will be home, but I want this lot in bed by then.'

Half an hour later, Kathleen had a fire almost blazing, the sixpences were in the meter, the lights were on and Peggy's boys sat in a semi-circle in front of the fire, laughing and filling their faces with sweets, Nellie helping the youngest. Kathleen had a good poke about the kitchen. The bread crock was empty, the cold shelf was bare – there was not a scrap of food or a drop of milk to be had. Kathleen placed the milk Nellie had returned with on the cold shelf then opened each of the drawers and was amazed to see that the cutlery had gone. She opened the smallest drawer in the press where she knew that Peggy kept the rent book and the letter with the dock board address on the top caught her eye. 'Aye aye, what's this, then?'

Peering over the top of her glasses, what she was reading began to sink in and it felt as though icy water trickled down her spine. Holy Mother of God, Peggy and the children and her lazy good-for-nothing husband were being evicted. They'd be out on the street on Friday morning.

'Paddy...' Little Paddy was stuffing an Everton mint into his mouth and looked over. 'Paddy, has your mam said anything to you about this Friday? About anything special that might be happening?' Little Paddy looked confused and shook his head. 'All right, love, don't you be worrying.'

Kathleen took a deep sigh; she would need to talk to Jerry about this, but he was in the Anchor and Kathleen had a more pressing problem: holding a family together and keeping a roof over Peggy and her children in the very short time she had left.

'Paddy, I'm putting some more money here in the bread crock. In the morning, you go and buy some bread, butter, sugar and jam.'

Little Paddy felt as though it was Christmas morning and he felt tears burn at his eyes without knowing why. Before Peggy had left, they'd had the best tea in months.

Now they had sweets and the house was bright and warm, but the nagging worry was still at the back of his mind. 'Kathleen, is Ma all right?'

Kathleen felt her heart lurch for him. 'Of course she is, Paddy, your mam's just got a few things on her plate, but we're going to get those sorted out. The shopping, can you remember that? There's a good lad.' She ruffled little Paddy's hair and left the house with a heavy heart.

Chapter Twenty-one

A lice could hear a murmuring of voices out in the yard and a shuffling of feet as Nellie and Kathleen told her all that they had found around at Peggy's house.

'What can we do now?' asked Alice. 'Shall I make them some griddle scones? I can't leave because of Joseph but I have the buttermilk I got from Eric this morning.'

Nellie, desperate to do more to help, clapped her hands. 'Yes, I'll help.'

Kathleen nodded. 'I'm going to give it another hour and then I'm going to the pub to fetch Jerry and ask him what we will do, but, sure, look, it's gone eight; she'll be back soon enough wherever she is. Peggy would never leave her kids for long, she'll be back.'

They all turned as the back door flew open and Alice thought she was imagining things when Angela burst into her kitchen and then, with tears springing from her eyes, ran to Nellie and threw her arms around her and began to wail. Then the rest of the Doherty children filed in, Maura and Tommy behind them.

'Maura! Tommy!' Kathleen exclaimed. 'Feck, I think I'm going to faint!'

Seconds later the noise in the kitchen was so loud, Kathleen could hardly hear herself think and Joseph, who had woken, thundered down the stairs.

'Is that Captain Conor's ship in the dock?' said Tommy to Alice as Kathleen fussed over the kids and Maura.

'It is, Tommy, and you can guess where Jerry is?'

'What a night to come home. Is the haul waiting to come up?'

Alice had picked Niamh up and rocked with her on her hip. 'Not yet. It has a list and needs to go into dry dock after it's been unloaded. Jerry reckons there's nothing wrong with it, that Conor's overdone it with the barrels of dark rum from the Caribbean and he's gone to see him down the Anchor.'

Tommy winked at Alice, then said, 'I'm off to the pub, Maura, to see a man about a dog,' and without another word he was out of the door and down the backyard, whistling as he went.

'Tommy!' Maura stood at the back door with her hand out. Tommy knew exactly what she was there for, the money from the sale of the Talk of the Town. He slipped his hand inside his jacket and, removing the money, placed it in her own. 'Away with you,' she said, grumpily, but Tommy could feel her warm smile on his back as he almost ran through the gate.

*

Back in the kitchen, with tea in her hand and Nellie and Alice feeding the children with griddle scones, Maura felt as though she could relax for the first time in days.

'Sit down, Maura, leave them to us,' Alice had said as she mixed the batter in the bowl. 'They are far too excited so they need to get it out of their system and then, when they are done, I'm making some to take down to Peggy's.'

Kathleen was on her knees at the press and, staggering to her feet, held a bottle aloft. 'We definitely need a bit of this in our tea – Golden Knight, you can't beat it. Maura, I can't believe you are here, so much going on that I'll tell you about when this lot are asleep. Speaking of which, you can't sleep over the road, it'll be freezing.'

'We'll be fine, Tommy and I, especially with this inside me, but could the kids spend the night here, Kathleen? Do you mind, Alice?'

'Of course I don't mind! They can all squeeze in together and we can put extra blankets down on the floor. It may not be the most comfortable night they will ever spend, but it will at least be warm and they will sleep after the journey they have had. Are you really back for good?'

Maura sipped and winced. 'Jesus, that's just taken the lining off my stomach, Kathleen. We are, Alice, and I'll tell you this, we are never leaving again.'

Half an hour later, the kitchen table was filled with the crumbs from the scones and Maura was drying the faces of her children, lined up in a row, with a warm towel. Then Alice said, 'Say goodnight to your mam,' and Maura hugged each of her children.

'Mammy, can I go and see Paddy?' Harry muffled into her chest. 'I've slept all the way home.'

Maura looked up at Kathleen, her eyes asking what she should do. Kathleen, alight with the excitement of having Maura back, said, 'Go on, Harry, you go with Nellie and Angela and take the griddle scones.'

Minutes later, as the last of the murmurings came from upstairs, the three women sat before the fire, warm, alcohol-laden cups nursed in their hands. It only took seconds before the conversation turned to the shocking state that Peggy and Paddy were in – and the horrifying news to Maura that Frank the Skank thought he was about to move into her house. But it was the news about Peggy that concerned her the most.

'Frank the Skank might think he is, but I've paid the rent, I still have the rent book – and what's more, I have rights,' said Maura. 'Kathleen, are you sure the letter said the bailiffs were coming on Friday?'

Kathleen dug deep into her apron pocket. 'See for yourself, I brought it back with me because I wanted to speak to Peggy about it myself.'

Alice gasped. 'Kathleen, you didn't!'

Kathleen held the letter out to Maura. 'I did, Alice,

because I knew that something was badly wrong. When did Peggy ever disappear from her own house? Or faint down at the rent office, eh? She's quite obviously not been managing, but she never breathed a word, Maura. I knew things couldn't be right, but they didn't seem to be that wrong. Nothing that her fat lazy arse of a husband couldn't put right with a bit of hard work. I think she's been lost without you, Maura. You understood her better than any of us.'

Maura opened the letter. 'She fainted at the rent office? I've never known Peggy to faint at all. She's as strong as an ox.'

'Exactly, that's what I said to Dr Cole. She was a nervous wreck. I thought she must have been down at the office, paying the rent. And this morning she was shaking like a leaf when she came to ask for a loan for food.'

'Did you give her one?' asked Maura.

'Of course I did, but I've been giving her a loan every week and she's not paid a penny back. I gave her one and six for food. Paddy hasn't worked a full week since you left and I think it's just all got on top of her.'

Maura fell quiet as she read the letter. 'It says the arrears are over a month?'

Kathleen nodded. 'You have that look in your eye, Maura, do you have a plan?'

Maura drained the last of the whiskey-heavy tea in her cup. 'Have you ever know me not to, Kathleen?'

★

Peggy had made her way along the lower dock wall. It was so dark, she could barely see. She thought of the kids as she looked up the steps to the houses above, feeling lost and bewildered.

'Oi, what are you doing, missus?' a woman called out to her from the shadows of the administration building, which was now in darkness. 'Come here!'

Peggy peered through the gloom and knew straight away that the voice belonged to a woman of the night. A professional, who knew what she was doing and seemed none too pleased to see Peggy invading her patch. She wondered should she retrace her steps and go back home. Maybe she should take what money she had left from the pawnshop and throw herself on Mr Heartfelt's mercy... Even as the thought entered her mind, she knew it was useless, she had no time. They would be turfed out by the bailiffs and the door would be locked and boarded up behind them so that they couldn't possibly return and everyone would know. No, she had nowhere to go and every day the problems piled higher and higher. If she didn't drown in the Mersey, she would do so under the weight of despair – surely this was better for the kids? Mr Heartfelt would never be so mean as to turn her children out onto the street after their mother drowned. This way, she would be so much more use to all of them. A cold, watery grave for Peggy would give her family a reprieve and then, surely, big Paddy would realise that he had to work, for the kids would be his responsibility.

Turning from the woman with the unfriendly stare, Peggy looked towards the dark, uninviting water which lapped against the edge of the dock. It would only take one minute and then she would know nothing. There would be no more shame, no more trying so hard and always failing. It would be a sin, but could eternal damnation be worse than how she felt right now? How could she take a newborn baby out onto the street? She took a step towards the water, could hear the distant sound of men's voices from somewhere inside the ships.

'Oi! I said, come over here!'

Peggy had never been a woman who was easily intimidated and yet now she felt herself begin to tremble with fear. She decided to approach the woman, to tell her it was a mistake and that she was sorry, that she would be leaving, that it was all a mistake, that there was no point and she knew what it was she had to do. She would move along the dock and find a quiet spot where no one would disturb her...

'Oi, come here, deaf lugs!' The woman was older than she'd appeared at first. Her hair was bleached yellow and pinned up in folds and she wore fishnet stockings with long black boots and a white PVC raincoat which was open and revealed a black dress beneath. She was far too old for the clothes that she wore. She glared at

Peggy. 'There's only one reason any woman comes down here when it's getting dark,' she said before Peggy had reached her, 'so don't think I don't know what it is you're up to. The nerve of you, me and Stella come down here early to get a bit of business from the new ship and a cheeky old slapper like you comes along and thinks she can take our patch? What's your name and where the hell are you from, up there?' The woman nodded her head up to the streets and, taking out her cigarettes, lit one. 'You wait here until Stella gets back, she's got a bit of business herself on the *Morry*. Thought you could take us on in a pair of auld slippers, did you? Or did you just forget to get dressed. Drunk, are yer?'

Peggy could now see that her eyeliner was smudged and that the woman had a faint bruise on the side of her cheek. She took a long drag on her cigarette. 'Drunken housewife looking for drunken sailor who won't be fussy about what he's paying for, is it? Fancy yourself good enough for the game, did you? You've got nice hair, I'll give you that.' The woman laughed out loud, but the smile disappeared from her face as quickly as it came. She stepped forwards and, with her free hand, jabbed Peggy in the shoulder with her long painted fingernail, making Peggy step backwards and almost stumble.

'The friggin' state of you. Jesus, the likes of you give us a bad name and that's saying something.' As she exhaled the smoke into Peggy's face, she stared hard. 'I said, what's your name?'

Peggy's mouth felt dry and the pain in her belly was weighing her to the spot. All she wanted, all she needed, was the water's edge. She was trapped in a living hell where, minute by minute, everything got worse. The water, the lapping, it was calling her name, *Peggy... Peggy...* Up it slapped and down it fell, calling her to a dark peacefulness. That was where she had to reach, where the pain, the confusion, the hopeless despair, would all end. The lightness in her head made her dizzy.

'P-p-peggy,' she stammered.

'Oh, Jesus, she can't even talk proper! Well, Peggy, you just stand right there until Stella gets back. She's in charge around here and I'm guessing she will want to have a word or two with you – that's if you're lucky. She might want more than a word, get one of the fellas to help out. You see the thing is, Peggy, you can't just come down here and take someone's patch when you fancy. It doesn't work that way, because if you did, others might think it's easy and fancy their chances, and we can't have that, can we? I think someone needs to teach you a lesson, P-p-peggy.'

Peggy shuffled forwards; the water wasn't that far... if she could just get to the edge... but the woman stood in her way. 'Oh no yer don't! You aren't going anywhere, missus, you stand right there until I say otherwise.'

Chapter Twenty-two

Maggie Trott looked in the mirror and checked her newly applied make-up. Cindy had given her a list of essential items and she had made the trip into town and bought her own supplies, to match those Cindy had used. Coty foundation and blusher, Outdoor Girl mascara in a palette with a brush, liquid eyeliner in a bottle, Aqua-green eyeshadow which went well with her hair and Portrait Pink lipstick were lined up before her.

'Rub a bit of the lippy into your cheeks before you put it on your lips,' Cindy had said. 'It gives the blusher a boost and really makes a difference.'

When Cindy had finished restyling her fiery red hair and completed her makeover, Maggie had had to lean forward in the chair to check the reflection was really her. Her hair, which was normally straight unless she had slept in her curlers, crowned her head in ringlets. Her eyes peered back at her, twice as large as usual, and her lips pouted. She had always had good bone structure, but it had never looked as good as it did right now, defined by the powder and blush. Maggie was transformed. She looked thirty-five at the most. Her face had been spared the wrinkles and lines of other women her age, who spent their summers on the front step in a chair, watching the children play out in the street and her complexion was flawless.

Now she smiled at her own reflection. Her face looked just the way Cindy had made it up, earlier in the week.

'There you go, you look amazing,' Cindy had said as she spun Maggie around in her chair with a flourish.

'It – it doesn't look anything like me,' gasped Maggie.

Cindy laughed. 'I know, nothing like you, isn't it great? Honestly, I'm a magician. Women come in here and a couple of hours later they walk out with new hair and it changes them. Listen, me and our Reg are going down to the Admiral on Wednesday – why don't you come and join us? Shall I knock on for you at half seven?'

'Oh no, no. People will think I'm trying to be something I'm not at my age, mutton dressed as lamb.'

Cindy pushed Maggie back down into the chair. 'Maggie, look at you – you are *gorgeous*. It's been time to move on for years. Every other woman widowed in the war from around here has remarried and had a second lot of kids and they've moved on, but not you. You've carried a torch around for way too long. Everyone knows it and, what is more, you know it too. Look, come out with us, will you? Just once. And if you don't feel comfortable then, well, my Reg will walk you back, I promise. If you say no, I'll never do your hair again.'

Maggie had grinned and felt her resolve weaken. 'Oh, go on then – but first I'm going into town to get myself some of that tutty you've just put on my face!'

'Good, well, we'll be at your back gate at half seven. Tell you what, if you start coming out at night with us and you keep this look up, you won't be single for very long. Time for a quick ciggie before you go?'

Cindy had winked as she pulled the packet of cigarettes out of her pocket and Maggie longed to confide in her, to tell her there was only one man she ever thought she could trust. A man she had known since he was a thin and gangly teenager, about to go to war. A man who was completely unavailable, so Cindy's prediction would never come to pass.

Now, as she waited for Cindy and Reg to call for her, she felt excited and nervous at the same time, felt the familiar loneliness seep through her body, compounded by the silence of the house. She thought of Eric, of how she had let her life slip by, worrying about the little things, like making sure the front step was never dirty, that her nets were washed every third Monday. That her windows shone, the cat was fed, the range blackened and that she always had a bit put by. If she carried on as she was, she would wake up one morning and nothing would have changed and she would be past it. No, she could not let that happen. A clean step didn't make her laugh. The nets couldn't keep her warm at night.

Maggie took a deep breath and spoke to her reflection. 'Come on, you! Woman up, you're a long time dead.'

She tried to recall the face of her late husband, to hear his voice. She couldn't. Hadn't been able to for some time. He was gone and she was alive and free. Tonight would be a trial run. She would have one port and lemon and then ask Reg to walk her back home. Then she would leave the curlers out tonight and in the morning Eric might look at her through new eyes, might decide to take his cup of tea indoors, instead of on the step, give Annie O'Prey something to really talk about. She had been living only half a life, all this time. Tears filled her eyes for the children she had never known. How had she let this happen?

She thought of Eric's face, which sprang to her mind with no effort whatsoever. She thought of the kindness in his eyes, and she knew she was a wicked woman, but just the once, just the once, was that really wicked? And as soon as she had allowed that thought to run riot in her mind, she no longer cared. Whatever happened, it would be worth the confession at mass the following day and she could say, 'I have sinned, Father, and it will never happen again.' Because it really would be just the once.

She heard the rattle on the back gate, Cindy and Reg, bang on time to escort her for her first night ever in the pub as a single woman. 'I'll be home in an hour,' she said to the statue of the Virgin Mary on mantelpiece, as she placed the guard over the fire. In the flickering of the flames, the Holy Mother frowned down at her and Maggie knew it – but for the first time in her life, she didn't care...

Eric patted the money in his pocket and glanced down at his polished boots. Gladys wasn't as sharp as she thought she was; she had been to the stables twice to berate him and hadn't even noticed he wasn't wearing his wellies. He patted Daisy Bell, slid the bolt on the stable door as silently as he could and tiptoed across the yard and out of the back gate. In a valiant act of defiance, he was off to the pub to take up Cindy's invitation to join her and Reg. And one thing he was sure of was that Gladys was all about appearances. She would rather die than be one of those women who sent another man into the pub to turf her own out.

'I'm off to the pub!' he shouted back over the gate and, as the kitchen door flew open and the words, 'Oh no you aren't!' floated over the wall after him, he was off and around the corner as fast as his legs would carry him.

'Eric, Eric,' Gladys hissed down the entry, but the entry was clear and Gladys would never shout in case people heard her. Shouting in public would reduce her to the same level as the women on the four streets, or so she thought.

Eric, heading towards the lights shining from the windows of the Anchor, heard the chorus of noise that escaped onto the street as the door opened and his heart lifted for the first time since his hand had brushed against Maggie Trott's and Cindy had wrapped him in her cloak of kind words. He thrust his hands deep into his pockets and felt the pound notes crinkle beneath his fingers. He had taken them from the money bag and he didn't care. He thought of Cindy's words, of Maggie's hand which had been warm and soft against his own, of the look in her eye, and he swallowed hard.

'Get a grip, soft lad,' he said to himself, to calm the nerves in his stomach as he was met by the smell of hops, the sound of laughter and clinking glasses. And he felt the invisible cloak of tension that he wore day and night slip from his shoulders as a docker's voice called out, 'Well, look who it is! Eric the milky, here for a proper pint, come on in, man, come on in!'

Chapter Twenty-three

Nellie, Angela and Harry returned from Peggy's, still chattering away, nineteen to the dozen.

'Oh yes, we did so much fishing – your Uncle Liam took me with him all the time!' Harry was talking to Nellie who was keen to hear all the news she could about everyone in Ballynevin where she spent two weeks every August with her Nana Kathleen. 'I held the landing net and he heaved and heaved and he threw a big salmon into it. It was bigger than me. I almost couldn't stand up!'

Angela thumped him. 'Stop lying, Harry, you're better now, you can't get away with telling your whoppers any more. The salmon was no bigger than your little finger and he only took you the once because you almost fell in.'

Harry looked outraged at Angela's put-down but had no time to bite back as Maura's voice broke in. 'Excuse me, remember where you are, please, and that the little ones are asleep upstairs. Now, is Peggy back then?'

All three shook their heads, their faces solemn. 'We've lit the range in your house, Maura, I got the key from inside the copper boiler,' said Nellie.

Maura hugged Nellie and held her close, the girl as precious to her as one of her own. 'I was just going to do the same thing myself. Was big Paddy home, then?'

Once more all three shook their heads.

'Have the kids gone to bed?' asked Alice and all three nodded.

'Except little Paddy,' said Harry. 'He's going to sit up until his mam gets home – Ma, can I sit with him?'

Maura frowned. 'Harry, it's been an exhausting day and journey; I think I'd rather you stayed here, where it's warm.'

Harry lifted his face to her. 'Oh, it's boiling in there! Shelagh and Mrs Keating and Deirdre have all been in with buckets of coal – you would have said it was as busy as Lime Street, Ma. Shelagh said no one's going to be going to bed until they have seen you with their own eyes. They all knew you were here because Seamus came back for his pipe and told Shelagh that Tommy was in the pub. Deirdre has brought sheets in and is making the beds and Malachi says I can be in charge of the ball all day tomorrow.'

Kathleen looked concerned. 'Well, isn't that just grand? Plenty of heat now in Peggy's and they will have your house warmed through and sheets aired in no time, Maura, different altogether to next door. At Peggy's the lights are on and the kids have full bellies but they have bare feet, God love them.'

Alice walked over to her mother-in-law. 'Why are you looking so worried, Kathleen?'

'Because, Alice, I think we have a much bigger problem. Every bingo in Liverpool ended almost an hour ago so I think something awful is wrong; Peggy should have been long back by now. That feeling I had, Alice, all day, it must have been this.'

Alice was already lifting coats down from the back of the door. 'Maura, would you let Harry go back, so that little Paddy isn't alone if he needs help? Girls, will you stay here and look after Joseph and the others? We must all go and look for Peggy because, Kathleen, I'll put money on Paddy being in the pub, otherwise, he would have been back at his house or called into ours to let us know what was happening. He's been waylaid by the taste of the Guinness.'

'He will have seen Tommy and stayed with him, for it will be a right old lock-in with Tommy and Conor both home,' said Kathleen. 'I have a better idea, though: let's knock on with the mop, see who we can get around to help. That way we can decide who is looking where. It'll need more than two of us, Alice – I think we need a search party.'

'Shall we call the police?' said Alice.

Kathleen shook her head. 'No, not yet. Maura, are you up to it after the journey?'

'Of course I am! There's no way I'm sitting here while you are all out looking for Peggy. Where do we start?'

Alice picked up the mop. 'Kathleen, do you think you should read our tea leaves first, for a bit of a clue?' She banged on the wall, three long thuds in rapid succession, which meant: urgent.

Kathleen lifted the simmering kettle off the range, poured it over the tea leaves and threw in an extra scoop. 'Alice, that's the best idea you've had all day.'

Alice raised her eyebrows. 'Is it now, along with looking for Peggy and everything else I do around here? Welcome back, Maura!'

'We will be a woman down. Maggie Trott won't be answering the knock,' said Maura. 'We just saw her heading into the Anchor as we passed.'

Kathleen frowned and shook her head. 'Maggie Trott? No, you must be mistaken. Maggie hasn't been on a night out, ever. She's a martyr, is Maggie, she prefers to sit at home missing her husband, who has been dead for over twenty years. Maggie of Arc, I call her. She never misses mass, though, and for a woman who never goes out, she spends far too much time in confession.' Kathleen plumped up the cushions on the chairs beside the fire; despite the urgency of the situation, she could not allow anyone to come into her house unless it was tidy. 'The problem with Maggie is she is scared of her own shadow. She wouldn't admit it, but she is. The thing is, Maura, they think life lasts forever – and the thing about Maggie especially is, she should know better! No, she will be running up this path along with the rest of them any moment now.' Alice banged on the kitchen wall with the end of the mop, three ominous thuds. The three women held each other's gaze knowing all too well the sounds that would follow. They waited, they heard the echoing thuds on walls followed by the distant click of back yard gates. The women of the four streets were coming to the rescue as they always had, so many times before.

Chapter Twenty-four

Cindy gave Maggie's arm a reassuring squeeze as they approached the doors of the Anchor. She could sense her nervousness and, as they drew nearer, the quieter Maggie became.

'Come on, love, cheer up, you're just coming for a drink in the pub, it's Babs and Bill waiting inside, not Pierrepoint the old hangman! And you never know, you might just meet someone nice, a fella, I mean; there are a few around here worth a second look.'

Maggie pulled a disbelieving face and Cindy smiled. 'Oh, all right, I'm exaggerating.'

Reg snorted with derision. 'Cindy, you haven't even had a drink yet.' He leant forward to address Maggie. 'Not much chance of finding a decent fella in here, Maggie. You have to let us take you into town one night. You'd enjoy yourself because we know how to have a good night out.'

Maggie liked Reg. He had made a good show of not minding in the least that Maggie had joined them. 'Let me try the local, first, eh, Reg? But I do appreciate the thought. It can't be much fun for you, having me playing gooseberry when you thought it was just the two of you for the night – I'm very lucky to have been asked.'

Reg gasped in mock surprise. 'Maggie, I'm the lucky one. They'll all be asking me in the pub what aftershave I use.' He bent his head down to Maggie and whispered, 'On our second date, Maggie, I'm going to insist you take my other arm so that I have one of you on each side – and I'll tell you this for nothing, I'll be the proudest man on these streets. You see, that lot in there, they think I can't bag a wife because Cindy refuses to marry me.'

Maggie blushed. 'She will one day, Reg,' she whispered back. 'She's a modern miss, is our Cindy, so don't give up. You just keep trying.'

'Let's light up before we go in. I think you need one for your nerves, Maggie,' said Reg as he shuffled a packet of Benson and Hedges Gold and handed one to Maggie.

Cindy flicked open the silver lighter Reg had bought for her birthday. 'She'll soon cheer up once she's got a port and lemon inside her, won't you, Maggie? And here's my guess: tonight is going to be special, I can just feel it and I haven't even been to Kathleen to get my tea leaves read. Two port and lemons, please, Reg, as soon as we get in; me and Maggie will go straight to the table. Let's walk in like we're Princess Margaret arriving for a night out and show off your lovely coat – I haven't seen that before.'

Maggie blew her cigarette smoke high into the night air and smiled. 'Neither had I until this afternoon – I bought it in Blacklers, treated myself, along with the make-up.'

Cindy was delighted. 'Well, it's smashing – I'm jealous. And your hair looks lovely, even though I say so myself.'

There was no more time for conversation or sartorial scrutiny because Reg opened the pub door and the wall of noise hit them. The throng at the bar stood three deep and the overhead lights reflected from the pile of hair that was Babs's, her face shining with perspiration from pulling the tall mahogany pumps to serve a demanding throng of thirsty dockers.

The smell of hops, the smoke from the fire and cigarettes, lit a memory for Maggie of the last time she was in the Anchor, with her husband before he left for the war. Her throat almost closed. Why hadn't she remembered that before?

'Aye, aye, queen,' shouted Reg to Babs, as a sea of male drinkers parted to allow the ladies past. 'Go on, Cindy, get yourselves settled by the fire, it's damp out there.'

'It's always bleedin' damp,' shouted Babs, 'don't take your vest off until June, ladies!'

Cindy waved to Babs then whispered, 'Put a smile on

your face, Maggie, you must stop looking as frightened as your cat when Scamp gets into your backyard.'

Maggie tried to smile. 'I'm not even used to being Maggie,' she replied, 'never mind going to the pub. Everyone calls me Mrs Trott and they always have.'

'Aye, I know,' said Cindy, 'and it ages you. What's more, you let it happen because it made you feel comfortable and safe, didn't you?'

Maggie smiled. 'Who are you? Cindy the hairdresser, Dr Cole in disguise or Kathleen telling my fortune?'

Cindy threw back her head and laughed. 'That's better, now you're smiling. Do you know what, I think all those quacks need to learn to be a hairdresser first – you'd be amazed at the things women come out with while they're sat in my chair. I reckon I can even tell when they are going to get pregnant, though it seems to come as a shock to most of them!'

Maggie was not the least bit surprised; for many, need and survival had long since banished discretion and shame on the four streets.

'Evening, Cindy – oh, hello, Mrs Trott!' Babs called across.

One of the men in the crowd shouted, 'Oh, is it two ladies with you tonight, Reg? Is one not enough?' The crowd began to laugh and Maggie blushed to the roots of her hair.

Cindy squeezed her arm. 'Evening, fellas! Well, he's doing a lot better than any of you,' Cindy shouted back to the joker, as bold as brass. 'You can't even find yourself one and you've been trying for ten years that I know of! Remember when you asked me to go out with you and I said, not on your life? I told you that the rumour that I had been blinded by the peroxide was entirely false – and even if I had been as blind as a bat, I still wouldn't be that desperate that I'd want to go out with you.'

The crowd roared and Maggie found herself laughing with them as the joker looked wounded and then laughed himself. 'All lies,' he shouted. 'I was just after a free haircut.'

A cry went up from the men around the bar, 'What hair? You don't have any hair, baldy!'

'All right, Cindy, you win,' the joker shouted back, to the odd jeer of, 'You should never mess with Cindy,' from the crowd.

Cindy blew them a kiss and she and Maggie pushed through the crowd and found the table that was always waiting for Cindy. None of the men in the pub sat down and only a certain type of woman stood or sat near the bar; respectable women sat at a table. The table was nothing more than an upturned barrel with polished planks balanced on top. Maggie looked around nervously.

'Oh, look, there's the *Morry*'s crew in over by the fire. He's a good bloke, Captain Conor, Ena never stops talking about him,' said Cindy. 'How lucky are people around here that one of their own is the captain of a

tramp ship and gets the dockers all the knock-off gear?
I swear to God, if it wasn't for him, half of the kids on
this street would go hungry. Ena says the owner knows
that he only gets three-quarters of a ship, that the rest
is for the streets, and he doesn't mind. He tells Conor
to just make sure there's no trouble and that he gets the
right price for his load.'

'He's come just in time,' said Maggie, 'because, by all
accounts, only the fittest have had a full week in work
since January. It's going to be the most miserable carnival
in living memory on the four streets this year.'

Cindy crossed her legs and Maggie admired her
ladder-free sheer stockings. Cindy's boots were made of
red leather, with grey fur dotted with black leopard spots
folded over the top. Maggie's heart ached. She would
love just to try them on and then thought to herself for
the very first time, look what you have been missing out
on for so long. The warmth of the laughter in the room
worked its magic as well as the heat from the huge fire.
Maggie let her shoulders relax and gave a deep sigh.
Cindy leant forward and placed her elbows on the table.
'So, when was the last time you actually went out, then?
And, I don't mean to the bingo.'

Maggie didn't need to think. 'I've not been out anywhere since the war,' she said. 'Well, except to the odd
christening or wedding, and there was a party in the
street, remember, the night before the Dohertys left for
Ireland? But since then and you know, the war, well…'

'I know, I know,' said Cindy as she placed her hand over Maggie's. 'The war was tough, queen, but it was years ago and there's no reward in heaven for being a martyr, you know, it's a load of old guff. We all only have one life, it's here and now and oh, before you say anything back to me, because I know you are going to, you *can* spend this life cherishing the memories of the man you loved and lost, God love him and rest his soul...' Cindy blessed herself with the cross and then put her hand over Maggie's. 'You can live every day, honouring your vows – but you do know one of those vows was "till death do us part"? And that's just it, Maggie: death *did* part you.'

Cindy's words pierced Maggie, but they worked; death *had* parted them. Realisation of how stupid she had been washed over her with such a force that she gasped.

'I've been an idiot, haven't I?' She looked Cindy in the eye. 'People didn't think well of me for living like a hermit, did they? I did it in honour of him, but if he died for us, then the least I could do was be true to him.' Even as she spoke the words out loud, she knew that after all this time, they sounded ridiculous. 'They all think I'm pathetic, don't they, think I need their sympathy? Is that what the women around here say when they sit in your chair?'

'No, love, they don't.' Cindy's voice was gentle, her eyes tender. She could sense she had got through. 'That's not what they say at all. Some are jealous that you have no kids to run around after, but honestly, everyone just worries about you. Do you know what I think?' Cindy didn't wait for an answer. 'I think you became a war widow and you used it as a safety blanket. You don't have to try, do you, so it's an easy path to take. I think you dug yourself a trench that deep you didn't know how get back out – which is why I'm that glad you've come out tonight.'

Why had no one else ever said what Cindy just had? Maggie wondered. And then she remembered a conversation with Maura Doherty. 'Do you want to stay in that house every day and night, or do you need a lift out?' she had said once and Maggie had thought at the time she'd been joking. But now Maggie knew what she'd been getting at and the answer drifted into her thoughts almost as soon as she had finished asking herself the question.

'I should have walked out of the door myself,' she said to Cindy. 'Should have got myself a job and lived a life. It was just that with his mam and dad's bit of money, it was always easier not to try.'

Cindy removed her hand and sat upright. 'Well, it doesn't matter any more, you're here now.'

'Ah, it's Eric the milky,' shouted Babs over the heads of the men drinking at the bar. 'Has your Gladys fallen asleep, or what?'

'Eric? Good God, man, I never thought we would see you in here. Is it a man's drink you're after now?' asked

Reg who'd got caught by another customer and had only just reached the bar.

Eric laughed. 'I am – Babs, a pint of mild, if you would.'

'It's my pleasure, Eric. I take it you've escaped? The police won't be coming in, will they? We don't want no trouble with your Gladys.'

Eric looked shocked and stuttered, 'Oh, n-no, not at all...'

Babs chuckled. 'I'm kidding, Eric. Oh, it's good to see you. Now Reg, two port and lemons and your usual, is it?'

Eric peered towards the table where the ladies were sitting. 'I'll get those for you, Reg,' he said.

'Eric, it's a gentleman you are, thank you.'

A voice called out, 'Reg, would you and Cindy play some arrows? We have Denny's wife who wants to play a game and she can't if the other team doesn't have a woman to make it equal.'

Reg turned to Eric and behind his hand said, 'That's the nicest thing anyone has ever said about Denny's wife, that she's a woman. She can down a pint faster than any docker in here and she plays better arrows too! I can't,' he called back, 'we have a visitor with us.'

Eric who had spotted Maggie as soon as he had walked into the Anchor, did not let his moment pass. 'I'll keep your visitor company for you, Reg, if you and Cindy fancy a game?'

'Would you mind?'

Eric felt his heart lighten. 'No, not at all. She's one of my best customers is Maggie Trott, I wouldn't mind at all.'

Babs, listening, grinned and took a packet of arrows from the shelf next to the till and held them out to Reg who took them willingly. 'Right, I know my place, I'll take these drinks over and then we'll go and find the dart board.' Reg winked at Babs and scooped up the three drinks into his hands.

'I'll be over in a moment,' said Eric. He wanted to make sure Reg told Maggie in advance and she was comfortable with the idea.

'Here you are ladies,' Reg said as he approached the table. 'Cindy, we're needed for a game of arrows.'

'Thank you, Reg,' Maggie said. She had known that Reg wouldn't sit with them but felt suddenly alarmed that Cindy was about to leave her also.

'Oh, don't thank me, it was bought for you by an admirer, Maggie,' said Reg.

'An admirer, already? Who?' said Cindy, amazed, and craned her neck towards the bar, but it was Maggie who spotted him first, raising his glass to her. Eric!

'Oh, God, it's the milky, I thought you meant a real fella then, I thought your luck had changed, Maggie.' Cindy laughed before picking up her own drink and taking a sip, then continued, 'Imagine his Gladys letting him out. I told him he needed to get out to the pub – he's another one letting his life slip past him. He's a really good man, is Eric, but I swear to God, that wife of his will see him into the ground, she makes his life that miserable.' Cindy leant forward and whispered, 'Everyone knows he lives a dog's life with Gladys and I think the poor man is on the edge.'

Maggie raised her drink to her lips and recalled her conversation with Eric that morning. 'Are you watching that show, *Coronation Street*, on the television tonight?' Eric had asked as he walked back to the cart.

She had hesitated before she replied, her first instinct not to speak out loud her betrayal of martyrdom and admit she was going out to the Anchor with Cindy and Reg. 'No, not tonight, I don't think so,' she had faltered.

'Why not?' he'd asked. 'Got other plans?'

She had taken a breath, pushed the cat back indoors, smoothed down her sleeve, avoided his eyes and then decided to be truthful; she had no idea how she had been so bold, 'Well, actually, I'm going to the pub with Cindy and Reg.'

Eric had looked so surprised she thought he was about to faint. 'Which one? The Anchor?'

She nodded, her mouth dry. He didn't speak either and, instead, picking up the reins had said, 'Walk on, Daisy,' leaving her feeling incredibly foolish. But now here he was in the pub and he had known she would be there too. He was smiling at her, he had bought her a drink – and there was no doubt about it, admiration was shining from his eyes. She felt her heart pounding as he walked towards their table.

'Eric, what a sight for sore eyes you are,' said Cindy. 'I'm so glad you've come.'

'Well, a suggestion is as good as any order from you, Cindy,' said Eric.

'Right, Cindy,' Eric laughed, 'they need our help. They want a woman on the arrows.'

Cindy inclined her head towards Maggie. 'Reg, I can't, I've got Maggie with me.' Cindy would never leave Maggie on her own.

'I'll sit here with Maggie and look after her, if you would like to play, Cindy,' Eric said.

Cindy looked to Maggie for approval. 'Do you mind?' she asked.

Maggie shook her head. 'Of course not,' she replied as she took another sip of her drink.

Eric smiled down at her. He was wearing a cable knit sweater and unlike the other men in the bar who wore caps, his head was bare. His shoulders were broad and Maggie realised that his hat had hidden his good looks; with his dark hair and beard, he was a very handsome man. Maggie gulped on her port and lemon and had to stop herself when she realised she had swallowed almost half a glass. As Cindy walked away to join the arrows team, only Babs saw the wink that passed between Reg and Eric and the pat Reg gave Eric on the shoulder.

Eric placed his pint on the upturned barrel. 'I hope you don't mind,' he said as he sat and straddled the seat. The noise of the chatter swirled around them and Maggie felt as though they were sitting in a bubble, because all she could hear was Eric... She managed a smile.

'No, not at all, not just this once,' she teased as she raised her glass. 'Thank you for the drink.' He raised his own pint glass and clinked it against the side of her own. 'You are a married man, after all,' she said.

Eric had no response to that. He had stolen money from his own house to be here, had to run like a thief in the night to escape. He took in Maggie's hair, her make-up. 'You look stunning,' he said. 'Nothing like the Mrs Trott who gives me my tea each morning. Mind, she's a looker too.'

Maggie grimaced. 'It's Maggie,' she said quickly, 'you know that.'

He smiled. 'I was only teasing,' he said. 'So, here's another question: who is it I will be seeing in the morning, Mrs Trott or the new Maggie?'

With an audacity Maggie did not know she possessed, she returned his gaze full on and his eyes never wavered from their target.

'Maggie, if you like,' she said. Her mouth was dry, her head light, she wasn't sure who was talking, her or almost empty glass of port and lemon. His brown eyes devoured her face, and she felt their approving appraisal bore into her very soul.

'Just once is it, did you say?'

She sipped the last of her drink before she replied; she knew exactly what she was committing to and she was ready. 'Yes, just once. I'll try anything, just the once,' she replied. 'You never know, it might be enough.'

The frisson between them sizzled and to Maggie it felt as though the air had left the room. Her breath froze as her pulse raced.

'I'll refill these,' he said as he picked up her glass. 'We can have another before we leave.'

Maggie's breath caught in her chest and her stomach lurched. *Before we leave…* He had said it out loud, converted her fantasies and flirtations into an impending deed and, as he left for the bar he turned and said, 'Once would never be enough for me, Maggie.'

Chapter Twenty-five

It had taken only seconds for Shelagh to run to Deirdre Malone's house, even with a baby on her hip. She left doors open and a bin scattering in her wake and gasped the words out before she was even fully in the kitchen as the door flew open with Shelagh virtually swinging on the latch. 'Deirdre, have you heard the news?' She had intended to savour in the delight of holding something over Deirdre, but, carried away in the moment, she blurted out, 'Maura and Tommy are back, for good. Can you believe it?'

'No they're not,' Deirdre said, as cool as a cucumber.

'They are, I'm telling you. Seamus came back for his pipe and told me. I saw Nellie with my own eyes. The kids came for a shovel of coal and I asked them, what do you want it for and they said, Peggy was short and Maura's back. Honest to God, she's in Kathleen's but I don't think we will see her now until tomorrow, it's so late.'

Deirdre took her coat down from the kitchen door. 'Oh, I think we will. I need to see this with my own eyes.

Malachi!' Deirdre shouted up the stairs. 'Get down here in the kitchen until your da gets back and watch the kids don't make a mess.'

Shelagh juggled the baby onto her other hip. 'Where are you going?' she asked. 'We can't just go into Kathleen's, she's not knocked on with the mop yet.'

Deirdre fastened her headscarf under her chin. 'No, and she won't, will she? It's bloody Maura, always calling the shots, but no one's slept in Maura's house for months, there's no beds made. We can go and start getting it ready for her and that way we will have to see her, won't we? They can't leave us out because that wouldn't look very nice, would it? Mary, put that mop down, you're coming with us.'

Shelagh looked twice at the girl. 'Holy Mother of God, Mary, what happened to your hair?'

'Don't ask,' said Deirdre. 'God alone knows what Eugene will say when he sees the state of it, and she paid Cindy good money for that.'

Mary was about to say that she hadn't at all. That Cindy hadn't taken a penny off her, but instead she kept quiet and said, 'I can't, Mam. I'll have to go and fetch Biddy from the Seaman's Stop. Malcolm has a full house tonight from one of the ships and she's down there, helping.'

Deirdre wasn't listening, she was already away and out of the door. Shelagh, in her wake, popped her head back around the door and said, 'Mary, your hair looks lovely, so it does!' and as quick as a flash, she was gone.

An hour later, they had almost finished preparing the house for Maura's return and were slightly disappointed not to have been summoned, especially as Harry and little Paddy had arrived to see who was in the house and would obviously carry the news back to Maura that they were already there and using their own initiative. It had taken them less than an hour to do what would have taken a tired Maura much longer to complete alone. During the turning of the mattresses, the making of the beds and the lighting of the fires in both bedrooms, there had been a prolonged exchange.

'It seems to me, Shelagh, that if you've got a bit of money, you don't want to go and spend it on an empty house, do you? It's obvious they always intended to come back, isn't it?'

Shelagh was confused. 'I suppose so, because look at this place. Kathleen has been coming in once a week since they left and giving it the once-over. In fact, she had the nets out last week and there's nothing for us to do other than make the beds and light the fires. So Kathleen must have known, mustn't she? Or she probably read it in the tea leaves – that's the thing about Kathleen, she knows what's coming before the rest of us do. Nothing's a surprise to her. She can see into the future, 'tis a great gift she has.'

'Ma,' the back door opened and one of Shelagh's children ran in shouting up the stairs, 'you've got to go to Kathleen's now! She's banging on with the mop and it's three knocks.'

Shelagh picked her baby up from the floor and straightened her back with some effort. 'We're doing the beds. Tell her no one needed to tell us what to do, it's all done and dusted and when is Maura coming down?'

'Ma, she knows you're here, Nellie told her, Kathleen says you've got to come, right now!'

Deirdre tutted. 'There you go, Shelagh, we've been summoned. Finally, we get to see Queen Maura – and you see, that's the other thing about Maura, we get her house ready for her, but we have to go and have a formal introduction at Kathleen's house. She thinks she's flamin' royalty, that one.'

It took only minutes for Kathleen's house to fill and to calm everyone down due to the surprise at Maura's return.

'Oh, it was no surprise to us, was it, Shelagh?' said Deirdre. 'The minute Shelagh told me, I said, right, come on then, Shelagh, she will have tired kids on her hands to deal with and I knew those beds would need making.'

Deirdre had never been Maura's favourite neighbour, but she was grateful that Deirdre had done exactly what Maura would have done had the boot been on the other foot. 'Thank you, Deirdre, that's good of you. It's nice to know nothing and no one has changed.'

Deirdre folded her arms and preened. 'We've turned the beds down and lit the fires in both of the bedrooms.

It's a good job you came back in May; it's not too bad at all in there, just a bit damp maybe, but the fires are fierce so the house will soon be as warm as toast. The range is lit so you'll have hot water too and I've left the kettle warming on the corner.'

Annie O'Prey came in through the back door and clapped her hands together. 'Well, would you look at what the cat's dragged in!' she exclaimed.

Maura felt tears spring to her eyes and took a deep breath; she was home, amongst the women of the four streets, and she could not have felt more relieved. The women gathered around her, asking a hundred questions, and one thing was certain: everyone was delighted to see her.

Kathleen clapped her hands. 'Come on, everyone, there is something more important we have to attend to – Peggy is missing.'

Deirdre laughed out loud. 'She can't be missing, she was walking down the street this afternoon with Shelagh's pram.'

Shelagh frowned. 'Well, actually, little Paddy came to ours hours ago to see had Peggy brought the pram back and she had, but she just pushed it into the wash house; normally she would have come in and cadged a cuppa at the very least. Little Paddy was very worried, but I told him she's down the bingo.'

Kathleen shook her head. 'Our Nellie and I went and checked and I thought maybe she might have gone into town and then I thought how ridiculous that was. She's only got her slippers. She wouldn't go on the bus in her slippers.'

'Come on, everyone, you know the drill,' said Alice as she began to pour the tea. 'Put plenty of sugar in your cup so that the leaves stick to the side.'

'I'll put a drop of whiskey in too,' said Kathleen.

'Sorry we're late,' said Biddy who had arrived last with Mary in her wake. 'If you can't find Peggy, where is big Paddy?'

'Probably in the Anchor. I'm hoping that if we all read the leaves, we will be able to find a clue in the cups.'

Everyone fell quiet and an air of seriousness descended upon the kitchen as they waited for the help they had always turned to during a crisis, or simply to get them through hard times. Kathleen's reading of the tea leaves had guided each woman in managing even the most difficult problems. An unpaid bill, a sick child, an unwanted pregnancy – all were a way of life in the four streets and Kathleen's kitchen was open for readings every Friday morning. No one knocked at any other time because they knew they would be turned away.

'They would be filling my hands with the sixpences every day of the week instead of the kids' bellies with food,' Kathleen said to Alice when anyone knocked on the door, begging her to give them a reading because a mammy back home was ill, or a wage-earning brother was up before a magistrate in Dublin.

'That was a strange turn Peggy took down at the rent office – did Dr Cole say he could do anything?' asked Biddy as Alice filled her cup.

Kathleen shook her head. 'He said no bloody chance of helping with anything, other than trying to get Paddy into work and that her nerves were shot to pieces. He wanted...' Kathleen dropped her voice, 'to do an internal, *down there.*' It rose again. 'Wanted to check her fibroids to see if they were any worse but she refused. She was desperate to stop Frank the Skank from moving in next door, that's what's upset her, but Dr Cole said there was no chance of that, either.'

Kathleen, Maura and Alice exchanged a knowing look. They would not reveal the contents of the letter, would not bring further shame down on Peggy's head. Between them, they would rescue her. They would pay the rent and retrieve the shoes from the pawnshop.

The air was tense as Maura spoke. 'I've never known Peggy to go anywhere alone; you all know what she's like, she'd need a bit of company to help her. Has anyone been keeping an eye on her, has she kept up with the bills?'

Alice slipped the knitted tea cosy over the teapot. 'We've been feeding the kids, Maura. Hardly a day goes by when one of us doesn't do something. Maggie Trott only really bakes for Peggy's kids.'

Maura took a deep breath, her elation at returning home replaced with concern for Peggy. 'Say a prayer, ladies, as you drink the tea,' she said, knowing that her first task tomorrow would be confession, to ask forgiveness for having her tea leaves read.

'Saint Maura's definitely home,' Deirdre whispered to Shelagh as she took her cup and blew and sipped the tea.

Five minutes later Kathleen peered into the row of cups lined up before her. 'Right, did everyone have two sugars?' she asked as Mary drained the last drop, watching Biddy to see how it was done. It was the first time Mary had been amongst the women in a reading and she now fully absorbed the solemnity and seriousness of the occasion.

Mary had travelled a long way from the convent to Kathleen's kitchen via Cindy's in a very short time. She had fallen in love – and out of it just as fast – and here she was, a new boundary being crossed, having her teacup read.

The assembled women leant in close to the table and nodded their heads.

'Right then, let's go. Three swills to the right and make a wish for your family,' Kathleen said, and all the women picked up their cups and swilled them to the right. 'Now, three to the left and make a wish for Ireland, then one for Peggy as you tip, with no hesitation whatsoever, the cup upside down into the saucer.'

Silence accompanied the solemn cup-swilling until the clattering sound of upturned cups hitting saucers.

'Maura's right, we have to go to confession for this,' whispered Shelagh. 'With us doing it all together, the priest would be mad with us, for isn't it like a séance?'

Biddy placed her finger over her lips, telling Shelagh not to speak, but it was too late.

'I need quiet, Shelagh,' said Kathleen. 'I can't find the answers in the middle of chatter.'

Shelagh's eyes widened; the atmosphere in the room had changed, fear of the priest was replaced by a thrill of excitement and everyone almost stopped breathing as the warmth of the room was replaced by an icy chill. The candles that Alice had lit and placed on the table, 'to keep the bad spirits away,' flickered violently from side to side, as though someone had suddenly opened the back door, but no one had.

Kathleen took a deep breath and it took all of her willpower and reserve as she looked at Maura and saw, as plain as day, Kitty standing at her shoulder and, on her other side, her first daughter-in-law, Nellie's mother and Maura's closest friend, Bernadette, her long red hair iridescent against her whiteness. They had come together and Kathleen knew instinctively that this was not a good thing that they had come to warn her, to help her. Kitty inclined her head towards Maura's cup. She was urging her to read and Kathleen knew that the message contained within was from them.

The room was silent as Kathleen reached out and picked up Maura's cup; Kitty gazed at her and waited.

And from the moment she looked inside, Kathleen wished she hadn't.

'Oh, angels of mercy, why did we do this?' She looked around the table at the women waiting on her every word with bated breath.

'Why, what is it? What can you see?' asked Maura.

Kathleen took a shuddering breath. 'I can see water, deep water, black and deep,' said Kathleen. 'And I can see a new baby in here, too.'

Kathleen tipped Maura's cup to the side. 'Look, Maura, see, there's a babby on one side of your cup and trouble all over the other – but it's not for you. See those leaves there? They are a warning to us, to you.' She tipped up the cup for everyone to see and they nodded in unison. Not one of them had a clue what it was she was talking about. 'That's the dockers' steps, see, going down the side of the handle, there, and that crowd, that's us at the top, and trouble. See that side,' they all nodded, 'that's the water. There's a dark cloud hovering over us and it's waiting to do its worst. There is a baby and it's not a baby to be – that would be a different sign – this is a baby that's here. It's a dark cup this is.'

'Maybe one of the ships is going to sink?' said Deirdre. 'Have you seen the state of the *Morry*, it's leaning over to one side.'

'Good job all the men are sleeping in Malcolm's and not on board in that case,' said Biddy.

'I know what it is,' said Maura, 'we've just crossed

deep water to get here, the leaves are just a few hours behind, that's all.'

Shelagh, with hand shaking, held out her cup to be read and with an effort Kathleen took it. She did not want to see any more bad news. They all waited with eyes wide as she stared into Shelagh's cup. The only sounds were the clock ticking on the mantelpiece, the gentle hum of the kettle on the range and the coals shifting in the grate.

'It's the same! The two cups are identical and I think I might know why,' said Kathleen. They all knew better than to ask. It was not a question and they wouldn't usually interrupt without being invited to do so. Kathleen was a seer. The dead used her to commune with the living via the medium of a nice strong cup of tea with two sugars. It was Annie O'Prey who broke the silence.

'Anything about Frank the Skank moving in among us?' she whispered, almost too afraid to speak. They all knew that her question was rooted in good sense. Jimmy would not last at home for five minutes with Frank the Skank as his neighbour.

Mary shivered as she ran her hands up and down her arms. Next was Biddy's turn and this time Kathleen gasped and banged Biddy's cup onto the saucer. 'It's just the same! Never in all my years have I ever picked up two cups that were the same, never mind three of them, and that's the message. It's the steps, dark, deep water and trouble. Mary, pass me yours; it's your first time and surely to God the spirits won't make your cup a dark one for your first.'

Kathleen slipped a glance towards Kitty and Bernadette; they were both still there and she could tell there was no objection to reading Mary's cup, but the sense of urgency was building: they were letting her know she had to go.

Mary wasn't remotely nervous handing her cup over, she was excited.

'Ah, 'tis a long and happy life you have ahead of you, Mary, and big change is coming. See there,' she tipped the cup up, 'you are going to be a woman of means and love is around the corner and with it, not because of it, I see success, business and independence and lovely hair.'

Deirdre laughed. 'Kathleen, that's our Mary's cup, not Elizabeth Taylor's.'

They all laughed as Mary blushed, but nothing could dampen the girl's pleasure at Kathleen's words.

When she'd finished the last cup, and all the rest of them telling the same story, Katheen was as white as the sheets Deirdre and Shelagh had just placed on Maura's bed. She put both of her hands down on the table and pushed herself upright with all the energy she had left.

'Ladies, we need to put a guard on the top of the steps, see who goes down and, even though it's pitch black, see if we can see anything down there. That's where the leaves are taking us – and we need to split up too. It's ten o'clock and I think it's time for us to heave big Paddy out of the pub and tell the men we have trouble. There is no way Peggy would be out this late alone. Maura, do you want to stay here and keep an eye on the kids? Everyone else, I think Peggy is in real danger and we need to find her, urgently.'

'I do not,' said Maura just as Nellie walked in.

'Harry is with little Paddy,' said Nellie, who could sense that all was not right.

'Grand. Nellie, would you stay here and I'll go and check on my house – and Kathleen, I'm going to talk to little Paddy, see if he can remember anything about what Peggy said, and I'll take my bag into my own house.'

The warmth edged its way back into the kitchen and Kathleen was both sad and relieved to see that the ghosts of Kitty and Bernadette had left. Alice helped Kathleen on with her coat; she knew her mother-in-law well enough to sense that she hadn't told them everything. As they reached the door, she held Kathleen's arm and tugged her back.

'Kathleen, what's wrong?' she asked.

Kathleen grabbed her daughter-in-law's hand and in the light of the overhead bulb, Alice could see that her mother-in-law was pale and beads of perspiration stood out on her top lip. 'I couldn't look any more, Alice. Death was in every one of the cups but Mary's and I couldn't say that, could I? And Kitty... she was here, Alice, behind Maura's shoulder the whole time. I had to get everyone out.'

Kathleen couldn't tell Alice that Jerry's first love was also in the kitchen she once called her own. Though Kathleen and Alice had had their differences over the years, the love Jerry had for Bernadette, that still burnt in his heart, was never spoken of, and was the root cause of all they had been through as a family.

'Was it just Kitty?' Alice asked, her brow furrowed.

Kathleen squeezed her hand as she lied. 'Aye, just Kitty,' and as she walked out of the door ahead of Alice, she blessed herself.

Maura ran, fleet of foot, down the back entry, passing by houses where she knew every occupant, hearing the sounds of babies crying and familiar arguments taking place. As she drew alongside Peggy's gate, she heard a sound which was unfamiliar to her: the sound of silence. She thought, as it was so quiet, the children must be in her own house and was desperate to set foot in it. She opened the back gate and caught her breath. She had lived in this house all her married life and yet never had she seen it so empty and quiet. Closing the gate behind her, she tiptoed across the cobbles, wondering why Deirdre hadn't left the light on, and stopped dead as she reached her own back door; it was ajar and she could hear a man's voice, but not one that was familiar to her. Her heart beat fast against her ribs and she held her breath to listen. Someone was in the kitchen... And then she saw torchlight sweeping across the room. It's the flamin' O'Prey boys, on the rob, she thought.

A voice came clearly to her. 'I called you as soon as I saw there were people in here, but now there's no one and the place is empty but the fires are lit. What's going on? Are you stringing me along because if you are, you won't be getting your cut.'

Maura tiptoed to the window ledge and peered through the nets. Despite her fear, her first thought was one of relief that Kathleen had kept them nice and clean.

'Don't you come the big I am with me,' said a second voice. 'You seem to be forgetting who's the boss around here and who it is who employs you. Your Margaret should be very grateful she's not living in one of the police houses on the Dock Road. And you won't need this poxy house if you do your job right.'

'I need insurance, in case it doesn't come off.'

The second man sounded impatient. 'What are you talking about? I *am* your insurance. You have it already, if I turn a blind eye to the comings and goings.'

'I'm not talking about being caught, but make no mistake, it would be worse for me as a policeman. When I'm gone, I want to know Margaret has a roof over her head, I owe her that. And now the *Morry* is in, Captain Conor and his band of merry men.'

The second man snorted. 'You'll be wetting yourself next. A deal is a deal and tonight is the night. *Nothing* is going to go wrong.'

It dawned on Maura who the second voice belonged to; it was Heartfelt. She almost gasped out loud.

'All very well for you to say but something is going on, I tell you. I saw two women leave here, thought maybe they were squatting, but they've gone into a house down the road and we can't hide the money in the copper boiler here if there's women in and out.'

Heartfelt walked closer to the window. 'I think the Dohertys are back; I saw Tommy Doherty going into the Anchor with Jerry Deane. Don't worry, though, I'm evicting the Nolans from the house next door on Friday morning and you can have that one, although if I were you, I'd be off and forget about Margaret. No one is going to suspect you – and Tommy Doherty coming back is going to look very suspicious. It won't be difficult to point the finger of blame up the steps towards this house. Come to the administration building in the morning and I'll set the alert off at about ten.'

Frank looked around the kitchen; it would have been perfect for Margaret, so much nicer than the present tiny house they lived in, but still, as long as she had a house his conscience would be eased and she wouldn't even notice he was gone.

Maura heard footsteps. They were leaving! Praying that the wash-house door was open, she rushed in on tiptoe and closed the door behind her, peering through the gaps in the wood.

'I'm off down to the docks,' said Frank the Skank.

'The *Morry* is in and I reckon they will be trying for a haul any time now.'

'Why worry?' Heartfelt asked. 'You don't need the bother. Concentrate on getting your Margaret in next door and then plan what you are going to do with the money. We didn't clear the docks of bizzies so that you could go lifting collars, we did it to give us a free run, remember that. Don't go looking for enemies. If Tommy Doherty is back, he's not a man to be messed with, we need to be careful tonight.'

Frank sounded concerned. 'They reckon down at Whitechapel that it was him who murdered the priest; they just had nothing to nail it on him.'

'Aye, maybe,' Heartfelt said. 'Who knows? But that priest was a baddun and I believe there's more to that than we know about. It's all the more reason to take care,' he said and was away down the entry.

Maura bit her lip and closed her eyes as, only inches away from her, Frank unbuttoned his trousers and relieved himself against the backyard wall. You dirty sod, she thought, resisting the urge to lift the washing paddle and hit him over the head with it. Buttoning himself up, he turned and stared at the wash-house door for so long that Maura felt as though she would pass out if she had to hold her breath a second longer. Then Frank walked away and the backyard gate slammed shut and she counted his footsteps down the entry until they disappeared.

*

Stepping into her kitchen, Maura flicked the switch and the overhead light spluttered into life. The kitchen was spotless, and she was home.

'Oh, holy feck!' she screamed as a rat ran across the kitchen door and, grabbing a kitchen chair, jumped onto it. Suddenly the door to the stairs opened and little Paddy dashed in and scooped up the rat, followed by Harry.

'Paddy, what is that?' Maura demanded, pointing at the rat little Paddy was slipping into his pocket, the intrusion of Frank the Skank and Mr Heartfelt instantly forgotten.

'It's Max, Auntie Maura, but don't tell my da, please.'

Harry was grinning from ear to ear and then he said, 'Ma, did you hear all that? We were hiding on the stairs.'

Maura jumped down from the chair as little Paddy said, '*I* did, and Frank the Skank is a bad man.'

'He is, Paddy, and it would seem Mr Heartfelt isn't the upstanding citizen he likes everyone to think he is.' Maura pushed the chair back under the table as little Paddy walked over to show her Max.

'Would you like to stroke him?' he asked. 'And Auntie Maura, who is being turfed out into the street? Maybe we should go and warn them. Is our mam back yet. Where is she, Maura?'

Maura grabbed little Paddy by the shoulders and pulled him into her. 'She will be here soon and no one is being turfed out, Paddy, no one.'

Harry stood close to them and said to Paddy, 'There's no point struggling, Paddy. She does that to me too, you just have to grin and bear it. It won't last for long.'

And as Harry smiled up at Maura, he looked the happiest Maura had seen him since the last time he had been with his best friend in her kitchen. 'You're more like brothers, you two. I should never have let you be separated,' she said as she stroked little Paddy's hair.

After a few moments he said, 'Auntie Maura? You're crushing Max.'

'Well, I'm very sorry, Max. But shouldn't he be in bed now, Paddy?'

'Oh, no, Auntie Maura, rats are nocturnal, they run around the streets, they come up from the river and...'

Maura shuddered. 'Paddy, I've only been this close to a rat before when I was trying to clobber him with the end of the mop.' She was keen to begin her search of the Nolans' house for clues as to where Peggy might be. 'Now I'm just going to check the fires upstairs, so you take Max back to his own house now, I'm sure he will be more comfortable in there.'

'Ma might be back now,' Paddy said hopefully. Maura smiled, but in her heart, she was not convinced.

'Maybe, Paddy,' she lied. 'Off you run now, boys, and I'll follow you in five minutes.'

*

As she made her way up the scrubbed wooden staircase, pleasure at the warmth of her house quickly replaced her anger at finding Frank the Skank in her kitchen. She could not fault the efforts of Shelagh and Deirdre – there was nothing at all for her to do and so she did what she had wanted to do for so long. She went into the children's bedroom and there it stood, the old oak wardrobe and Kitty's bed. She turned the key in the lock, the sound as old and as familiar to her as any, and reaching in, she removed Kitty's dress, one she had never washed. Pulling it towards her, she held it to her face and inhaled deeply. The smell of Kitty assailed her senses, her eldest daughter, her best friend, her heart. She stood for a moment and let the fabric of the dress absorb her tears that fell every day without fail as she whispered, 'I'm home, Kitty, I'm home...'

Chapter Twenty-six

Maggie had finished her second port and lemon far quicker than she had intended as a cheer rang out around the pub.

'Jesus, are my eyes deceiving me?' A voice rang above the cheers and Eric swivelled around in his chair and looked behind him to see who it was.

'What's the commotion about?' asked Maggie.

'I have no idea,' said Eric, 'but what or whoever it is, the entire pub is moving towards the door.' Eric looked knowingly in the opposite direction, towards the back door. 'I'm guessing that this would be a good time for anyone who wanted to, to leave and not be seen?'

His question hung on the air and Maggie made her decision in a heartbeat. She stood, and feeling like a woman she had never met before, said, 'Can you pass my coat, please? It's behind you.'

Eric, feeling like the man he had always wished he had been, picked up a bright green coat and said, 'This one?'

Maggie nodded, and without another word he slipped

the coat up her arms as she scanned the bar. No one had noticed them, all eyes were on the front; and with a glance between them which conveyed a lifetime of everything both needed to know, she walked towards the back door, holding her breath and hoping and praying that he had no last-minute fears or hesitation.

It was Harry who noticed the woman acting suspiciously in the entry ahead of them and both boys pressed themselves into the wall so that they could see what was happening.

'Who is it?' whispered Harry.

'I don't know,' said Paddy and they watched as a man turned into the entry and crept around the corner after her, but not until he had looked up and down the street and all around. 'It's Mrs Trott,' said little Paddy then, 'but she never goes out anywhere. No, it can't be. There's a mister with her and Mrs Trott doesn't have a Mr Trott, that's why I get all the biscuits she makes.' And then, to his total surprise, the couple stopped at Mrs Trott's back gate. Paddy gasped and couldn't help himself as he said out loud, 'Harry! It *is* Mrs Trott, and she's with Eric, the milky!'

'Come here,' said Eric as they reached the back gate and, reaching out, took hold of Maggie's hand, relieved to find it was shaking as much as his own. 'Maggie, are you sure about this?' he asked.

Maggie made to answer then frowned and said, 'Did you hear something then?'

Eric looked down the entry. 'No. There's no one there, it's just the river rats come up the steps to the street because it's getting cold down there.'

For a fleeting moment the diversion had dragged his thoughts to the dairy, to Gladys, to his marriage. Was there something? Was it Gladys? A cat howled and Maggie, looking up at Eric, smiled.

'Yes, I'm sure,' she said. 'It'll be that cat – and I'm as nervous as a kitten myself.'

His hand left hers and stroked her arm. 'Are you sure you are sure?'

Maggie didn't hesitate; hadn't she been dreaming about this possibility for longer than she cared to remember? Wasn't it this thought that kept driving her to confession? Her wicked thoughts were all here as one, standing before her in the form of this married man she had known for more than half of her life.

'I'm sure, Eric. By tomorrow I'll be another day older. I do think I need another drink though, do you? I've got a bottle of sherry in, no stout though, I'm afraid.'

Eric smiled and, bending, kissed her gently on the lips. He had never known a kiss like it. Her lips were soft and yielding and tasted warm and sweet. He just stopped himself from emitting a moan of appreciation. His hands slipped inside her new coat and wrapped around her and Maggie swayed in his arms as their lips met again. Eric pulled away.

'We had better step indoors,' he said as he glanced down the entry and, as he lifted the latch, guided her into her own yard.

At the sound of the gate closing, little Paddy opened his eyes which, revolted by what he had seen, had tightly closed the moment Eric bent to kiss Maggie.

'Oh my giddy aunt,' said Harry, in shock, 'was that the milky kissing Mrs Trott?'

'It was,' said little Paddy. 'Do you think we had better tell someone?'

'I think we better had,' said Harry. 'It's really changed around here and we haven't even been gone that long.'

'Tommy Doherty, is it really you?' the assembled crowd shouted almost at once. 'Are ye back for good? Will you be coming down the steps?'

One question after another hit Tommy like a volley of shots as, laughing, Jerry grabbed him and steered him through the crowd. 'You couldn't have picked a better night to come home for a visit,' said Jerry, as he slapped Tommy on the back.

'It's no visit, Jer,' said Tommy as he grinned up to the man who had been his closest friend since they were both new arrivals in Liverpool. 'We're home for good.'

Whilst Tommy bantered with the men and answered the questions, Jerry, being one of the tallest men on the four streets, scanned the pub in search of Captain Conor and located him standing close to the fire. He winked, indicating towards the back room and grabbed Tommy by the arm.

'Come on, mate, Captain Conor is here, work to do, 'tis a proper welcome home we have for you.'

Maura walked in through Peggy's back door and little Paddy's face lit up. The worry of his mother missing and the excitement of his friend returning was all too much for him but he knew instinctively that whatever it was that was ailing his mother and making her cry so often, and wherever she was, could be cured by the joy of having her best friend back next door and that she would make it all better.

'Mam, Mam, guess what we saw!' said Harry.

'The nasty woman won't be moving into your house now will she, Auntie Maura?' little Paddy asked her as she pulled the back door behind her.

'No, they will not, Paddy.' But she knew Tommy would need to get down to the docks the following morning and get taken on to secure their tenancy. 'Oh, dear, Paddy,' she said, 'I think I've got back just in time, don't you?'

Harry stood next to her and pulled on her sleeve. 'Mam, guess who we saw?'

Maura, distracted, looked about Peggy's kitchen and her heart sank. Peggy's pride and joy, her mother's clock, had gone from the mantelshelf and the side of the fire, where Maura knew Peggy lined up the shoes each night, as Maura had taught her, was bare. Little Paddy knew what she was looking at and felt a sense of shame.

'She took the blankets as well,' he said.

Maura looked shocked. 'The blankets? What have the boys got covering them upstairs?'

'Da's coat,' said Paddy. 'And I left their clothes on.'

Maura looked around the bleak and empty kitchen. Her own next door, which hadn't been lived in for months, was warmer and more homely. She looked down at little Paddy and her heart bled.

'It has to be unloaded tonight,' said Conor. 'The *Morry*'s in a bad way and the owner has said he's going to come to the dock tomorrow to see her. I'm supposed to have ditched half of the load into the Indian Ocean, and we staggered home, didn't we, Blinks? This one thought we were going to sink.'

Blinks looked shamefaced. 'Ah, I never doubted you, skipper; I knew we would reach Liverpool.'

Jerry whistled. 'We'll have to work through the night if it has to be unloaded by tomorrow,' he said.

'We can get that organised,' said Tommy, 'we've done it before.'

'Can you get it organised in half an hour?' said Conor as he lifted his pint of Guinness to his lips.

'Why half an hour?'

Conor wiped the foam of his beard with the sleeve of his jumper. 'The harbour master told me – he has no idea why or how – there's only one policeman on tonight but he's the one to watch, a guy called Frank the Skank.'

Jerry whistled. 'He's the one to watch, all right.' He turned to Tommy. 'He's supposed to be moving into your house.'

Tommy shook his head. 'Not unless the dock board have changed the rules. We have paid the rent every week we have been away, they can't move us.'

'So, if he's down there, why are we moving it tonight?' asked Jerry.

'Ah, well, there's a method in me madness; a crate of rum is making its way back to the harbour master's house right now – and in return, he has set up a problem ship due to come in on the bore down on the Clarence and asked Heartfelt to send your man to intercept stolen goods. Blinks took a second crate down to the Clarence and the gaffer down there is going to keep Frank the Skank busy until the early hours, when he is going to be informed the ship has moored up out at the bar.'

'What ship is it?' asked Tommy and Conor grinned.

'Tommy, it's a ghost ship, it doesn't exist. I set it up to give you time to get everything off and up the steps.'

Tommy looked over at Jerry, who said, 'Right, we

need to get to work. Tommy, you and Seamus can get the word round that it's all hands on deck, but this deck up at the top. I'll ask Seamus to start knocking on with you and get the fellas out. If we can get a strong line going from the dock up the steps to the top, and then have some of the older lads on Nelson Street ready to act as runners to get it into your wash house, then in the morning the women can start to dish it out around the streets.'

At that moment there was a timid knock on the door and they all turned to see big Paddy pop his head around the door.

'Jerry, your mam is here; she says our Peggy is missing.'

'Tell her I'm coming,' said Jerry, 'and you go home to your kids, Paddy.'

Paddy did not look pleased. 'Behave, Jerry, I can't go now; Reg has just bought me a pint,' and without waiting for a reply, he closed the door.

'The useless lump of shite,' said Tommy. 'He's gone backwards since I left.'

'They all have; Mam says Peggy's in a right mess,' said Jerry. 'I'll go and see what Mam wants and Tommy, you go and tell Seamus to start knocking on – Eugene can help him. We'll need at least fifteen strong men to form the chain up the steps and as many lads at the top. We'd better act fast.'

Jerry placed his pint on the table and, as he turned, Conor looked embarrassed as he said, 'Jerry, I don't think Peggy is missing, I saw her not an hour since.' Even with his tanned and weather-beaten skin, Jerry could see Conor was blushing. 'She was, er, down on the docks, with the whores. I was going to ask her was she all right, like, but then I thought that if she saw me it might shame her and so I left it.'

A look of utter disbelief crossed the faces of Tommy and Jerry. 'No, Conor, you've got that wrong,' said Tommy. 'Peggy? Never.'

'Well, she's not the usual sort, I'll give you that, but the thing about sailors is, they go that long without and, well, it's any port in a storm so to speak...'

Maura began to check like Kathleen had before her, looking for a clue as to where Peggy could be. She found the money and the pawnbroker's ticket in the bread bin and, taking it out, checked the date. It had been that very afternoon and she had been all the way down the Dock Road. Despite her tiredness, itching to roll up her sleeves and clean the kitchen, Maura slowly climbed the stairs towards the bedrooms.

She turned into Peggy's room and flicked on the light switch, but no light bulbs were working. Something felt wrong, it *smelt* wrong. Her eyes adjusted to the light coming through the window from the street lamp outside. She knew the room well, had once stood at that window with a newly born little Paddy in her arms as she rocked him and watched as big Paddy and Tommy made their way down Nelson Street to the Anchor, to wet the baby's head. Her eyes adjusted and she looked down to the floor and could make out a grey bundle where Peggy's bloodstained clothes lay. As she bent to pick them up, a metallic smell filled the air and she reeled backwards.

'Oh Peggy! What in God's name is this?'

All manner of things that could have gone wrong ran through her head. After all, the worst that possibly could happen to anyone had happened in Maura's life. She heard a noise coming from the children's room and, dropping the clothes and in a state of shock, crossed the landing and opened the door. There was no borrowed light in the back room and she stood in the doorway, her ears and eyes straining. Then she heard it again, a mewing, a weak cry. Her heart stopped.

'Paddy,' she shouted down the stairs, 'where is your rat?'

Paddy's face appeared at the bottom framed in the stairwell in the only light in the house, from the kitchen. 'He's here, Auntie Maura,' he said as he held him up.

Maura heard the noise again. 'Paddy, do you have more than one rat?'

'No, Auntie Maura.'

'Where's Scamp?'

For the first time little Paddy was stumped for an answer. 'He was here, in the kitchen. He's probably out looking for rats to kill. The only one he likes is Max.'

The noise came again and Maura stepped into the room as the boys began to mount the stairs. It was coming from under the boys' bed and they were all sleeping soundly on the top of the mattress, despite only having a coat to cover them. The sound came again; it was weak and thready, a wail, a cry for attention. Maura dropped to her knees and there, sticking out from the corner of the bed, was a drawer from the press in Peggy's room. Maura knew that drawer and what it had been used for seven times before. She reached under the bed and pulled it out. She could just about make out the form of a baby.

'Oh, Holy Mary Mother of God,' said Maura as she scooped the child up into her arms, 'by all the angels in heaven… Peggy, what have you done?'

Stella tottered down the gangplank of the *Morry* and almost fell over a number of times on her high heels as she made her way over to her friend, Betty, who appeared to be holding prisoner a woman who was looking very sorry for herself.

'What do you want here then, love?' she said as she drew closer.

Betty folded her arms. 'Our business, that's what she's after. Tell her, Stella, she can't just come down here and take our jobs, can she?'

Stella looked Peggy up and down and what she saw was a woman in extreme distress. She looked over at

Betty. 'If you had been born with a brain, Betty, you would be dangerous, you know that, don't you?'

Betty looked very put out as she struggled to work out what it was that Stella actually meant and Stella spoke to Peggy again. 'Didn't I see you before, love? With a pramload of stuff, heading towards the pawnshop? I saw you again coming out, didn't I, the pram empty? You on hard times, are you?'

Peggy nodded her head. Even in front of women who sold their honour for a living, she felt ashamed.

'Oh bloody hell, we even have a dog down here now!' exclaimed Betty as Scamp appeared, slowly edging his way towards Peggy, softly growling.

'Is that your dog?' asked Stella.

Peggy nodded. For the second time in her life, she felt as though she were about to faint. Her nipples tingled sharply, her daughter was calling her... The water was so close, if only she could escape...

'Can I just go? I don't want your business,' she said. 'I don't want to cause any bother.'

'No, you cannot,' said Betty.

'Shut up, Betty!' said Stella. 'There's no one on the *Morry* anyway, now. No business to be had. So you go on, love, you do whatever you were doing, walking your dog, or whatever it is you are down here for. We've all been there, but there's no business to be had tonight. We've all known hard times, love – why do you think we do what we do?'

'Ooer, Stella, speak for yourself! I've never looked as bad as *that*. And have you lost your marbles or what? Just letting her go like that? Jeez, it's tough enough as it is. I've only had one turn and Fred won't like it when I tell him.'

Stella turned her full gaze on Betty. 'Fred won't know, Betty, because if he does, you will be the only person who could have told him – and you will regret that very much, do you understand? I'm still the queen bee around here and you had better remember that.'

Betty's face flushed and she looked very put out. Scamp sidled up to Peggy, his eyes never leaving the two women, his lips pulled back, his teeth exposed, a low, constant growl coming from his throat.

Stella said in a lower voice, 'There but for the grace of God, Betty.'

Peggy took a step, but it was difficult; she was losing blood. She took another as Scamp brushed up against her leg and he whined and looked up at her, his ears down, his eyes asking her a million questions. A dozen more steps and she would be at the water's edge. She heard the clippety-clop of two pairs of stilettos walk towards the next dock, and Stella's voice carried to her on the air, cutting off Betty's grumblings mid flow.

'Leave her alone, Betty. She doesn't have a pair of shoes to her name, God love her. That could be us one day.'

Betty laughed. 'No way! I'd rather die.'

Chapter Twenty-seven

The only sound was the creaking of the cranes down on the dock and the odd jangling of chains on the *Morry*. Seamus gave each man very clear instructions.

'One man every five steps,' he whispered as his obedient dockers descended the steps. They needed no light, for it was a journey they made most days of their lives. The air was tense – the customs men could have walked out of the bond warehouse at any time and caught them red-handed.

Outside the pub, Jerry licked his lips, nervously, his mouth dry. 'Conor should be on board by now,' said Tommy.

'Aye, it's business as usual, Tommy. I can hardly believe my eyes you're back. I feel like this is my lucky night. Where's Maura? She's the big organiser on the top, we've never done it without her before.'

'She might have gone down the steps with Kathleen and Alice to look for Peggy, though I can't believe Conor was right. I mean, who could confuse Peggy with a whore?'

Jerry shook his head. 'I don't know, it's an odd one. I'm sorry for Maura that your return home has been spoilt by a haul, Tommy. Would have been nice if it could have been before you got here. Your wash house won't be Maura's own for a day or two.'

Tommy grinned. 'Are you fecking kidding me or what? I've missed all this; it couldn't be a better welcome home.'

After what felt like an eternity, Seamus let out the awaited whistle from the bottom of the steps to let Jerry know that everyone was in place and they were about to start unloading. The decision not to tell Paddy that Conor had seen Peggy down on the dockside had been taken by Tommy.

'Nah, let the women go and check it out. They will be down and back up in twenty minutes.'

'They'd better carry a few crates of rum each with them on the way back up,' said Jerry and they both began to laugh at the thought.

'I don't know what you're laughing at Jerry,' said Tommy.

'I'm laughing at what your mam and Alice would do to you if they heard you.'

Deirdre was washing the cups in Kathleen's sink, Shelagh was drying and they were less than happy.

'I'd just like to know what's going on,' said Deirdre.

'We all go off looking for her, Kathleen pops into the pub to speak to Paddy and we all get sent back.'

Shelagh began to stack the cups and saucers. 'Well, I suppose if that means they know where she is, so it doesn't matter, does it, really?'

Mary was in the parlour, looking through the front window with Annie O'Prey and Biddy, who had heard Deirdre and shouted back, 'We've got a job to do, Deirdre, you won't be missing out.'

'Look, Mary, there's our Callum going down the steps. He's strong, he is, can carry as much as two men together, he can.'

Mary saw Callum, lithe and quick, speak to Seamus, take his instructions and then disappear down the steps. She made no comment, but her heart stirred. Not in the way it had for Jimmy, but somewhere deeper and slower and she knew he was the one whose safe return she would be waiting for.

Deirdre came and stood next to them. 'Has your da gone down, Mary?'

'He has, he's near the top though.'

'He'll be helping to run it round the back then, to Maura's wash house.'

'We will have a busy day on tomorrow, so we will, doling that lot out,' said Biddy as the back door crashed open. 'Sshh,' said Biddy, without knowing who it was she was talking to. 'There's a haul on and everyone has to be quiet.'

Maura appeared not to have heard her; she was carrying a bundle in her arms and the bundle was wailing. 'Shelagh, are you still feeding?'

Shelagh stood stock-still. 'I am. But whose baby is that, Maura? I was the last to have a baby on the streets.'

'No you weren't, Shelagh, Peggy was. I just found this baby girl under the bed and I think poor Peggy has lost her mind.'

The women crowded around. 'God love her,' Shelagh said, 'is this all there is on her?' She turned to Mary and Nellie. 'Girls, would you go to my house and bring me some nappies off the airer? There's a jam jar with pins in it on the mantelpiece and a jar of zinc and castor oil there too. There's a couple of winceyette nighties and vests on the airer. Oh, God love her! Sshh, sshh; there, don't you be crying, baby, we've got you now. And if you knock on at Mrs Keating, ask her does she have any spare matinee coats and booties. Sure, she will give you a few, for she never stops knitting.'

Her orders given, Shelagh sat down on the comfortable chair next to the fire and, without a second thought, she undid the top buttons on her blouse and placed Peggy's crying baby to her breast. The eyes of every woman in the room met and they blessed themselves. For the first time they feared for Peggy's life...

★

Cindy and Reg returned to their table to find it empty. 'Oh, they've gone,' said Cindy. 'Do you think they left together or separately?'

Reg rubbed his chin. 'Well, that's a difficult one. What do you think? Eric lives with a harridan who scares him and half of his customers to death and she's lived alone for the past twenty years. I think they've definitely gone together, Cindy.'

Cindy gasped and then she grinned. 'Well, I hope so; it's about time she had a bit of fun. Now, Reg, sit down, I've been thinking.'

Reg grinned. 'Oh, hang on, this calls for a top-up, don't go away.'

Cindy turned to the fire and, bending down, picked up a log and threw it on. She lost herself in the soporific warmth and the flickering flames as she thought about what she was about to do. It had taken someone like Mary to walk into her shop to make her realise that her shop was her baby and all she had needed was someone she could trust. Mary was special; it was obvious that she was smart and in her, Cindy had seen someone who needed to be rescued and who, in turn, would rescue Cindy.

Reg returned and placed the glasses on the table and straddled a stool opposite Cindy. 'You look lovely tonight,' he said before he took a sip of his drink.

Cindy smiled. 'I don't deserve you, Reg, you are a good man.'

Reg grinned. 'I know.'

Cindy laughed. 'You know that ring I told you to put away until I was ready?'

Reg's eyes opened wide. 'Yes...'

'Well, do you still have it?'

Reg was almost too afraid to speak. 'Yes...'

Cindy grinned because the colour had left his face. 'Good, because I'd like you to ask me again, sometime soon. I'm ready, Reg, to do the settling down thing. Oh, I still want to keep the salon going, for now, but I think I've found someone who, once she's trained up, I'd be happy to hand my baby over to.'

Reg swallowed hard. 'Cindy, I-I don't know what to say, except – of course I will!'

Cindy picked up her drink and gave him a mock toast. 'I'll look forward to it, then, this time. So, here's to us, Reg!'

The pub suddenly fell totally silent and for an awful moment, Cindy thought they had been overheard.

'Aye, aye,' said Reg, 'have the bizzies come in?'

Cindy craned her neck around. 'Oops, they might as well have done! It's Gladys and she has thunder in her eyes.'

'Jesus, I wish they would get a move on. I can feel the cold in my back something wicked,' said big Paddy who had been dragged out of the pub by Eugene and was now next to Jerry as they shuffled forward. Jerry could see some activity down at the water's edge. Too much activity. He had a strange feeling and wanted to get rid of Paddy.

'You go back to the pub, Paddy, and I'll send Callum in for you when the load starts rising.' He had a suspicion that Kathleen was due back up the steps and it would take some explaining to make him understand why Peggy might be with her.

'Well, you know where I'll be if you need me,' said Paddy, and before Jerry could answer him he was gone.

Turning back to the dockside, Jerry noted that the customs hall was empty. So, too, were the harbour master's office, the administration building and the office of the meanest man on the dockside, Mr Heartfelt. A haul was a huge operation, unlike the odd bag of spuds or flour or a crate of tea or barrel of molasses. Conor had left him in no doubt that there would be sacks needing to be sliced, spilt and collected as they hung in the net, suspended from the hook of a crane that he was using to move the bigger loads out. They would store the bigger bags in lucky shed seven with the broken lock, ready to be separated and carried up in smaller loads. The rolls of fabric would be stored in the shed built into the sandstone ridge and would take a week to transfer up.

Jerry scanned the dock for a sight of the bizzies, his nerves on edge. There were none. Seamus trotted up to him silently.

'What's the cargo?' asked Jerry.

'Tea, coffee, raisins, flour, almonds, tons of material on rolls, hard nuts, potatoes, rum, ciggies, molasses, bananas, cocoa powder, weird-sounding big hams – you name it, he has it. Conor has pulled a blinder this time.'

Jerry thrust his hands into his jacket. 'Makes a change from unloading smelted iron. You can't feed a family on a lump of iron.'

Callum joined them bringing a message from Conor. 'We can't start yet; something's going on down on the bottom but he says not to worry, it's not the bizzies. I'll go back down and see if he needs me for anything.'

Jerry didn't like it at all. 'Whatever it is, I hope it's sorted soon; if the bizzies arrive, it's each man for himself. Pass the word down the line, Tommy…'

Tommy didn't like it either; each minute of delay was a risk and he hadn't come back from Ireland to find himself up before a magistrate on his first morning home.

Chapter Twenty-eight

It was Scamp barking that had alerted Alice.

'Kathleen, is that Scamp? It's coming from over here, quick.'

As she walked past the *Morry*, Blinks whispered down from the deck, 'Kathleen, you're a bit old to be working the docks! Short of a bob or two, are you?'

Kathleen scowled and craned her neck backwards to look up. 'You wait until I can reach you, you cheeky bugger,' she hissed back up at him. 'I'll be telling Conor on you. He said he saw Peggy down here and she's been missing since this afternoon. Have you seen her?'

Blinks shook his head. 'Not since earlier and we're just getting ready to unload. The coast is clear, but not sure how long for, so we need to be getting on before your man realises he's been had and comes back.'

Kathleen tutted. 'We're just going to walk along here and see if we can find her; Alice can hear a dog barking.'

'Be careful,' said Blinks, 'it's dark now. You only have

the moon and that suits us, but don't you go slipping. Watch out for the ropes.'

'I will,' said Kathleen. 'I can't swim, but who can?'

Blinks laughed. 'Me! So good job I can then – I'll dive in and pull you out if I have to.'

Kathleen and Alice hurried along the dock edge, following the sound of the barking.

'Look, there she is!' Alice exclaimed and from the light of the moon on the water, they could see Peggy sitting on the edge, Scamp dragging her backwards by her cardigan, barking between tugs.

'Alice, go back and fetch Blinks,' said Kathleen. 'Go on! I'll go to Peggy but we will need his help. And tell him to bring one of those trolleys he uses for unloading.'

Alice turned and ran back to the *Morry* as Kathleen edged closer to Peggy. 'Peggy love, what are you doing there?' she asked.

Peggy didn't answer Kathleen; she appeared to be unaware that she was even there.

'Peggy, Peggy love…' Kathleen stepped closer and this time Peggy turned.

'Go away, Kathleen,' she said. 'Leave me alone.' She was shaking violently and her teeth chattered as she spoke.

'I can't do that, Peggy, I've got to take you back up – the kids need you and even that lazy oaf of a husband of yours needs you too.'

As Kathleen drew nearer she was stunned to see that

Peggy's feet were in the Mersey and that she was sitting on the very edge of the dock, inches away from the water. It would take just one move, one lunge, and she would be in. One of her slippers floated on the surface of the water while the other had sunk and was visible just below the waterline. Kathleen's heart beat hard against her chest wall as she edged closer until she was behind Peggy, intending to hold on to the back of her blouse and thinking to herself, what use would that be?

Peggy was rambling incoherently; Kathleen tried again. 'Peggy, Peggy love, come on, what are you doing down here? Little Paddy says your chips are cold and we've Maura and Tommy home. I'll open a bottle of the Golden Knight sherry to celebrate – you love a glass of that, don't you? Come on now, lift your legs up out of that water and let's go and see Maura.'

Bending as best she could, Kathleen placed a hand on one shoulder and with her other grabbed a handful of fabric. This would be her leverage, all she had to help her if Peggy should slip over the edge – and if she wasn't careful, take Kathleen with her into the Mersey.

'Come on, Peggy, shuffle your bum back. I'll feel much better when your feet are out of that water and you're upright. Let's get you home.'

Peggy shook her head. 'There's no home to go to, I've lost it. I've been a terrible mother. My kids deserve better and they'll be better off without me. Leave me alone, Kathleen, just go away.' She finished on a sob and, in the reflected light from the water, Kathleen could see the tears rolling down her cheeks.

Kathleen let Peggy cry it out for a few moments and then tried again. 'Peggy, I know all about it. About the letter from Heartfelt, about the bailiffs coming – and you've got nothing to worry about; we are going to sort it all out for you, me and Maura. She has a plan to make everything right.'

Peggy stopped crying and, looking up at Kathleen, she said, 'But Maura's not here. I'm lost without her, I did it all wrong.'

Kathleen patted Peggy's back. 'No you didn't, Peggy. It's not your fault your Paddy never went down the docks, it's all his fault, not yours. You were managing the best you could.' Kathleen got down and sat next to Peggy, and took her hand in her own. 'The thing is, Peggy, and it's my fault. I should have taken better care of you – and Jerry, he should have been firmer with your Paddy. I'll tell you a secret, shall I?' She looked sideways and saw she had Peggy's attention. 'They are going to make our Jerry the new gaffer on this dock and you know what that means, don't you? It means every man on the four streets will be in work because they will get priority, for that's how it works. And Jerry, he is going to make sure your Paddy is down there with him, give him a bit of responsibility, like. Put him in charge of the sheds.'

Kathleen looked out across the Mersey, at the

shimmering moon, allowed her words to sink in, and then looking to her right and down towards Liverpool, she said, 'I never knew how lovely it was down here. Really lovely, isn't it? And I've other news for you that's going to put a smile on your face: Maura is home for good and between us, her and me are going to sort out your rent arrears. Don't worry, it's a loan; you can pay us a back a shilling a week so you don't have to feel like you're in our debt. We will sort it for you, Peggy, and we'll go to the pawnshop and get the kids' shoes and your mam's clock back.'

Peggy's hand felt like ice in her own and she was shaking so violently Kathleen was half afraid she would shake them both over the edge. Peggy was completely unresponsive and, worryingly, staring down at the water. The bore was in, the level was high and then, just as Kathleen thought, *Alice, where the hell are you?* she heard her daughter-in-law arrive at a trot, closely followed by Blinks pushing a trolley.

Then Peggy whispered something Kathleen thought she had misheard. 'What did you say, Peggy love?'

'Kathleen, I had a baby, can you save her? And I'm sorry, Kathleen, but I have to go. Even Paddy will be better off without me.'

Just as Peggy shook herself away from Kathleen and shuffled herself to the edge, to slip into the water, two arms caught her from behind and she found herself being hauled six feet backwards to the concrete floor of the dock. Before either woman had time to speak, Blinks said, 'Right, now you, Kathleen,' and before she knew what was happening, Blinks did the same to her and stood her on her feet.

'By God, you're strong,' said Kathleen, impressed.

He grinned. 'Come on now, Peggy,' he said and bent down again. Then, as though he were guiding and lifting a load from a crane into the ship's hold, he placed Peggy on the trolley.

'Hang on, hang on,' Kathleen said. She had lived through the births of many unwanted babies, had persuaded women not to roll on their babies in their sleep, or leave them on the steps of the convent so she had recognised the voice of a mother in anguish when she heard it. 'Peggy, Peggy, what did you say, you had a baby? Where?'

Alice was removing her coat to place over Peggy and Blinks, who had thrown some blankets over the handle of the trolley, was wrapping them around Peggy's shoulders.

'What baby, Peggy?' Alice placed the coat over Peggy's wet legs. 'Kathleen, she's rambling, she probably means one of the boys. We need to get Dr Cole.'

Kathleen was not convinced. 'No, Alice, she's distraught and she's upset, but she's not totally lost her mind. Also she said "she" and all Peggy's babies were boys. Peggy, what did you mean, you had a baby? When? When did this happen, Peggy love?'

Peggy blinked and looked down at her hands. 'I don't

know... Before, in the outhouse... We're being thrown out onto the street, Kathleen, in front of everyone. They won't let me keep her. The welfare will take them all off me.'

It was obvious, Peggy hadn't taken in a word Kathleen had said. Blinks turned the trolley around.

'Come on, Pegs, let's get you back up the top, will we?'

Peggy was whimpering, 'Let me go, let me go, please, that's all I want to do.'

They all turned as Scamp barked into the dark. 'Who is that, Alice?' said Kathleen. 'I can hear footsteps.'

Scamp, obviously satisfied that Peggy was in good hands, ran off into the darkness with his tail wagging just as they heard a voice shout, 'Peggy! Peggy!'

Peggy turned, blinking. It was Maura's voice and Kathleen had said something about Maura, but she couldn't remember what. They heard the running footsteps, Scamp's excited barks. All eyes were on Peggy as Maura, guided by Callum, came into view and said, 'I'm home, Peggy!'

Maura took in the scene. Peggy shaking, the dripping feet, water puddled on the concrete, the look on Alice's face and her hand flew to her mouth.

'Peggy, you weren't! Why would you do that? I've found your baby, Peggy, your baby. She's with Shelagh and, oh Peggy, she's so beautiful, just like her mam.' Maura fell to her knees and took the hands of her friend into her own, as tears filled her eyes. 'I'm back in the house, Peggy, back to help. Jer and Tommy will make sure your Paddy is down the docks every day and we will pay the rent arrears; we know all about it and you aren't going anywhere. I'm home to help you, Pegs, I missed you.'

Peggy looked into Maura's eyes and she couldn't believe what she could see. She wrapped her hands around Maura's face. 'Are you an angel?' she said through a river of tears.

Maura, almost too choked up to speak, said, 'No... well, I am if you want me to be. I can be your angel, Peggy.' Then, on an upbeat note, 'Yes of course I'm your angel, and everything is going to be just fine now. I hadn't realised, Peggy, you just needed that little bit of help, didn't you? And here was me thinking I was an old bossy boots and you would be glad to be rid of me.' Then Maura sprang to her feet. 'Peggy has a beautiful baby girl,' she announced as she took her handkerchief out of her pocket and wiped her eyes. 'What better home-coming present could I have than that, eh? Blinks, let's get this trolley up to the top and Kathleen, we'll knock on at the midwife's on the way past. Come on, Peggy, put this on you, we are taking you home.'

Chapter Twenty-nine

The light flashed from the bottom of the steps to the top, the sign Jerry had been waiting for. 'At last,' he said, 'let's go. Fetch Paddy out of the pub, Tommy – he doesn't get a drop if he doesn't pull his weight. And they've found Peggy, praise the Lord.'

The men blessed themselves and carried on with the business in hand. Little Paddy and Harry, who knew the call was out for the older boys to help move the goods from the top of the steps to the Dohertys' backyard, tried their luck and ran up to Jerry. 'Can we help, Jer?' they asked.

Jerry looked down at them and he couldn't resist the urge to scoop Harry into his arms and hug him. 'God, you are a grand lad and we've missed you,' he said, 'but, no, Harry, you cannot help because you've been sick in hospital, so you can both get home to bed. I know you will have sneaked out.'

Little Paddy grinned. 'Ma's at your house, Jerry; she's had a baby, we have a sister.'

Jerry looked stunned, but he could tell the boy wasn't lying. 'Well, it's going to be a double celebration tonight then,' he said. 'I'll send a bottle back, just for your mam, as soon as the last crate is up and we'll be round to wet the baby's head. Now, both of you boys, out of the way – don't break the chain.'

As the boys, keen not to upset Jerry, started do as they were told, they saw Gladys storming up the street.

'Oh-oh, here comes Gladys!' Little Paddy pulled Jerry by the sleeve and to Harry he said, 'My ma says it's a wonder she works in the dairy, because one look from her and the milk turns sour. Can you imagine that? She must have to stay in the house all day.'

'That's why she's out now,' said Harry, 'because it's dark.'

Gladys stormed up to the two boys and they froze. 'Have you seen Eric, the milkman?' she demanded. The two boys, open-mouthed, looked at each other. 'Well, have you? Is he helping out with this illegal affair? Because if he is, I'll be calling the police, I will. Jerry Deane, come here,' she shouted across the street and Jerry, not wanting any trouble, sprinted across the street.

'What's wrong, Gladys?' Jerry asked. 'What's the problem?'

Gladys had her arms folded, her black hat was jammed down over her brow and in the light of the street lamp, the yellow glow made her look jaundiced. Her head was bent low, her shoulders jutted upwards like two wing nubs.

'She looks like a bat,' whispered little Paddy to Harry and both boys put their hands over their mouths to stifle their giggles.

'I know what you're doing here is illegal,' she said. 'Is Eric down there? Because if he is, I'm calling the police.'

Jerry's head jerked back in surprise. 'If he is?'

'Aye, you heard me, is he?'

Jerry's brow furrowed and, lifting his cap, he rubbed his hand across his hair. 'What if he isn't? Will you be calling the police then?'

Gladys snorted. 'No, what you do is your affair. I'm not interested in *you* but if he's helping, you'll all cop it because if I have to walk into Whitechapel myself to do it, I'll be fetching the police.'

Tommy looked over from the other side of the street. Everyone knew Gladys was trouble but no one really wanted to have to face her.

'See that,' said Tommy to Eugene, 'that's why Jerry will get the gaffer's job; he's a natural leader. He'd face Hitler, that man would.'

Eugene looked across to where Tommy was indicating. 'To be honest, Tommy, I think most would rather face Hitler than Gladys – she's a scold, that one.'

Jerry spoke to Gladys in his softest tone, his most conciliatory manner. 'Gladys, honestly, I've no idea where Eric is. Is he not at home? Have you tried the Anchor?'

Jerry did not want to say that he had seen Eric in the Anchor earlier, that was a line men did not cross. No man had ever seen another in the pub when questioned.

'I've been in there and that whore behind the bar with the ton of make-up on her face says she's never seen him, so he must be here.'

Little Paddy shot out from round the back of Jerry's legs. Harry grabbed his sleeve to try and stop him, but he was too late. 'I've seen him,' little Paddy called out. 'He was kissing Mrs Trott in the entry.'

Harry's statement stunned the onlookers.

'Fecking hell,' Tommy whispered.

'That kid has a death wish,' said Eugene.

'And Eric is a dead man walking,' said Seamus.

The air trembled as they all stared at Gladys.

'You what?' she roared at little Paddy, who no longer felt as confident as he had only seconds before and he said again, with a little less volume, 'We saw him, didn't we, Harry?' He pulled Harry out from behind Jerry to stand next to him. 'We saw him and he was kissing Mrs Trott.'

It looked to Paddy as though Gladys's eyes were going to explode and then she said five words before she turned her back on all of them and marched back down the street. 'He. Is. Dead. To. Me.'

Eric stood naked, peeping through the net curtains of Maggie Trott's bedroom down into the street below.

Maggie came and stood at his side and slipped under his arm.

'If you are regretting this, Eric… don't,' she whispered. 'I understand, you are a married man and one night really was enough for you.'

Eric pulled her into his side. 'Good job you didn't say just the once was enough,' he said as he grinned down at her, 'for you would already be a liar.'

Maggie laid her head on his shoulder. 'But it's an impossible situation, isn't it?'

Eric took in a deep breath. 'No, it isn't. I'm not going to go back to my old life ever again. Even if you don't want me, Maggie, I have to walk a new path. The old one was destroying me and I can't go back.'

Eric led her back to the bed. 'I'll have to go,' he said. 'I have to collect the milk and load up the float and I have to face Gladys. I'm going to tell her everything and my guess is she will pack her bags and move to her sister's on the Wirral. She's been looking for an excuse to do that for years, anyway; all she wants is the money. I'll tell her to take every penny we have and I'll start over again.' He tucked the covers in over Maggie's shoulders.

'Eric, if she doesn't, put your bag on the float as well as the milk. You can move in here.' Her heart raced; she had broken the spell of loneliness and she didn't want to return to that life ever again. This big giant of a soft and gentle man was the one she wanted to be with.

'What will they say on the street? I couldn't bear to ruin your good name,' he said.

Maggie smiled. 'Eric, you were married to Gladys – they will be relieved for you, 'tis only the priest who will make life difficult. It's not like I had to fight for my honour, is it?'

Eric looked down on her and smiled. 'Maggie, as far as I am concerned, I was never married before God; according to the Holy Catholic Church, I'm probably still a single man.'

Maggie smiled, and freeing her arms from the bed-clothes, reached up. 'It just gets better and better,' she said in the moment before his lips came down on hers.

Dr Cole left Kathleen's house, smiling. The midwife had called him to check on mother and baby and little was said about the birth. The midwife, no stranger to the acts of desperation mothers were driven into in the face of extreme poverty, was just relieved that Peggy and the baby were still alive.

'It's grand to see you back home, Mrs Doherty,' Dr Cole had said. 'Mammy said she saw you in the hospital in Galway.'

Maura preened; having the doctor speak to you in the way Dr Cole just had was on a par with being a favourite of the Mother Superior. Her pleasure was heightened

by imagining the peevish look on Deirdre's face had she
been there to witness it.

'Are you staying here tonight?' Dr Cole asked Peggy,
but Maura answered for her. 'She's a bit overwhelmed,
doctor. There are women now, down at her house, giving
it a good clean and getting it ready for the baby. She was
a bit of a surprise, that baby, so we're having to beg,
borrow and steal around the streets for a crib and clothes
and nappies, but another hour and Peggy will be tucked
up in her own bed, won't you, Peg?'

There was no reply. Peggy was laid back on a pillow
Alice had tucked in behind her on the day bed, her
eyes closed. She was wearing Kathleen's clean clothes
and Maura and Alice had given her a bed bath, during
which Peggy had not spoken a word. Dr Cole fastened
the clasps on his bag. 'I'll be off, then,' he said. 'I saw
some... er, *activity*, as I came up the street so I left the
car at the bottom and walked up the entry. I didn't want
to disturb anything.' He winked at Maura as he spoke.

'Well, don't be surprised to find a nice bottle of rum
at the surgery tomorrow,' said Maura and she winked
back.

'What I don't understand,' he said as he placed his
hat on his head, 'is why a good Irishman who sails the
seven seas like Conor, can't bring in a nice haul of Irish
whiskey, in the name of God, why does it have to be
rum?' They both laughed as he walked through the door
and back out into the entry. 'Goodnight, Mrs Doherty,

I'm relieved you are back on the four streets, it's a better place for you being here.'

Maura watched him retreat until he was swallowed by the darkness. She looked up to the sky before she closed the door. So much had happened since she had arrived home, it was already beginning to feel as though she had never left.

It was Conor who saw the torchlight, who let out the short burst whistle, followed by the long, low return and everyone stopped dead. Blinks crept up the gangway to the hold door.

'What is it?' he whispered.

Conor was standing in the dark shadow at the side of the deck. 'There's torchlight in the administration building, I just saw it sweep across the back. Something's up. It could be an ambush, it's not safe, so it's not.'

Blinks looked out along the dock and towards the long, low hut. 'Fecking hell. That's all we need. Conor, we can't be caught on our first night home, you'll have a mutiny on your hands. This lot will string you up. They think you risk too much for this lot as it is; you know this cargo should have been dumped.' Blinks had tipped his head first towards the crew, who were in the hold, and the men on the four streets who were in the dock.

Conor held up his hand. 'Our men needn't worry. We can hide on the ship and on the first bore we can sail out – they can't. Every one of them would be in a cell tonight and up before the magistrate tomorrow if there is someone out there.'

Callum appeared at the top of the gangway. 'What's going on? Why have we stopped?'

Blinks sounded rattled. 'Because Conor saw a torch-light in the administration building. It seems our plan of getting rid of Frank the Skank hasn't worked.'

'What shall we do then?' said Callum, who was more afraid of being sent back to prison than he was willing to see the load make it to the top of the steps. He would never be able to win Mary over if that happened. He wanted to get away from the dockside as fast as he could. 'Shall I go and fetch Jerry? Maura told me she had a message for him when we were pushing Peggy back up. She said they had a visit at the house from Frank the Skank and Heartfelt. They didn't see her, but she wanted me to tell him.'

'Good lad, Callum,' Conor said. 'There's something going on down here and I don't like it. The coast is sup-posed to be clear and it isn't. I'm half-expecting to see a fleet of Black Marias coming along the docks. Run as fast as you can, lad.'

Callum grinned. 'That's what I do best, Conor.'

Tommy and Jerry ran down the steps together, giving instructions to each man as they passed him. 'Don't light up your ciggie until we tell you. Don't move or talk, just wait.'

Jerry gave Conor the whistle once they reached the bottom of the steps. Both men crouched down onto their haunches and made their way like crabs until they were on a level with the administration building. They both stared until their eyes watered, but they saw nothing.

'Conor is seeing things,' whispered Tommy, 'there's no one there.'

Jerry agreed. 'I think you're right but let's just give it one more minute.'

Just as they were about to leave, their legs aching from crouching in one place, they both saw the dim sweep of torchlight.

'Feck, right,' Jerry said, 'let's get on our bellies and crawl under the window to where that light came from and see if we can take a gander and find out what is going on.'

In seconds, they were crossing the moonlit slab of concrete that exposed them, aware that all eyes up on the top and all eyes on the ship were watching them. They stopped and, with stealthy moves, shifted into place and then rested their backs against the wall. The two men froze as they heard voices coming from inside. The two men winked at each other in the moonlight as they silently turned and pressed their ears against the wall of the wooden hut.

'How much is it?' said Frank the Skank.

'Nearly two thousand pounds. The dock board don't even know it's here. They have a separate account for the rents and trust me to look after it – I just haven't banked it for a while.'

'That's no heart-at-all-felt,' mouthed Jerry to Tommy.

'What are you going to do with your share?' Frank's voice again.

'Same as you, matey. I'm going to hold my nerve and tough it out. You can settle your Margaret in once the bailiffs have done their job on Nelson Street and I can help the police with their enquiries. Christ, the return of Tommy Doherty is a godsend, he's a sitting duck. We were obviously meant to have this and when the coast is clear, I'm off to New Zealand. I'll wave to you in Australia.'

The two men laughed. 'How are you going to get it out, Frank? It's a bit obvious, walking along the dock with a bag that size full of one-pound and ten-shilling notes.'

'I'm going to drop it out here at the back on the dock. Don't want to be seen walking out of the front door with it over my shoulder like a bag of swag.' Frank the Skank began to chuckle. 'There's a trolley tucked at the side and I'm going to wheel it to the cutting. Anyone who notices me from on top will think it's a dead dog from the dock. And when I get there, I have the police car waiting which I got for the week. I said to them, if there's only me on two docks, I can't police them properly on foot and they fell for it. I'm going to drive it to our house and store it in the coalhouse. Margaret doesn't like to get her hands dirty so she never goes down there. But first I'll plant a small bundle of notes down the back of the Dohertys' boiler and I'll find them there myself tomorrow, once the alarm is raised. They didn't get him for the murder of the priest, but they'll have him for this.'

Heartfelt let out a long whistle and Jerry and Tommy looked at each other, eyes wide. They heard the sound of wood on wood as a sash window slid open above them and then, as if an angel had appeared and delivered them a heavenly gift, a sack landed in their laps. Both men looked to the left and saw the trolley Frank had talked about. 'That'll do nicely, thanks, Frank,' whispered Tommy with a grin. Their eyes met as the window closed above them. They heard the front door on the street side of the administration building open and close and the sound of footsteps which they assumed to be Heartfelt retreating.

When Frank the Skank turned the corner, he visibly jumped as his torch lit up the two men with his sack at their feet. He looked down at the sack then up at the men and licked his thin, tight lips as his hand went to his truncheon.

'Don't even try it,' said Jerry. 'We know everything.

We know you were in the Doherty kitchen and you were heard. It's the end of the road, Skank.'

Tommy felt his blood boil with anger. 'You scumbag! You were going to try and nail me, put me down, separate me from my family because of your thieving ways.'

Jerry looked sideways at Tommy; the thought that they were up to no good themselves was lost on his friend. Then he spoke. 'You can take your money – we are better off without the likes of you two around here, but take this message to Heartfelt…'

Tommy swallowed; he couldn't believe Jerry was going to let the Skank walk and with the money too.

'Tell Heartfelt I've taken five hundred pounds. You two can have the rest. I'll be using this to help the people up there who, due to Heartfelt's mismanagement of the docks, are on half-pay most of the time. There are families who are suffering, kids who aren't being fed properly because of him, men who do a day's work on near-empty bellies. You can also tell him that if there are any rent arrears on the four streets, he's to wipe the slate clean from today – have you got that?'

Frank the Skank didn't speak.

'Oh, and tell your wife, never to walk down the four streets again telling us what we can and cannot do, and that goes for you too. Watch my back,' he said to Tommy as he bent to untie the sack. Then he counted notes until he had what he wanted and handed the money to Tommy. Jerry tied the sack up again and threw it at Frank's feet.

'There you go, there's enough left to do your runner to Australia, but you had better be quick, before one of us pops in to see your Margaret and tell her what you were up to' – Frank's mouth dropped and even in the torchlight, Jerry saw the blood leave his face – 'Oh, aye, we know everything, don't we Tommy? And just in case you were thinking of bluffing this one out and think you can still blame us...' He let out a long whistle and looked up the steps. 'See that there?' he said.

Frank looked over to the steps and along the ridge. One by one fifty orange flames illuminated the steps and the ridge along the top at the all-clear to light up. 'They are all our witnesses – they've seen everything.'

Frank the Skank looked as though he were in shock. A rat ran along the dock and stopped, sniffing his boot. 'See, you even smell like shite! Go – go now,' said Jerry and, picking up the sack, Frank shuffled off and didn't look over his shoulder once.

Chapter Thirty

The operation ran for three hours by the time they had finished and almost everything was stored neatly and filled Maura's wash house and backyard. The rest, despite Malcolm's protestations, was stored in the Seaman's Stop.

'If I end up in prison because of this I will never forgive you. I said so, Biddy, didn't I? I would not have a drop stored in my establishment.'

'You did, Malcolm, but you would also hate to see the carnival cancelled because there was nothing to hold it on the back of, wouldn't you? Now stop your moaning and help stack these crates.'

Malcolm, defeated, did as he was told and grumbled all the way through until the call went out for everyone to assemble at the top of the steps, to break open a crate. Callum passed around the bottles, one to each man who had passed the crates up the steps and helped with the operation.

'One for now, fellas,' Jerry said. 'And would you look

at this, the best haul ever and a carnival in just over a week.'

Those who had been unable to help and had bided their time in the Anchor, sauntered across the road to hear Jerry speak.

'Give a bottle to everyone here, Eugene, we have plenty to go around.'

'Eh, don't be giving it away for free, Jerry Deane! You'll be putting me out of business,' came the call from Babs, there to collect her own bottle, while Malcolm nursed his close to his chest and, looking sideways, saw Biddy grinning.

'What are you laughing at?' he said.

'You,' said Biddy. 'You and all your moans and groans and look at you, can't wait to open that and see what it tastes like, can you?' Malcolm looked affronted and, not for the first time, wondered was Biddy a mind reader.

Callum saw Mary standing alone. She was tired, but she didn't care. When the streets suffered, they were all in pain. The good times were few and far between and, when one arrived, she was happy to be in the middle of it. Callum moved across the back of the crowd and stood next to her.

'You've worked hard tonight,' he said.

Mary suppressed her desire to laugh. 'All women work hard,' she said.

Callum looked hurt. 'Aye, but not many work like you

do. I've watched you for a long time and I've always liked you, Mary, but you were always working.'

Mary turned to look at him. 'You're right,' she said. 'It's been my lot but I'm going to change something, Callum, I'm going to choose myself what work it is I do from now on. Someone else has always decided for me.' She smiled, to reassure him that she meant no offence.

'Sure, why wouldn't you?' he said. 'I chose my life. I chose the docks, not the jail. Being in control of your own way, that's the path to happiness.'

'I have a plan, Callum. I'm going to go and work for Cindy and I haven't told me ma yet, but I'm going to leave home and live in the flat above the salon. Cindy is going to teach me and I'm going to be a hairdresser.' Even though she was tired, her eyes were bright with excitement.

'Does that mean I'll be getting free haircuts for the rest of me life then?' said Callum. Mary blushed to her roots and looked down to her feet. 'Mary, I've asked your da and he says I can take you to the picture house tomorrow night. I wouldn't have felt right calling at your house if I hadn't asked him.'

Mary looked back up and her eyes met his. She had never been to town in her life at night. 'I don't mind,' she said. 'It's the four streets, not Carnaby Street and Da would like that you asked him.'

Callum grinned as he slipped his hand into hers. 'Good, because I can't wait to kiss you, Mary.'

Mary shook his hand playfully away, but her stomach did a somersault at his words. She couldn't wait either – but it would all be on her terms and Cindy would be her guide.

'Are you going to tell them about the money?' Tommy asked quietly as they handed the bottles around.

'No, not yet. Them bizzies will be all over the docks like a rash tomorrow, so we'll wait for it to die down before we let them all know about that.'

They walked Peggy back to her house, Kathleen, Maura and Alice – the rest of the women were already in there and the house was spotless. Even Deirdre was soft-spoken as they made their way in.

'I've brought the settle in from yours, Maura, and made it up by the fire, for she'll be better off down here. I had to use your spare bedding, though.'

'Don't be worrying about that, Deirdre,' said Maura. ''Tis only blankets.'

'Has anyone told Paddy yet?' asked Alice and they all turned as her husband answered, 'I have and he's here.'

They parted to let big Paddy through and he removed his cap to sit on the side of the settle. Peggy's daughter lay in her arms; she'd refused to put her down since Shelagh had given the baby to her.

'A girl, Pegs?' Paddy said, looking at his wife, who had eyes only for her daughter.

'It is,' she said, 'she's a beautiful colleen.'

'Have we a name?' asked Paddy, who felt as though he were looking at their firstborn.

'I do. Kitty. I'm calling her Kitty.'

Maura, watching the scene from the side, blinked away the tears that sprang to her eyes.

'Jerry's going to be the new gaffer,' said Paddy. 'He's putting me on the sheds and I'll be working every day now, I promise.'

Peggy looked up at her husband and smiled and then around at the women who had saved her. Jerry had told Paddy how close he had come to losing his wife and instead of the angry reaction he had expected, Paddy had been filled with remorse. Little Paddy came into the room, still wide awake at one in the morning. He sat on the opposite side of the settle and peered over the blanket at his new baby sister.

'Did you say her name was Kitty, Ma?' he asked.

'I did, Paddy, is that all right with you?'

Paddy, wide-eyed, nodded his head. 'Oh, aye, Kitty will love that. I'll tell her next time I see her.'

They all looked at Paddy; for a simple boy, he said the strangest things.

'God, that lad, he's away with the fairies,' said Deirdre, as Jerry and Tommy joined them.

'We're here to wet the baby's head,' said Jerry. 'And did you all know that little Paddy saw Gladys off tonight, or we might not have had this?' He held a large bottle of rum aloft. 'He did a grand job, didn't you, Paddy? She was about to call the police, but Paddy saved the night.'

Little Paddy beamed from ear to ear with pride.

'Oh, really?' said Maura. 'How did you do that, Paddy?'

Little Paddy stood up for effect. 'Oh, that was easy, I just told her I'd seen Eric the milky kissing Mrs Trott in the entry.'

Everyone in the room looked at each other, mouths fell open and then closed before the laughter began. Peggy laughed along too, one hand on her belly and the other wrapped around her daughter as love shone out of her eyes and down on the bundle swaddled in borrowed clothes. No one ever visited her house; she knew her neighbours were more inclined to avoid having to cross her threshold, but here they all were, drinking and laughing in her kitchen and she had a daughter in her arms and a repentant husband who had promised to stay in work.

Tommy slipped his hand around his Maura's waist. 'Where's Biddy?' he asked.

Mary, who was helping Deirdre dish out the drinks, said, 'She's taken Shelagh's pram to put Ena in it and wheel her home from the Anchor.'

Tommy almost spat out his drink as Maura raised her eyebrows. 'Are you glad to be home?' he asked her quietly and Maura whispered back, 'Honest to God, we were gone six months? Maggie Trott and married Eric the Milky! It's like Sodom and Gomorrah.' And she blessed herself.

'Good job you're back then, to keep them all in order.'

Maura smiled at her husband as Deirdre placed a rum-laden cup of tea in her hand. 'This is home, Tommy. I never want to leave the four streets ever again.'

Nadine Dorries grew up in a working-class family in Liverpool. She spent part of her childhood living on a farm with her grandmother in the west of Ireland. She trained as a nurse, then followed with a successful career in which she established and then sold her own business. She is an MP, presently serving as Minister of State in the Department of Health and Social Care, and has three daughters.